MISSILE MOUSE

THE *STAR CRUSHER*

BY
JAKE PARKER

AN IMPRINT OF

■SCHOLASTIC

New York   Toronto   London   Auckland   Sydney   Mexico City   New Delhi   Hong Kong

OFFICIAL
GSA
DOCUMENT

FOR
EYES
ONLY

ACKNOWLEDGMENTS

Big galactic thanks to Anthony Wu, Jason Caffoe, Kohl Glass, Katie Smith, Tom Saville, Mike Lee, Dave Strick, and Phil Falco for giving their time and talents to the creation of this book. And a stellar thank-you to Judy Hansen, Sheila Keenan, and David Saylor for your faith in me. Most importantly, thanks to my wife, Alison, for her whip cracking, her wrangling of kids, and her patience. This book would still be fiddling around in the recesses of my imagination if not for her.

ISBN: 978-0-545-11714-2 (hardcover)
ISBN: 978-0-545-11715-9 (paperback)

Library of Congress Cataloging-in-Publication Data Available

10 9 8 7 6 5 4 3 2 1   10 11 12 13 14

First edition, January 2010
Edited by Sheila Keenan
Creative Director: David Saylor
Book design by Phil Falco
Printed in Singapore   46

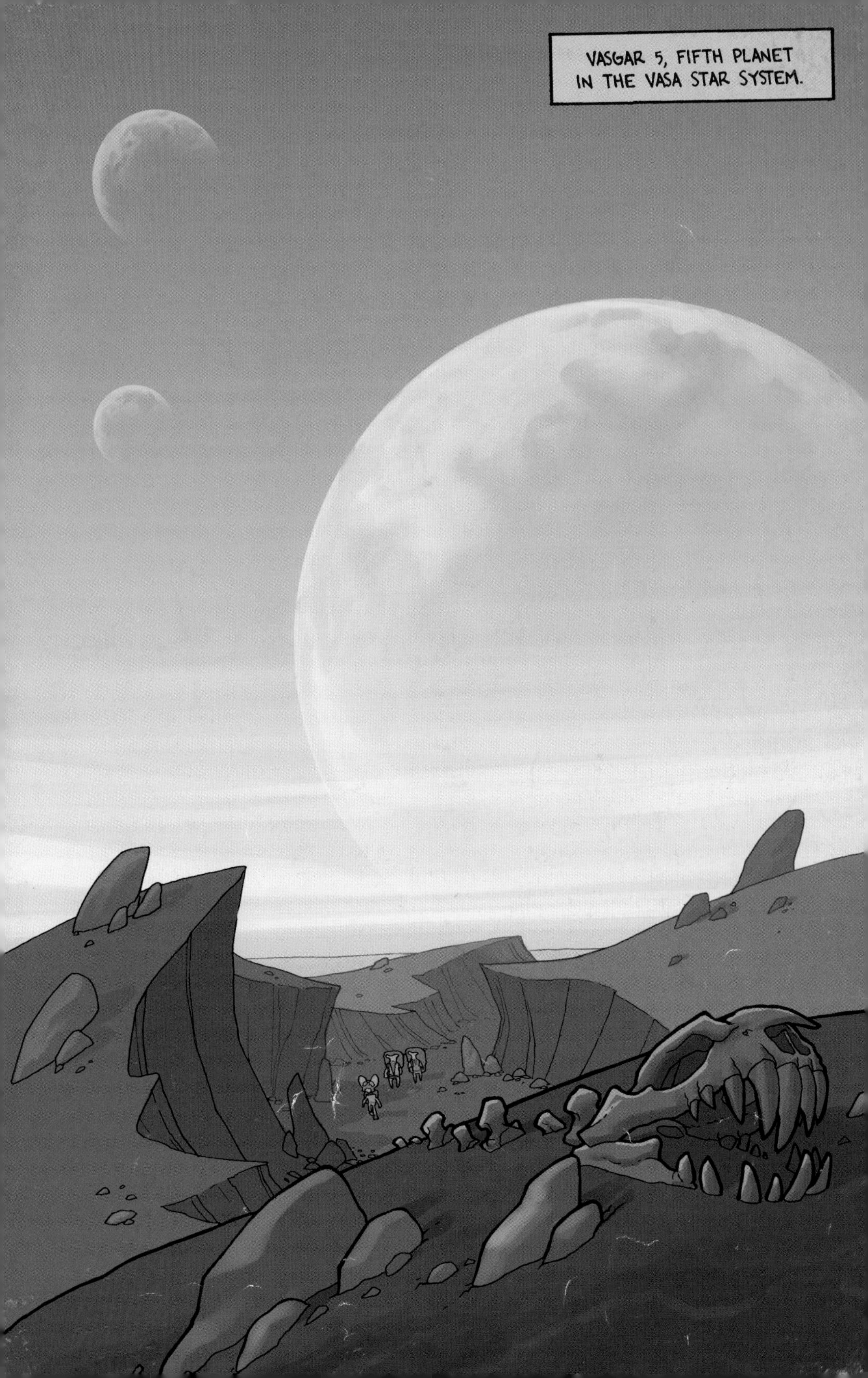
VASGAR 5, FIFTH PLANET IN THE VASA STAR SYSTEM.

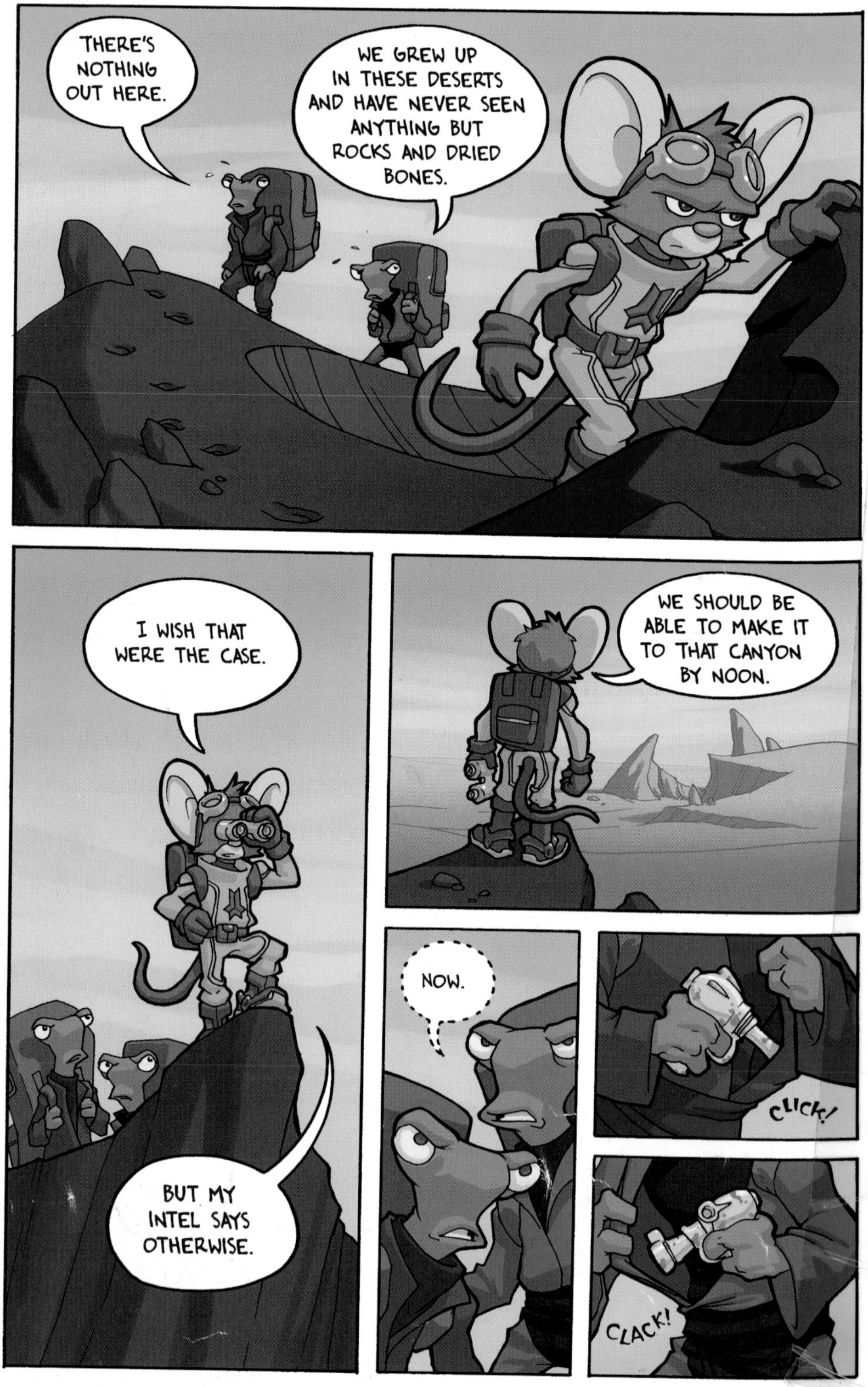
THERE'S NOTHING OUT HERE.
WE GREW UP IN THESE DESERTS AND HAVE NEVER SEEN ANYTHING BUT ROCKS AND DRIED BONES.
I WISH THAT WERE THE CASE.
BUT MY INTEL SAYS OTHERWISE.
WE SHOULD BE ABLE TO MAKE IT TO THAT CANYON BY NOON.
NOW.
CLICK!
CLACK!

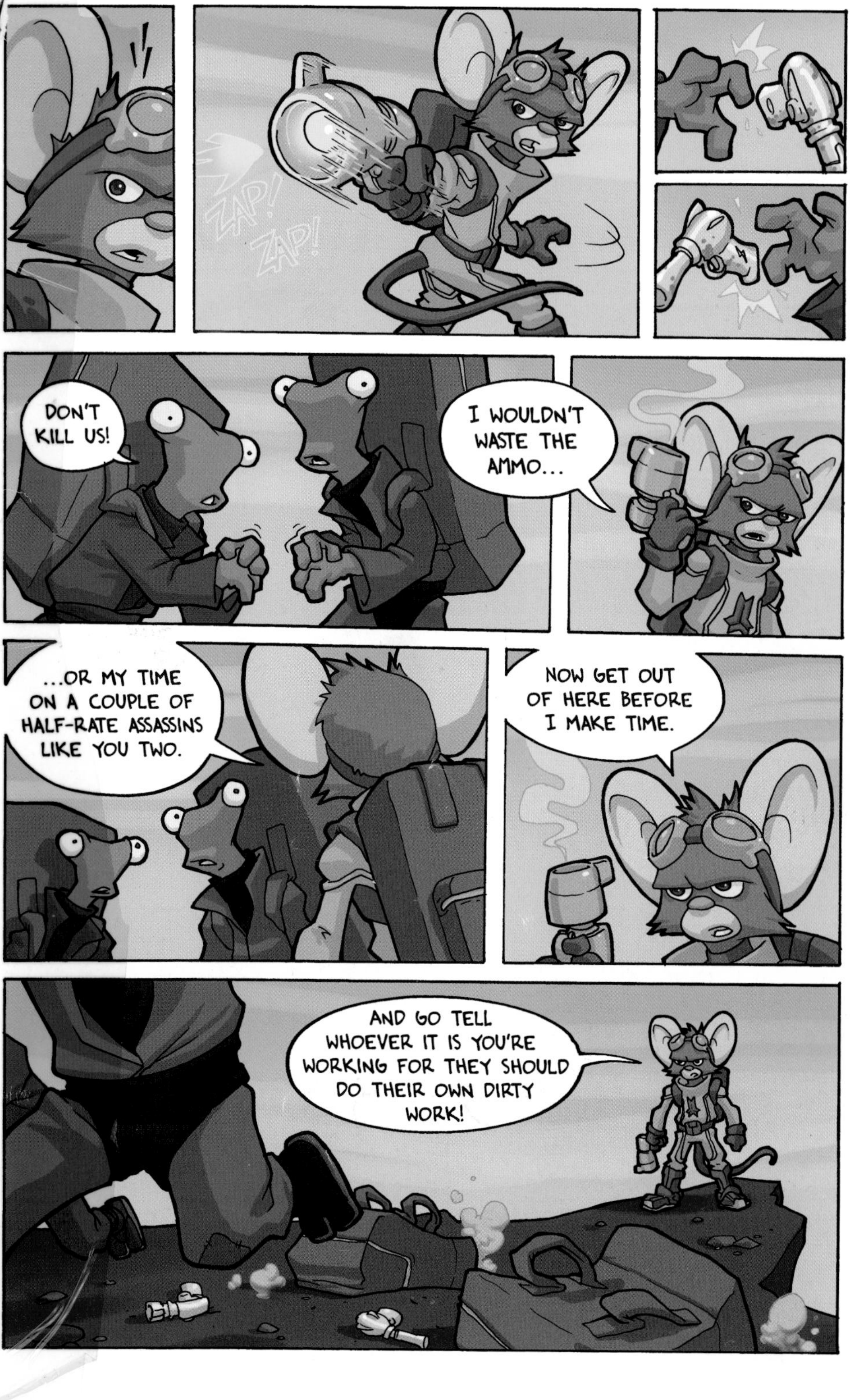
ZAP!
ZAP!
DON'T KILL US!
I WOULDN'T WASTE THE AMMO...
...OR MY TIME ON A COUPLE OF HALF-RATE ASSASSINS LIKE YOU TWO.
NOW GET OUT OF HERE BEFORE I MAKE TIME.
AND GO TELL WHOEVER IT IS YOU'RE WORKING FOR THEY SHOULD DO THEIR OWN DIRTY WORK!

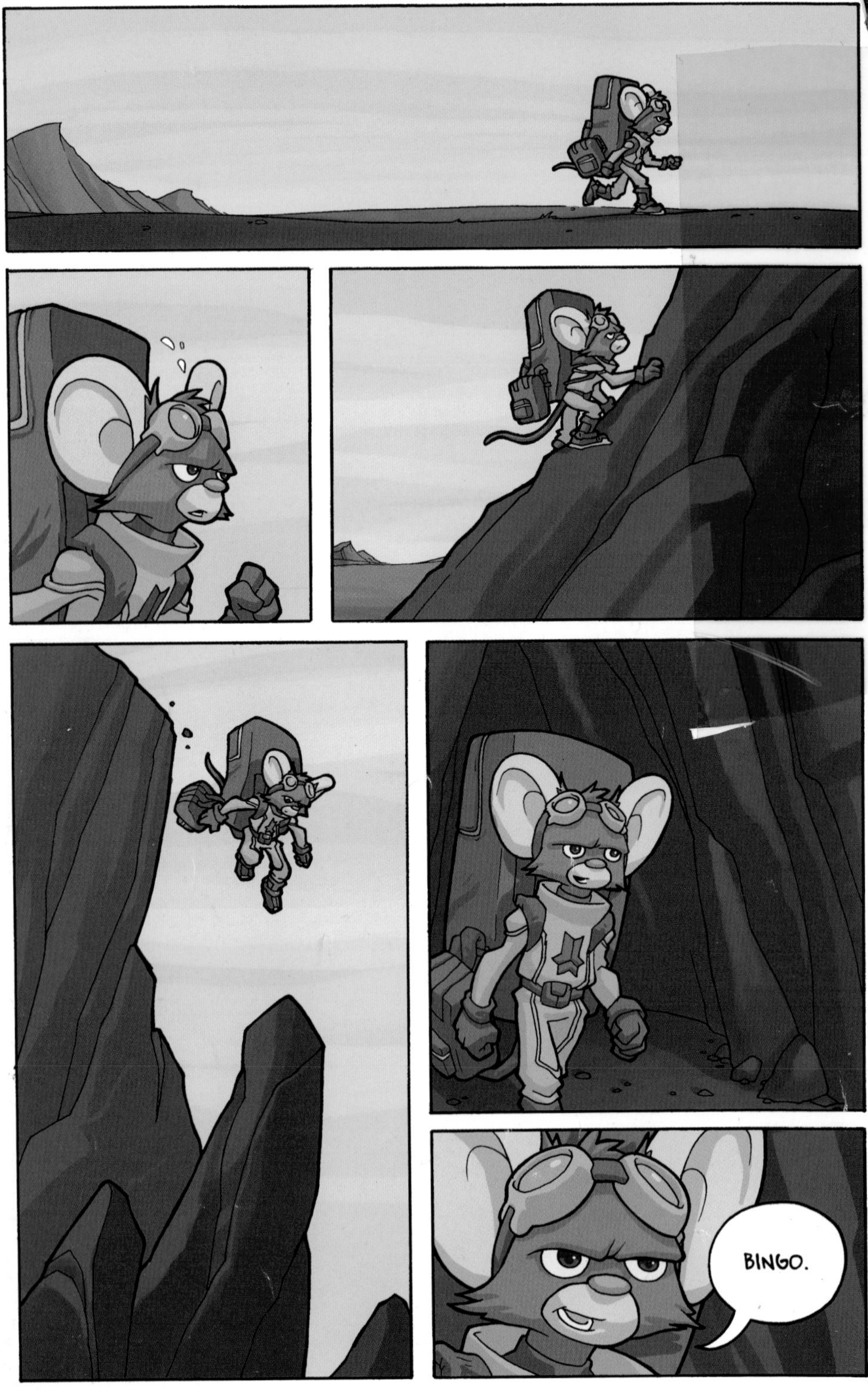
BINGO.

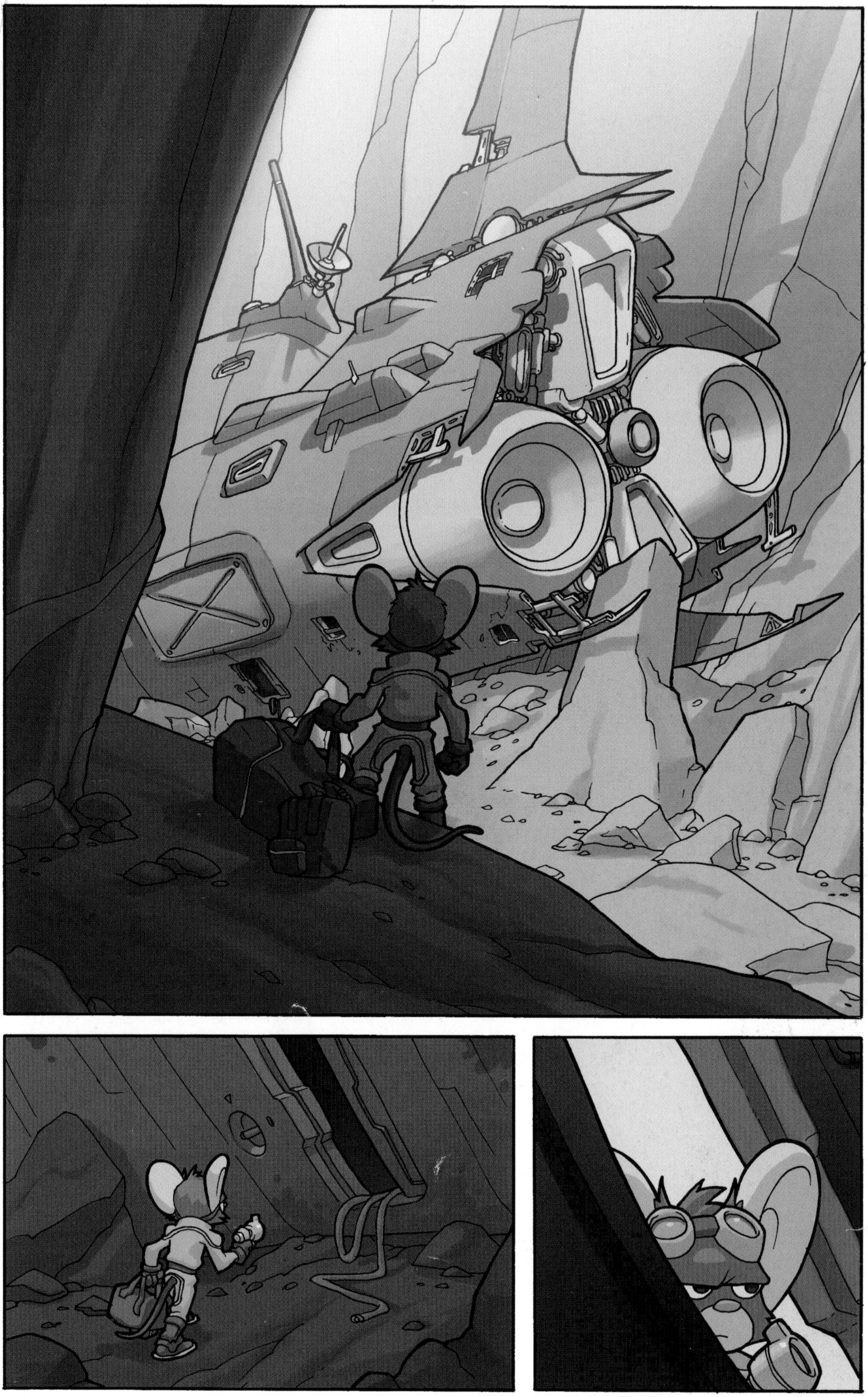

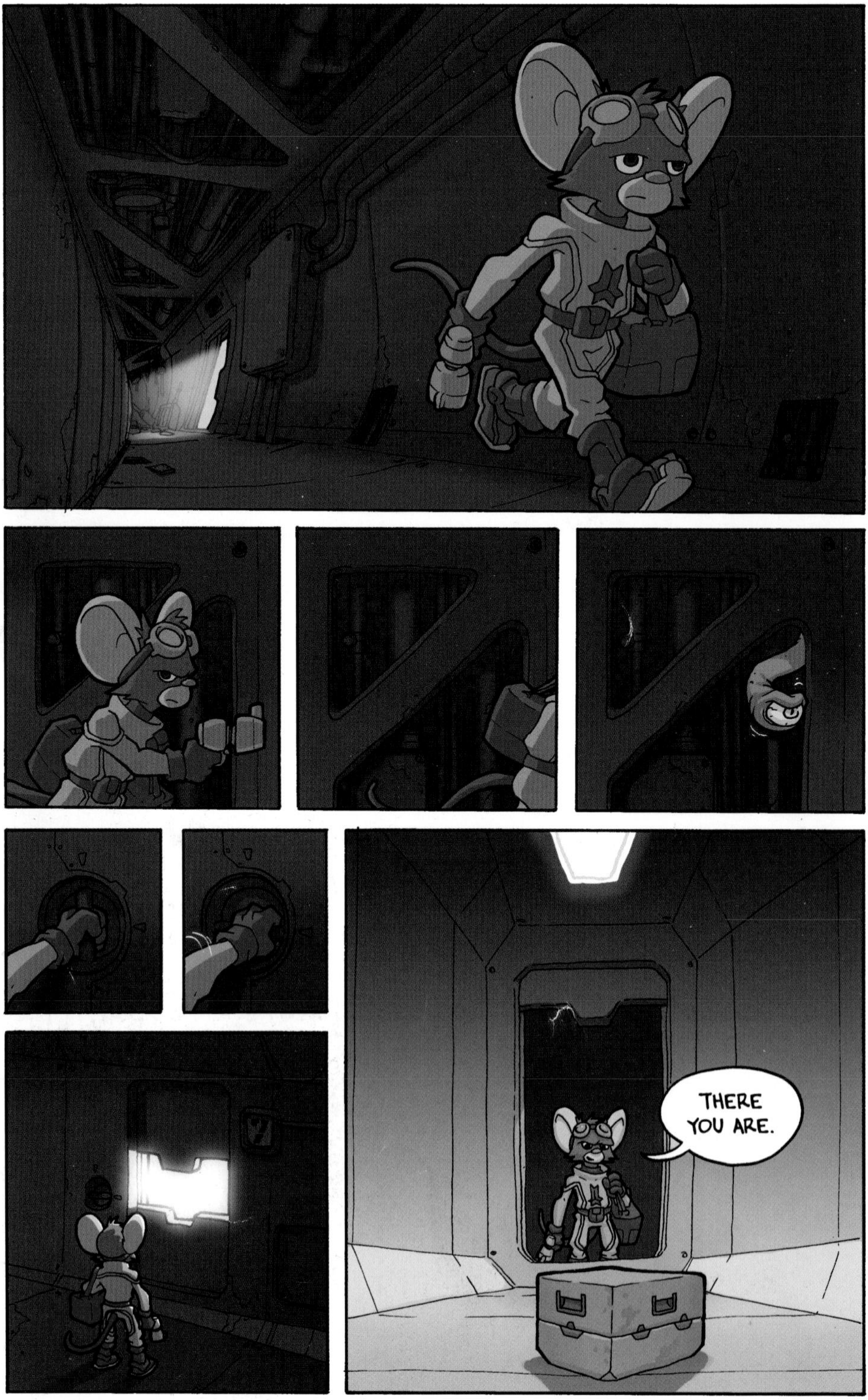
THERE YOU ARE.

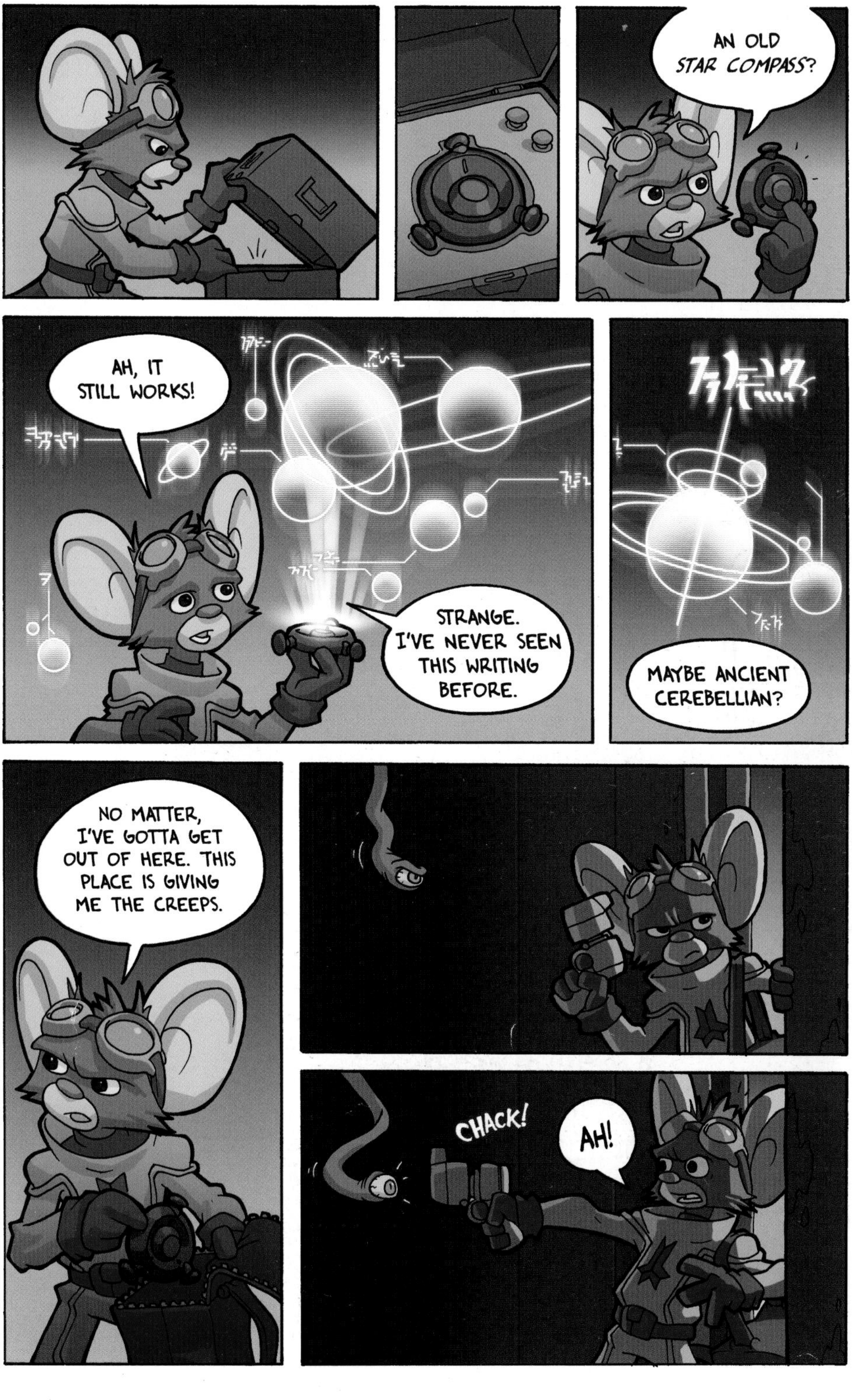
AN OLD STAR COMPASS?
AH, IT STILL WORKS!
STRANGE. I'VE NEVER SEEN THIS WRITING BEFORE.
MAYBE ANCIENT CEREBELLIAN?
NO MATTER, I'VE GOTTA GET OUT OF HERE. THIS PLACE IS GIVING ME THE CREEPS.
CHACK!
AH!

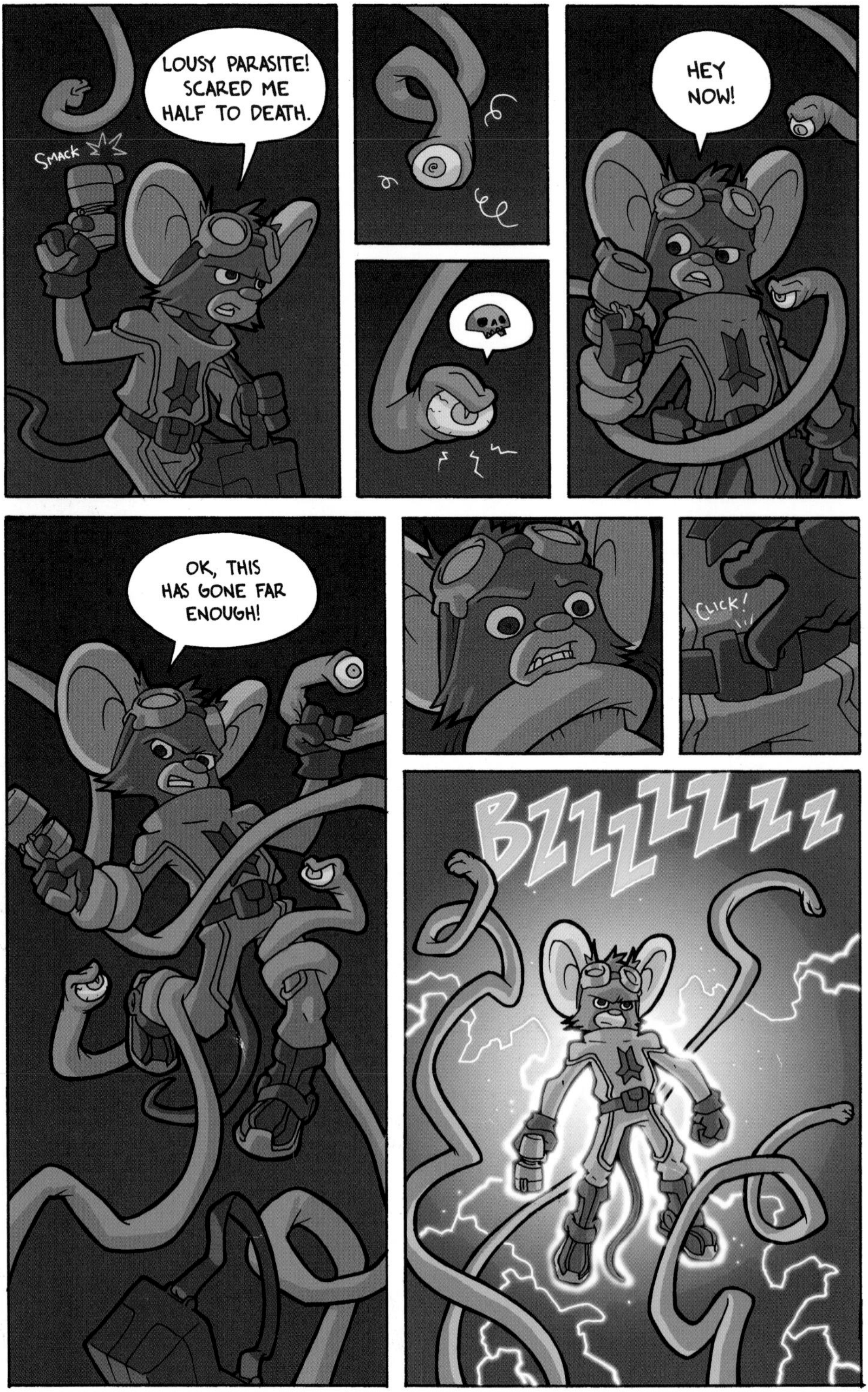
LOUSY PARASITE! SCARED ME HALF TO DEATH.
SMACK
HEY NOW!
OK, THIS HAS GONE FAR ENOUGH!
CLICK!
BZZZZZZZ

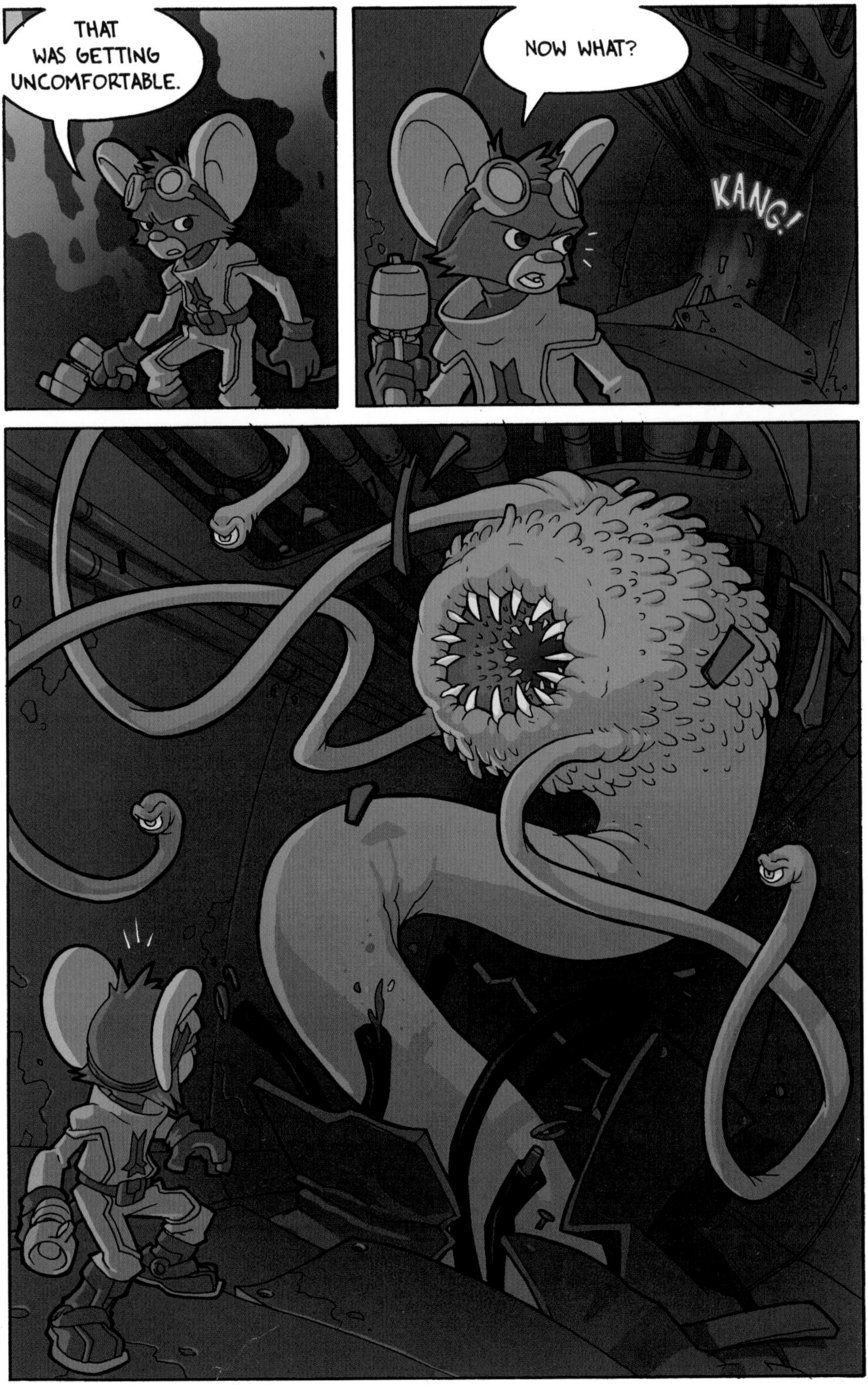
THAT WAS GETTING UNCOMFORTABLE.
NOW WHAT?
KANG!

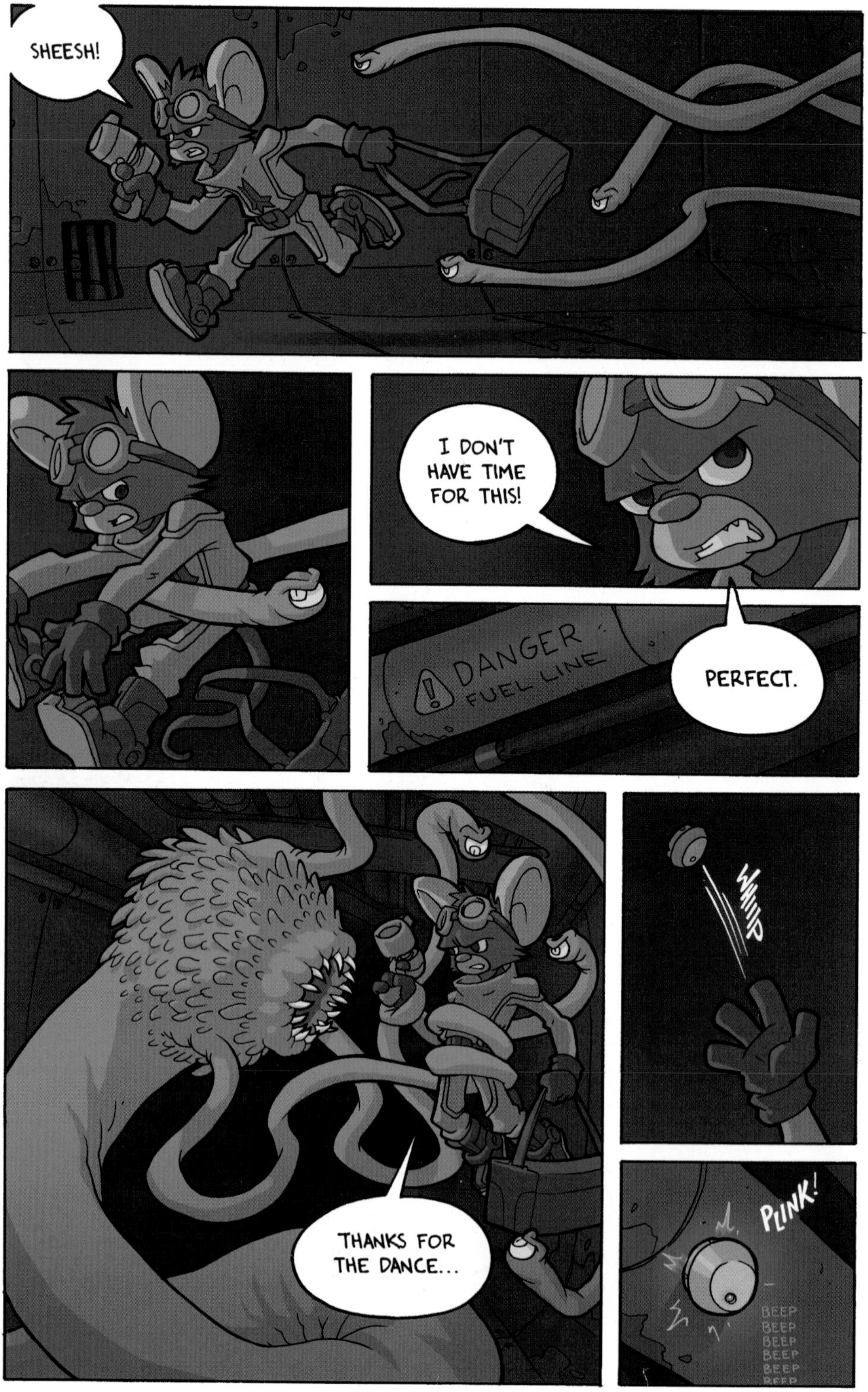

SHEESH!
I DON'T HAVE TIME FOR THIS!
DANGER
FUEL LINE
PERFECT.
THANKS FOR THE DANCE...
WHIP
PLINK!
BEEP
BEEP
BEEP
BEEP
BEEP

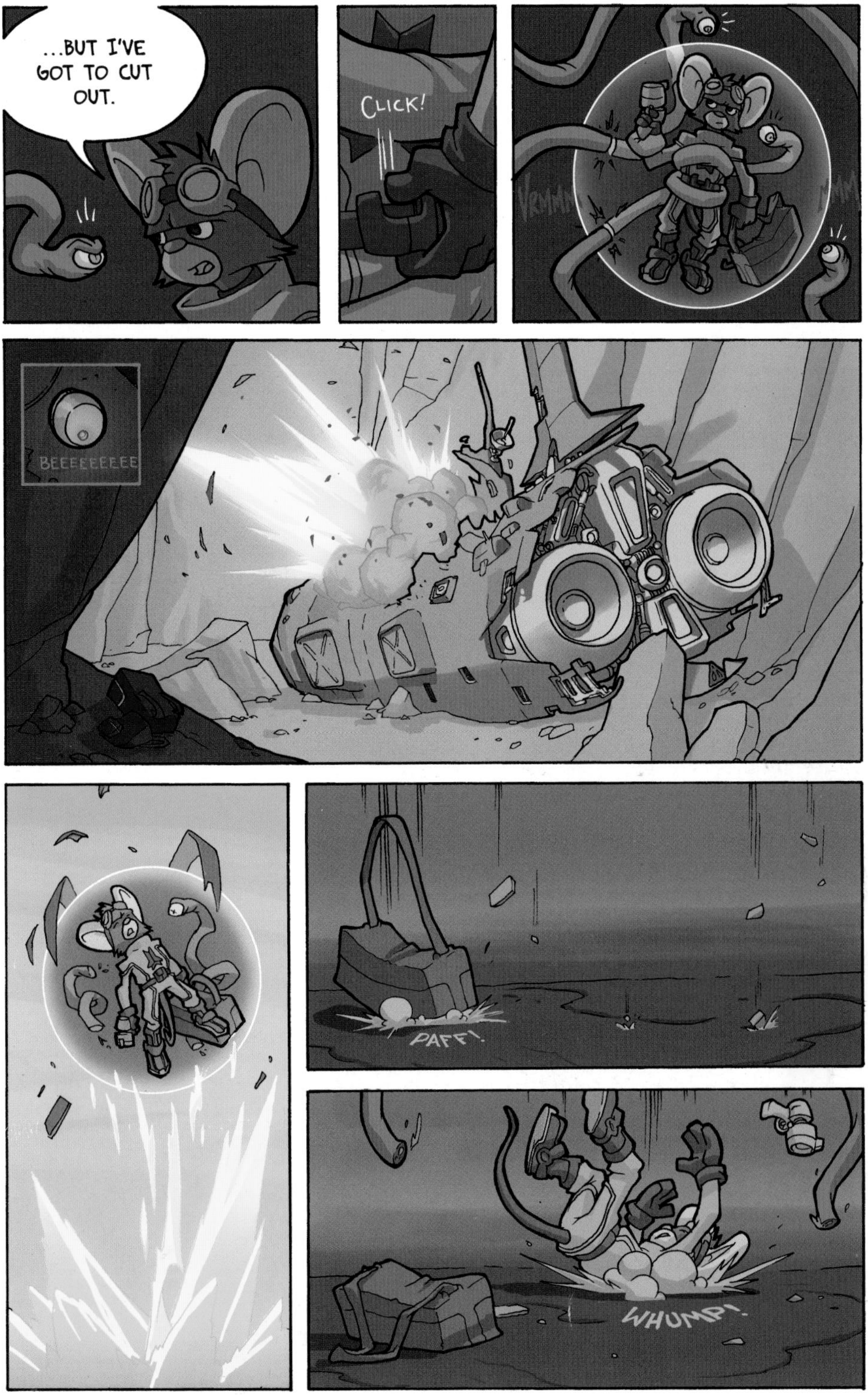
...BUT I'VE GOT TO CUT OUT.
CLICK!
BEEEEEEEEE
PAFF!
WHUMP!

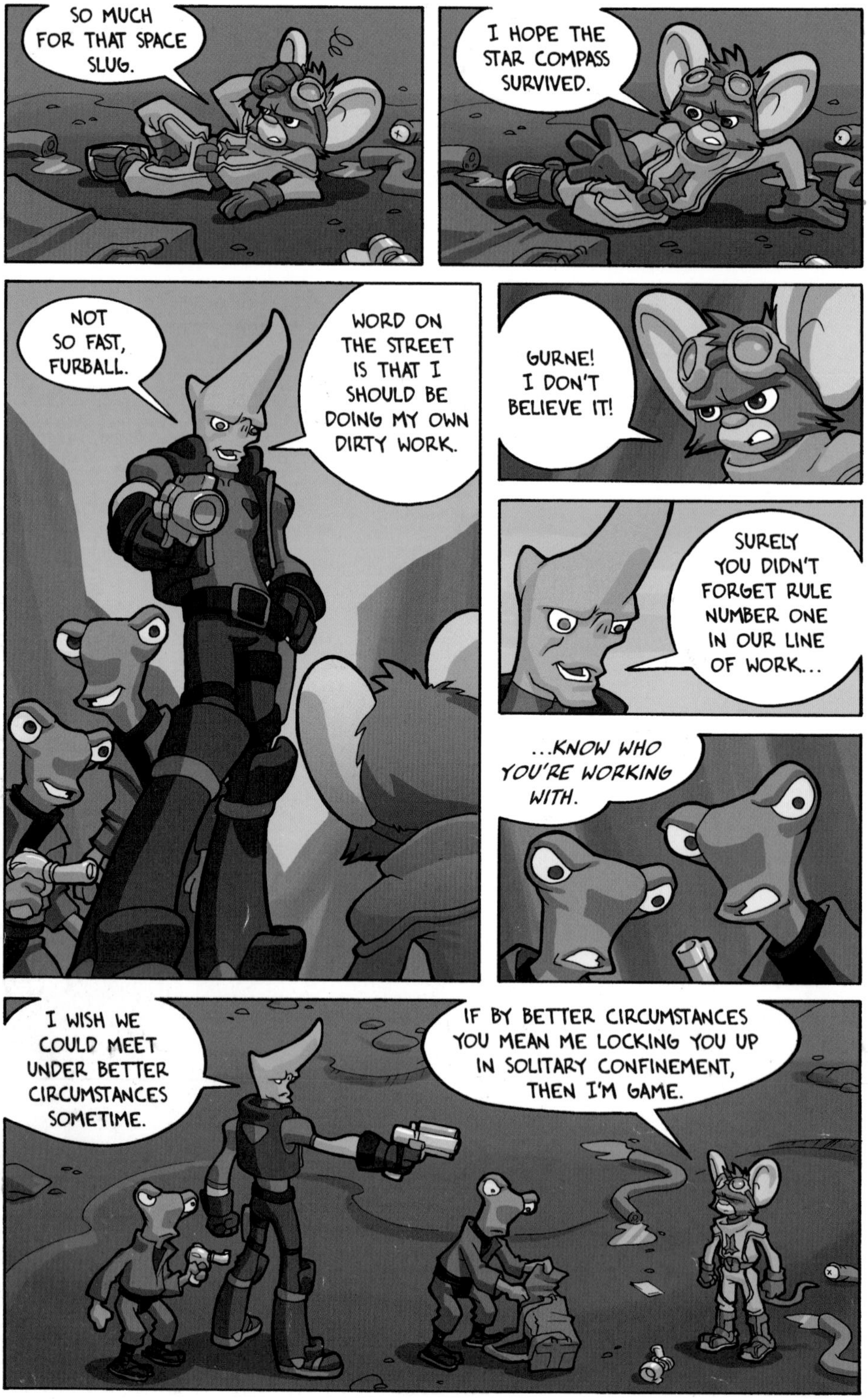
SO MUCH FOR THAT SPACE SLUG.
I HOPE THE STAR COMPASS SURVIVED.
NOT SO FAST, FURBALL.
WORD ON THE STREET IS THAT I SHOULD BE DOING MY OWN DIRTY WORK.
GURNE! I DON'T BELIEVE IT!
SURELY YOU DIDN'T FORGET RULE NUMBER ONE IN OUR LINE OF WORK...
...KNOW WHO YOU'RE WORKING WITH.
I WISH WE COULD MEET UNDER BETTER CIRCUMSTANCES SOMETIME.
IF BY BETTER CIRCUMSTANCES YOU MEAN ME LOCKING YOU UP IN SOLITARY CONFINEMENT, THEN I'M GAME.

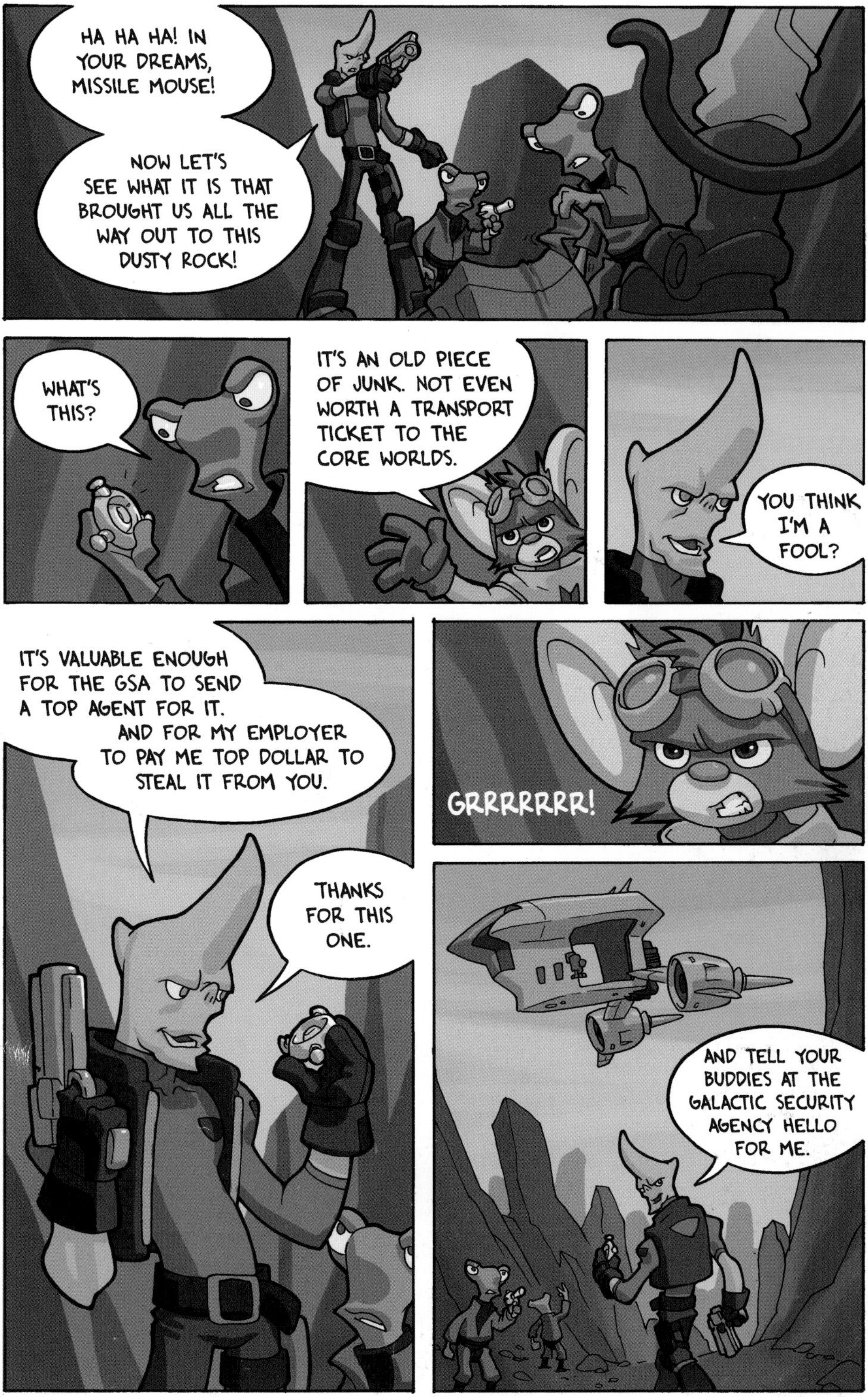
HA HA HA! IN YOUR DREAMS, MISSILE MOUSE!
NOW LET'S SEE WHAT IT IS THAT BROUGHT US ALL THE WAY OUT TO THIS DUSTY ROCK!
WHAT'S THIS?
IT'S AN OLD PIECE OF JUNK. NOT EVEN WORTH A TRANSPORT TICKET TO THE CORE WORLDS.
YOU THINK I'M A FOOL?
IT'S VALUABLE ENOUGH FOR THE GSA TO SEND A TOP AGENT FOR IT.
AND FOR MY EMPLOYER TO PAY ME TOP DOLLAR TO STEAL IT FROM YOU.
GRRRRRRR!
THANKS FOR THIS ONE.
AND TELL YOUR BUDDIES AT THE GALACTIC SECURITY AGENCY HELLO FOR ME.

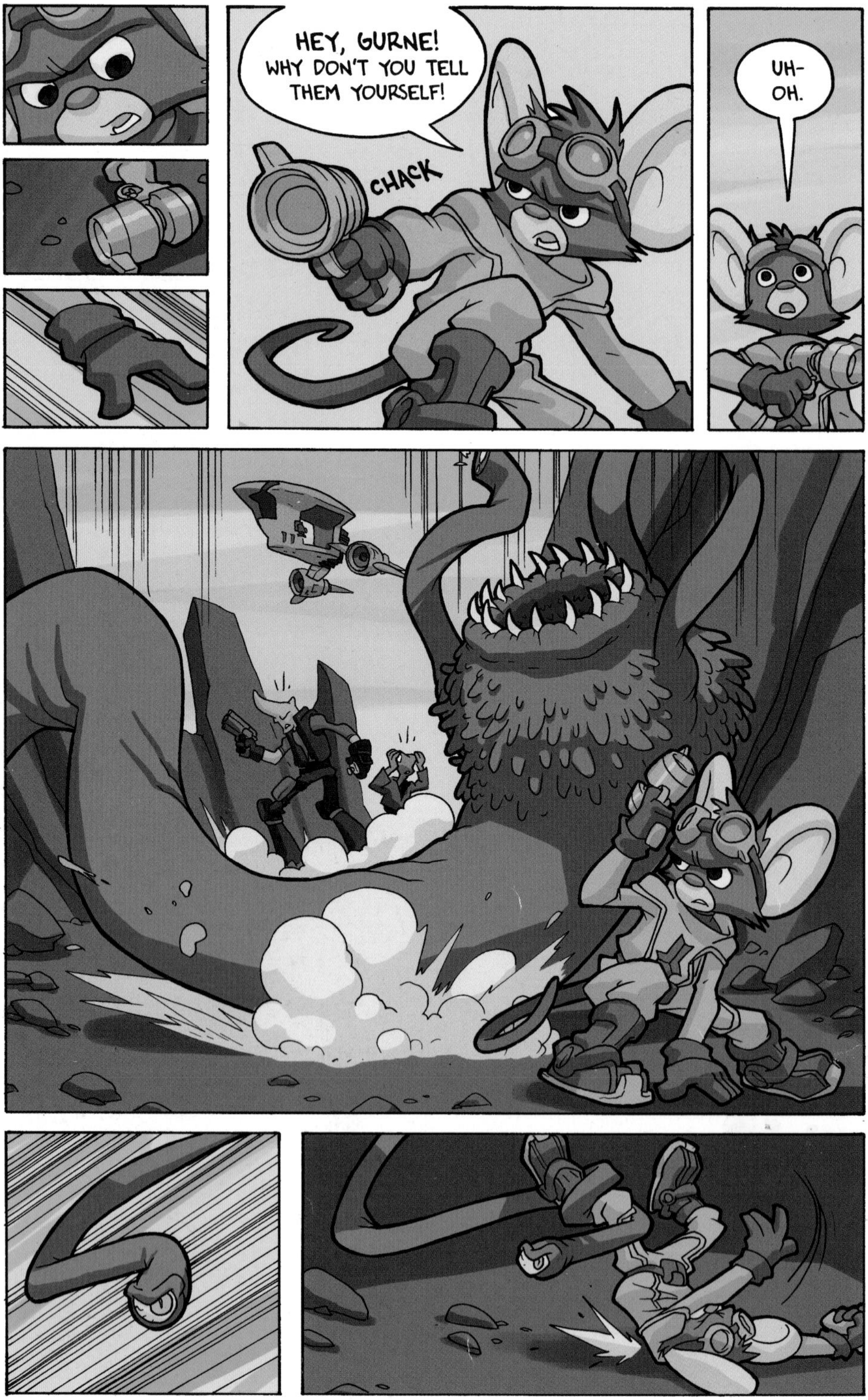
HEY, GURNE! WHY DON'T YOU TELL THEM YOURSELF!
CHACK
UH-OH.

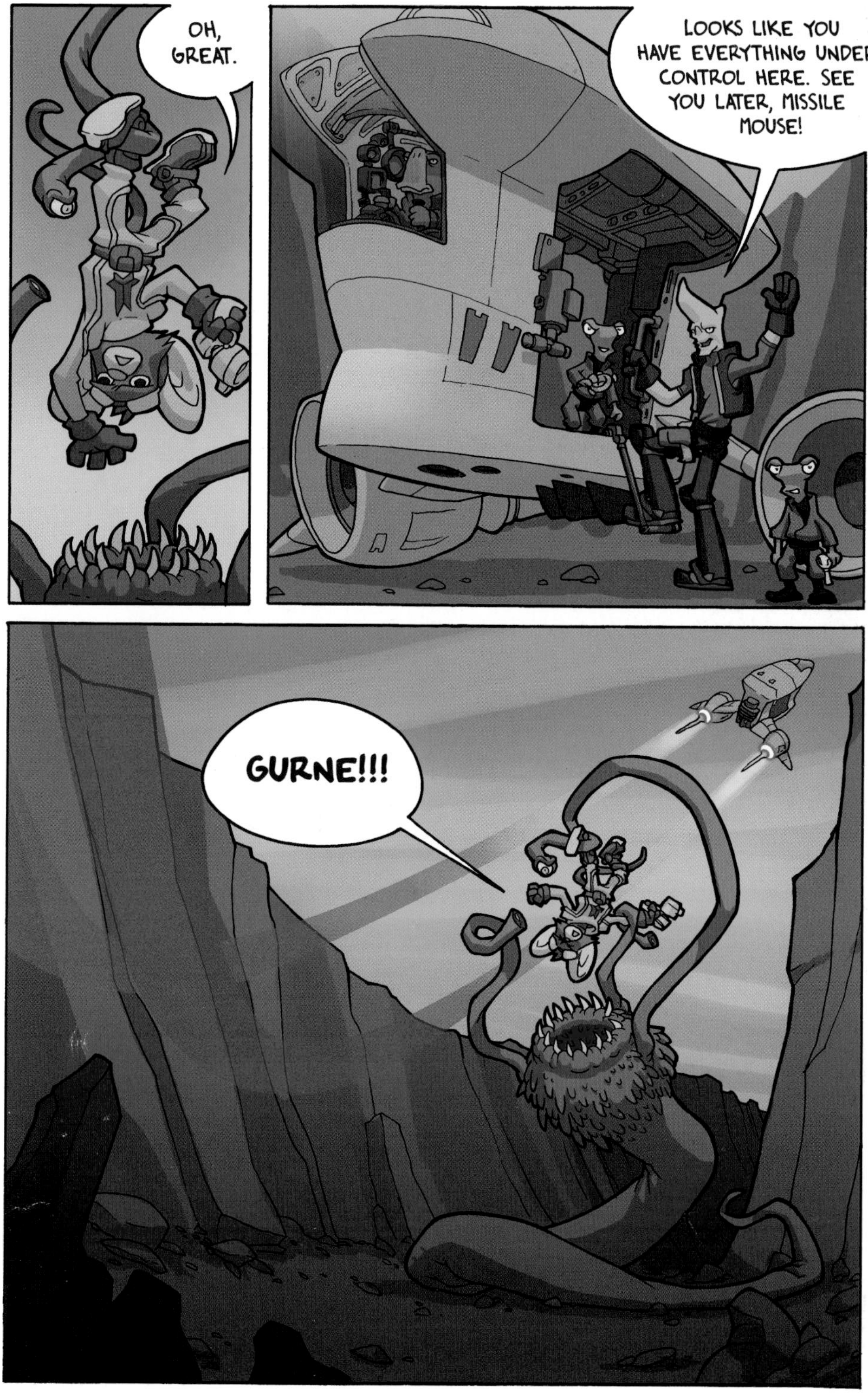
OH, GREAT.
LOOKS LIKE YOU HAVE EVERYTHING UNDER CONTROL HERE. SEE YOU LATER, MISSILE MOUSE!
GURNE!!!

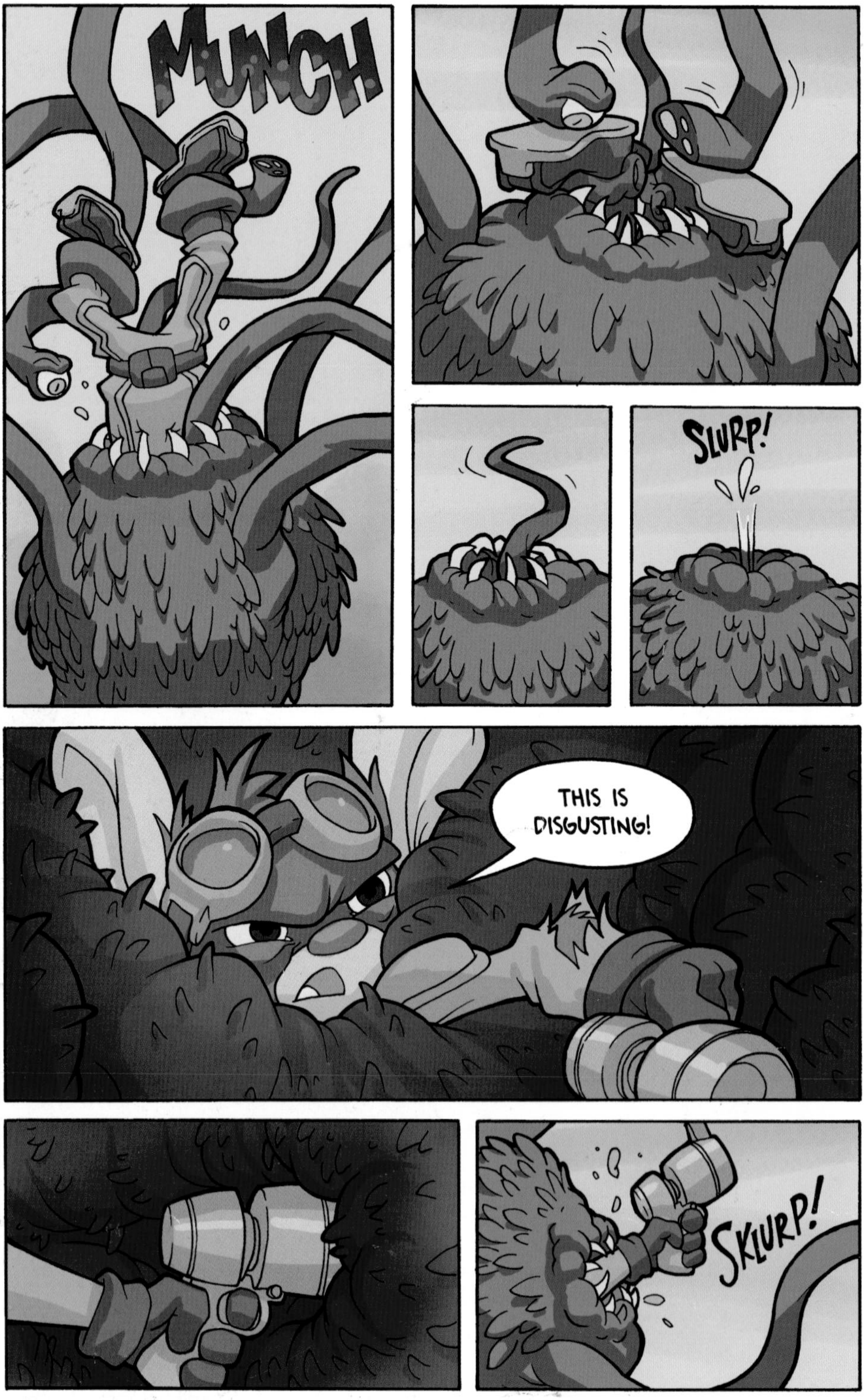
MUNCH
SLURP!
THIS IS DISGUSTING!
SKLURP!

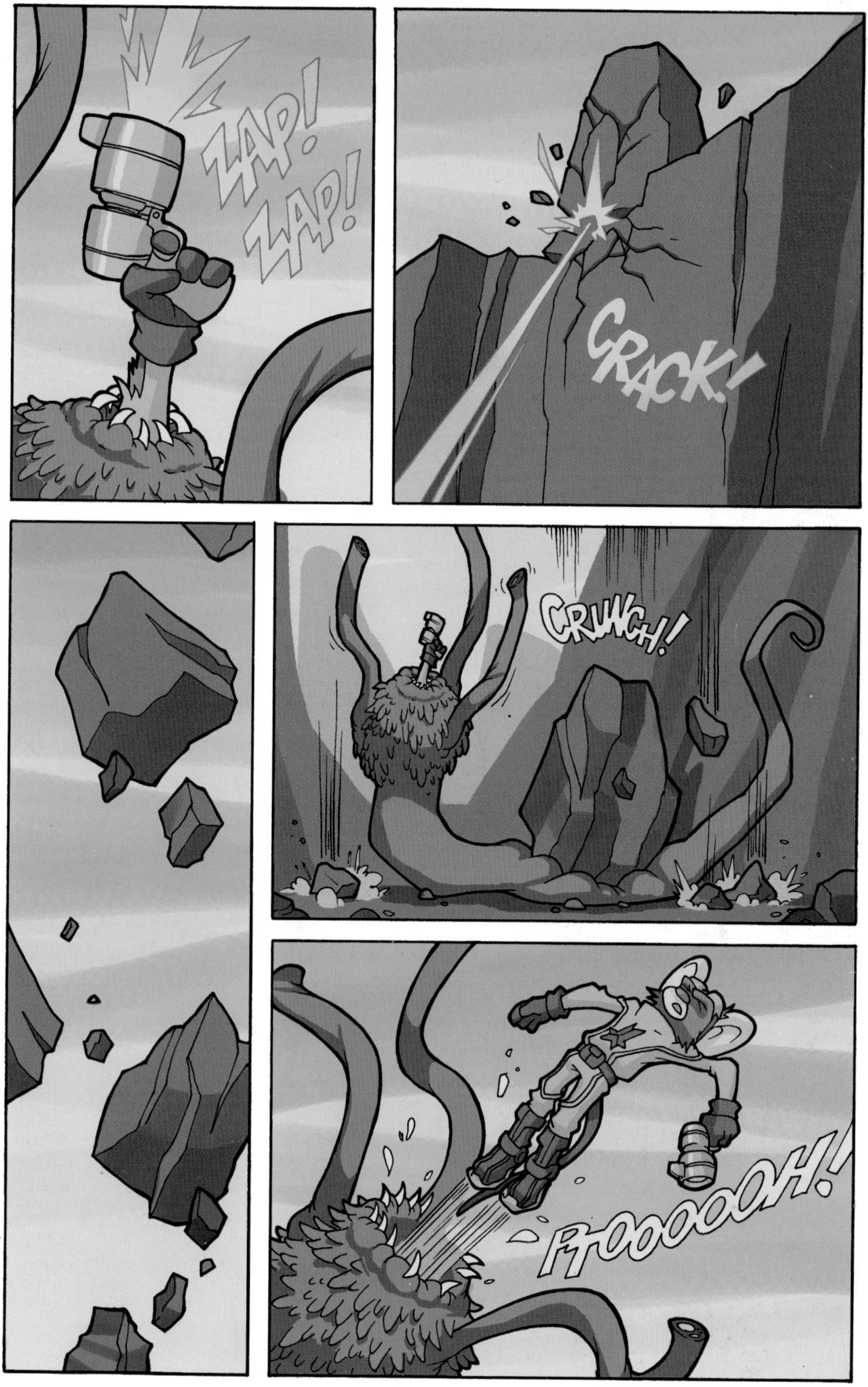
ZAP!
ZAP!
CRACK!
CRUNCH!
PTOOOOOOH!

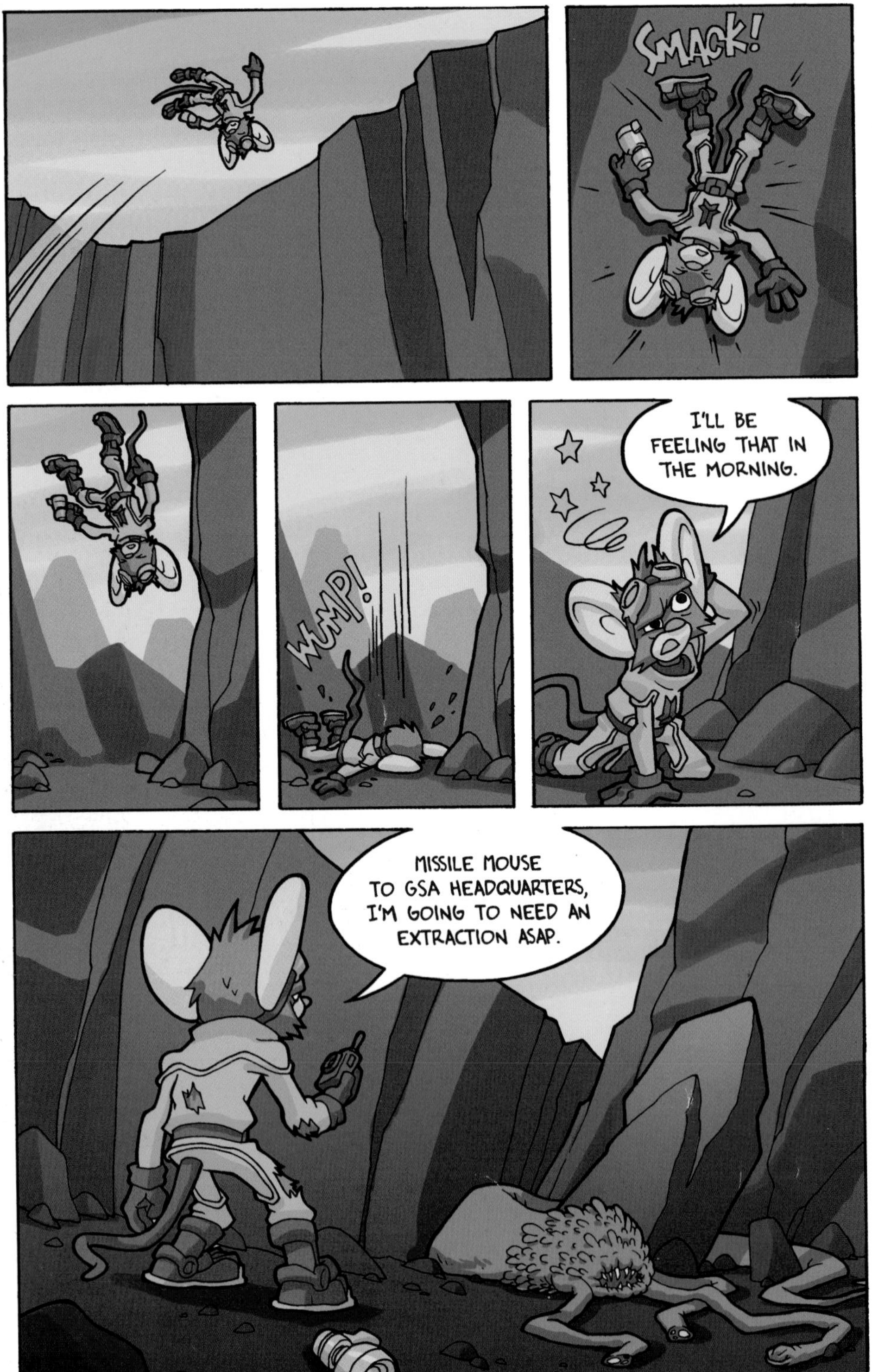
SMACK!
WUMP!
I'LL BE FEELING THAT IN THE MORNING.
MISSILE MOUSE TO GSA HEADQUARTERS, I'M GOING TO NEED AN EXTRACTION ASAP.

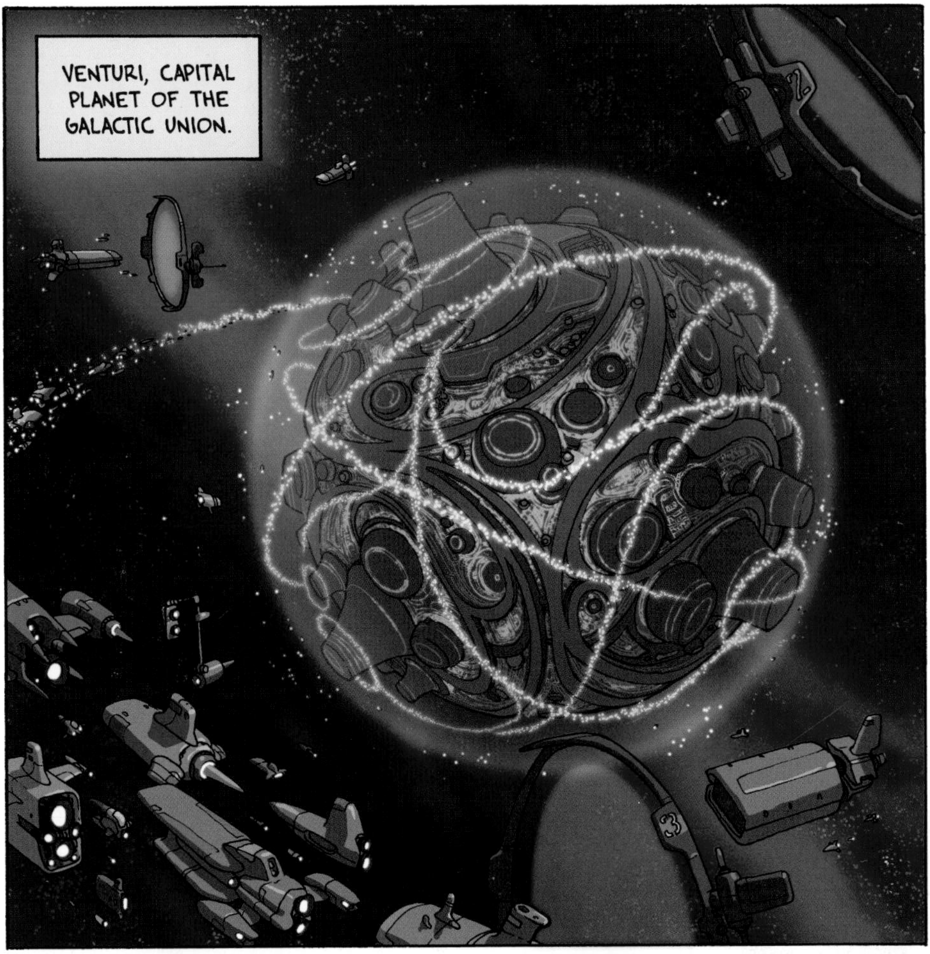
VENTURI, CAPITAL PLANET OF THE GALACTIC UNION.

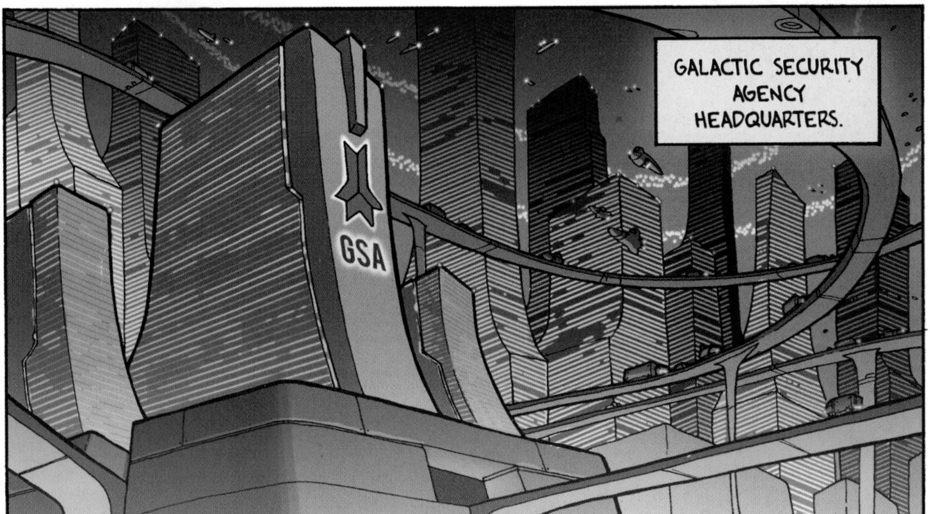
GALACTIC SECURITY AGENCY HEADQUARTERS.
GSA

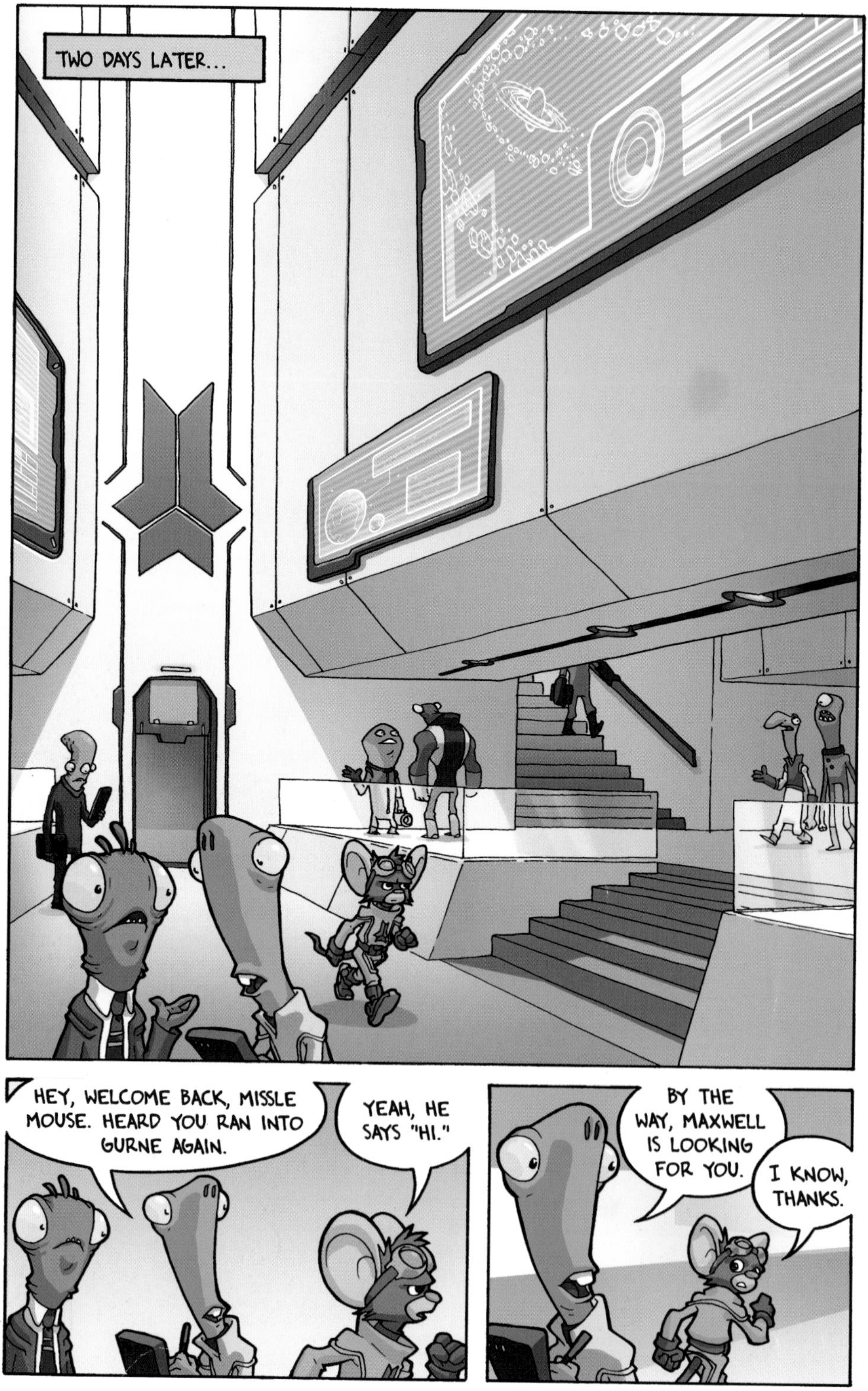
TWO DAYS LATER...
HEY, WELCOME BACK, MISSLE MOUSE. HEARD YOU RAN INTO GURNE AGAIN.
YEAH, HE SAYS "HI."
BY THE WAY, MAXWELL IS LOOKING FOR YOU.
I KNOW, THANKS.

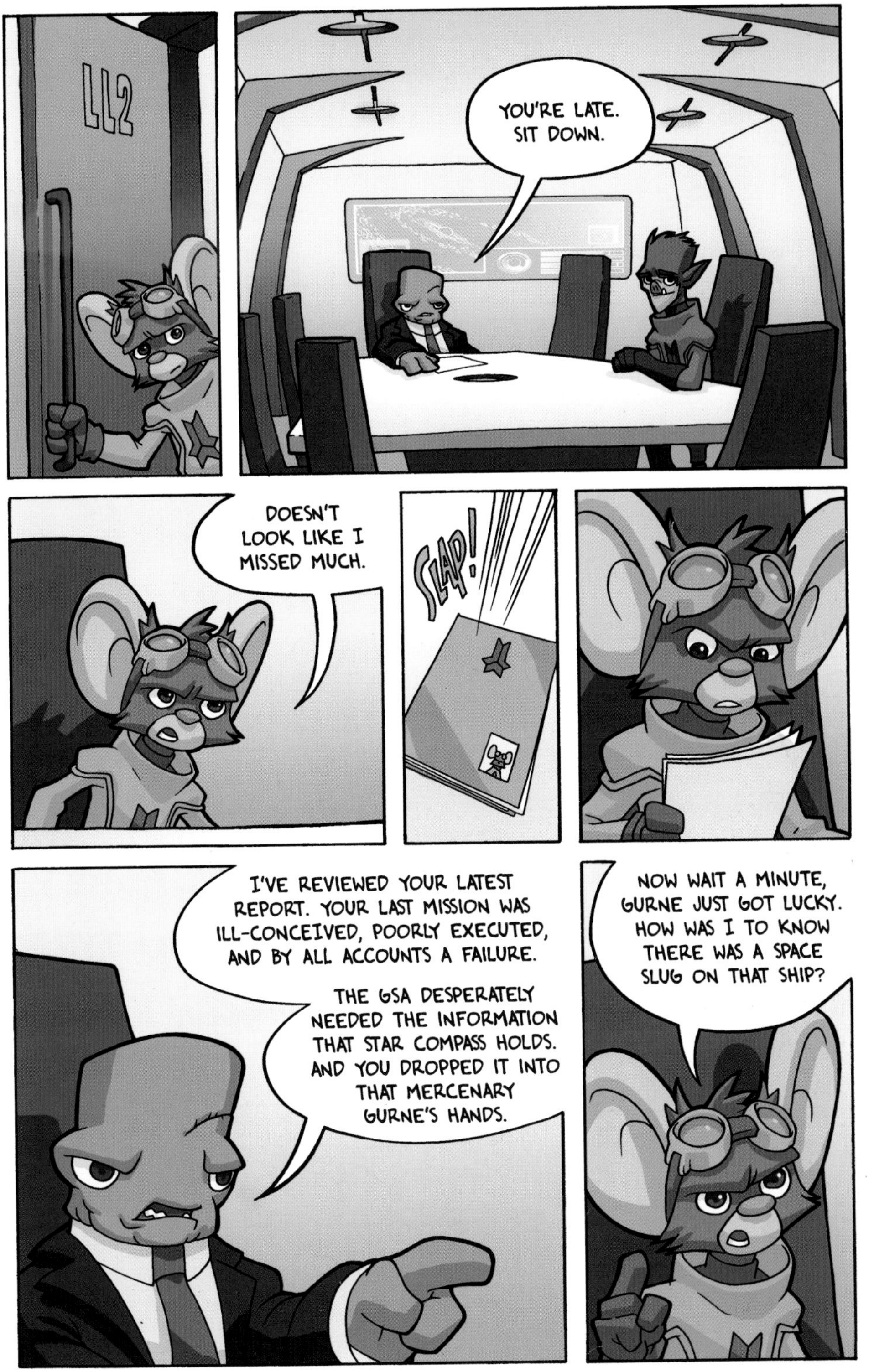
LL2
YOU'RE LATE. SIT DOWN.
DOESN'T LOOK LIKE I MISSED MUCH.
SLAP!
I'VE REVIEWED YOUR LATEST REPORT. YOUR LAST MISSION WAS ILL-CONCEIVED, POORLY EXECUTED, AND BY ALL ACCOUNTS A FAILURE.
THE GSA DESPERATELY NEEDED THE INFORMATION THAT STAR COMPASS HOLDS. AND YOU DROPPED IT INTO THAT MERCENARY GURNE'S HANDS.
NOW WAIT A MINUTE, GURNE JUST GOT LUCKY. HOW WAS I TO KNOW THERE WAS A SPACE SLUG ON THAT SHIP?

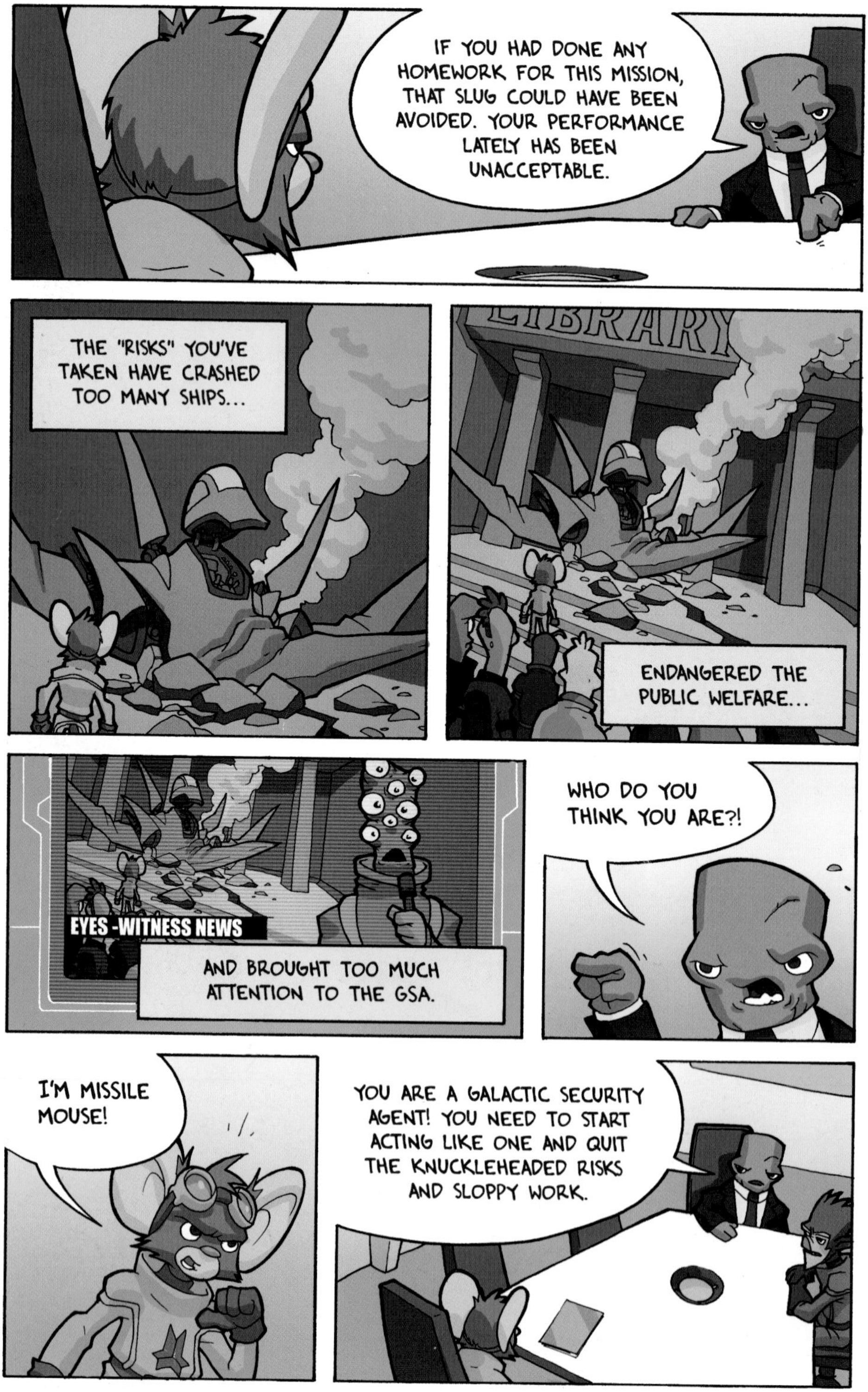
IF YOU HAD DONE ANY HOMEWORK FOR THIS MISSION, THAT SLUG COULD HAVE BEEN AVOIDED. YOUR PERFORMANCE LATELY HAS BEEN UNACCEPTABLE.
THE "RISKS" YOU'VE TAKEN HAVE CRASHED TOO MANY SHIPS...
LIBRARY
ENDANGERED THE PUBLIC WELFARE...
EYES -WITNESS NEWS
AND BROUGHT TOO MUCH ATTENTION TO THE GSA.
WHO DO YOU THINK YOU ARE?!
I'M MISSILE MOUSE!
YOU ARE A GALACTIC SECURITY AGENT! YOU NEED TO START ACTING LIKE ONE AND QUIT THE KNUCKLEHEADED RISKS AND SLOPPY WORK.

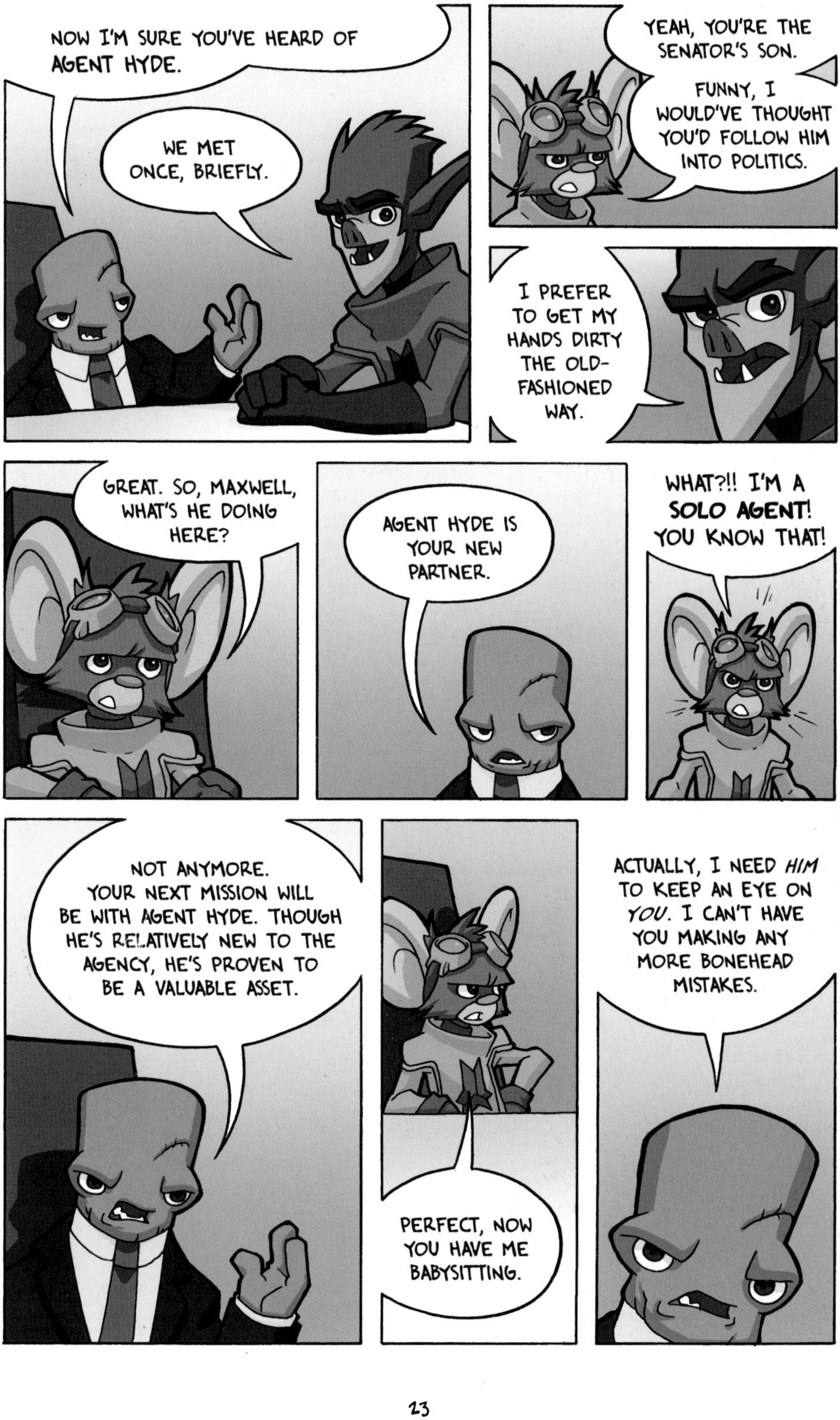
NOW I'M SURE YOU'VE HEARD OF AGENT HYDE.
WE MET ONCE, BRIEFLY.
YEAH, YOU'RE THE SENATOR'S SON.
FUNNY, I WOULD'VE THOUGHT YOU'D FOLLOW HIM INTO POLITICS.
I PREFER TO GET MY HANDS DIRTY THE OLD-FASHIONED WAY.
GREAT. SO, MAXWELL, WHAT'S HE DOING HERE?
AGENT HYDE IS YOUR NEW PARTNER.
WHAT?!! I'M A **SOLO AGENT**! YOU KNOW THAT!
NOT ANYMORE. YOUR NEXT MISSION WILL BE WITH AGENT HYDE. THOUGH HE'S RELATIVELY NEW TO THE AGENCY, HE'S PROVEN TO BE A VALUABLE ASSET.
PERFECT, NOW YOU HAVE ME BABYSITTING.
ACTUALLY, I NEED *HIM* TO KEEP AN EYE ON *YOU*. I CAN'T HAVE YOU MAKING ANY MORE BONEHEAD MISTAKES.

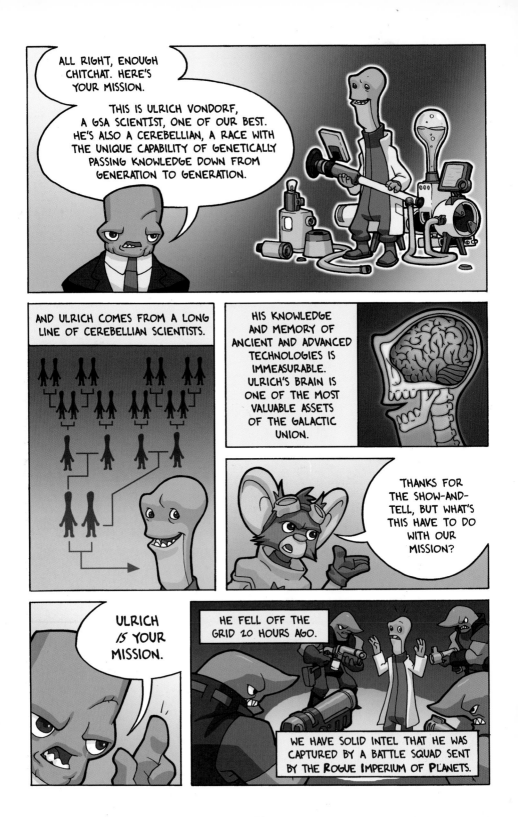

ALL RIGHT, ENOUGH CHITCHAT. HERE'S YOUR MISSION.

THIS IS ULRICH VONDORF, A GSA SCIENTIST, ONE OF OUR BEST. HE'S ALSO A CEREBELLIAN, A RACE WITH THE UNIQUE CAPABILITY OF GENETICALLY PASSING KNOWLEDGE DOWN FROM GENERATION TO GENERATION.

AND ULRICH COMES FROM A LONG LINE OF CEREBELLIAN SCIENTISTS.

HIS KNOWLEDGE AND MEMORY OF ANCIENT AND ADVANCED TECHNOLOGIES IS IMMEASURABLE. ULRICH'S BRAIN IS ONE OF THE MOST VALUABLE ASSETS OF THE GALACTIC UNION.

THANKS FOR THE SHOW-AND-TELL, BUT WHAT'S THIS HAVE TO DO WITH OUR MISSION?

ULRICH *IS* YOUR MISSION.

HE FELL OFF THE GRID 20 HOURS AGO.

WE HAVE SOLID INTEL THAT HE WAS CAPTURED BY A BATTLE SQUAD SENT BY THE ROGUE IMPERIUM OF PLANETS.

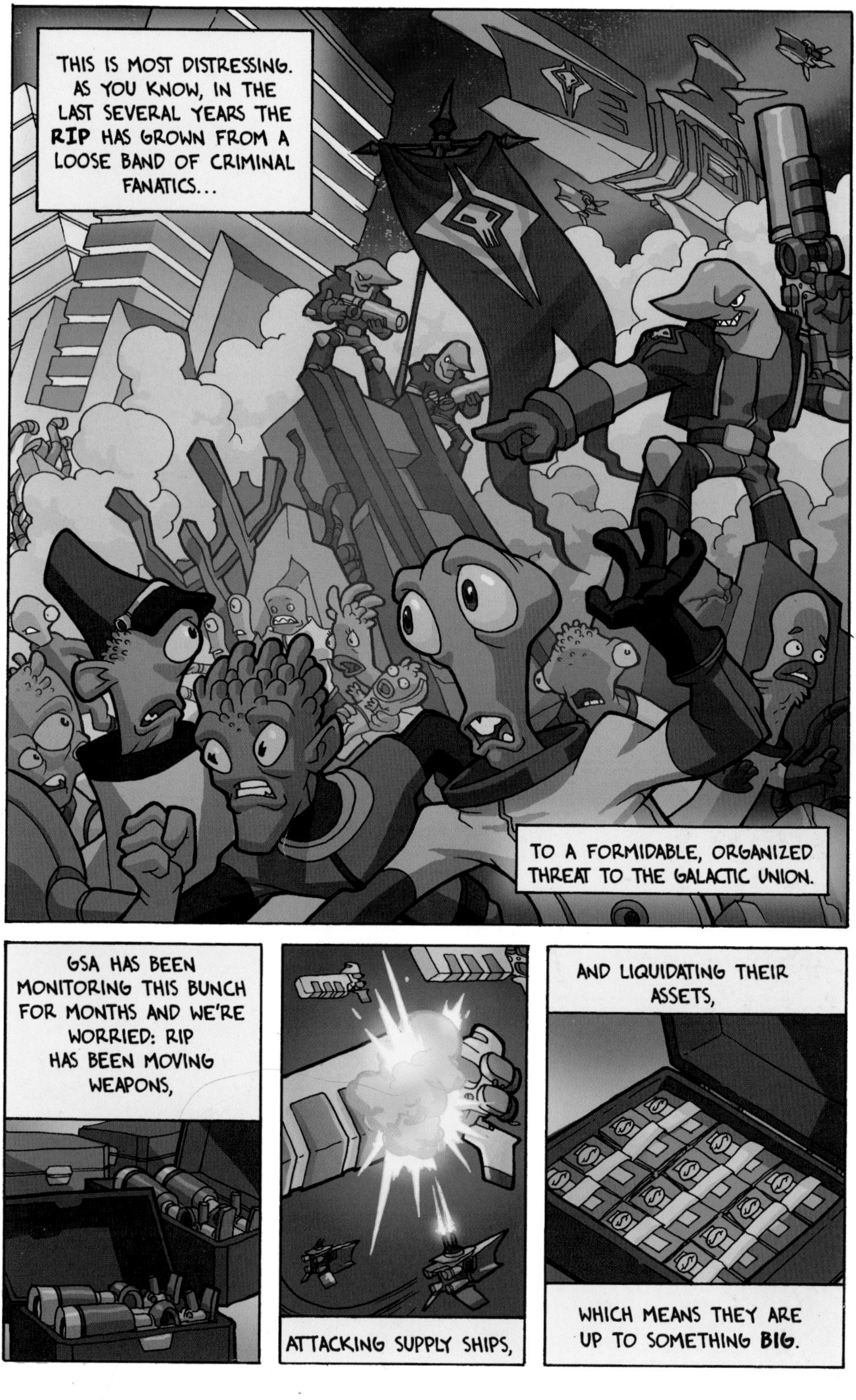
THIS IS MOST DISTRESSING. AS YOU KNOW, IN THE LAST SEVERAL YEARS THE RIP HAS GROWN FROM A LOOSE BAND OF CRIMINAL FANATICS...
TO A FORMIDABLE, ORGANIZED THREAT TO THE GALACTIC UNION.
GSA HAS BEEN MONITORING THIS BUNCH FOR MONTHS AND WE'RE WORRIED: RIP HAS BEEN MOVING WEAPONS,
ATTACKING SUPPLY SHIPS,
AND LIQUIDATING THEIR ASSETS,
WHICH MEANS THEY ARE UP TO SOMETHING BIG.

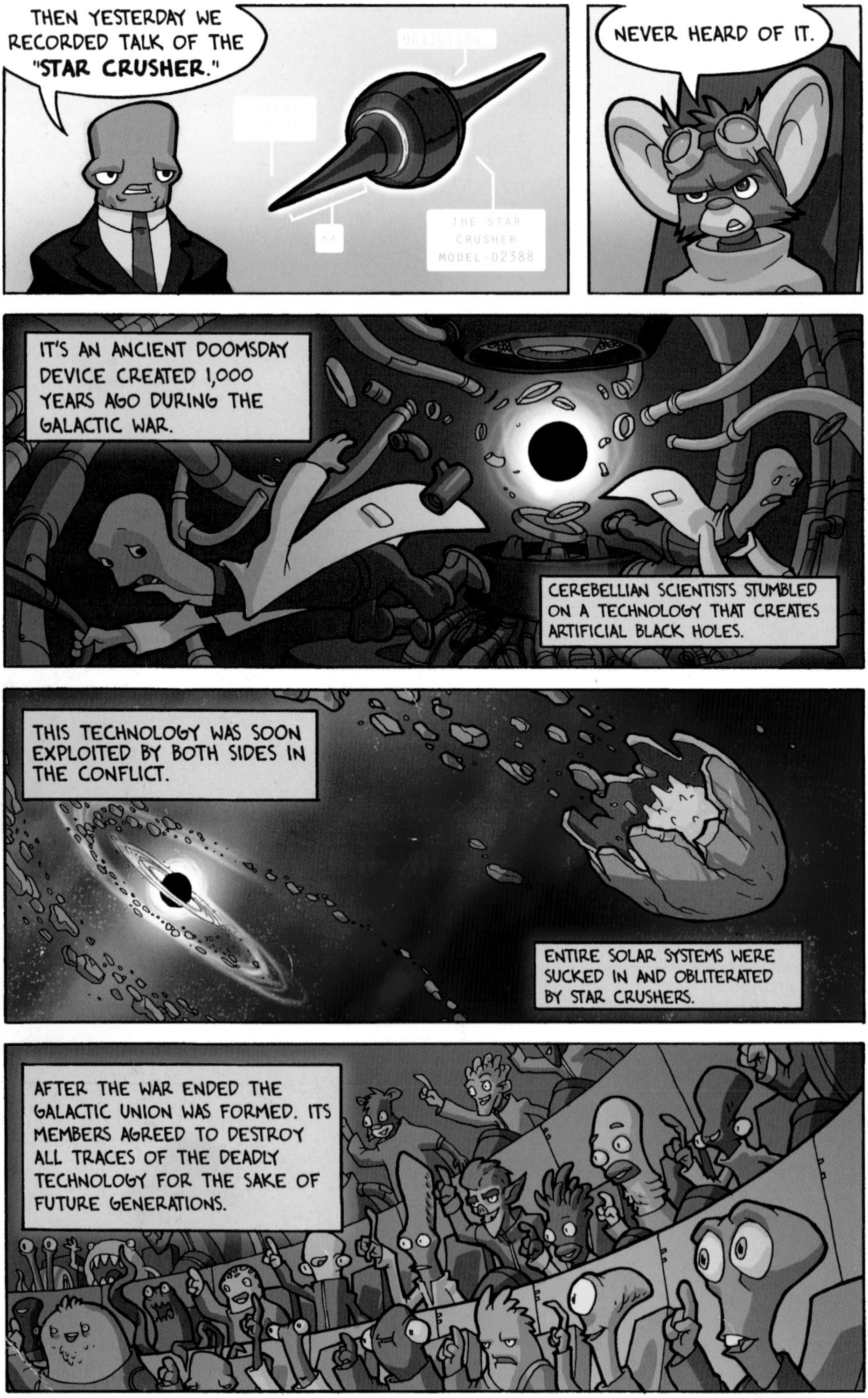
THEN YESTERDAY WE RECORDED TALK OF THE "STAR CRUSHER."
THE STAR CRUSHER MODEL-02388
NEVER HEARD OF IT.
IT'S AN ANCIENT DOOMSDAY DEVICE CREATED 1,000 YEARS AGO DURING THE GALACTIC WAR.
CEREBELLIAN SCIENTISTS STUMBLED ON A TECHNOLOGY THAT CREATES ARTIFICIAL BLACK HOLES.
THIS TECHNOLOGY WAS SOON EXPLOITED BY BOTH SIDES IN THE CONFLICT.
ENTIRE SOLAR SYSTEMS WERE SUCKED IN AND OBLITERATED BY STAR CRUSHERS.
AFTER THE WAR ENDED THE GALACTIC UNION WAS FORMED. ITS MEMBERS AGREED TO DESTROY ALL TRACES OF THE DEADLY TECHNOLOGY FOR THE SAKE OF FUTURE GENERATIONS.

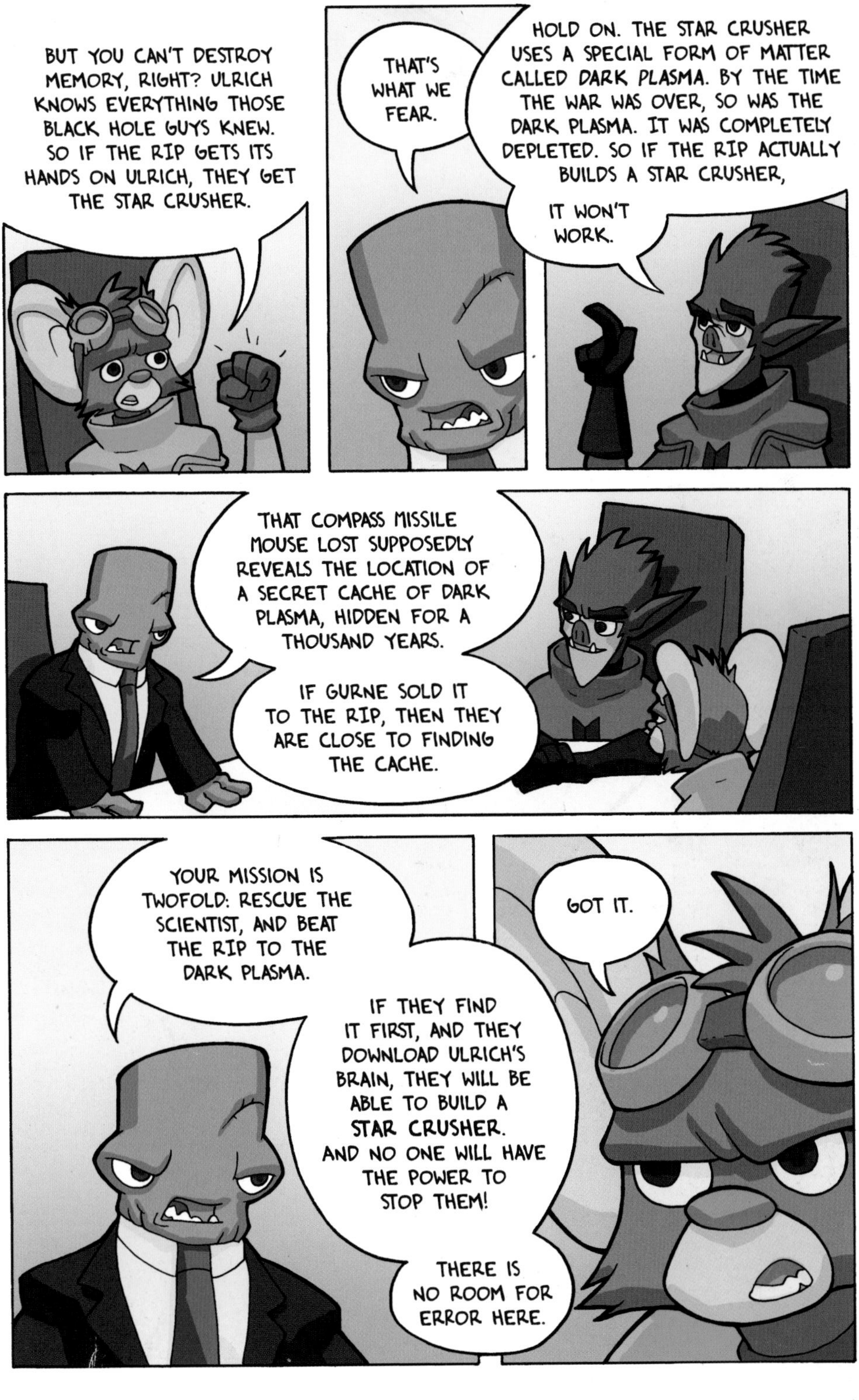
BUT YOU CAN'T DESTROY MEMORY, RIGHT? ULRICH KNOWS EVERYTHING THOSE BLACK HOLE GUYS KNEW. SO IF THE RIP GETS ITS HANDS ON ULRICH, THEY GET THE STAR CRUSHER.
THAT'S WHAT WE FEAR.
HOLD ON. THE STAR CRUSHER USES A SPECIAL FORM OF MATTER CALLED DARK PLASMA. BY THE TIME THE WAR WAS OVER, SO WAS THE DARK PLASMA. IT WAS COMPLETELY DEPLETED. SO IF THE RIP ACTUALLY BUILDS A STAR CRUSHER,
IT WON'T WORK.
THAT COMPASS MISSILE MOUSE LOST SUPPOSEDLY REVEALS THE LOCATION OF A SECRET CACHE OF DARK PLASMA, HIDDEN FOR A THOUSAND YEARS.
IF GURNE SOLD IT TO THE RIP, THEN THEY ARE CLOSE TO FINDING THE CACHE.
YOUR MISSION IS TWOFOLD: RESCUE THE SCIENTIST, AND BEAT THE RIP TO THE DARK PLASMA.
IF THEY FIND IT FIRST, AND THEY DOWNLOAD ULRICH'S BRAIN, THEY WILL BE ABLE TO BUILD A STAR CRUSHER. AND NO ONE WILL HAVE THE POWER TO STOP THEM!
THERE IS NO ROOM FOR ERROR HERE.
GOT IT.

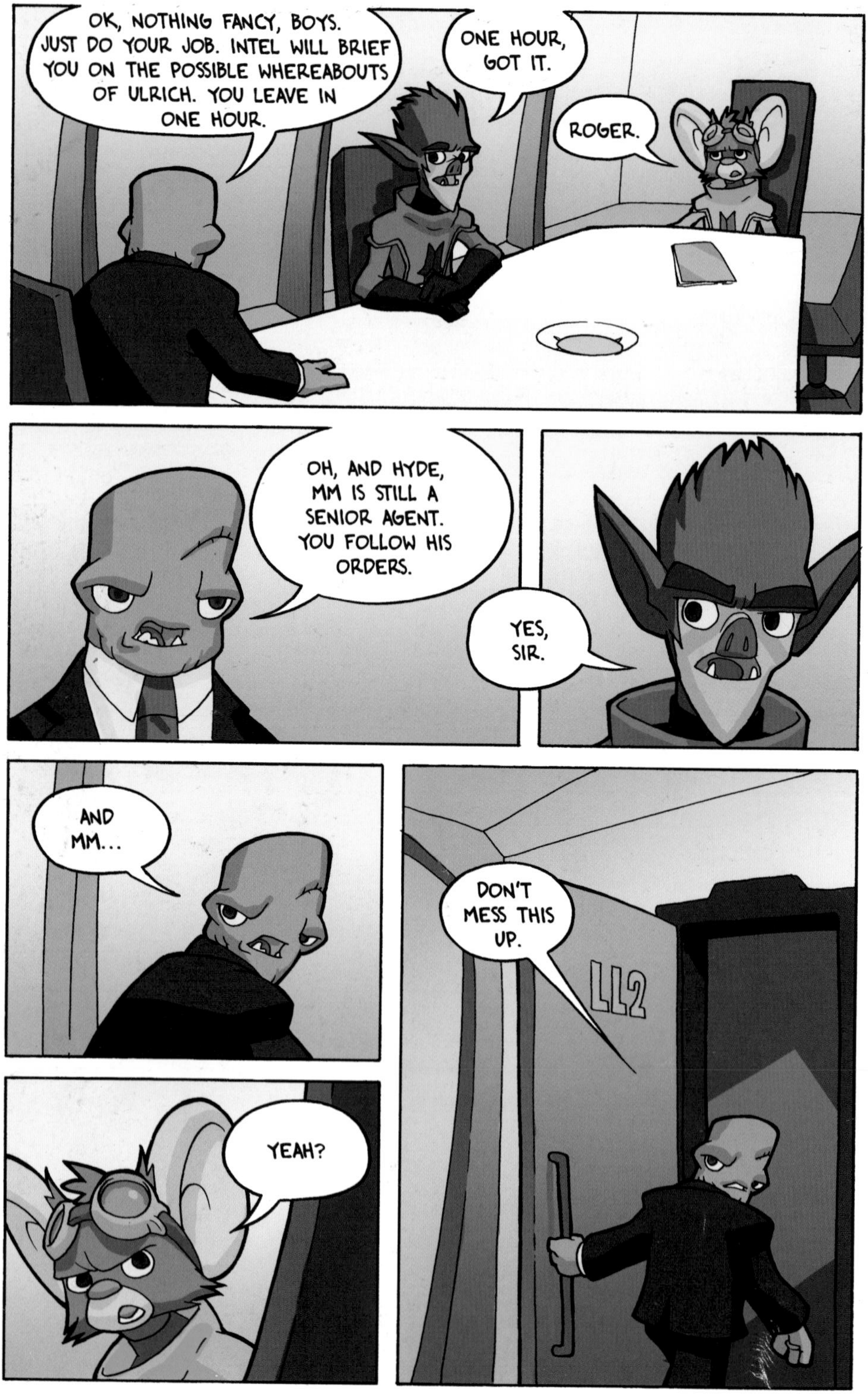
OK, NOTHING FANCY, BOYS. JUST DO YOUR JOB. INTEL WILL BRIEF YOU ON THE POSSIBLE WHEREABOUTS OF ULRICH. YOU LEAVE IN ONE HOUR.
ONE HOUR, GOT IT.
ROGER.
OH, AND HYDE, MM IS STILL A SENIOR AGENT. YOU FOLLOW HIS ORDERS.
YES, SIR.
AND MM...
YEAH?
DON'T MESS THIS UP.
LL2

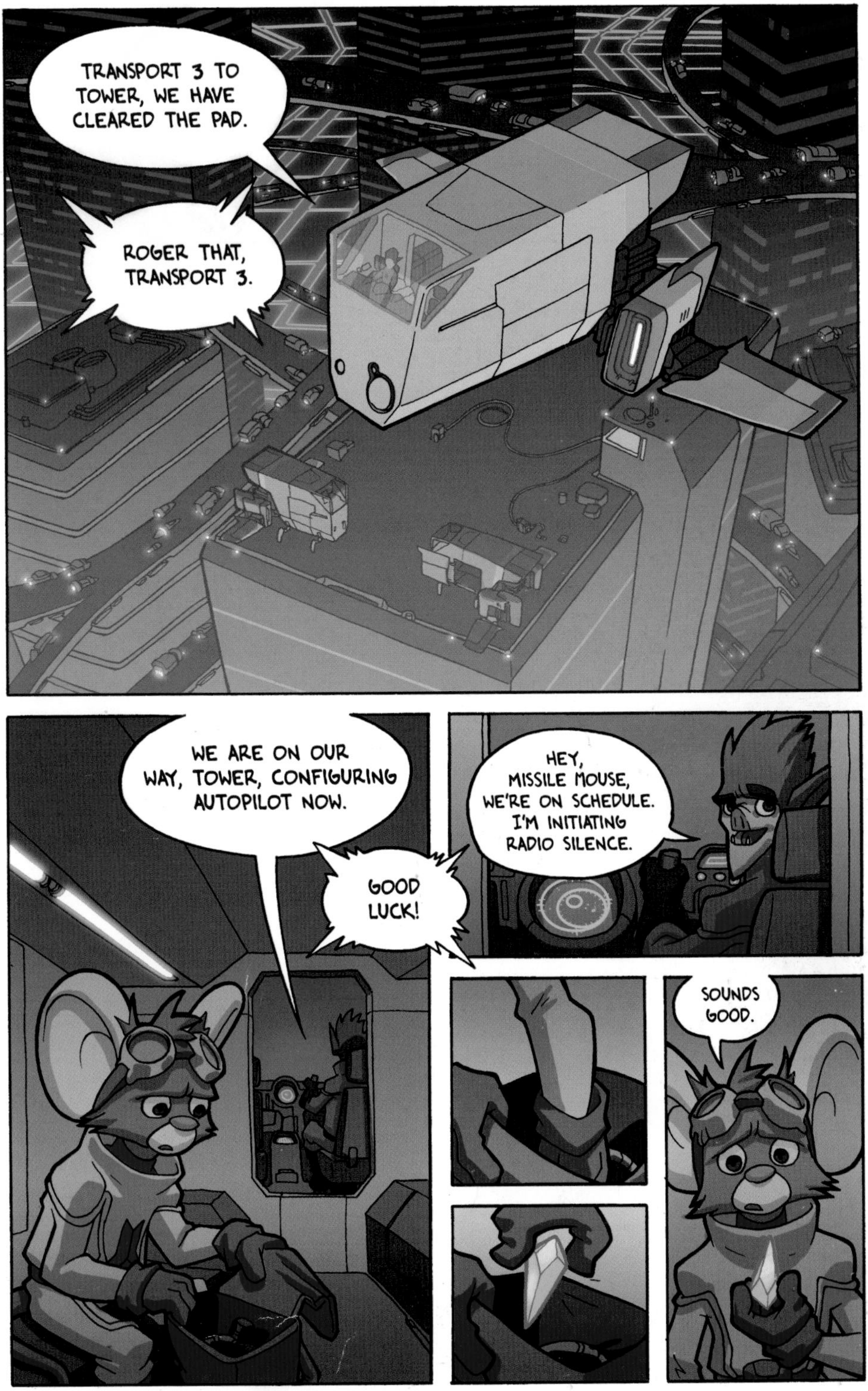
TRANSPORT 3 TO TOWER, WE HAVE CLEARED THE PAD.
ROGER THAT, TRANSPORT 3.
WE ARE ON OUR WAY, TOWER, CONFIGURING AUTOPILOT NOW.
GOOD LUCK!
HEY, MISSILE MOUSE, WE'RE ON SCHEDULE. I'M INITIATING RADIO SILENCE.
SOUNDS GOOD.

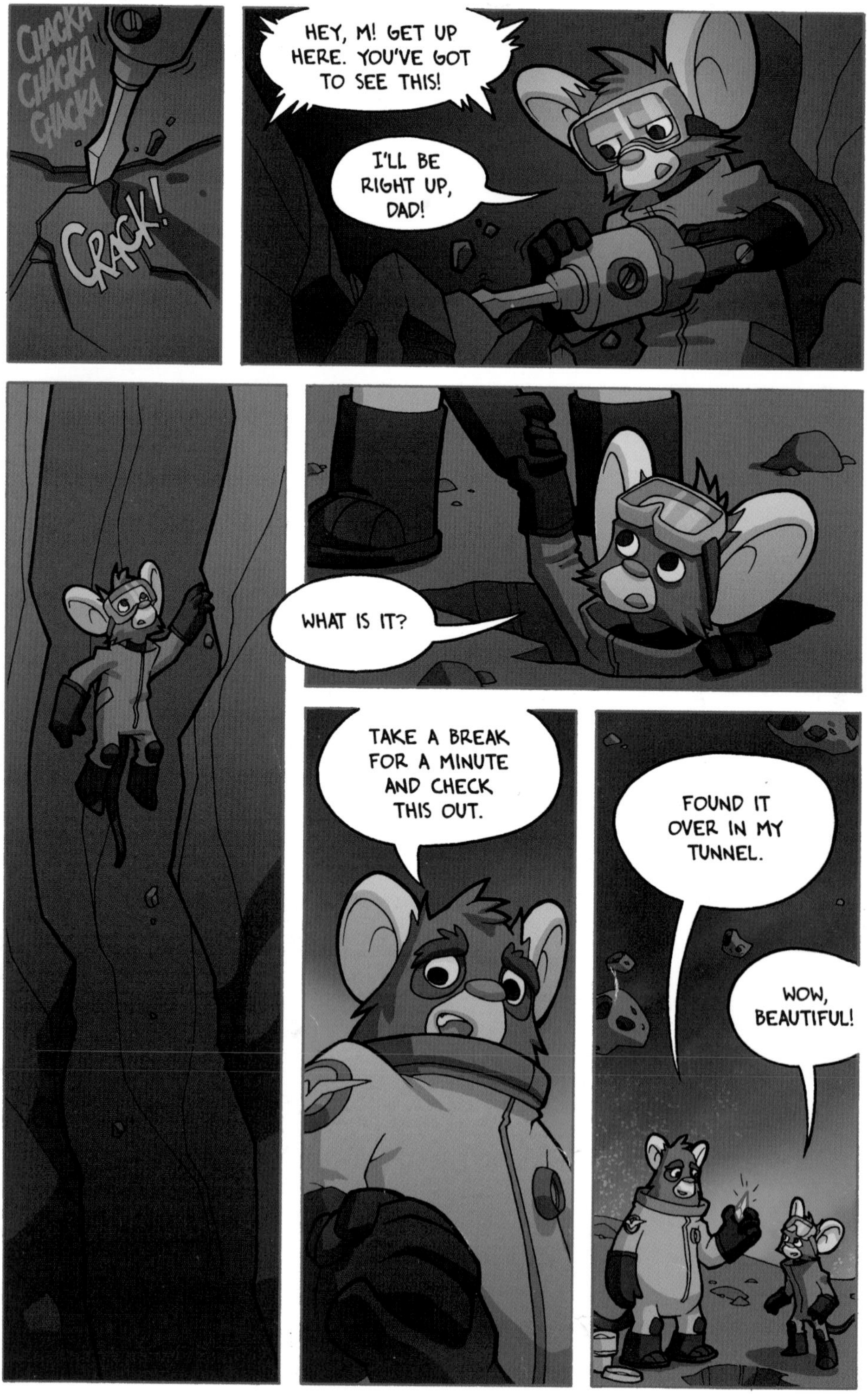
CHACKA
CHACKA
CHACKA
CRACK!
HEY, M! GET UP HERE. YOU'VE GOT TO SEE THIS!
I'LL BE RIGHT UP, DAD!
WHAT IS IT?
TAKE A BREAK FOR A MINUTE AND CHECK THIS OUT.
FOUND IT OVER IN MY TUNNEL.
WOW, BEAUTIFUL!

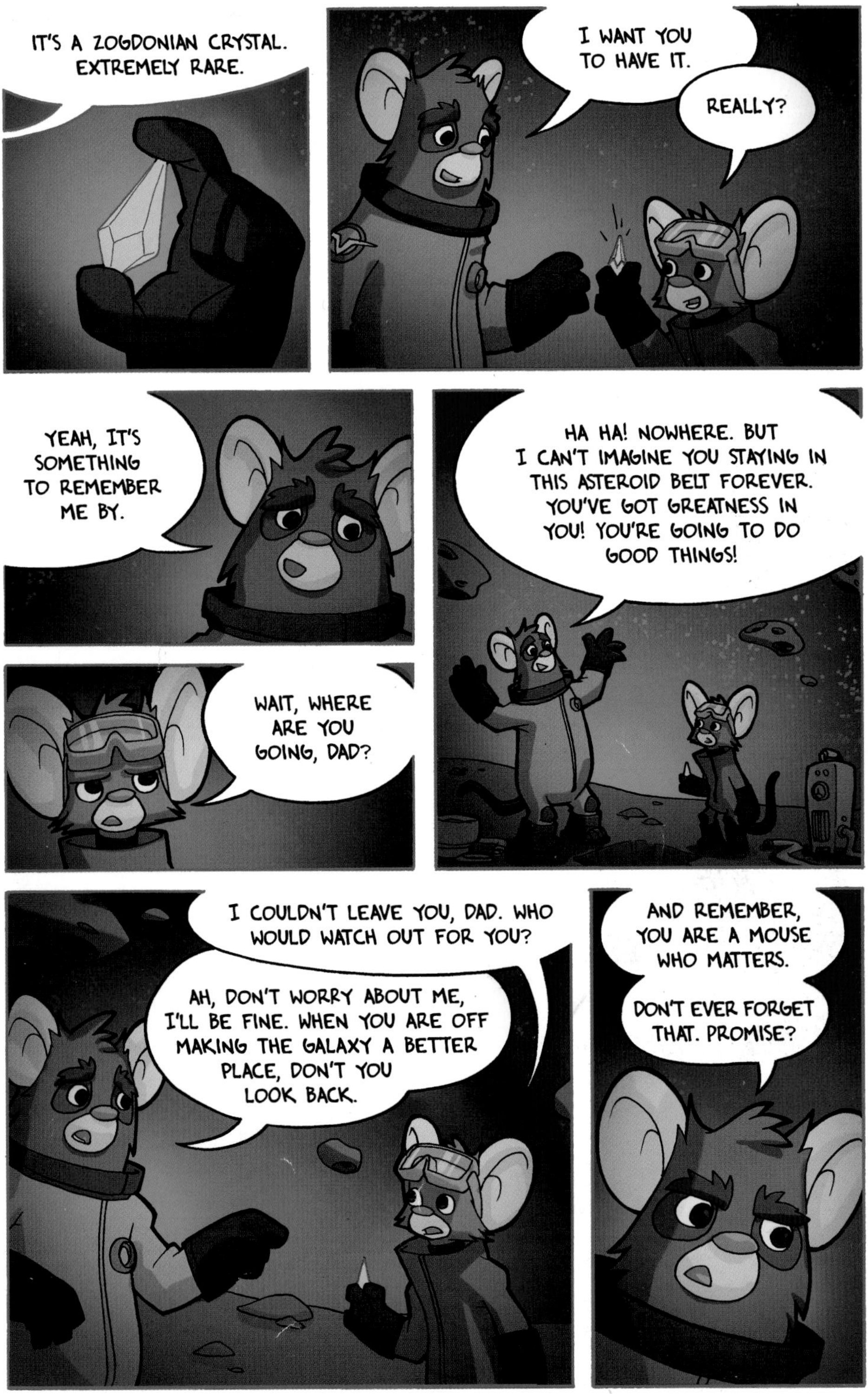
IT'S A ZOGDONIAN CRYSTAL. EXTREMELY RARE.
I WANT YOU TO HAVE IT.
REALLY?
YEAH, IT'S SOMETHING TO REMEMBER ME BY.
WAIT, WHERE ARE YOU GOING, DAD?
HA HA! NOWHERE. BUT I CAN'T IMAGINE YOU STAYING IN THIS ASTEROID BELT FOREVER. YOU'VE GOT GREATNESS IN YOU! YOU'RE GOING TO DO GOOD THINGS!
I COULDN'T LEAVE YOU, DAD. WHO WOULD WATCH OUT FOR YOU?
AH, DON'T WORRY ABOUT ME, I'LL BE FINE. WHEN YOU ARE OFF MAKING THE GALAXY A BETTER PLACE, DON'T YOU LOOK BACK.
AND REMEMBER, YOU ARE A MOUSE WHO MATTERS.
DON'T EVER FORGET THAT. PROMISE?

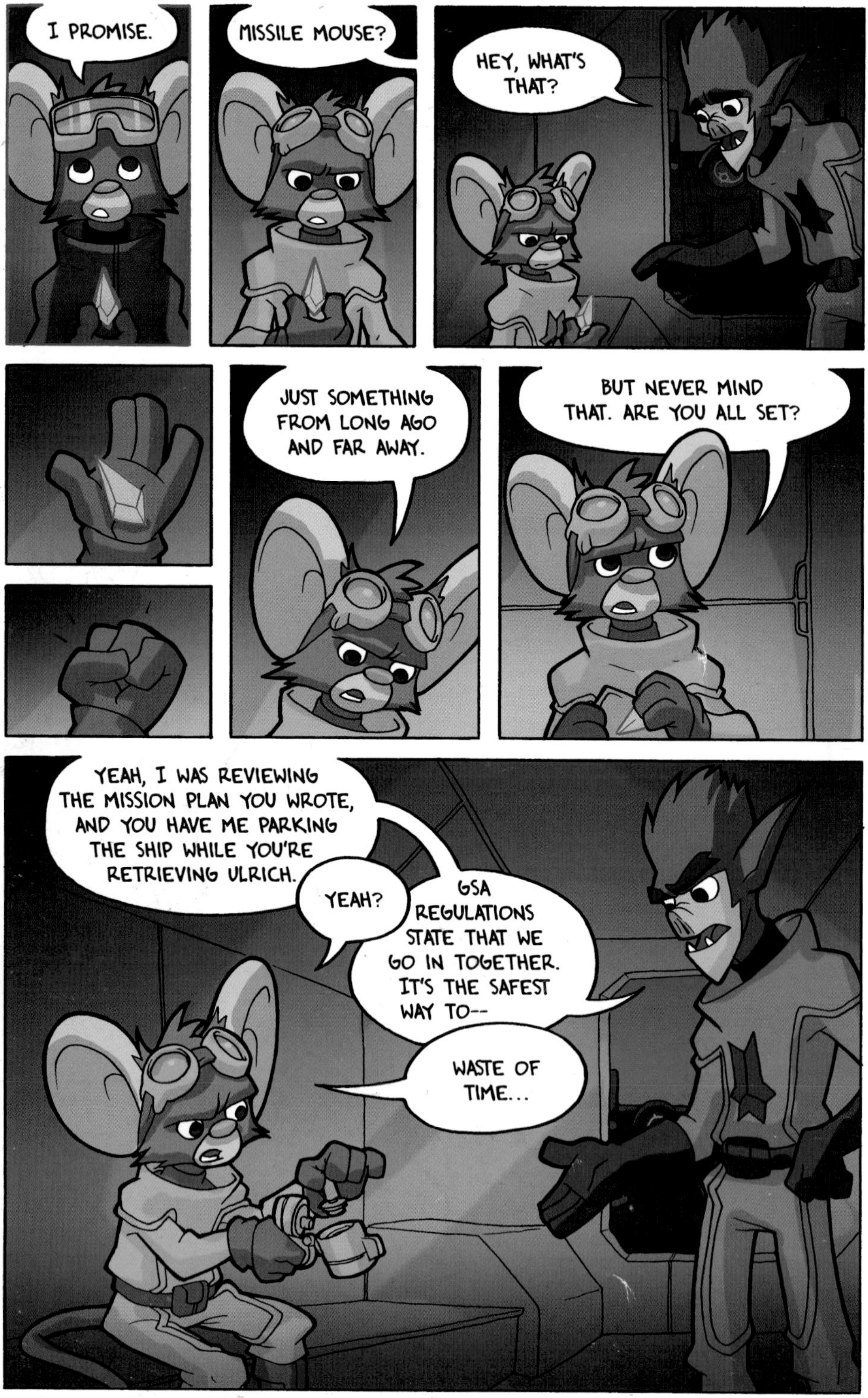
I PROMISE.
MISSILE MOUSE?
HEY, WHAT'S THAT?
JUST SOMETHING FROM LONG AGO AND FAR AWAY.
BUT NEVER MIND THAT. ARE YOU ALL SET?
YEAH, I WAS REVIEWING THE MISSION PLAN YOU WROTE, AND YOU HAVE ME PARKING THE SHIP WHILE YOU'RE RETRIEVING ULRICH.
YEAH?
GSA REGULATIONS STATE THAT WE GO IN TOGETHER. IT'S THE SAFEST WAY TO--
WASTE OF TIME...

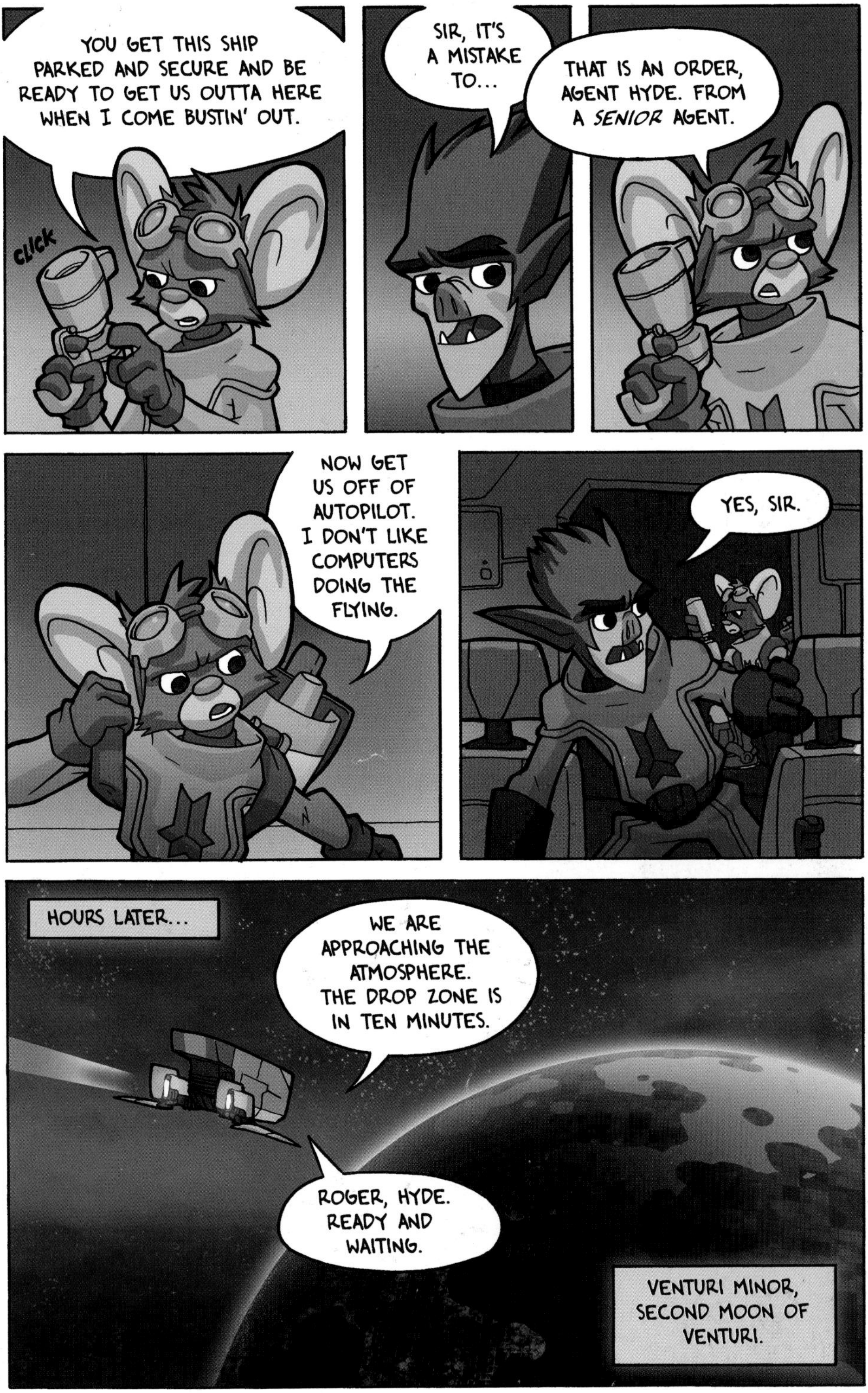
YOU GET THIS SHIP PARKED AND SECURE AND BE READY TO GET US OUTTA HERE WHEN I COME BUSTIN' OUT.
CLICK
SIR, IT'S A MISTAKE TO...
THAT IS AN ORDER, AGENT HYDE. FROM A *SENIOR* AGENT.
NOW GET US OFF OF AUTOPILOT. I DON'T LIKE COMPUTERS DOING THE FLYING.
YES, SIR.
HOURS LATER...
WE ARE APPROACHING THE ATMOSPHERE. THE DROP ZONE IS IN TEN MINUTES.
ROGER, HYDE. READY AND WAITING.
VENTURI MINOR, SECOND MOON OF VENTURI.

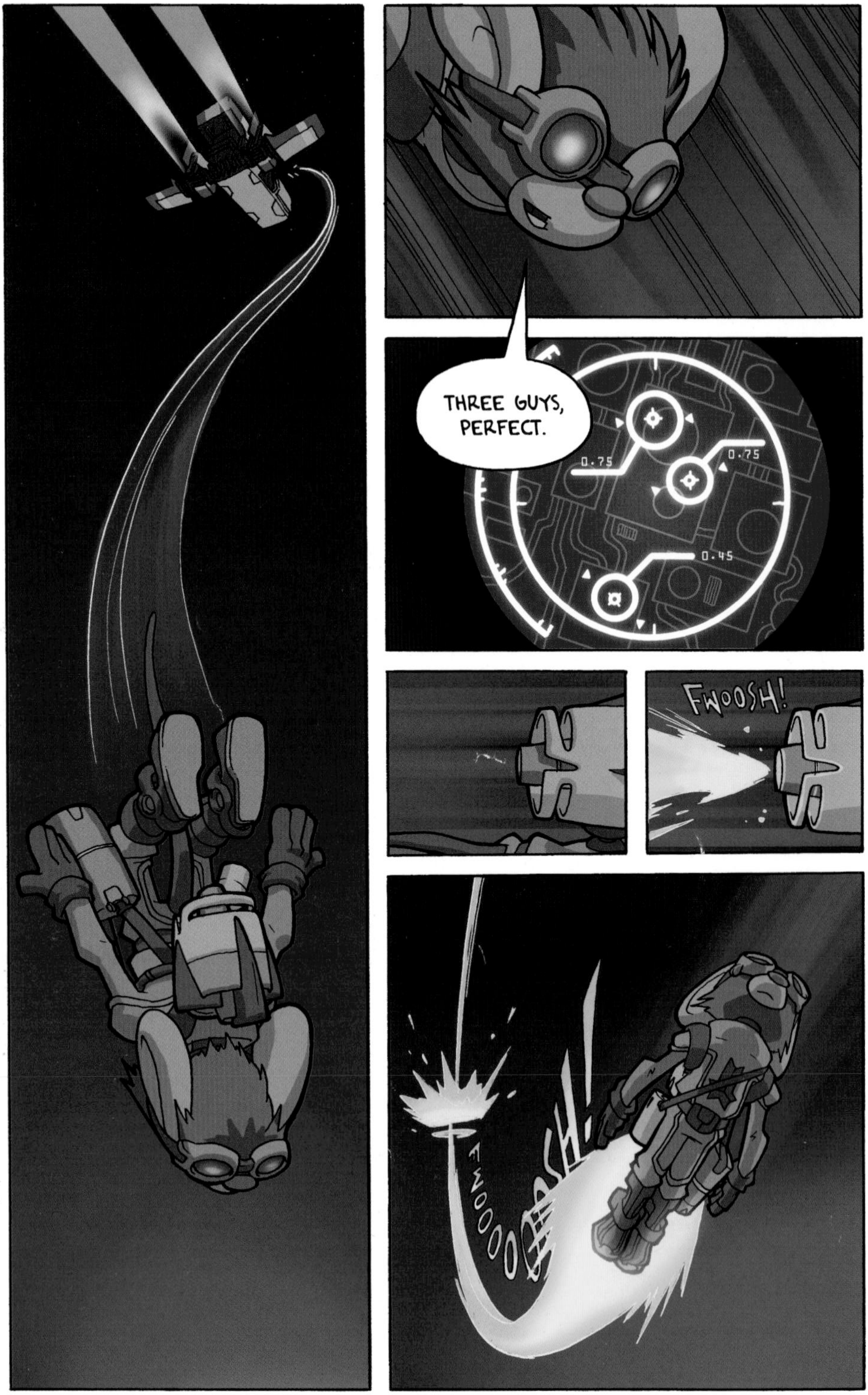
THREE GUYS, PERFECT.
0.75
0.75
0.45
FWOOSH!
FWOOOOOSH!

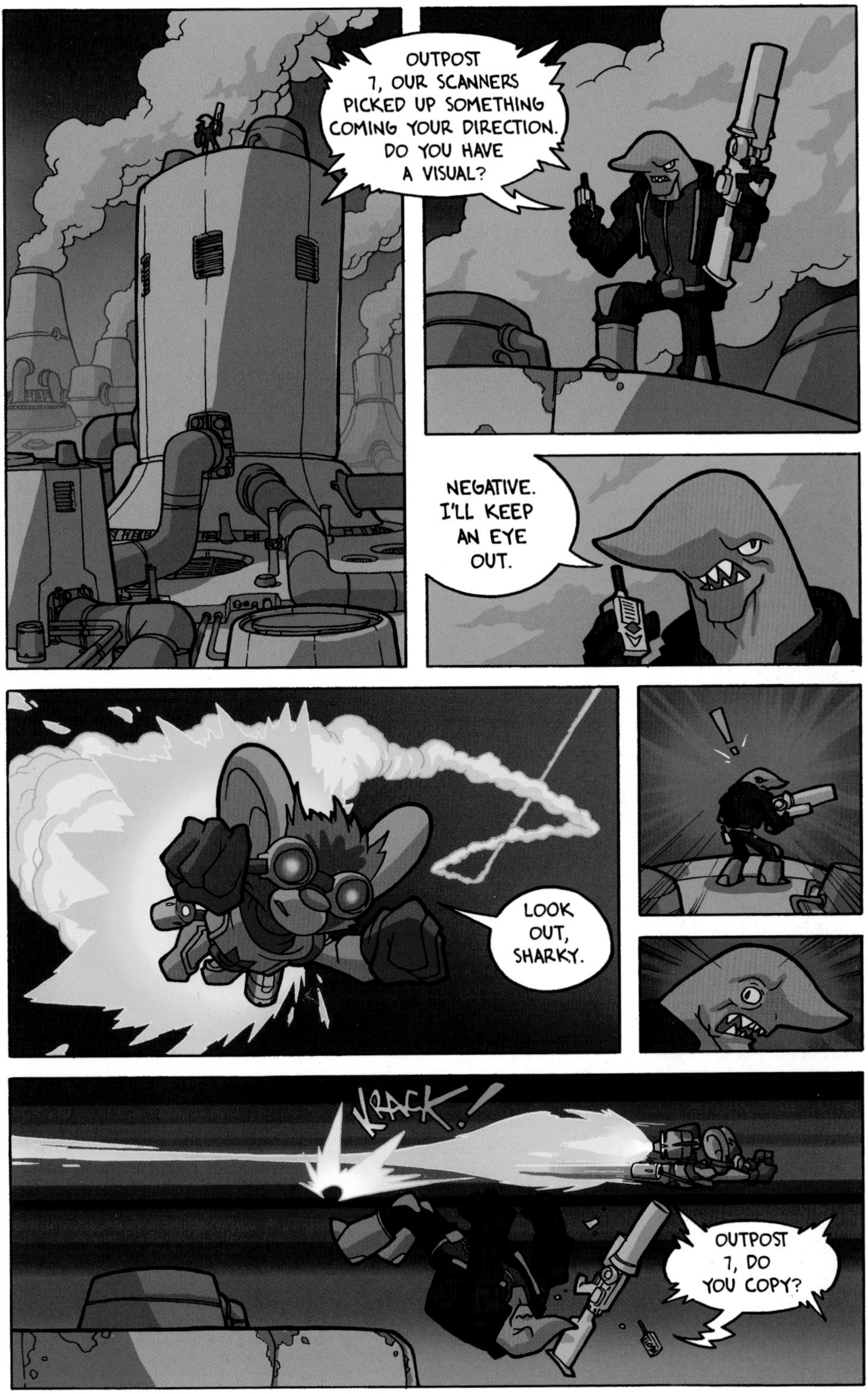
OUTPOST 7, OUR SCANNERS PICKED UP SOMETHING COMING YOUR DIRECTION. DO YOU HAVE A VISUAL?
NEGATIVE. I'LL KEEP AN EYE OUT.
LOOK OUT, SHARKY.
!
KRACK!
OUTPOST 7, DO YOU COPY?

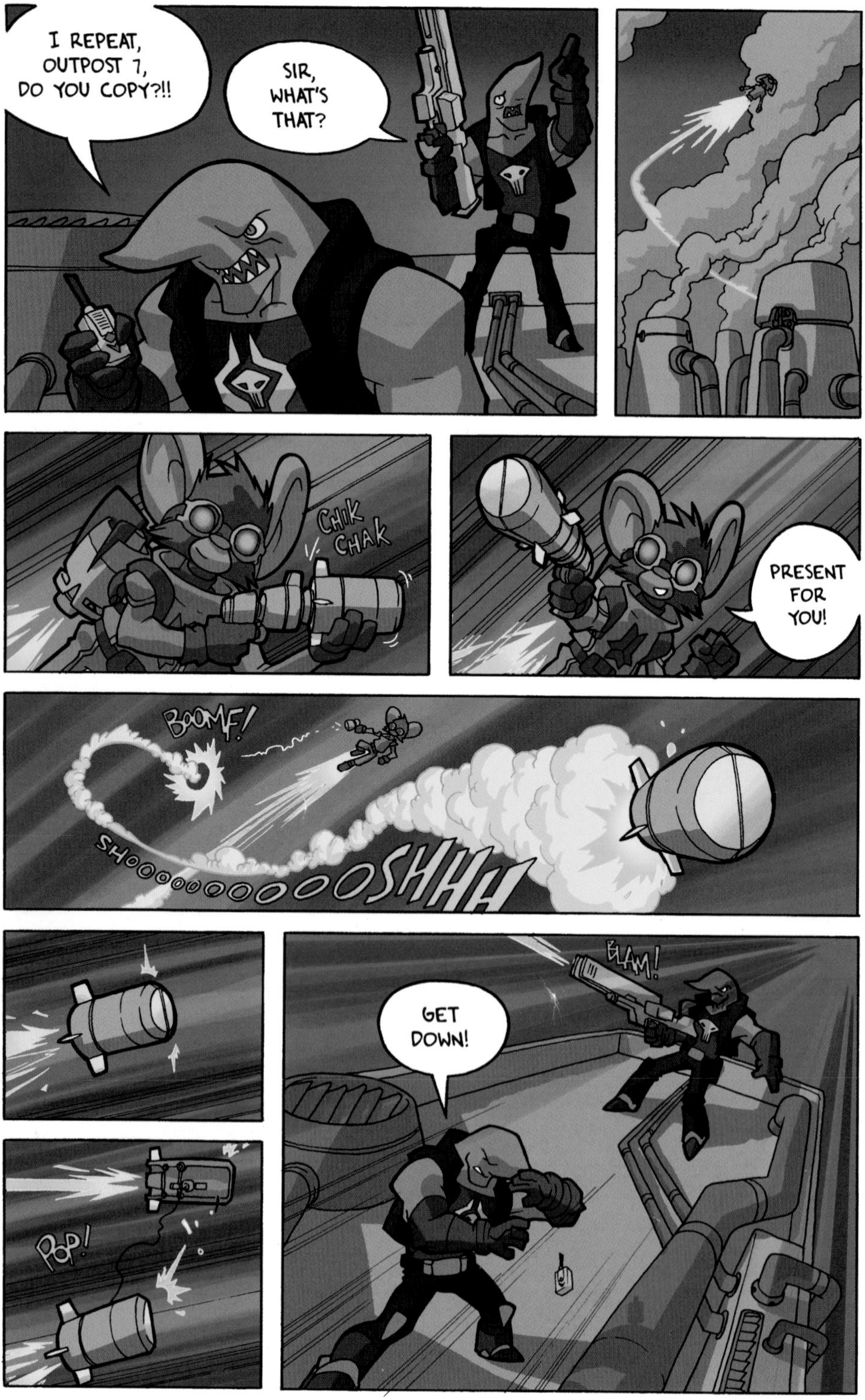

I REPEAT, OUTPOST 7, DO YOU COPY?!!
SIR, WHAT'S THAT?
CHIK CHAK
PRESENT FOR YOU!
BOOMF!
SHOOOOOOOOOOOOOSHHH
POP!
BLAM!
GET DOWN!

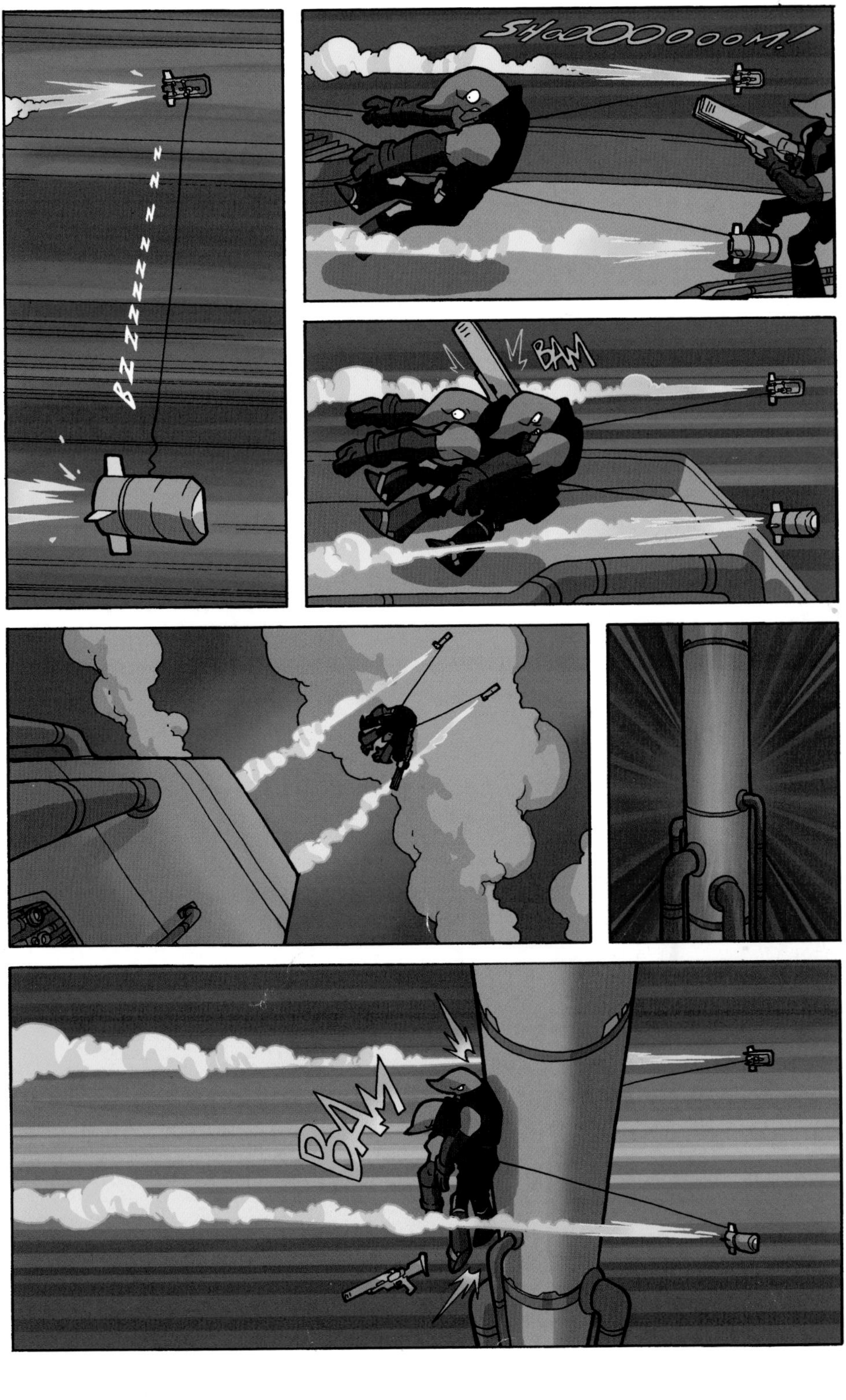

BZZZZZZZZZZZZ
SHOOOOOOOOOM!
BAM
BAM

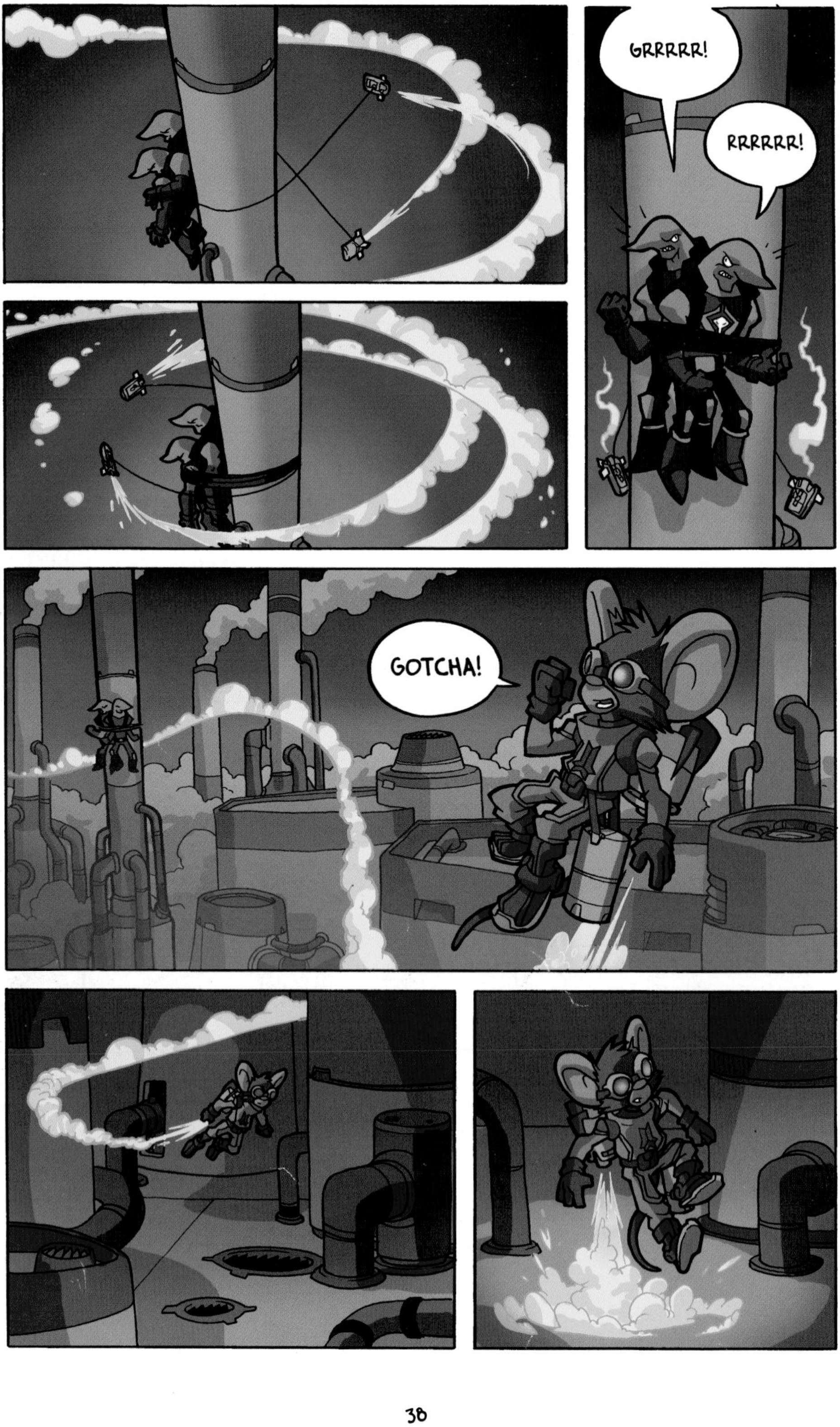
GRRRRR!
RRRRRR!
GOTCHA!

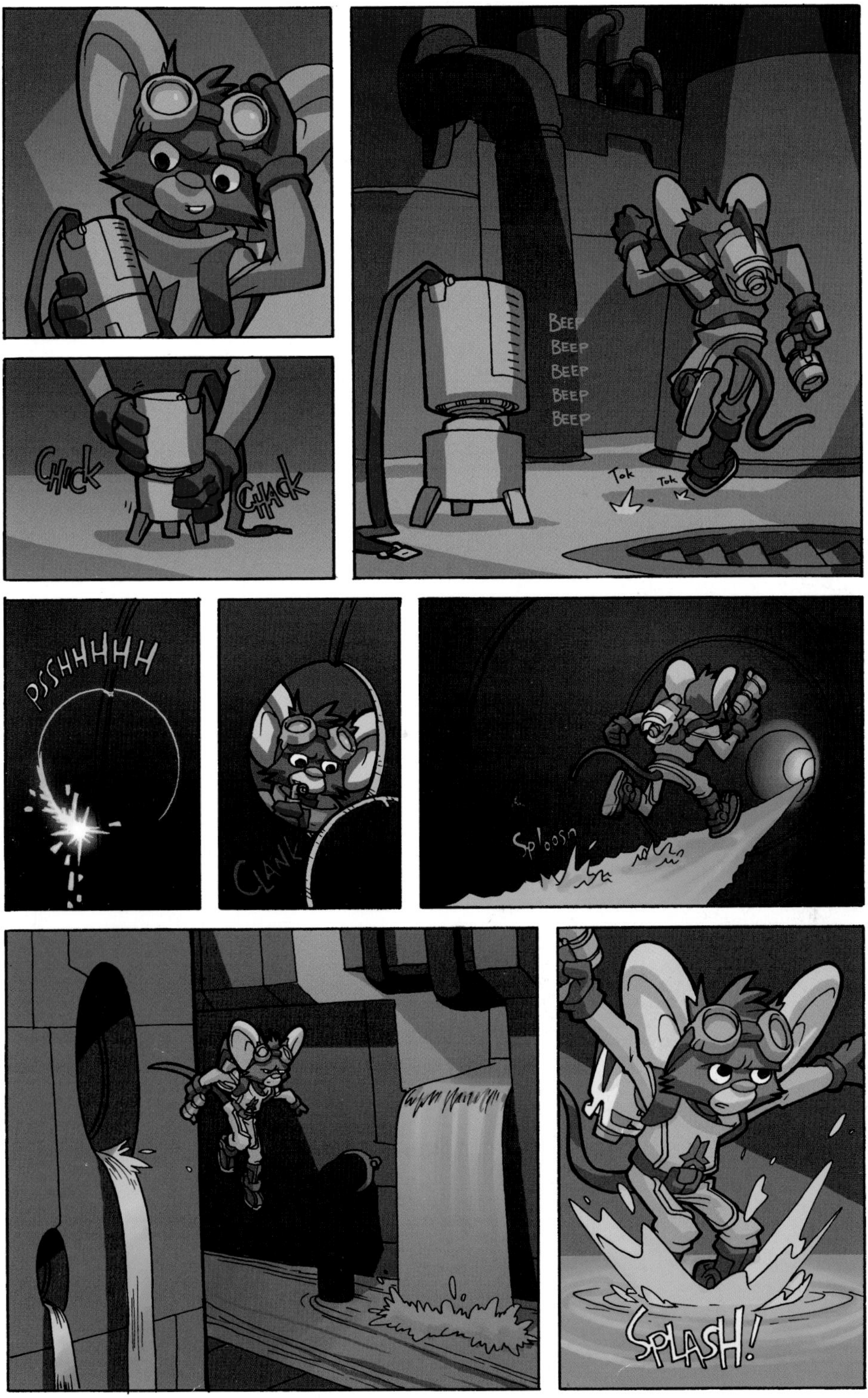
CHICK
CHACK
BEEP
BEEP
BEEP
BEEP
BEEP
Tok
Tok
PSSHHHHH
CLANK
Sploosh
SPLASH!

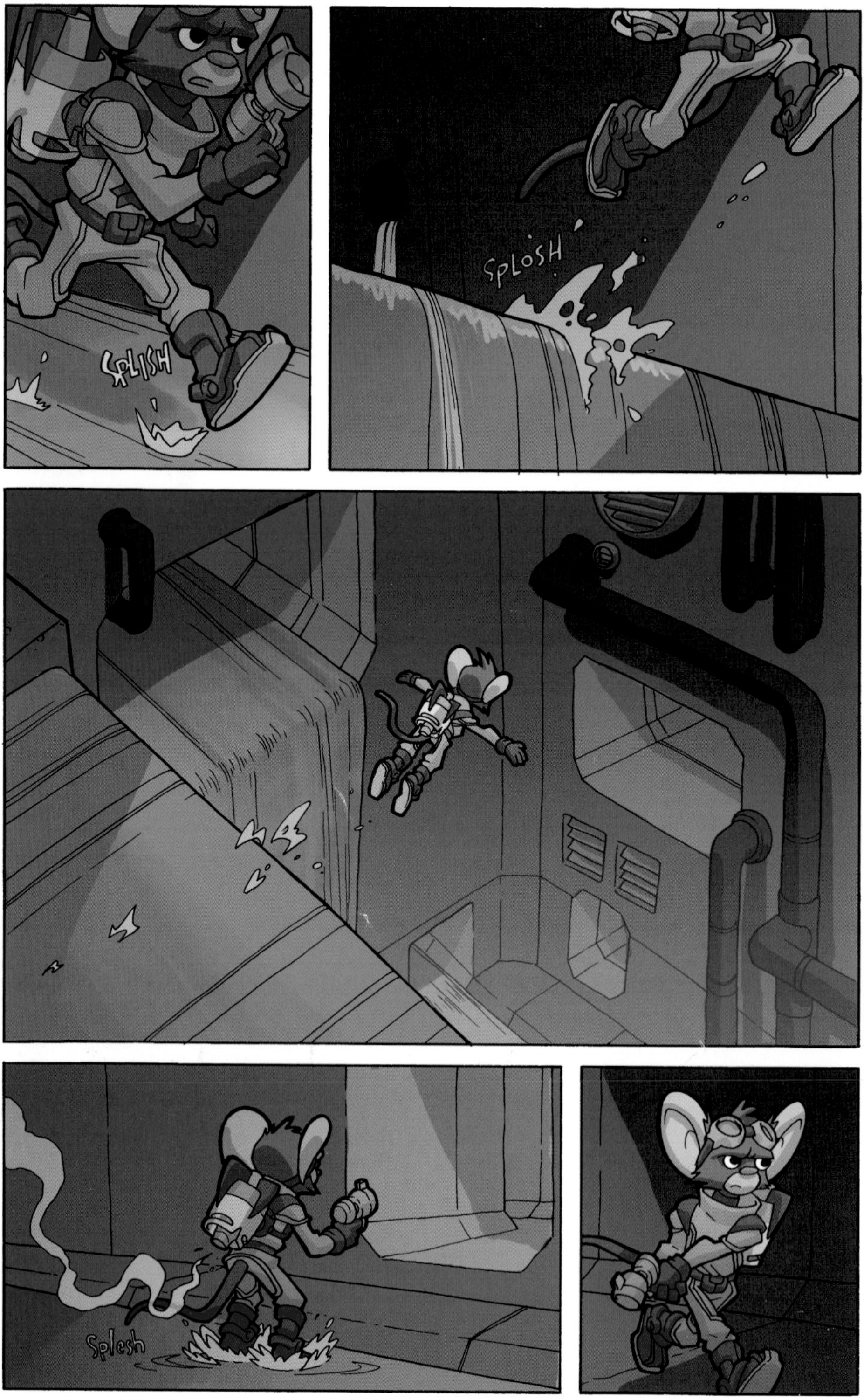
SPLISH
SPLOSH
Splesh

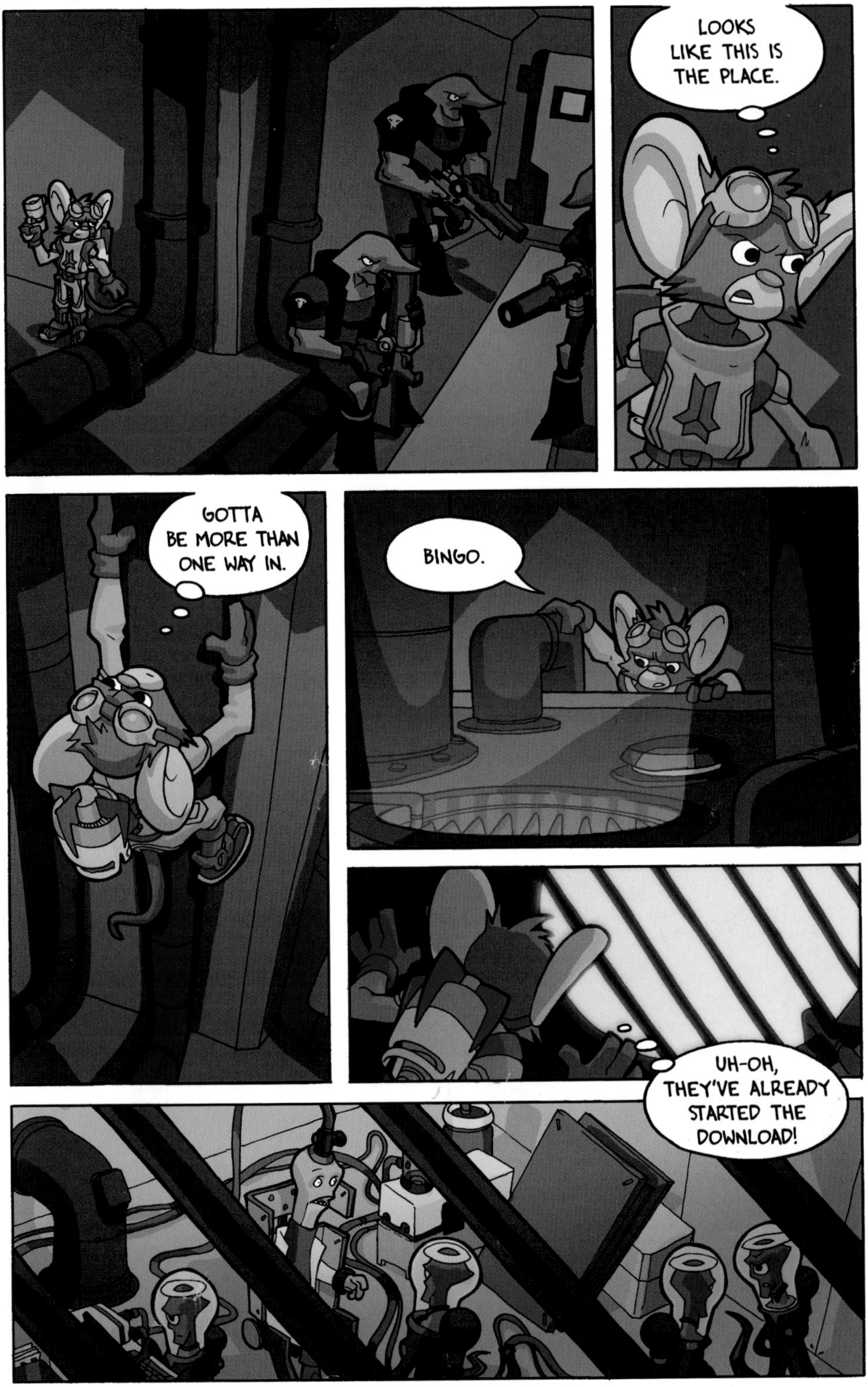
LOOKS LIKE THIS IS THE PLACE.
GOTTA BE MORE THAN ONE WAY IN.
BINGO.
UH-OH, THEY'VE ALREADY STARTED THE DOWNLOAD!

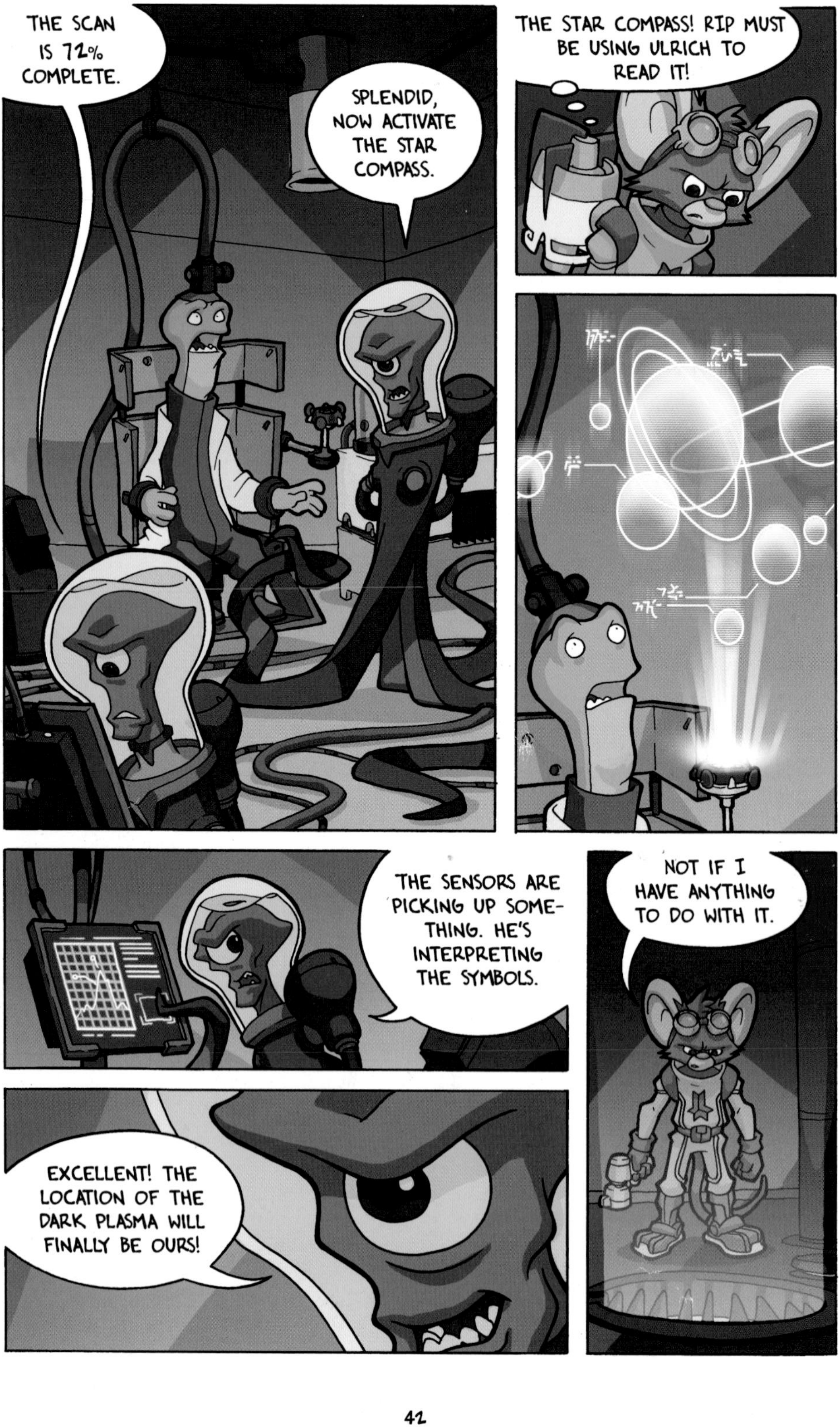
THE SCAN IS 72% COMPLETE.
SPLENDID, NOW ACTIVATE THE STAR COMPASS.
THE STAR COMPASS! RIP MUST BE USING ULRICH TO READ IT!
THE SENSORS ARE PICKING UP SOME-THING. HE'S INTERPRETING THE SYMBOLS.
EXCELLENT! THE LOCATION OF THE DARK PLASMA WILL FINALLY BE OURS!
NOT IF I HAVE ANYTHING TO DO WITH IT.

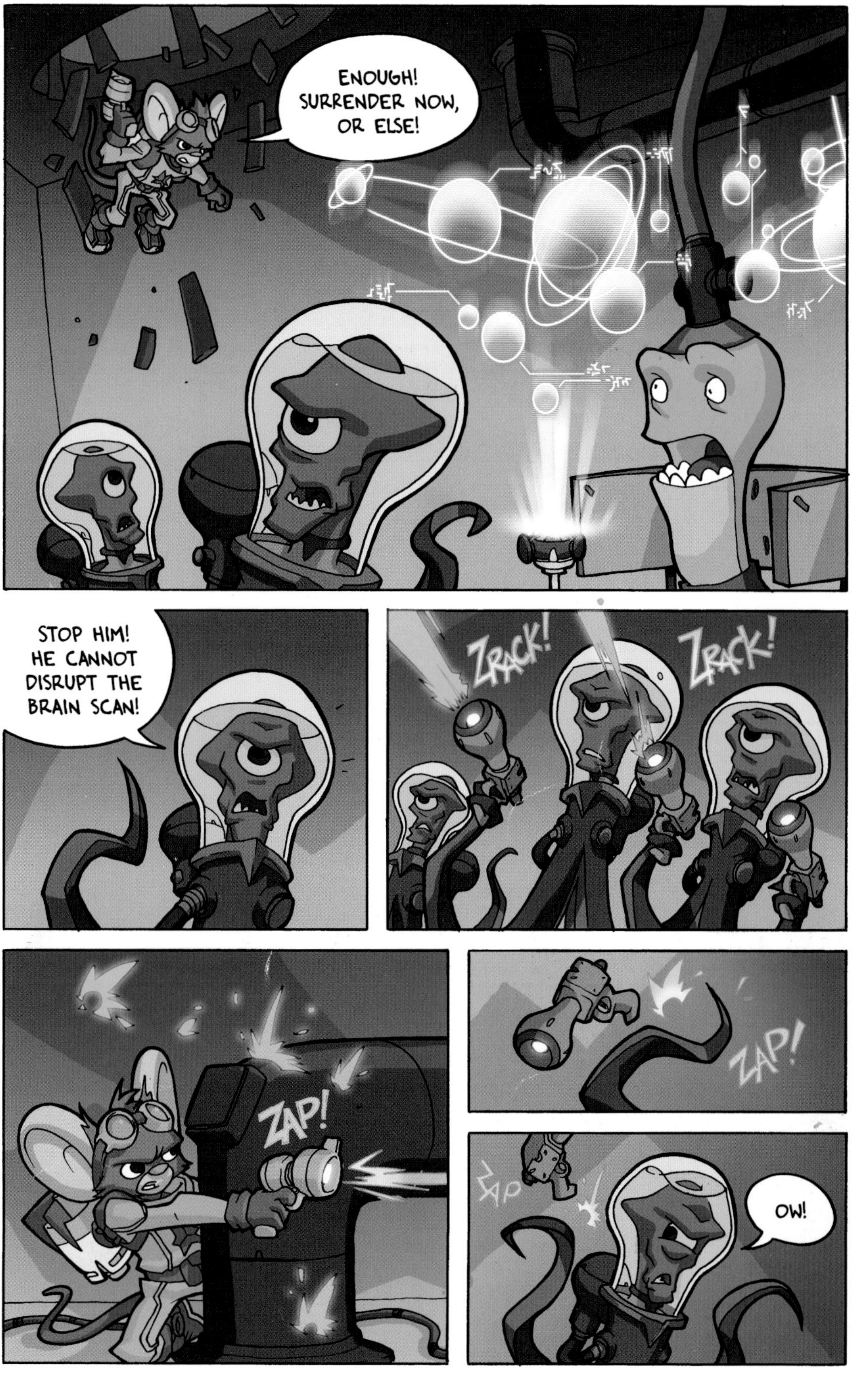
ENOUGH! SURRENDER NOW, OR ELSE!
STOP HIM! HE CANNOT DISRUPT THE BRAIN SCAN!
ZRACK!
ZRACK!
ZAP!
ZAP!
ZAP
OW!

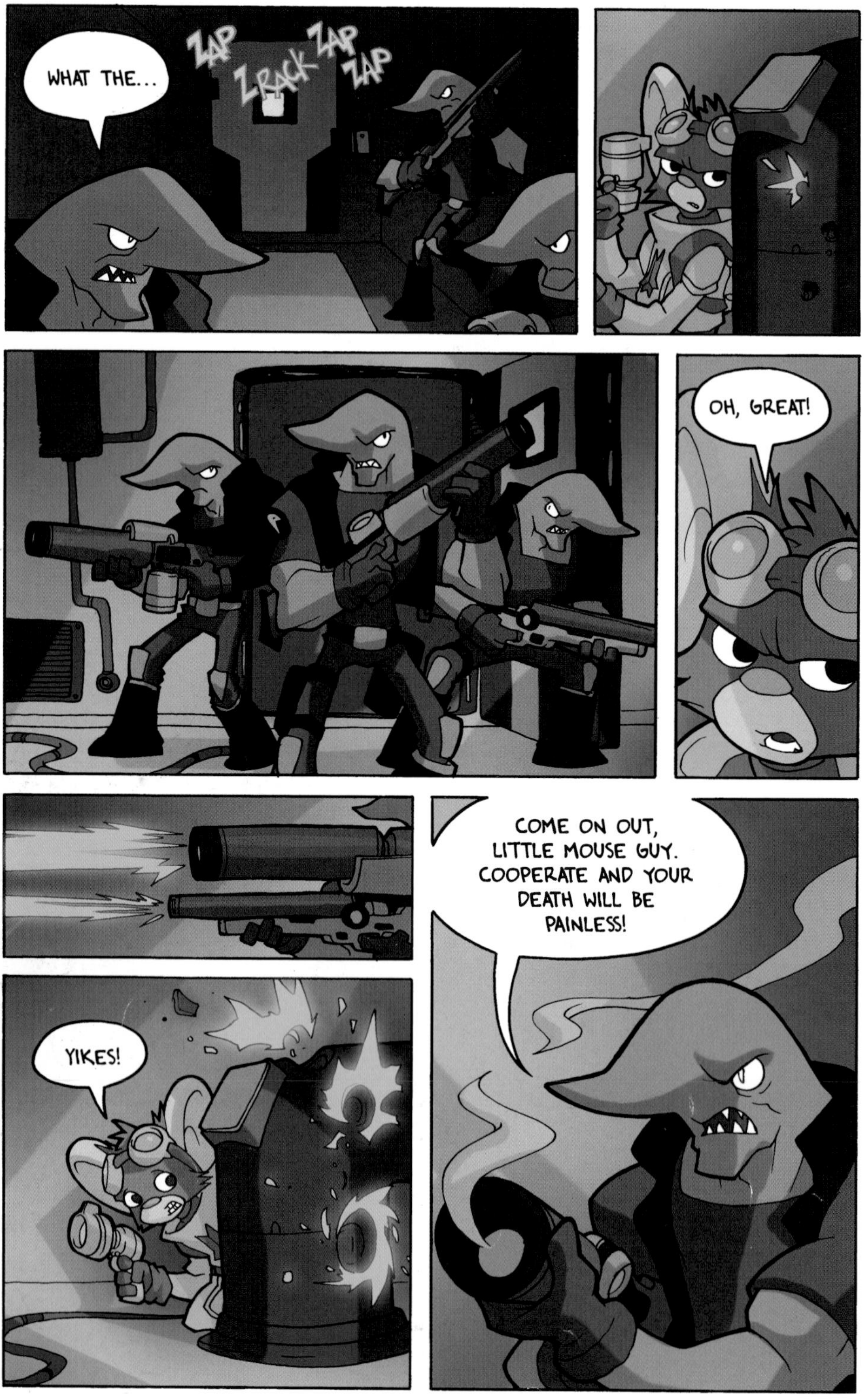
WHAT THE...
ZAP
ZRACK
ZAP
ZAP
OH, GREAT!
YIKES!
COME ON OUT, LITTLE MOUSE GUY. COOPERATE AND YOUR DEATH WILL BE PAINLESS!

OH YEAH? THIS IS YOUR LAST CHANCE TO DROP YOUR WEAPONS AND SURRENDER!

HA HA HA HA HA HAHAH HA HA H

OK, HERE GOES NOTHING.

BOOM

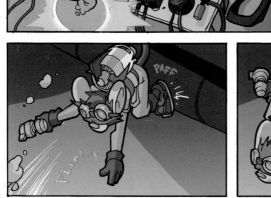

PAFF.

FLIP!

SPRING!

45

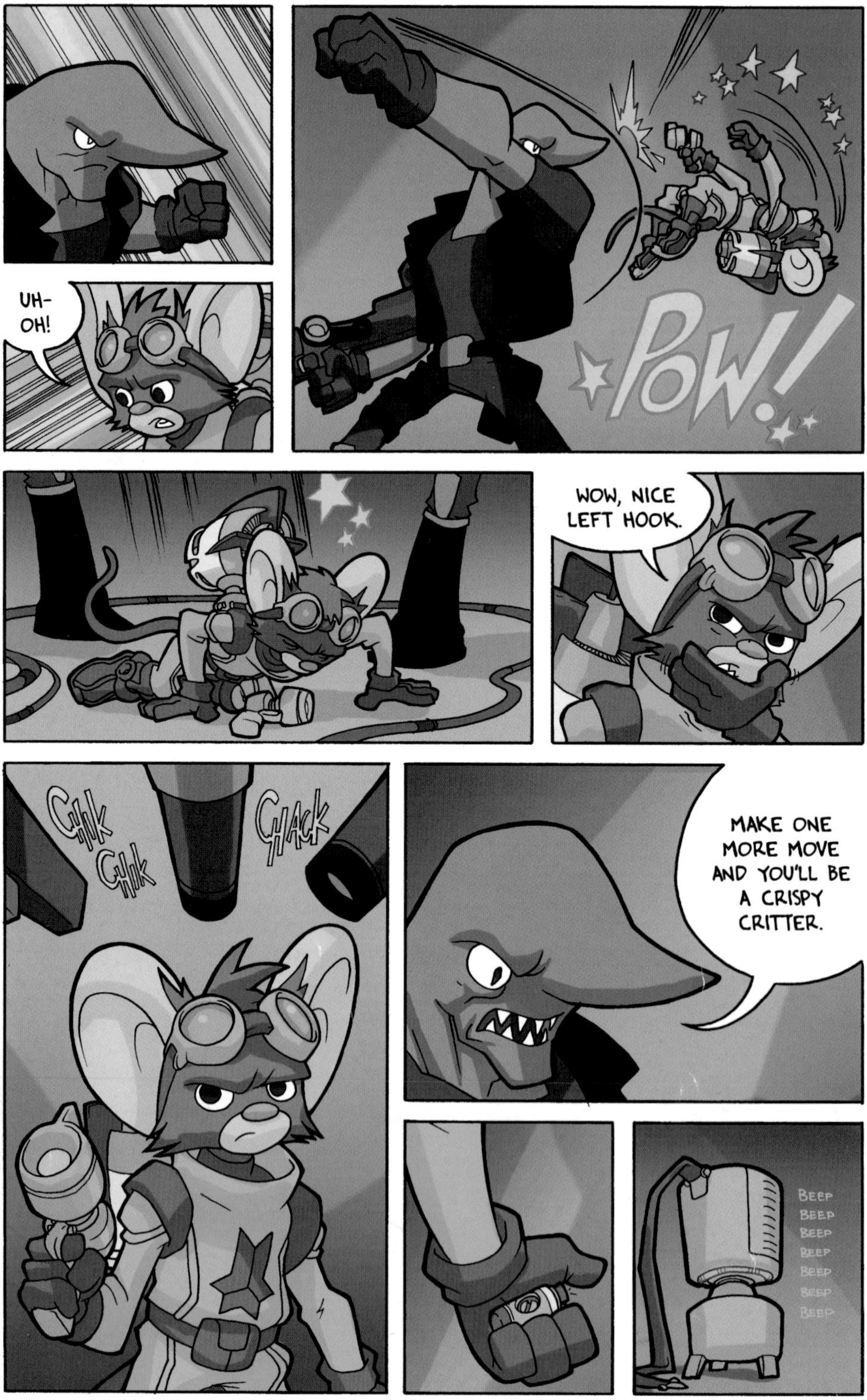
UH-OH!
POW!
WOW, NICE LEFT HOOK.
CHIK
CHIK
CHACK
MAKE ONE MORE MOVE AND YOU'LL BE A CRISPY CRITTER.
BEEP
BEEP
BEEP
BEEP
BEEP
BEEP
BEEP

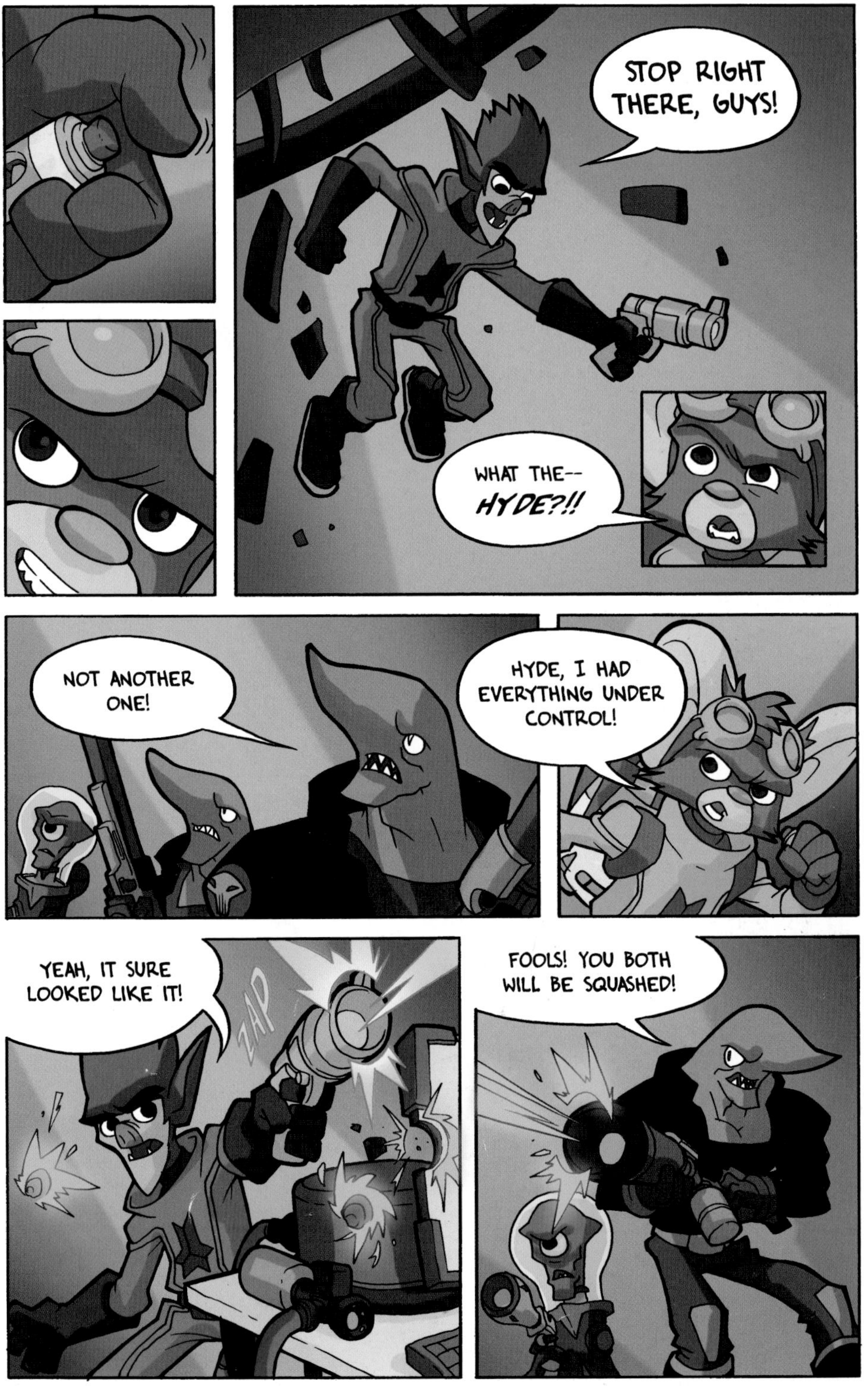
STOP RIGHT THERE, GUYS!
WHAT THE-- HYDE?!!
NOT ANOTHER ONE!
HYDE, I HAD EVERYTHING UNDER CONTROL!
YEAH, IT SURE LOOKED LIKE IT!
ZAP
FOOLS! YOU BOTH WILL BE SQUASHED!

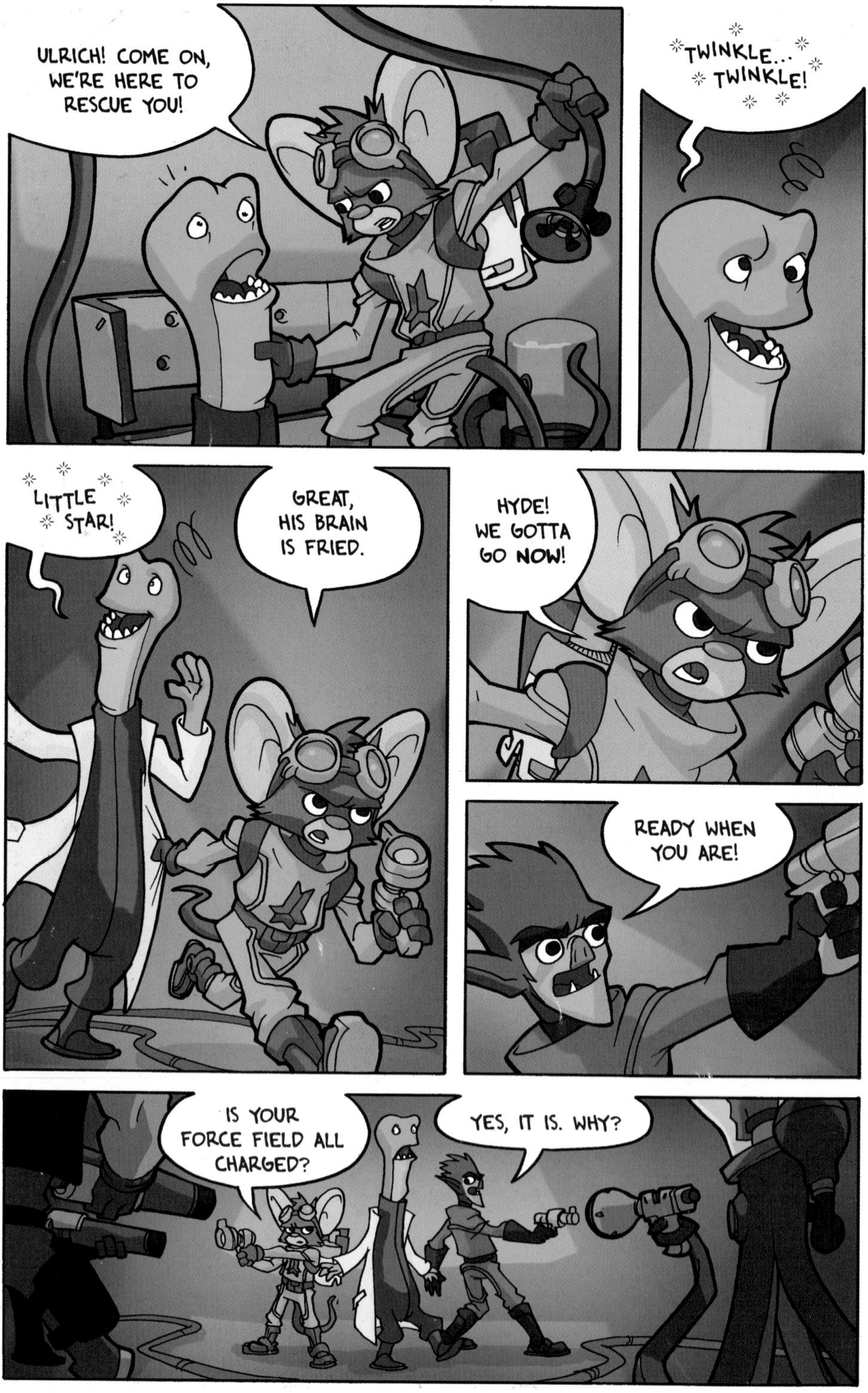
ULRICH! COME ON, WE'RE HERE TO RESCUE YOU!
TWINKLE... TWINKLE!
LITTLE STAR!
GREAT, HIS BRAIN IS FRIED.
HYDE! WE GOTTA GO NOW!
READY WHEN YOU ARE!
IS YOUR FORCE FIELD ALL CHARGED?
YES, IT IS. WHY?

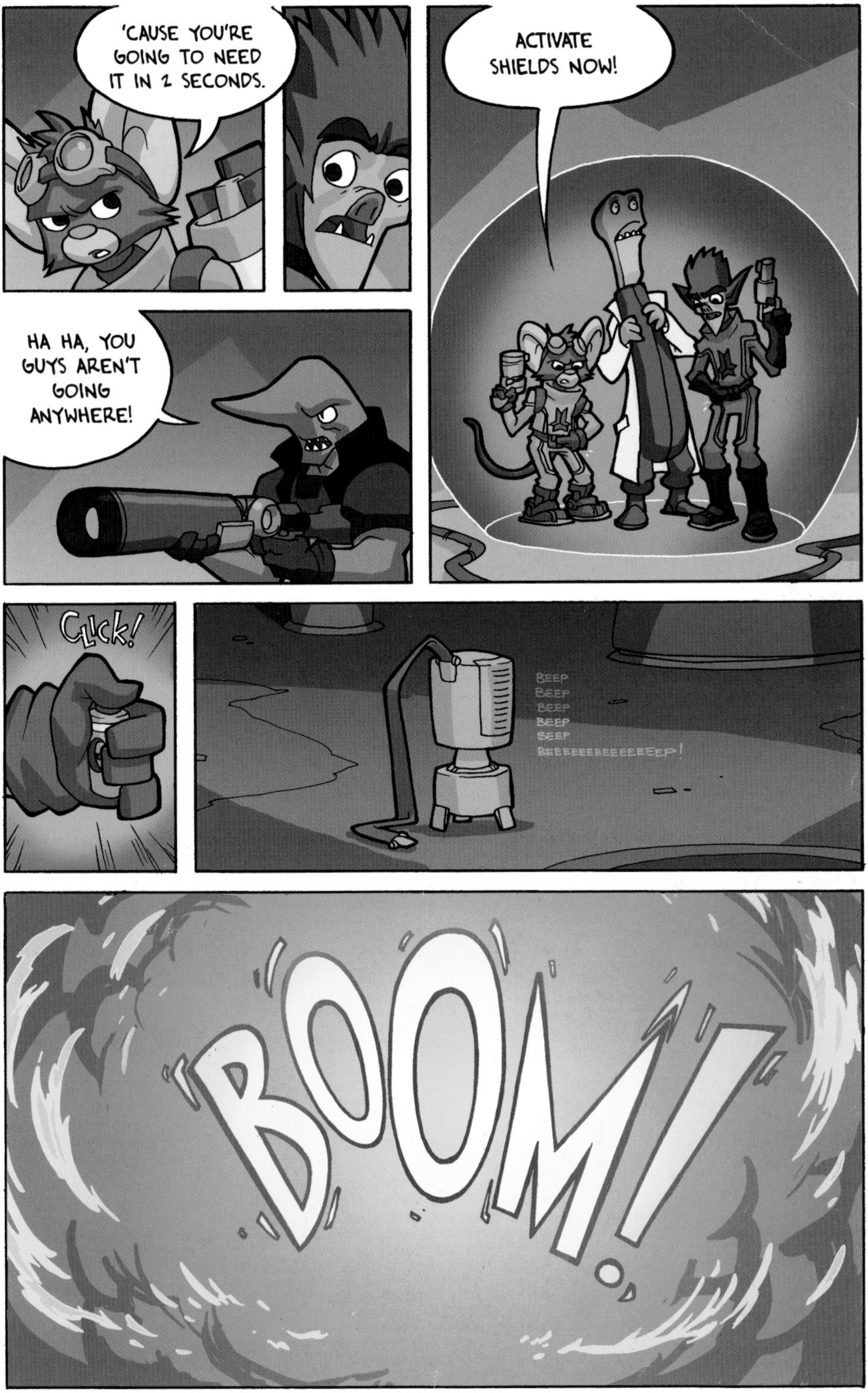
'CAUSE YOU'RE GOING TO NEED IT IN 2 SECONDS.
ACTIVATE SHIELDS NOW!
HA HA, YOU GUYS AREN'T GOING ANYWHERE!
CLICK!
BEEP
BEEP
BEEP
BEEP
BEEP
BEEEEEEEEEEEEEEP!
BOOM!

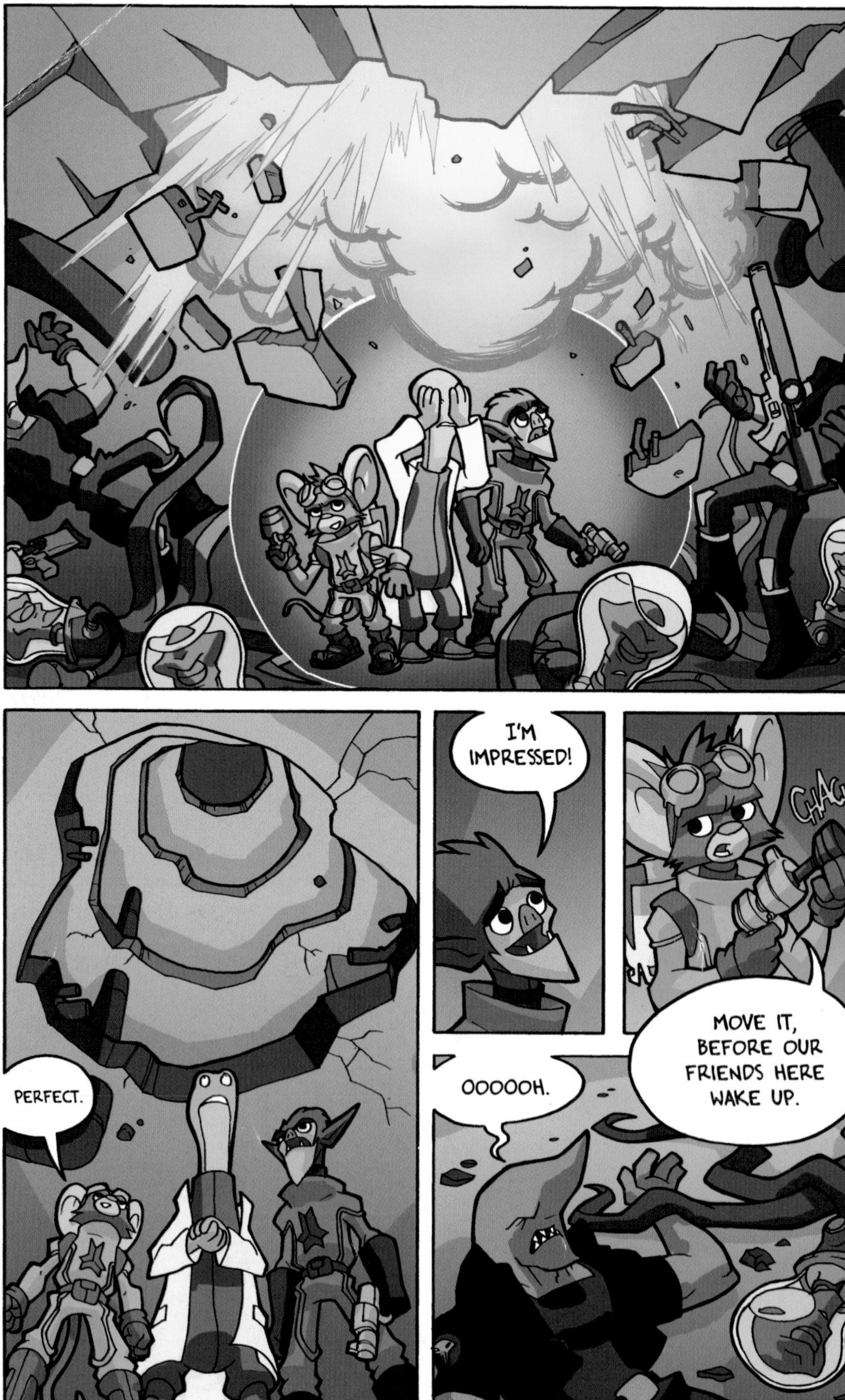
PERFECT.
I'M IMPRESSED!
CHACK
MOVE IT, BEFORE OUR FRIENDS HERE WAKE UP.
OOOOOH.

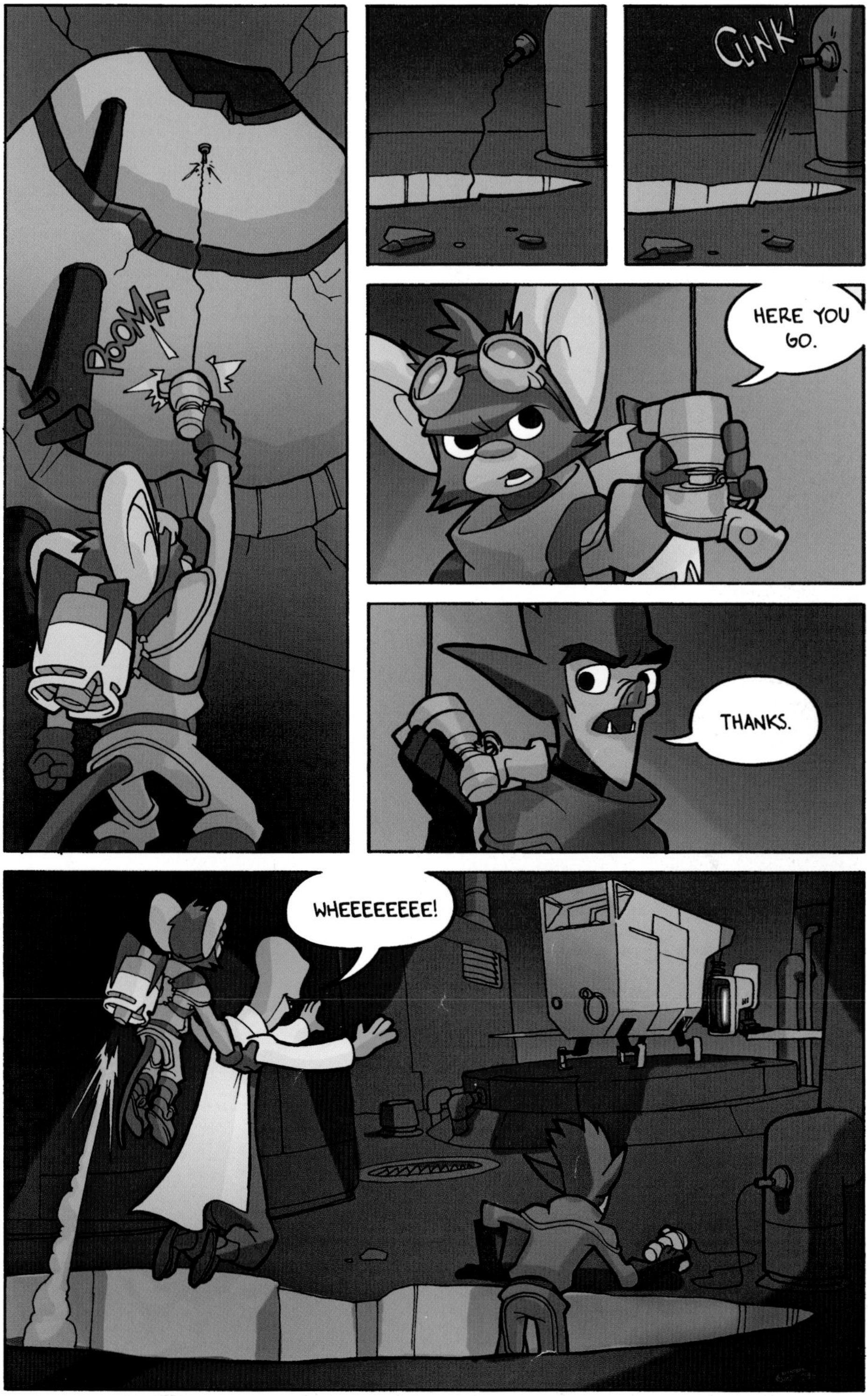
POOMF
CLINK!
HERE YOU GO.
THANKS.
WHEEEEEEEE!

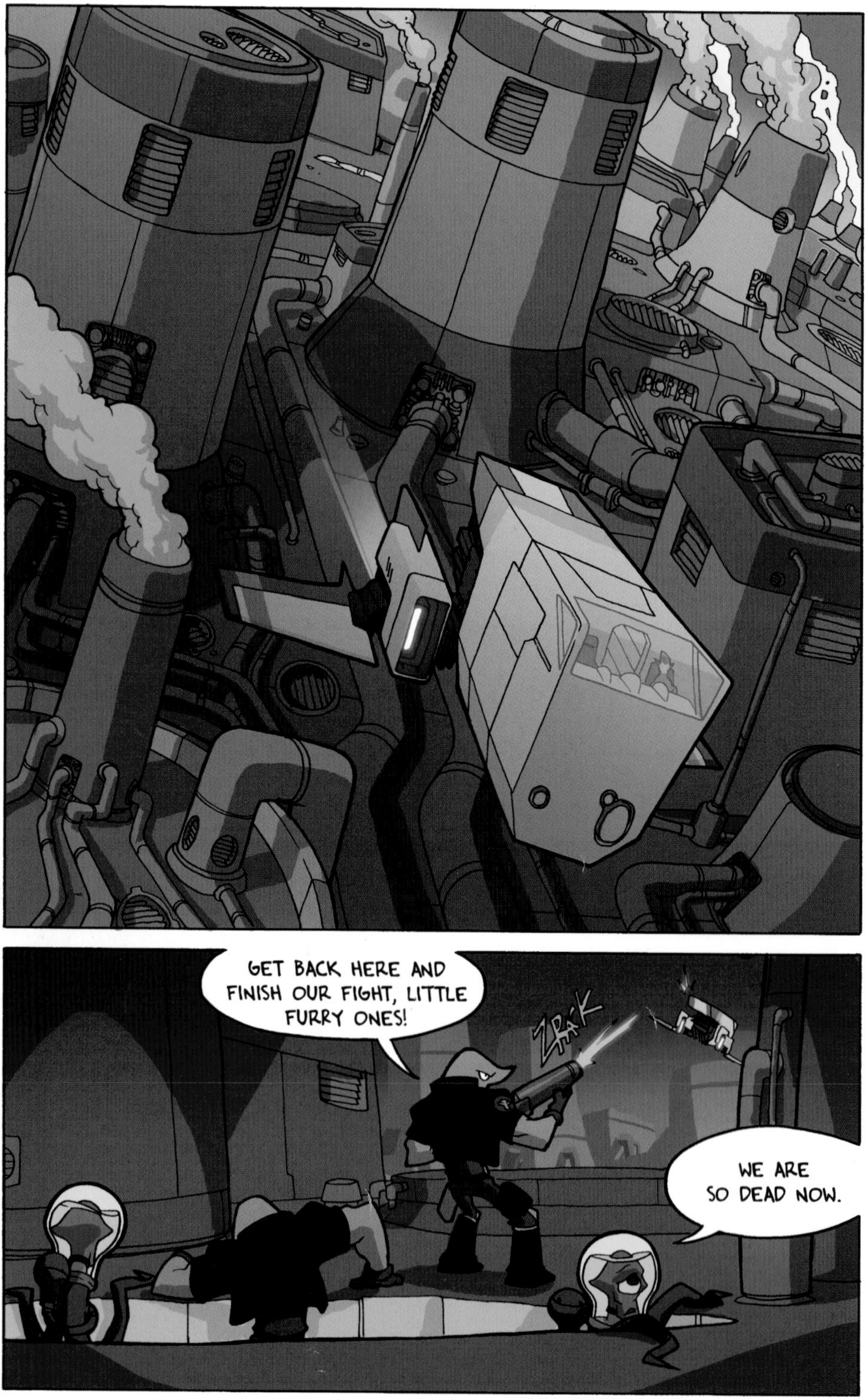
GET BACK HERE AND FINISH OUR FIGHT, LITTLE FURRY ONES!
ZRAK
WE ARE SO DEAD NOW.

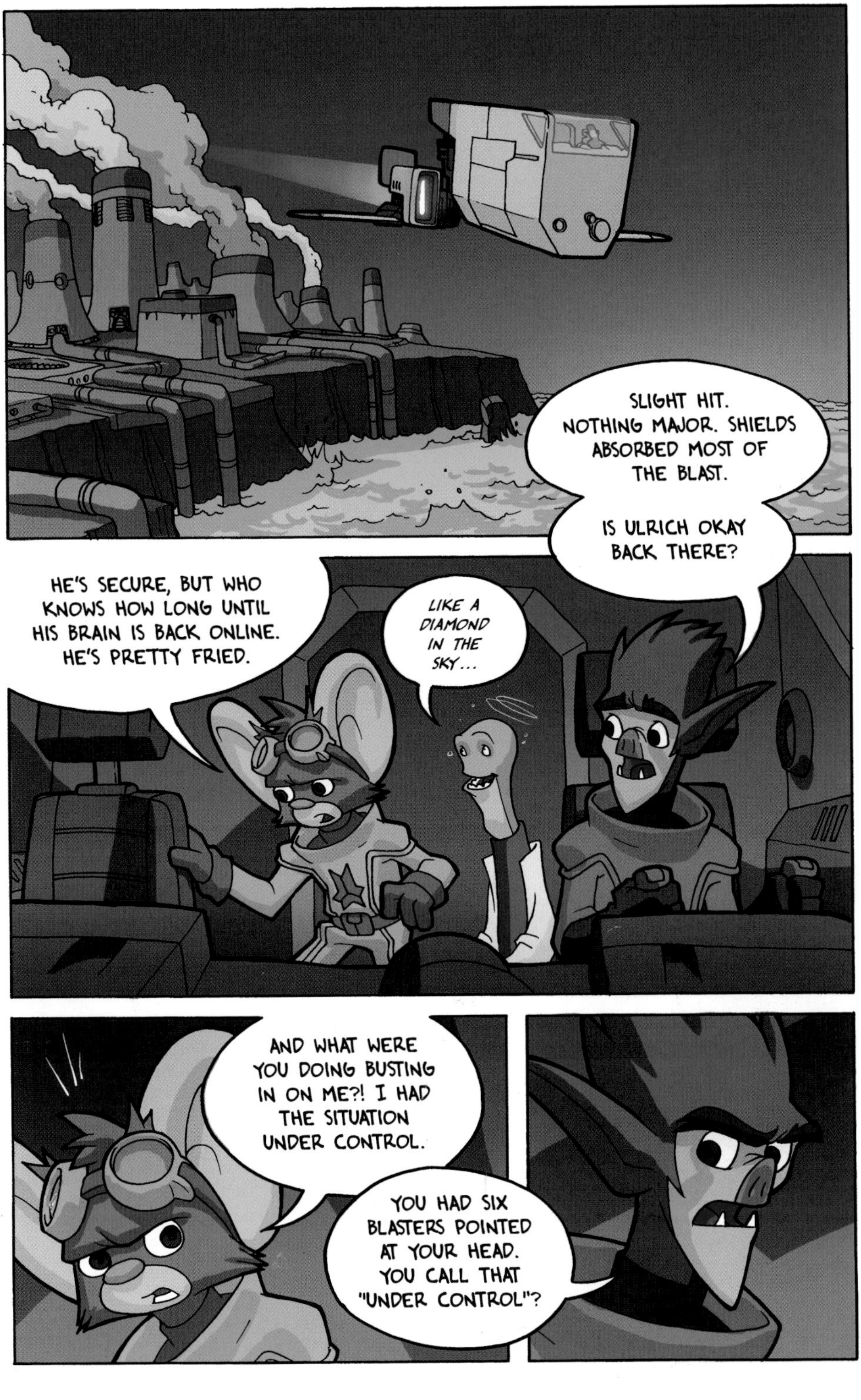
SLIGHT HIT. NOTHING MAJOR. SHIELDS ABSORBED MOST OF THE BLAST.
IS ULRICH OKAY BACK THERE?
HE'S SECURE, BUT WHO KNOWS HOW LONG UNTIL HIS BRAIN IS BACK ONLINE. HE'S PRETTY FRIED.
LIKE A DIAMOND IN THE SKY...
AND WHAT WERE YOU DOING BUSTING IN ON ME?! I HAD THE SITUATION UNDER CONTROL.
YOU HAD SIX BLASTERS POINTED AT YOUR HEAD. YOU CALL THAT "UNDER CONTROL"?

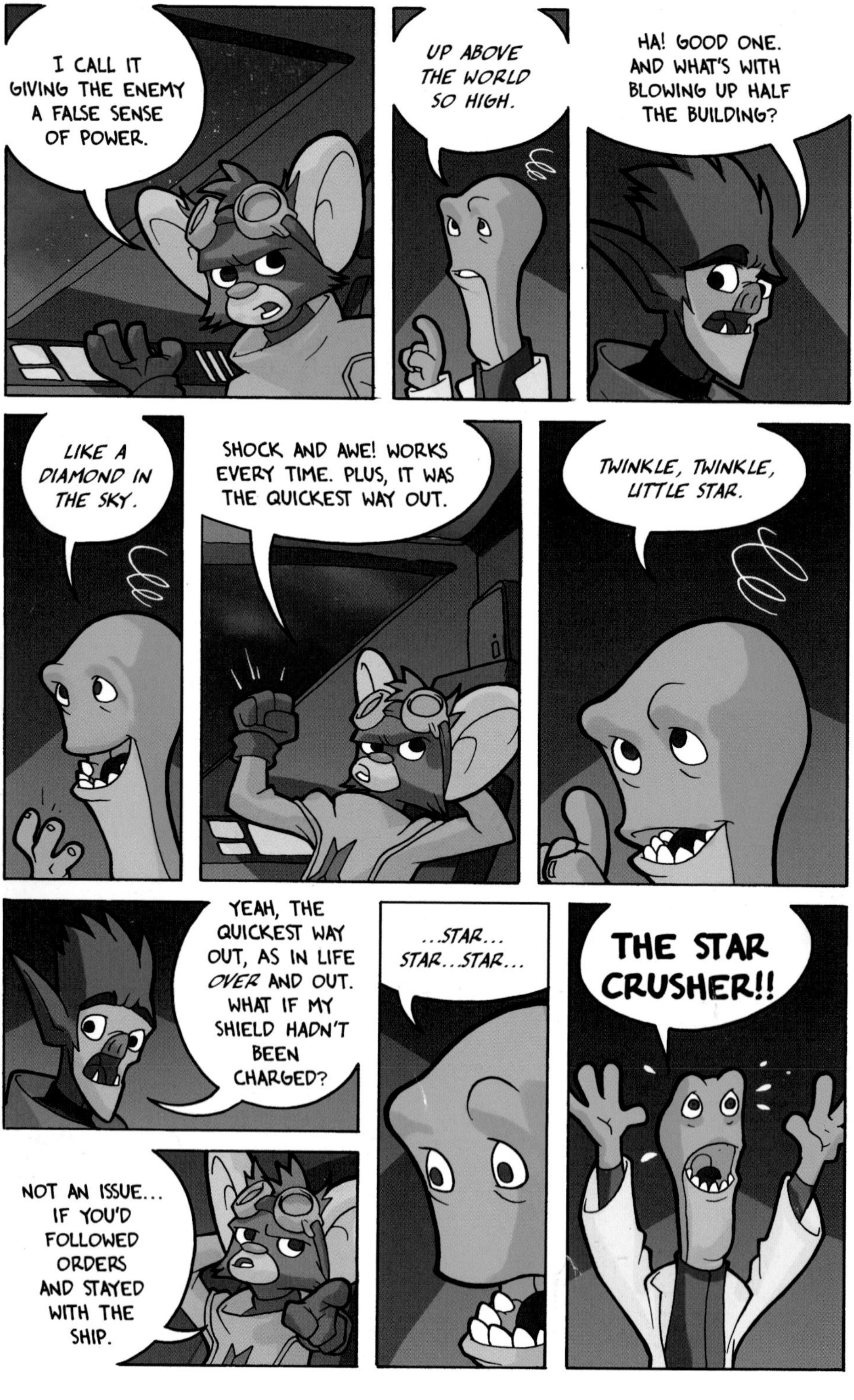
I CALL IT GIVING THE ENEMY A FALSE SENSE OF POWER.
UP ABOVE THE WORLD SO HIGH.
HA! GOOD ONE. AND WHAT'S WITH BLOWING UP HALF THE BUILDING?
LIKE A DIAMOND IN THE SKY.
SHOCK AND AWE! WORKS EVERY TIME. PLUS, IT WAS THE QUICKEST WAY OUT.
TWINKLE, TWINKLE, LITTLE STAR.
YEAH, THE QUICKEST WAY OUT, AS IN LIFE *OVER* AND OUT. WHAT IF MY SHIELD HADN'T BEEN CHARGED?
NOT AN ISSUE... IF YOU'D FOLLOWED ORDERS AND STAYED WITH THE SHIP.
...STAR... STAR...STAR...
THE STAR CRUSHER!!

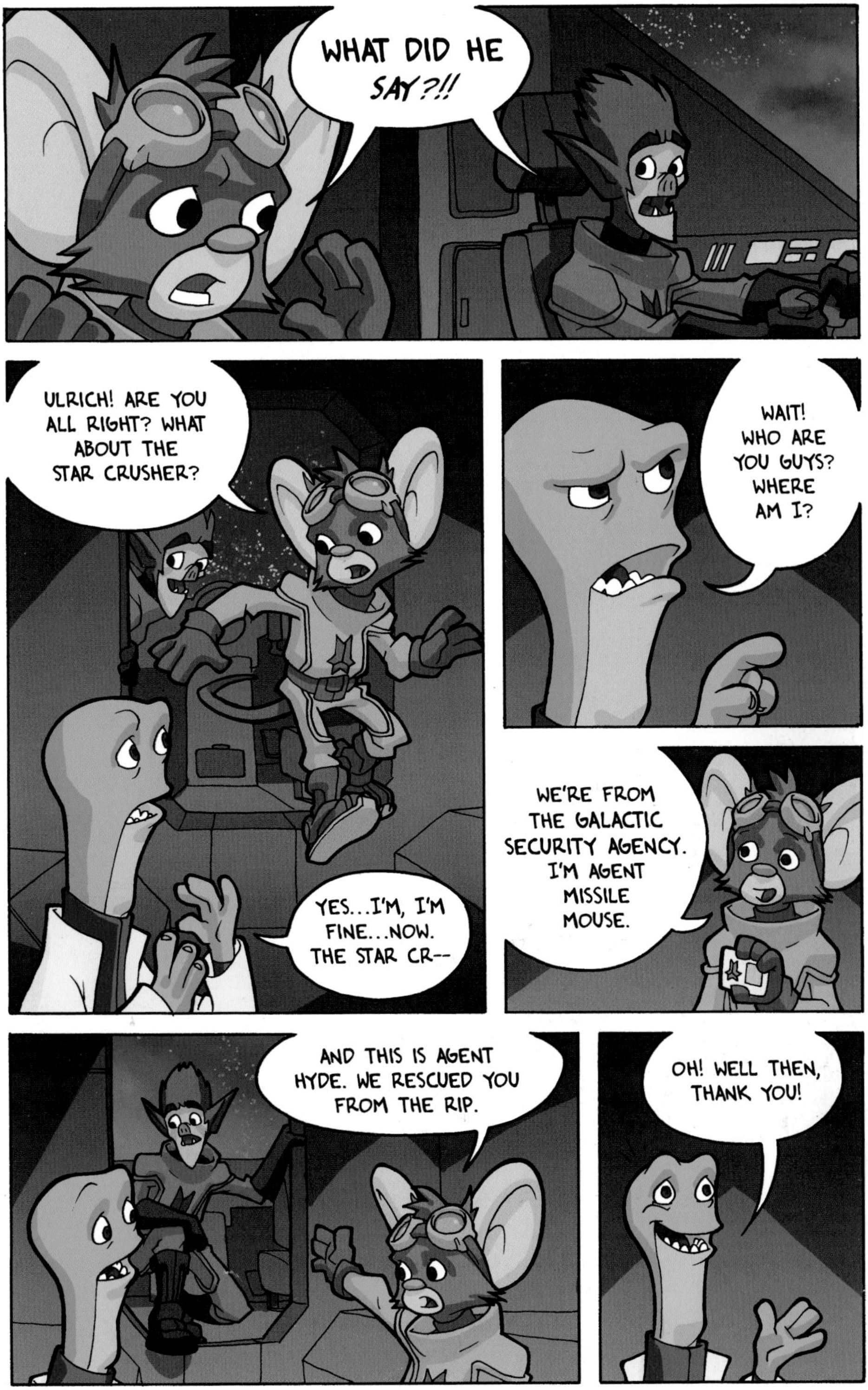
WHAT DID HE SAY?!!
ULRICH! ARE YOU ALL RIGHT? WHAT ABOUT THE STAR CRUSHER?
YES...I'M, I'M FINE...NOW. THE STAR CR--
WAIT! WHO ARE YOU GUYS? WHERE AM I?
WE'RE FROM THE GALACTIC SECURITY AGENCY. I'M AGENT MISSILE MOUSE.
AND THIS IS AGENT HYDE. WE RESCUED YOU FROM THE RIP.
OH! WELL THEN, THANK YOU!

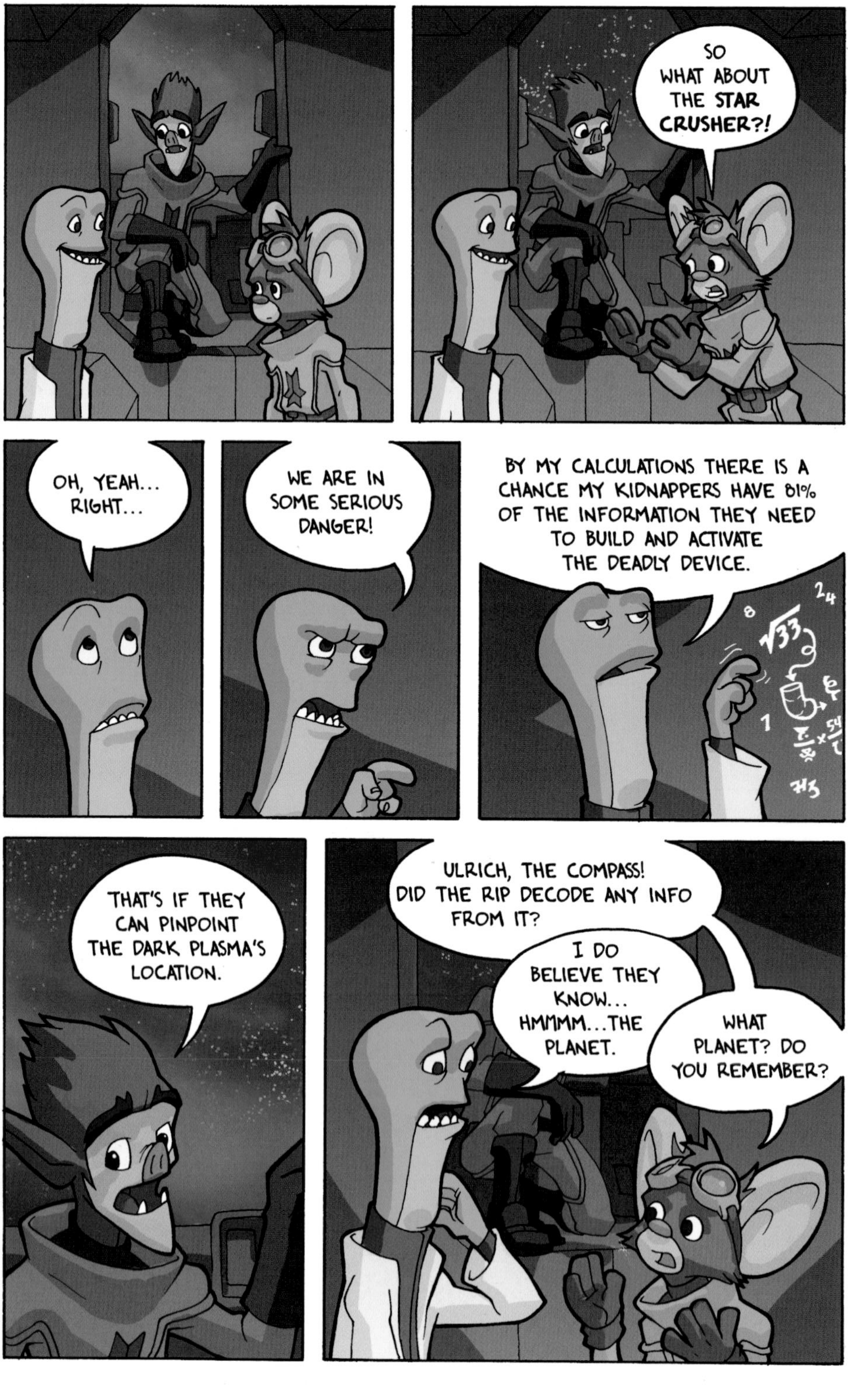
SO
WHAT ABOUT
THE STAR
CRUSHER?!
OH, YEAH...
RIGHT...
WE ARE IN
SOME SERIOUS
DANGER!
BY MY CALCULATIONS THERE IS A CHANCE MY KIDNAPPERS HAVE 81% OF THE INFORMATION THEY NEED TO BUILD AND ACTIVATE THE DEADLY DEVICE.
THAT'S IF THEY CAN PINPOINT THE DARK PLASMA'S LOCATION.
ULRICH, THE COMPASS! DID THE RIP DECODE ANY INFO FROM IT?
I DO BELIEVE THEY KNOW... HMMMM...THE PLANET.
WHAT PLANET? DO YOU REMEMBER?

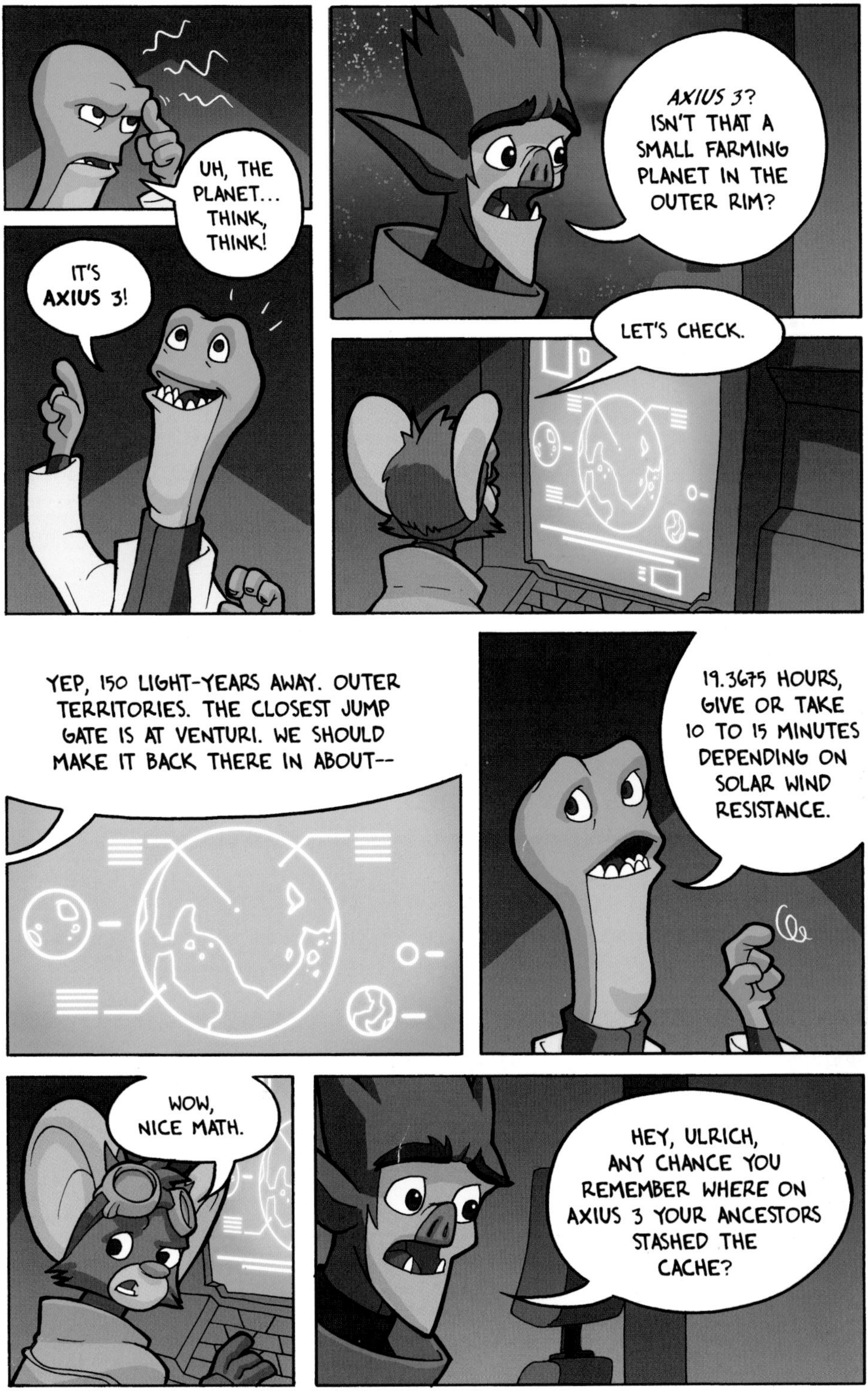
UH, THE PLANET... THINK, THINK!
AXIUS 3? ISN'T THAT A SMALL FARMING PLANET IN THE OUTER RIM?
IT'S AXIUS 3!
LET'S CHECK.
YEP, 150 LIGHT-YEARS AWAY. OUTER TERRITORIES. THE CLOSEST JUMP GATE IS AT VENTURI. WE SHOULD MAKE IT BACK THERE IN ABOUT--
19.3675 HOURS, GIVE OR TAKE 10 TO 15 MINUTES DEPENDING ON SOLAR WIND RESISTANCE.
WOW, NICE MATH.
HEY, ULRICH, ANY CHANCE YOU REMEMBER WHERE ON AXIUS 3 YOUR ANCESTORS STASHED THE CACHE?

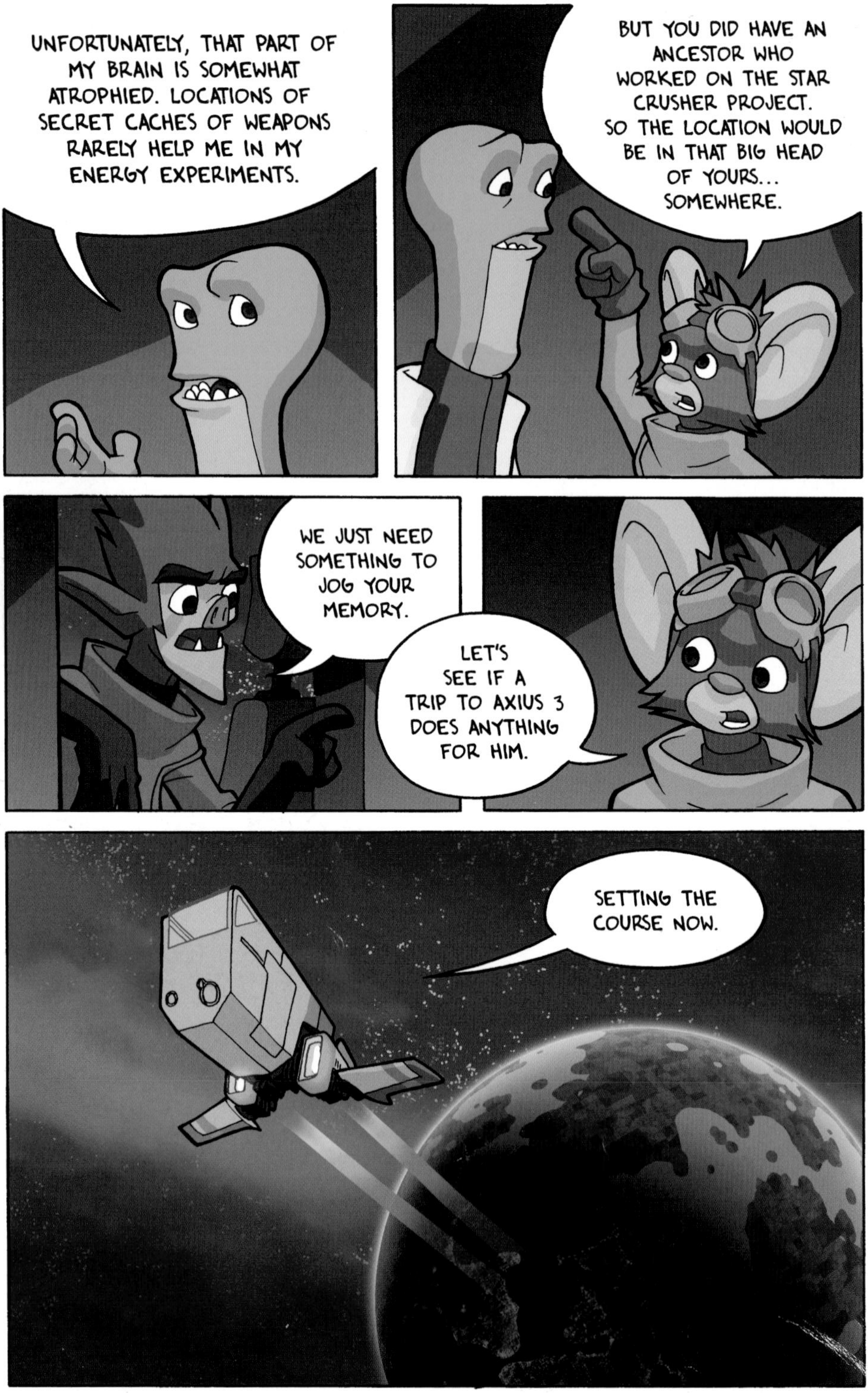
UNFORTUNATELY, THAT PART OF MY BRAIN IS SOMEWHAT ATROPHIED. LOCATIONS OF SECRET CACHES OF WEAPONS RARELY HELP ME IN MY ENERGY EXPERIMENTS.
BUT YOU DID HAVE AN ANCESTOR WHO WORKED ON THE STAR CRUSHER PROJECT. SO THE LOCATION WOULD BE IN THAT BIG HEAD OF YOURS... SOMEWHERE.
WE JUST NEED SOMETHING TO JOG YOUR MEMORY.
LET'S SEE IF A TRIP TO AXIUS 3 DOES ANYTHING FOR HIM.
SETTING THE COURSE NOW.

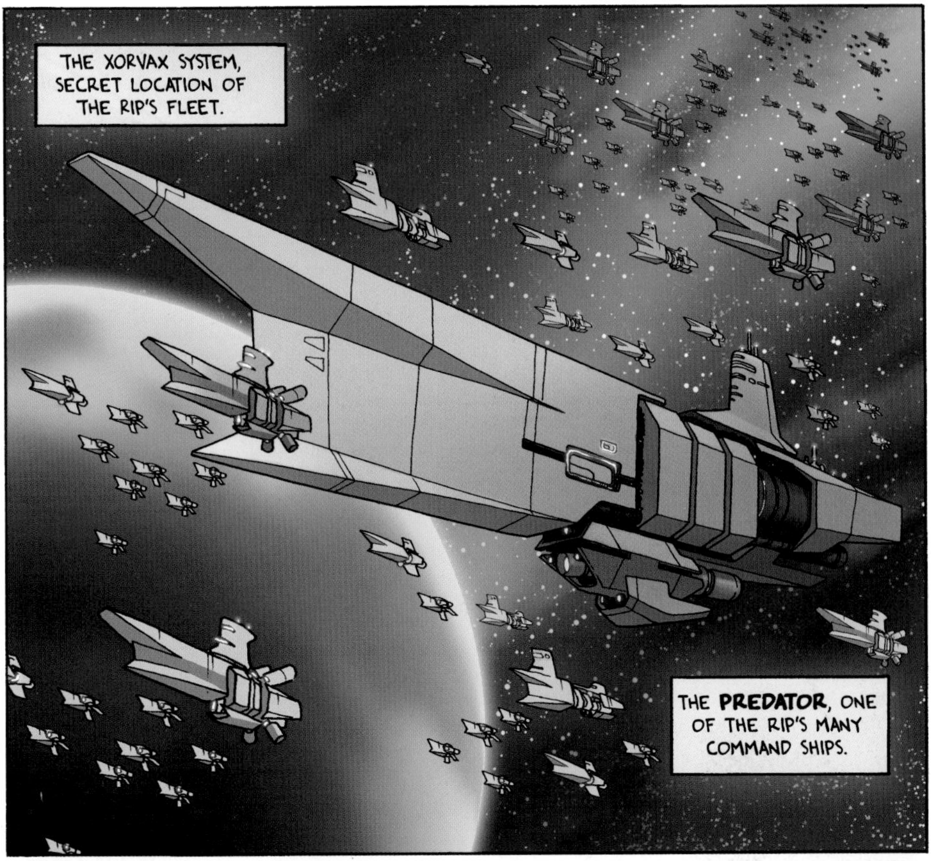
THE XORVAX SYSTEM, SECRET LOCATION OF THE RIP'S FLEET.
THE **PREDATOR**, ONE OF THE RIP'S MANY COMMAND SHIPS.

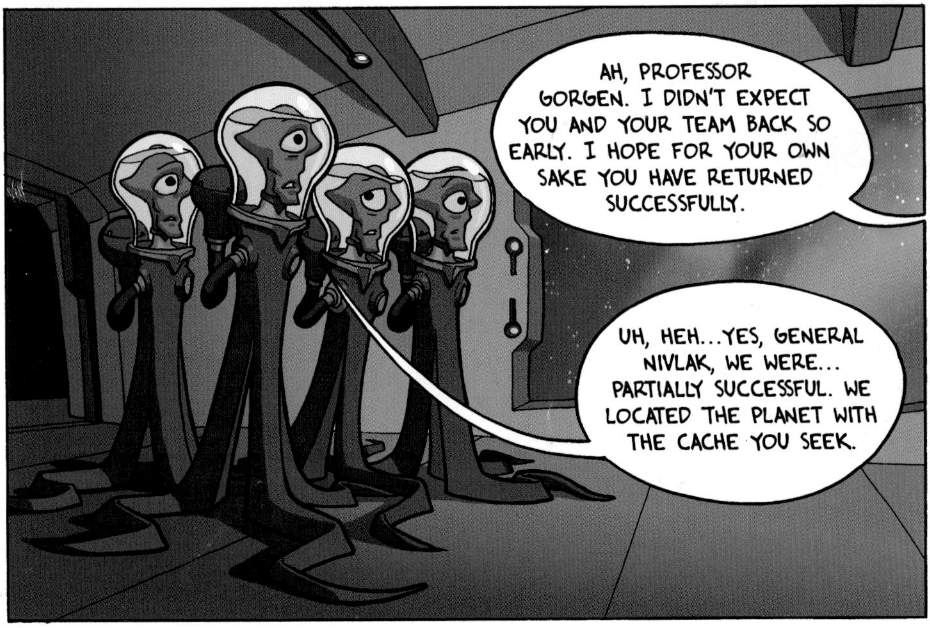
AH, PROFESSOR GORGEN. I DIDN'T EXPECT YOU AND YOUR TEAM BACK SO EARLY. I HOPE FOR YOUR OWN SAKE YOU HAVE RETURNED SUCCESSFULLY.
UH, HEH...YES, GENERAL NIVLAK, WE WERE... PARTIALLY SUCCESSFUL. WE LOCATED THE PLANET WITH THE CACHE YOU SEEK.

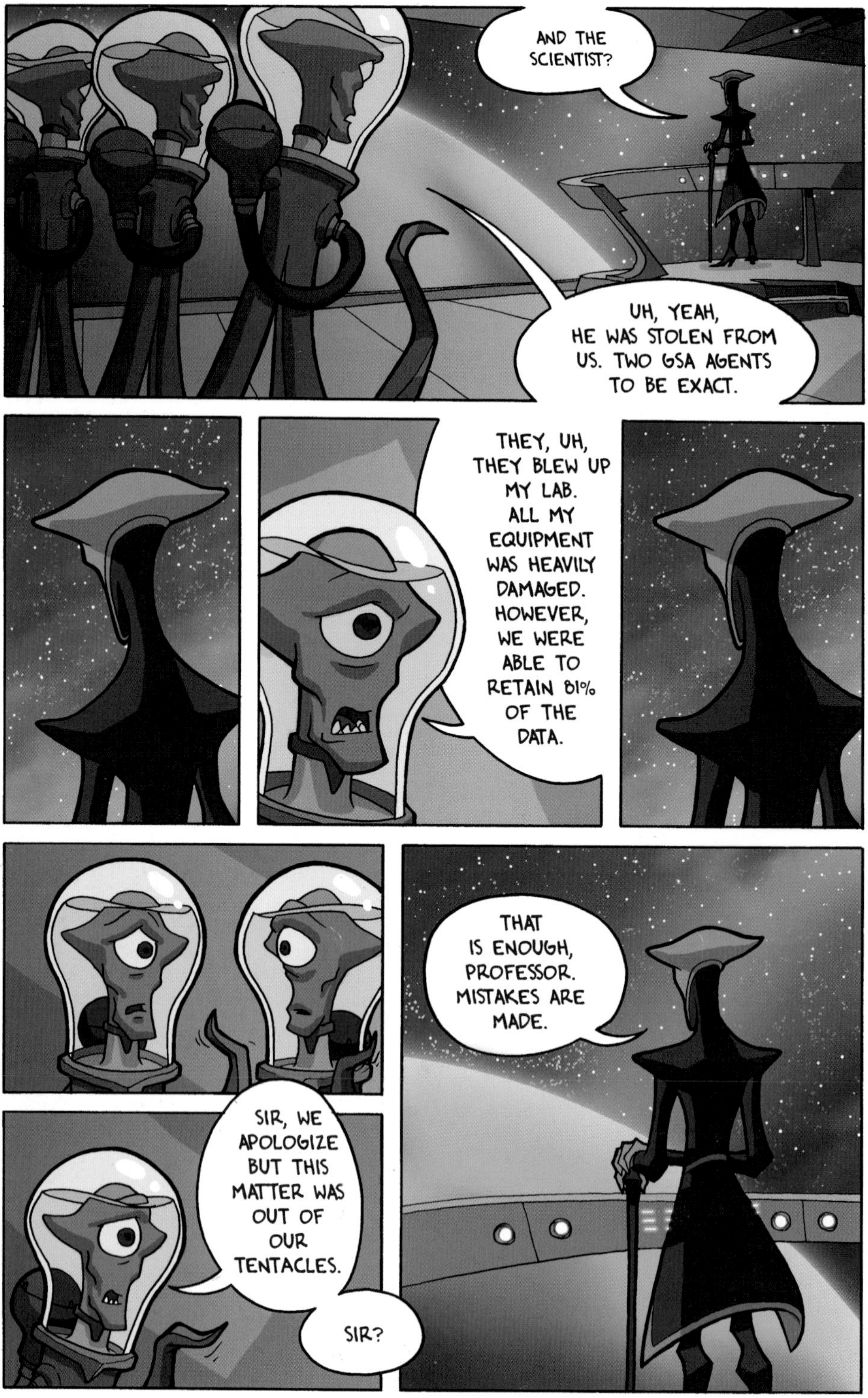
AND THE SCIENTIST?
UH, YEAH, HE WAS STOLEN FROM US. TWO GSA AGENTS TO BE EXACT.
THEY, UH, THEY BLEW UP MY LAB. ALL MY EQUIPMENT WAS HEAVILY DAMAGED. HOWEVER, WE WERE ABLE TO RETAIN 81% OF THE DATA.
SIR, WE APOLOGIZE BUT THIS MATTER WAS OUT OF OUR TENTACLES.
SIR?
THAT IS ENOUGH, PROFESSOR. MISTAKES ARE MADE.

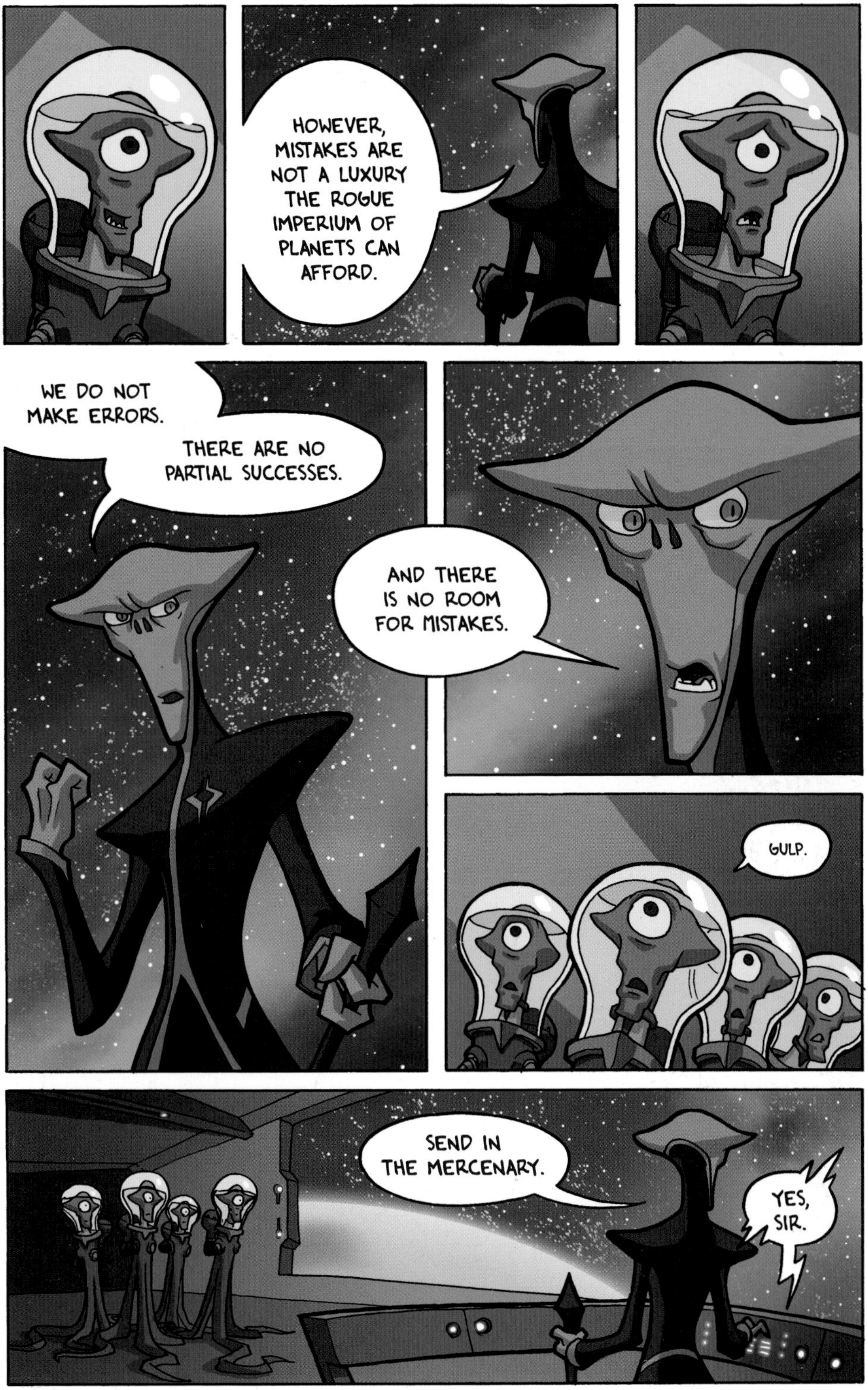
HOWEVER, MISTAKES ARE NOT A LUXURY THE ROGUE IMPERIUM OF PLANETS CAN AFFORD.
WE DO NOT MAKE ERRORS.
THERE ARE NO PARTIAL SUCCESSES.
AND THERE IS NO ROOM FOR MISTAKES.
GULP.
SEND IN THE MERCENARY.
YES, SIR.

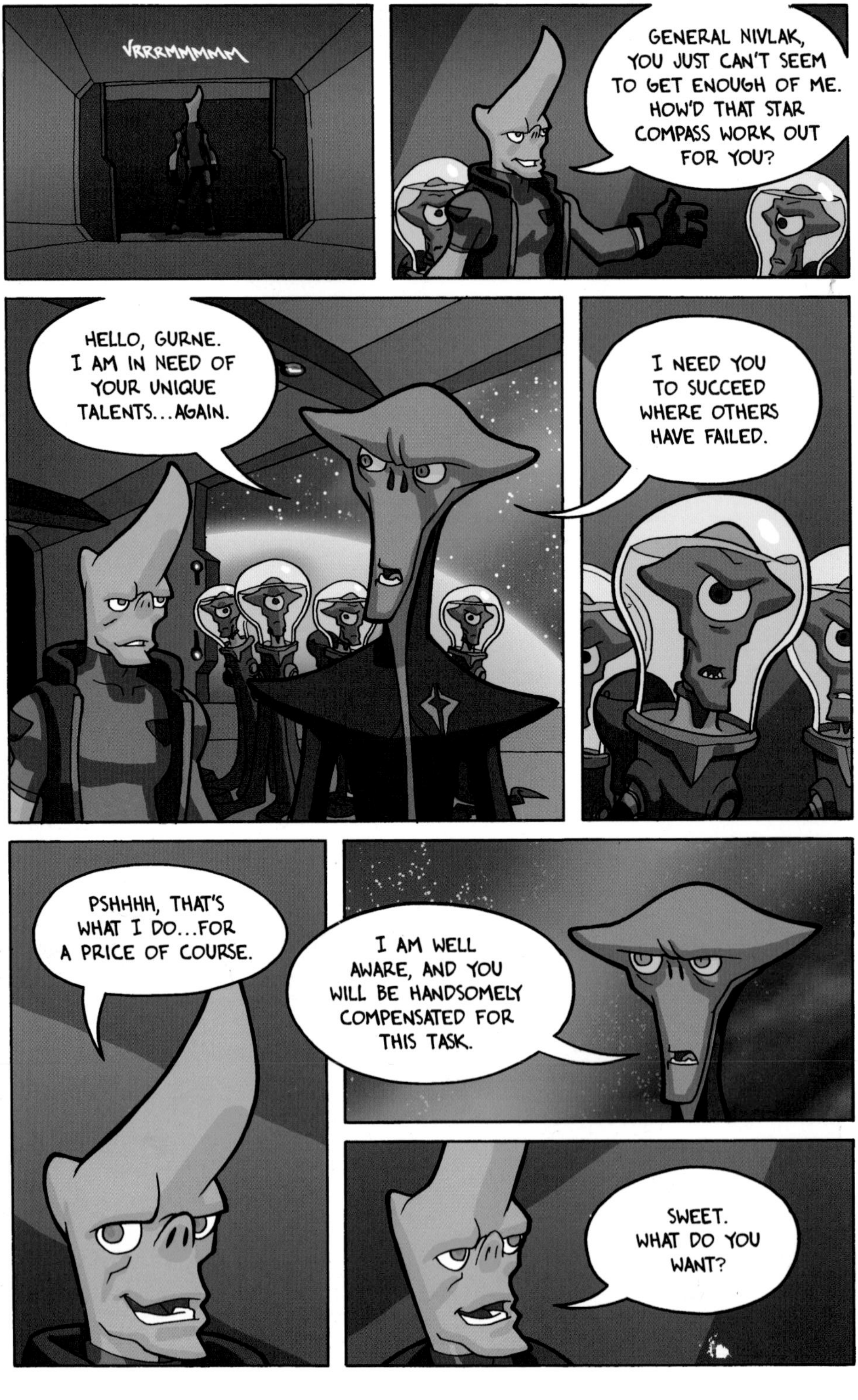

VRRRMMMMM
GENERAL NIVLAK, YOU JUST CAN'T SEEM TO GET ENOUGH OF ME. HOW'D THAT STAR COMPASS WORK OUT FOR YOU?
HELLO, GURNE. I AM IN NEED OF YOUR UNIQUE TALENTS...AGAIN.
I NEED YOU TO SUCCEED WHERE OTHERS HAVE FAILED.
PSHHHH, THAT'S WHAT I DO...FOR A PRICE OF COURSE.
I AM WELL AWARE, AND YOU WILL BE HANDSOMELY COMPENSATED FOR THIS TASK.
SWEET. WHAT DO YOU WANT?

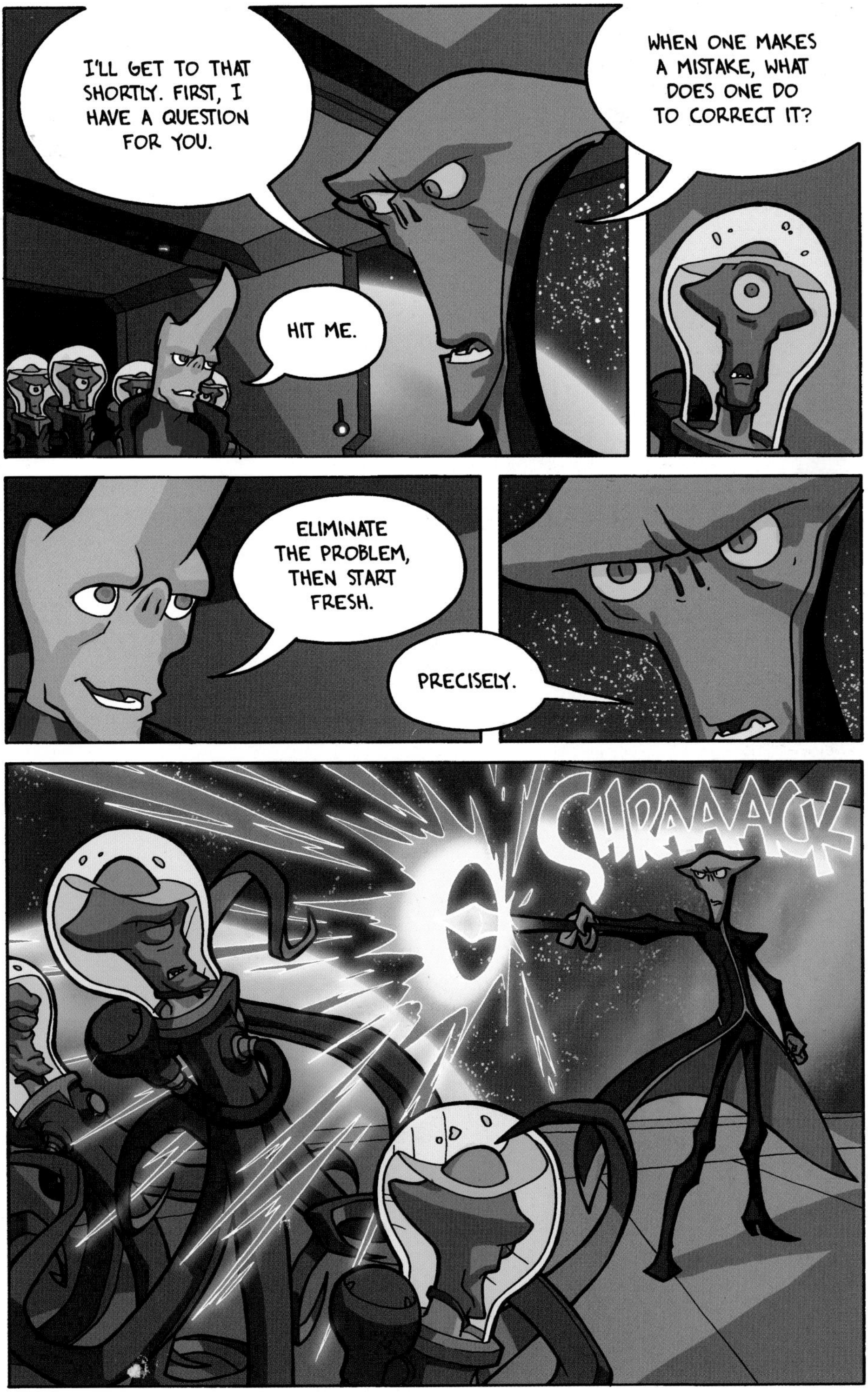
I'LL GET TO THAT SHORTLY. FIRST, I HAVE A QUESTION FOR YOU.
HIT ME.
WHEN ONE MAKES A MISTAKE, WHAT DOES ONE DO TO CORRECT IT?
ELIMINATE THE PROBLEM, THEN START FRESH.
PRECISELY.
SHRAAACK

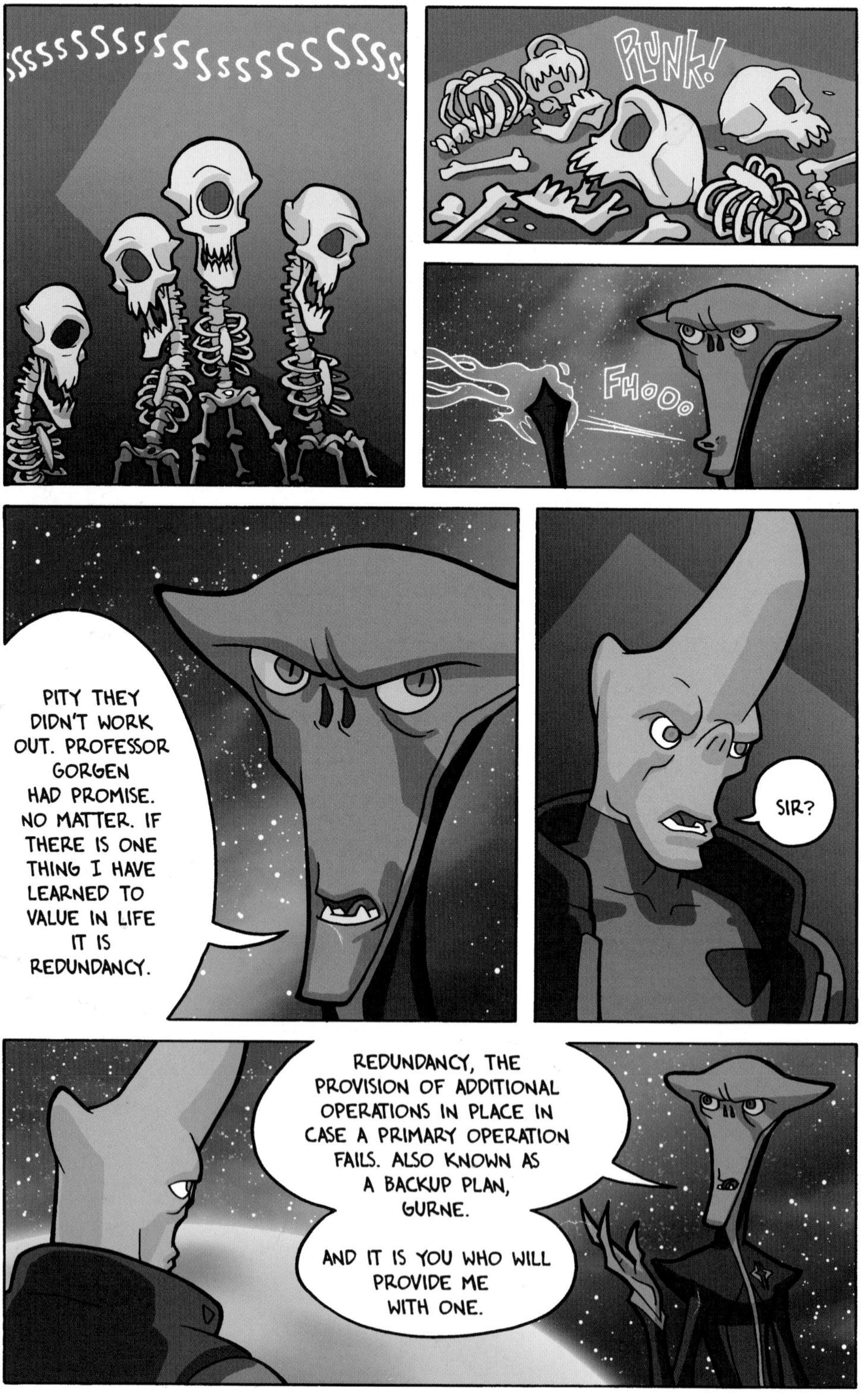
sSSSSSSSSSSSSSSSSSSSs
PLUNK!
FHOOo
PITY THEY DIDN'T WORK OUT. PROFESSOR GORGEN HAD PROMISE. NO MATTER. IF THERE IS ONE THING I HAVE LEARNED TO VALUE IN LIFE IT IS REDUNDANCY.
SIR?
REDUNDANCY, THE PROVISION OF ADDITIONAL OPERATIONS IN PLACE IN CASE A PRIMARY OPERATION FAILS. ALSO KNOWN AS A BACKUP PLAN, GURNE.
AND IT IS YOU WHO WILL PROVIDE ME WITH ONE.

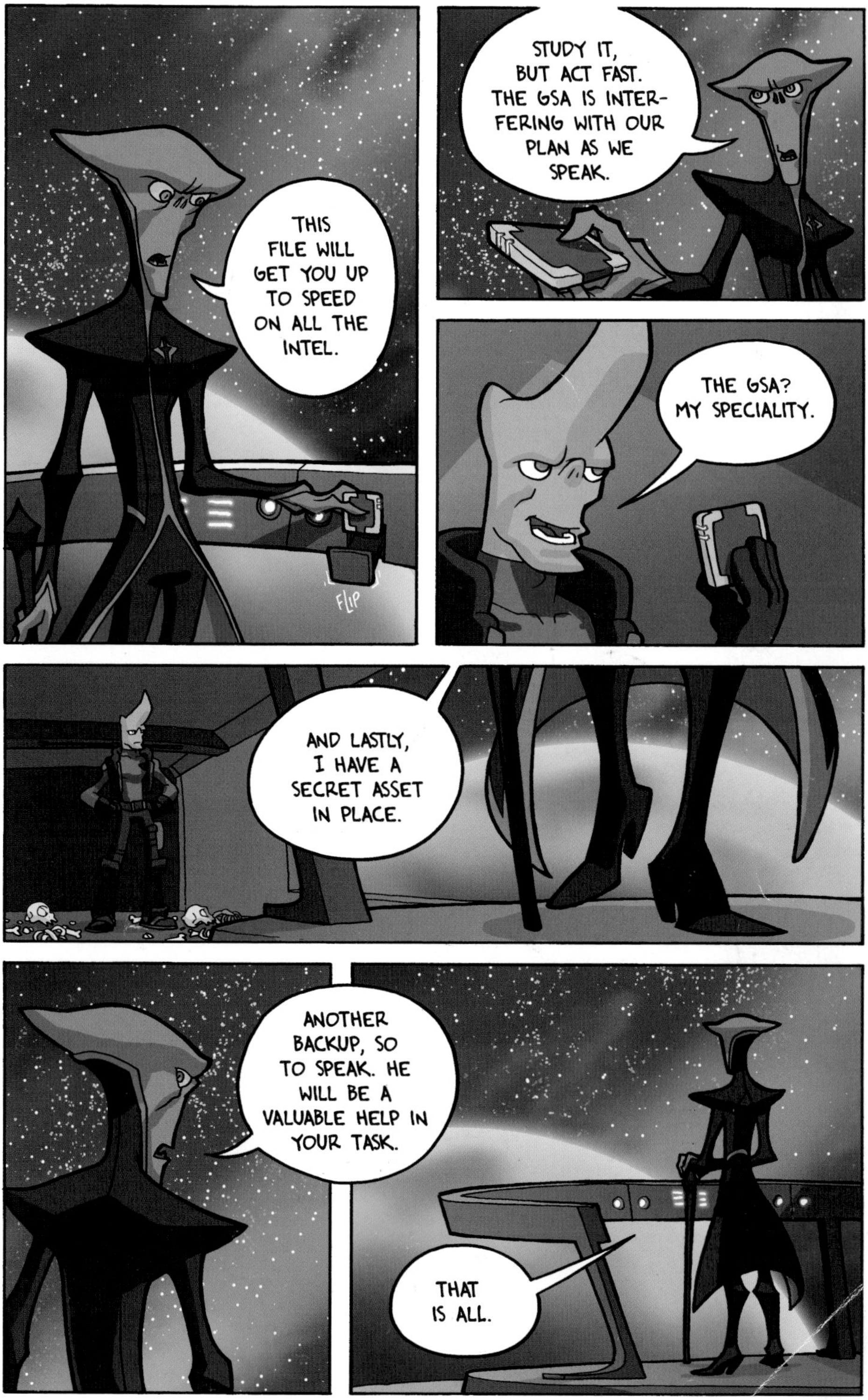
THIS FILE WILL GET YOU UP TO SPEED ON ALL THE INTEL.
FLIP
STUDY IT, BUT ACT FAST. THE GSA IS INTERFERING WITH OUR PLAN AS WE SPEAK.
THE GSA? MY SPECIALITY.
AND LASTLY, I HAVE A SECRET ASSET IN PLACE.
ANOTHER BACKUP, SO TO SPEAK. HE WILL BE A VALUABLE HELP IN YOUR TASK.
THAT IS ALL.

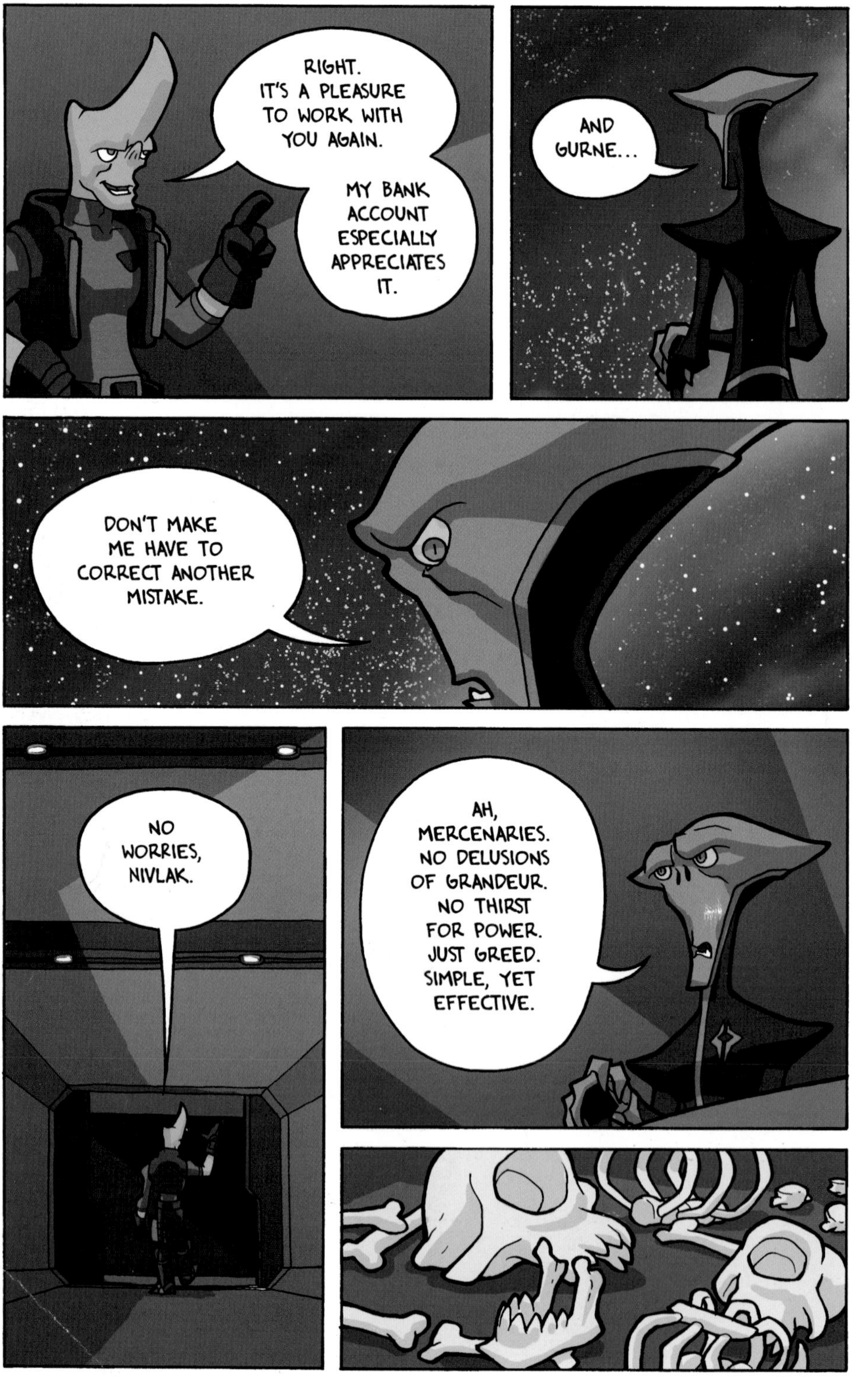
RIGHT. IT'S A PLEASURE TO WORK WITH YOU AGAIN.
MY BANK ACCOUNT ESPECIALLY APPRECIATES IT.
AND GURNE...
DON'T MAKE ME HAVE TO CORRECT ANOTHER MISTAKE.
NO WORRIES, NIVLAK.
AH, MERCENARIES. NO DELUSIONS OF GRANDEUR. NO THIRST FOR POWER. JUST GREED. SIMPLE, YET EFFECTIVE.

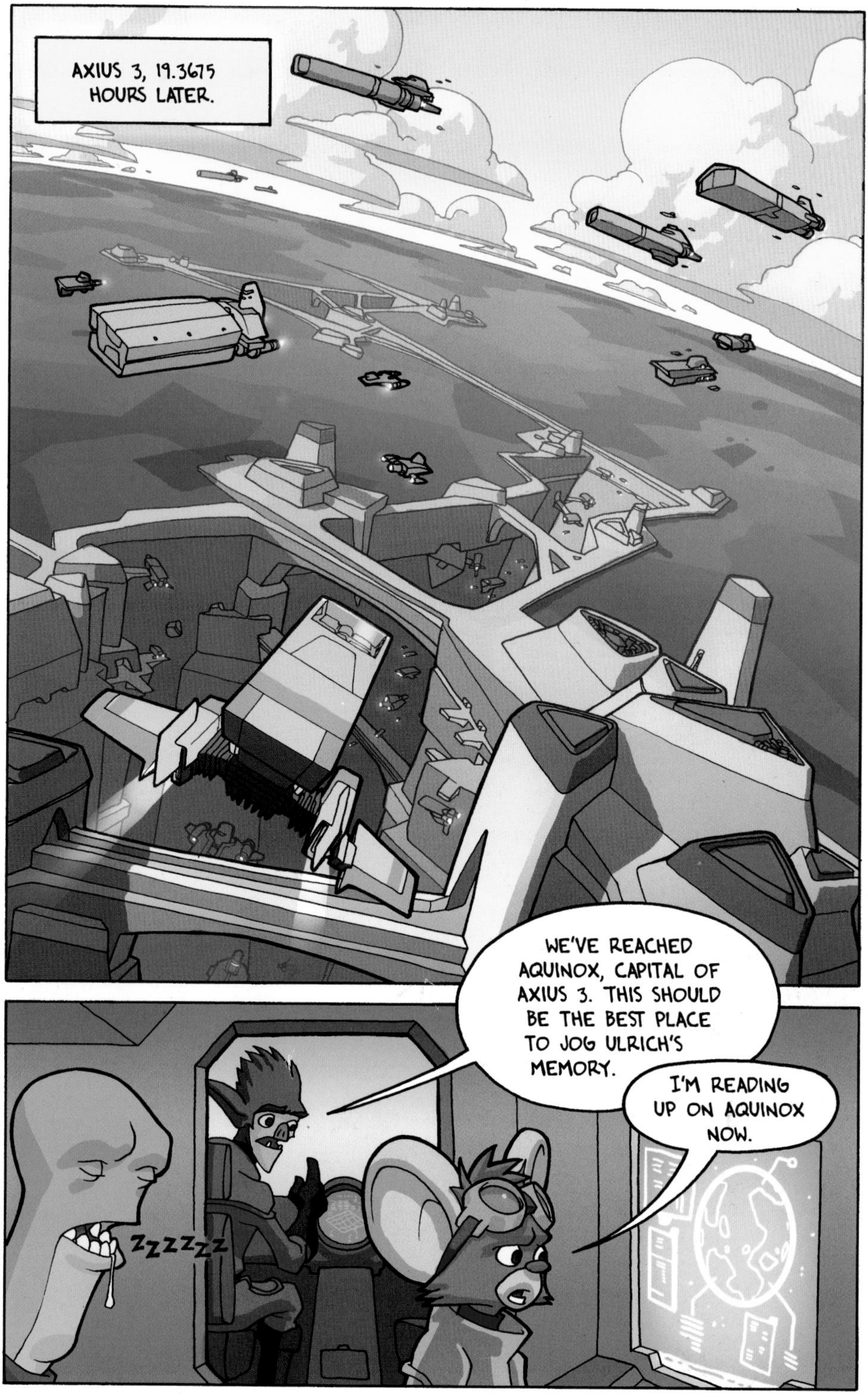
AXIUS 3, 19.3675 HOURS LATER.
WE'VE REACHED AQUINOX, CAPITAL OF AXIUS 3. THIS SHOULD BE THE BEST PLACE TO JOG ULRICH'S MEMORY.
I'M READING UP ON AQUINOX NOW.
ZZZZZZ

ACCORDING TO OUR DATA FILE THERE'S A GSA CONTACT NOT FAR FROM HERE.

SAYS HE OWNS AND OPERATES A LITTLE PLACE CALLED ONE-EYED JACK'S ON THE LOWER LEVELS. LOTS OF OFF-WORLDERS COME THROUGH WITH INFORMATION.

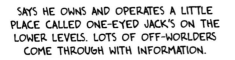

GSA CONTACT

PERFECT. WE'LL NEED TO DISGUISE OURSELVES SO WE BLEND IN A LITTLE BETTER.

YAWN

OKAY, REMEMBER WE'RE TRYING TO KEEP A LOW PROFILE. THERE COULD BE RIP SPIES ANYWHERE.

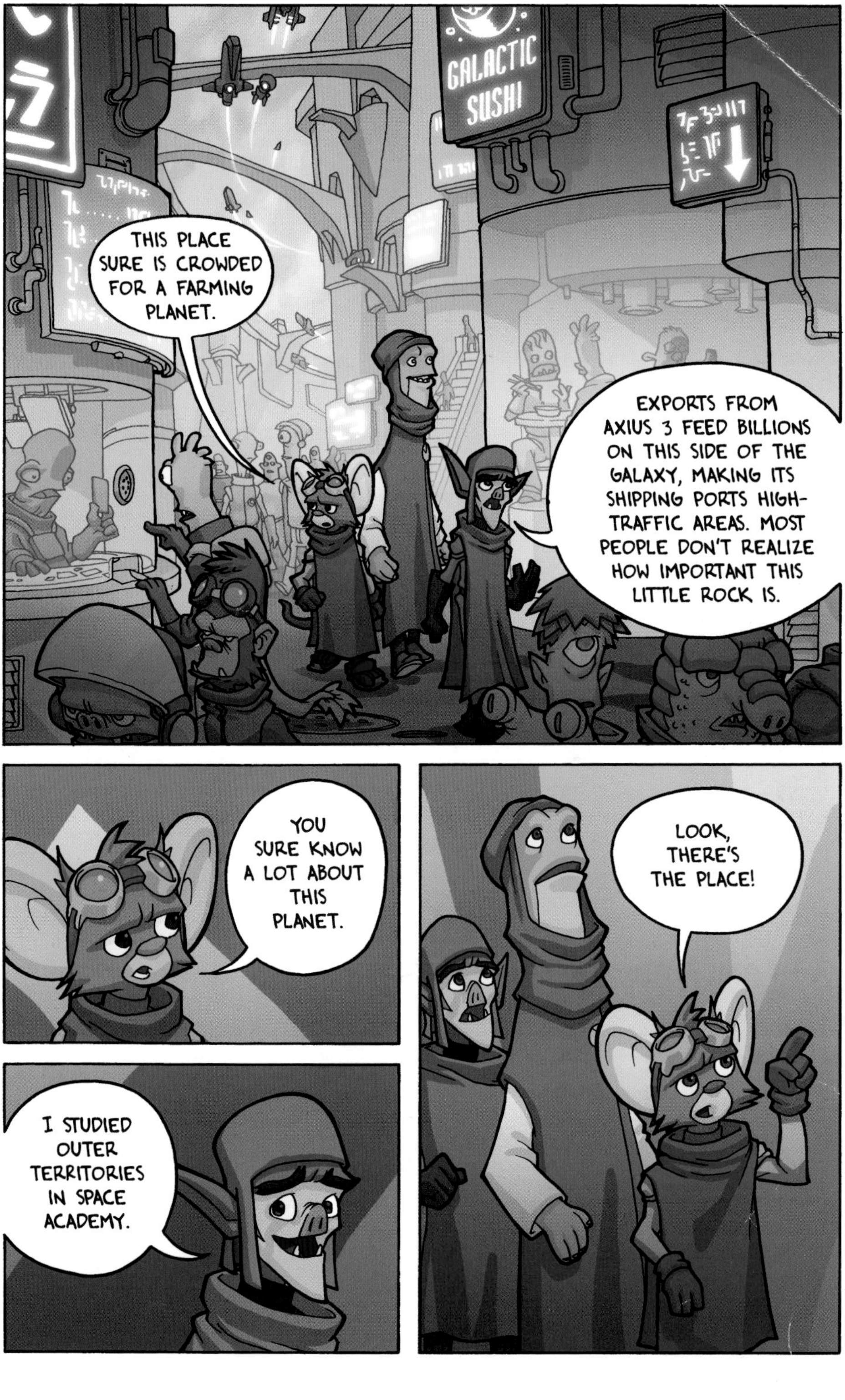
GALACTIC SUSHI
THIS PLACE SURE IS CROWDED FOR A FARMING PLANET.
EXPORTS FROM AXIUS 3 FEED BILLIONS ON THIS SIDE OF THE GALAXY, MAKING ITS SHIPPING PORTS HIGH-TRAFFIC AREAS. MOST PEOPLE DON'T REALIZE HOW IMPORTANT THIS LITTLE ROCK IS.
YOU SURE KNOW A LOT ABOUT THIS PLANET.
I STUDIED OUTER TERRITORIES IN SPACE ACADEMY.
LOOK, THERE'S THE PLACE!

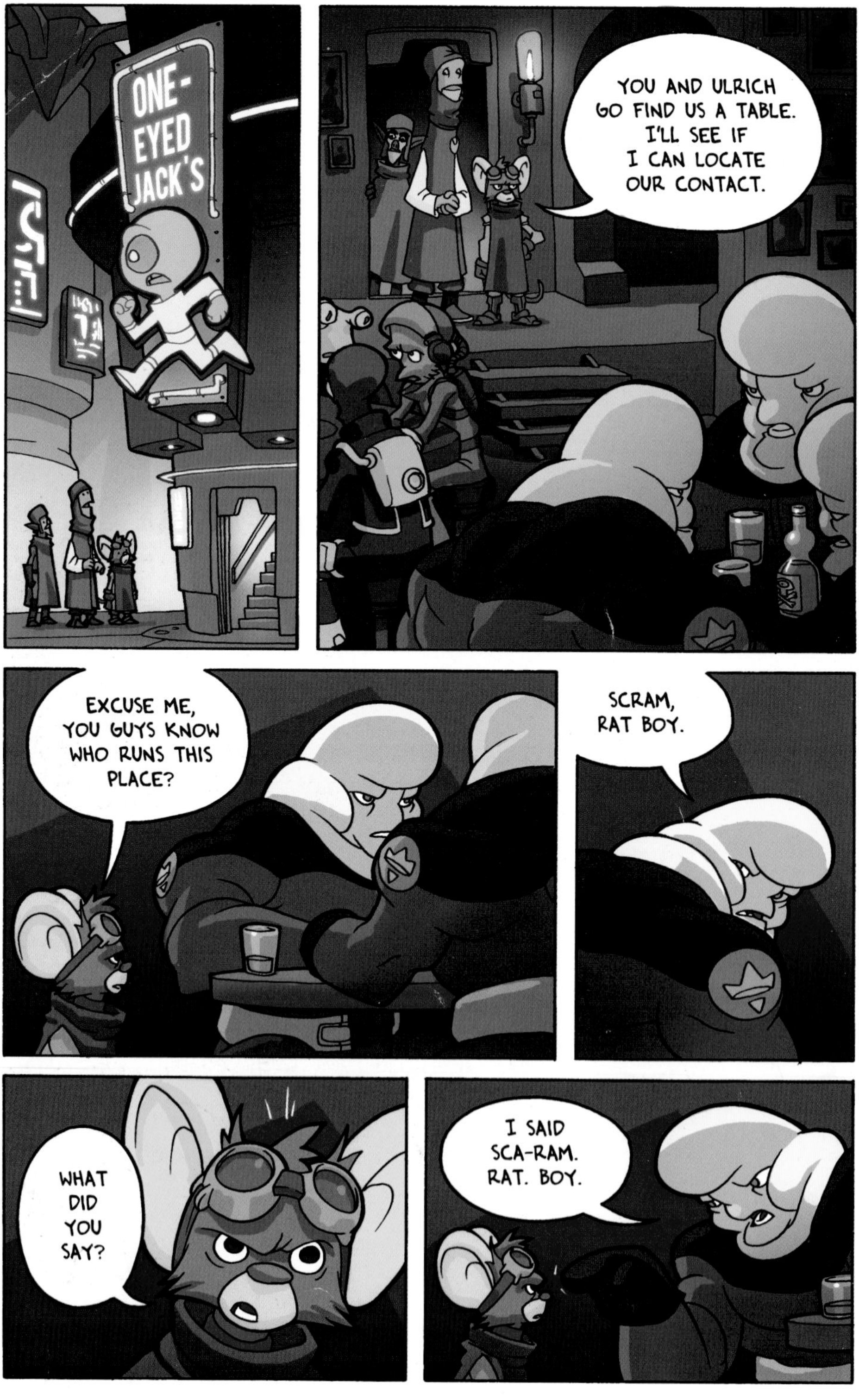
ONE-EYED JACK'S
YOU AND ULRICH GO FIND US A TABLE. I'LL SEE IF I CAN LOCATE OUR CONTACT.
EXCUSE ME, YOU GUYS KNOW WHO RUNS THIS PLACE?
SCRAM, RAT BOY.
WHAT DID YOU SAY?
I SAID SCA-RAM. RAT. BOY.

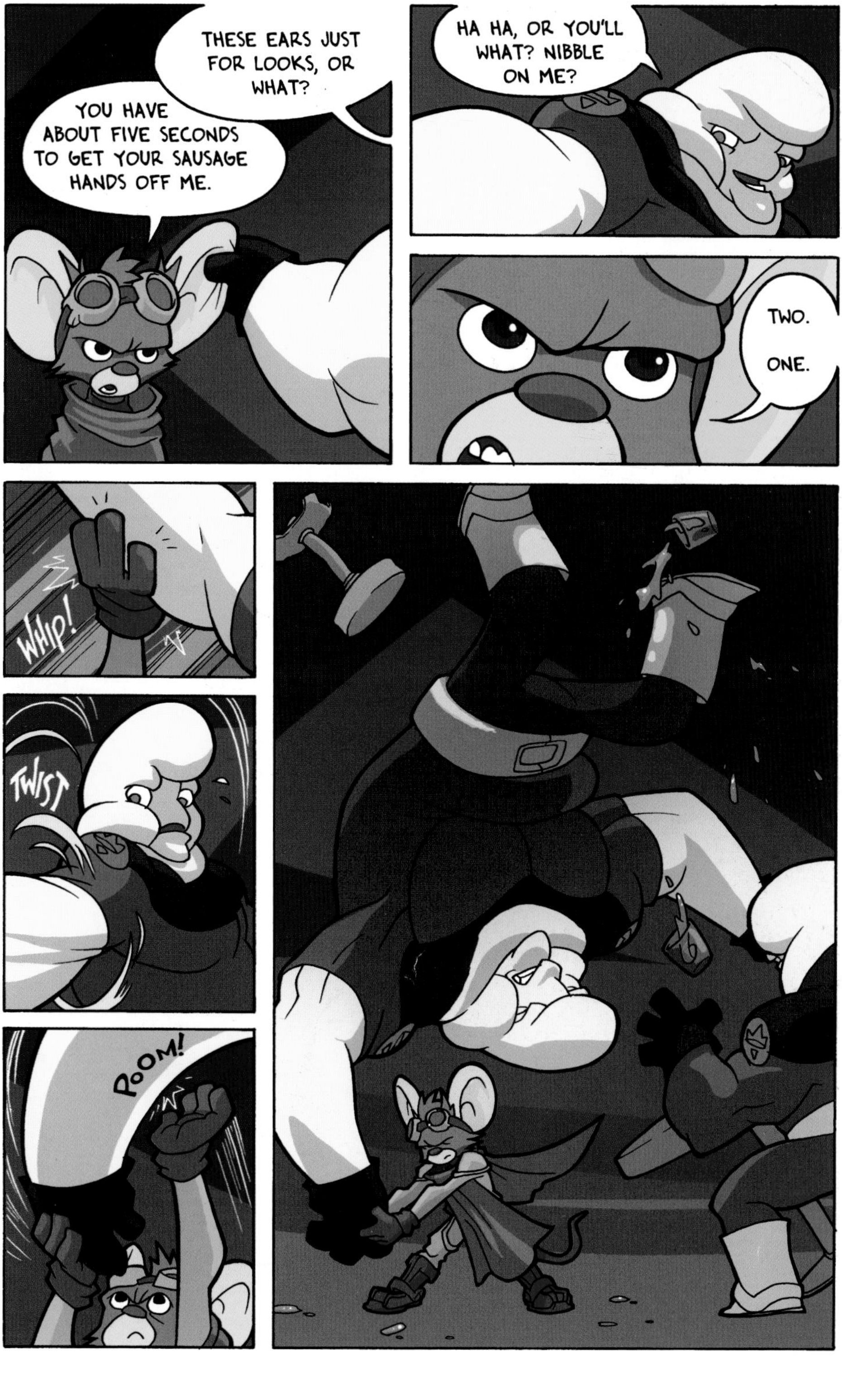
YOU HAVE ABOUT FIVE SECONDS TO GET YOUR SAUSAGE HANDS OFF ME.
THESE EARS JUST FOR LOOKS, OR WHAT?
HA HA, OR YOU'LL WHAT? NIBBLE ON ME?
TWO.
ONE.
WHIP!
TWIST
POOM!

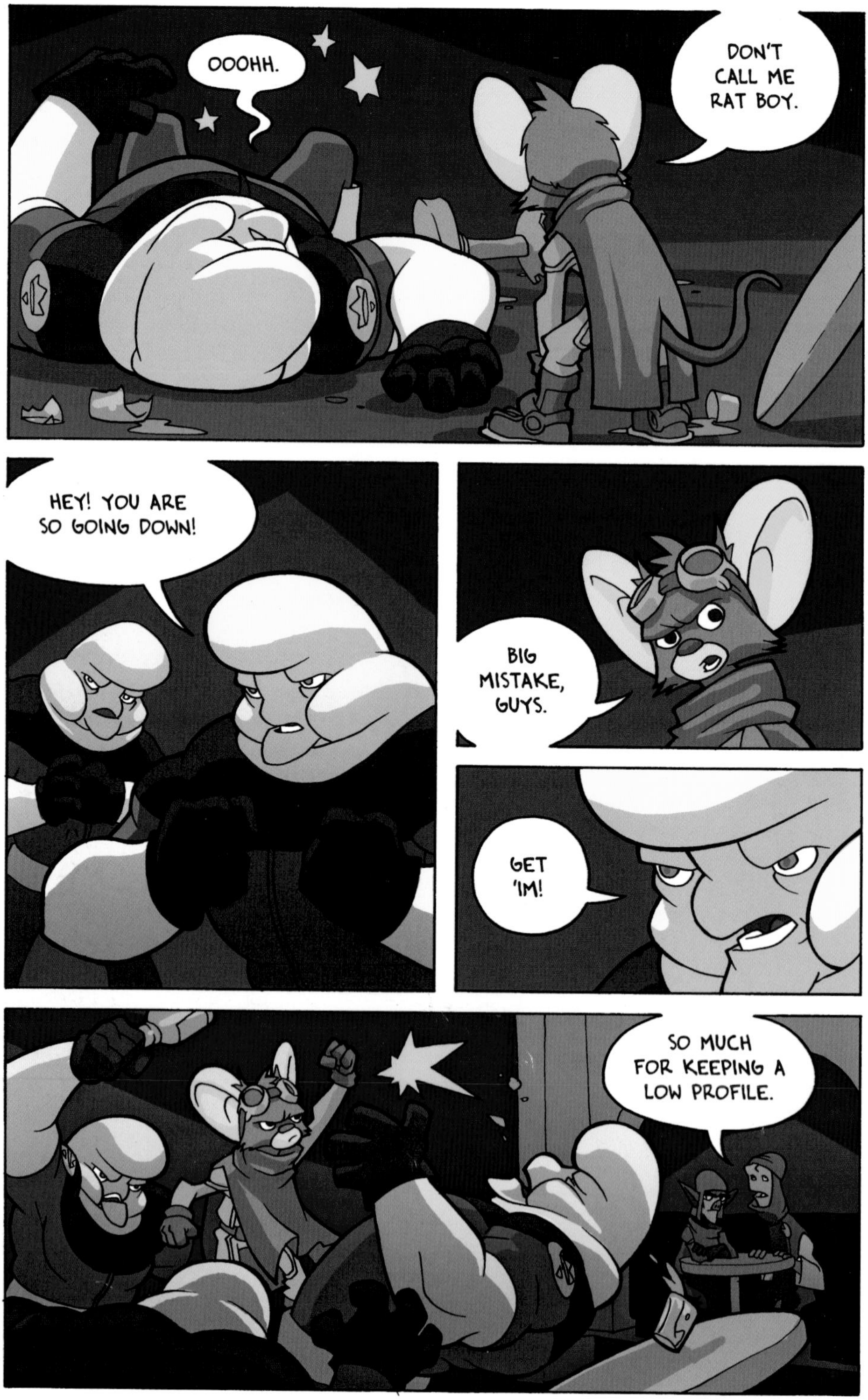
OOOHH.
DON'T CALL ME RAT BOY.
HEY! YOU ARE SO GOING DOWN!
BIG MISTAKE, GUYS.
GET 'IM!
SO MUCH FOR KEEPING A LOW PROFILE.

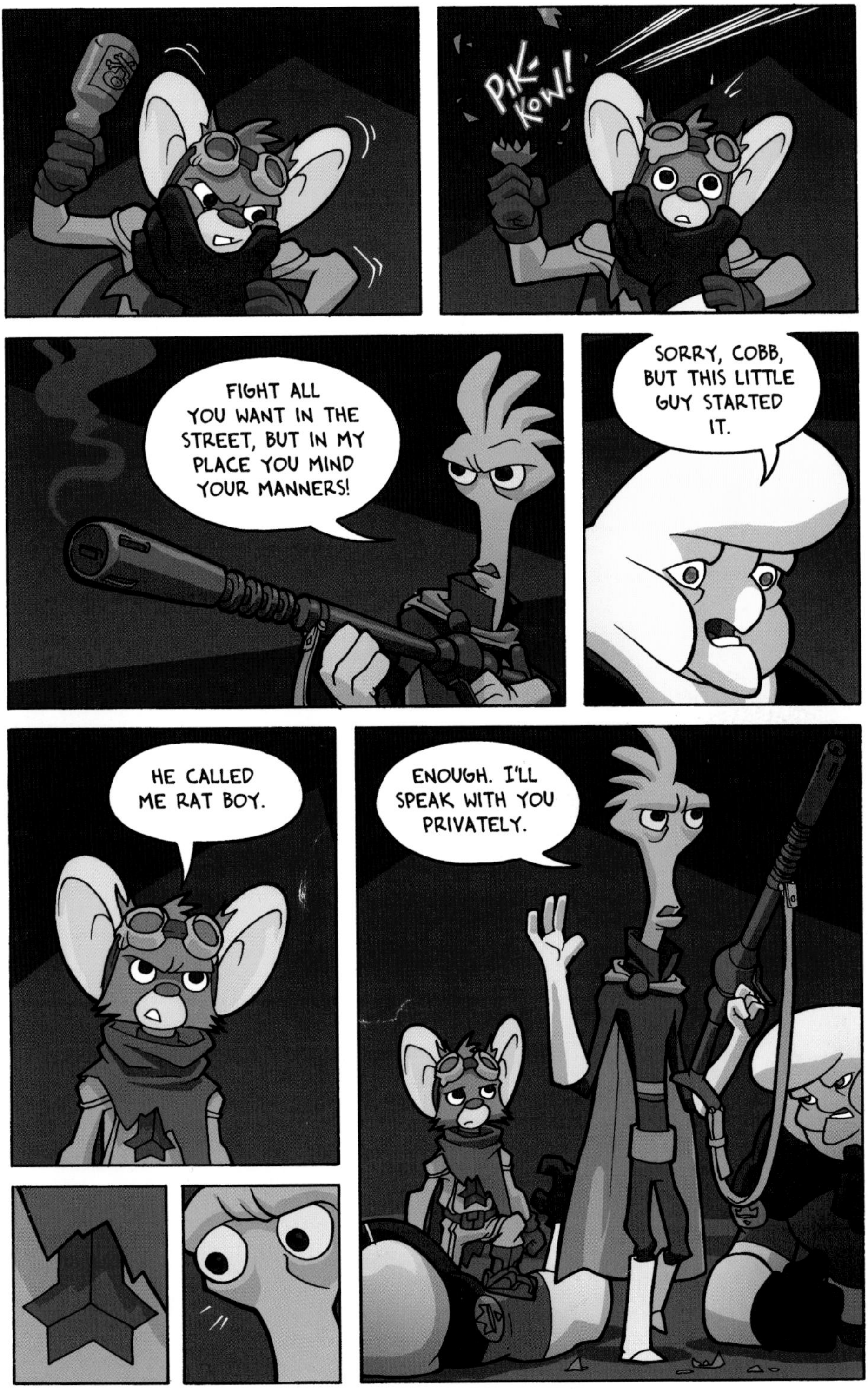
PIK-KOW!
FIGHT ALL YOU WANT IN THE STREET, BUT IN MY PLACE YOU MIND YOUR MANNERS!
SORRY, COBB, BUT THIS LITTLE GUY STARTED IT.
HE CALLED ME RAT BOY.
ENOUGH. I'LL SPEAK WITH YOU PRIVATELY.

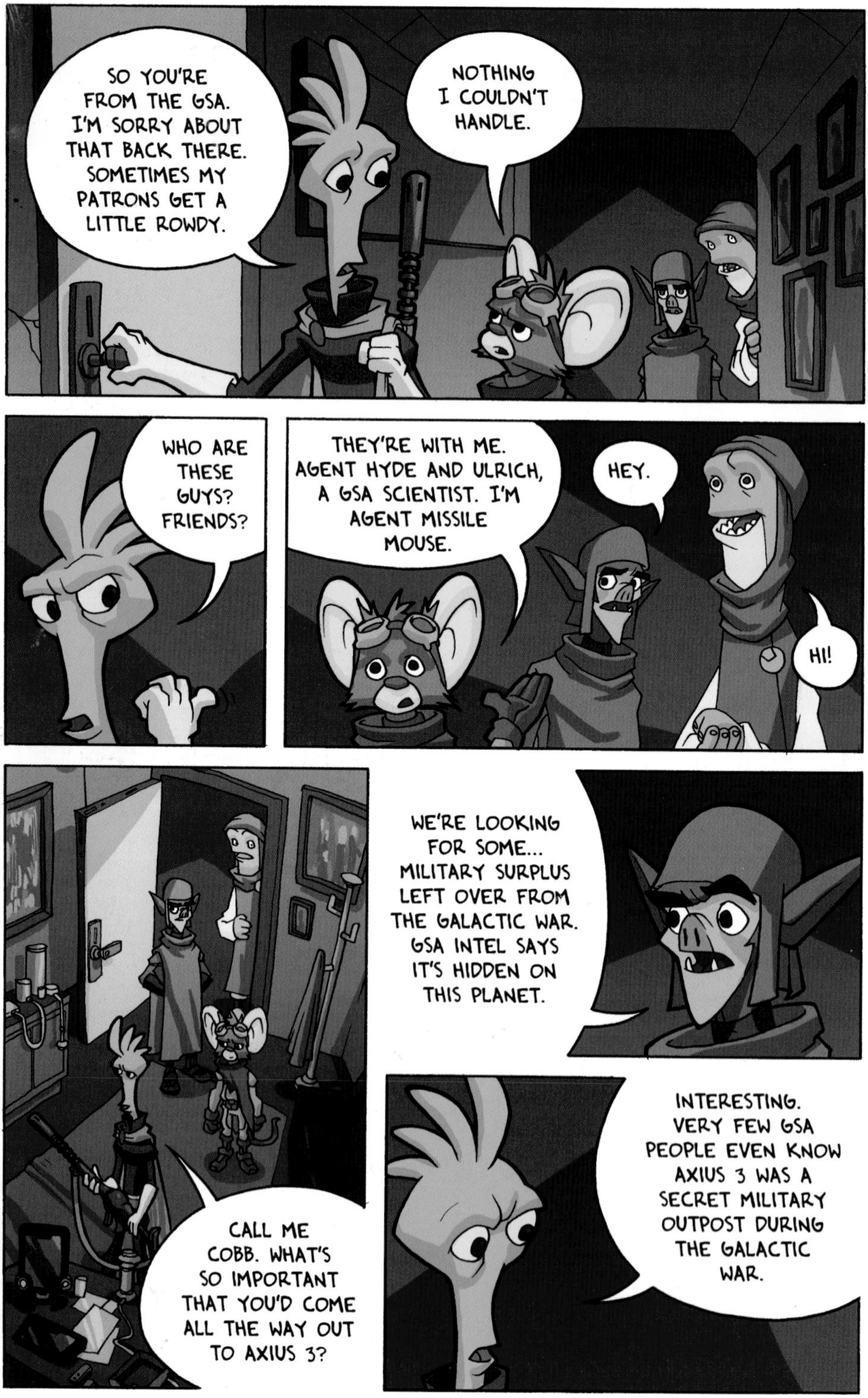
SO YOU'RE FROM THE GSA. I'M SORRY ABOUT THAT BACK THERE. SOMETIMES MY PATRONS GET A LITTLE ROWDY.
NOTHING I COULDN'T HANDLE.
WHO ARE THESE GUYS? FRIENDS?
THEY'RE WITH ME. AGENT HYDE AND ULRICH, A GSA SCIENTIST. I'M AGENT MISSILE MOUSE.
HEY.
HI!
CALL ME COBB. WHAT'S SO IMPORTANT THAT YOU'D COME ALL THE WAY OUT TO AXIUS 3?
WE'RE LOOKING FOR SOME... MILITARY SURPLUS LEFT OVER FROM THE GALACTIC WAR. GSA INTEL SAYS IT'S HIDDEN ON THIS PLANET.
INTERESTING. VERY FEW GSA PEOPLE EVEN KNOW AXIUS 3 WAS A SECRET MILITARY OUTPOST DURING THE GALACTIC WAR.

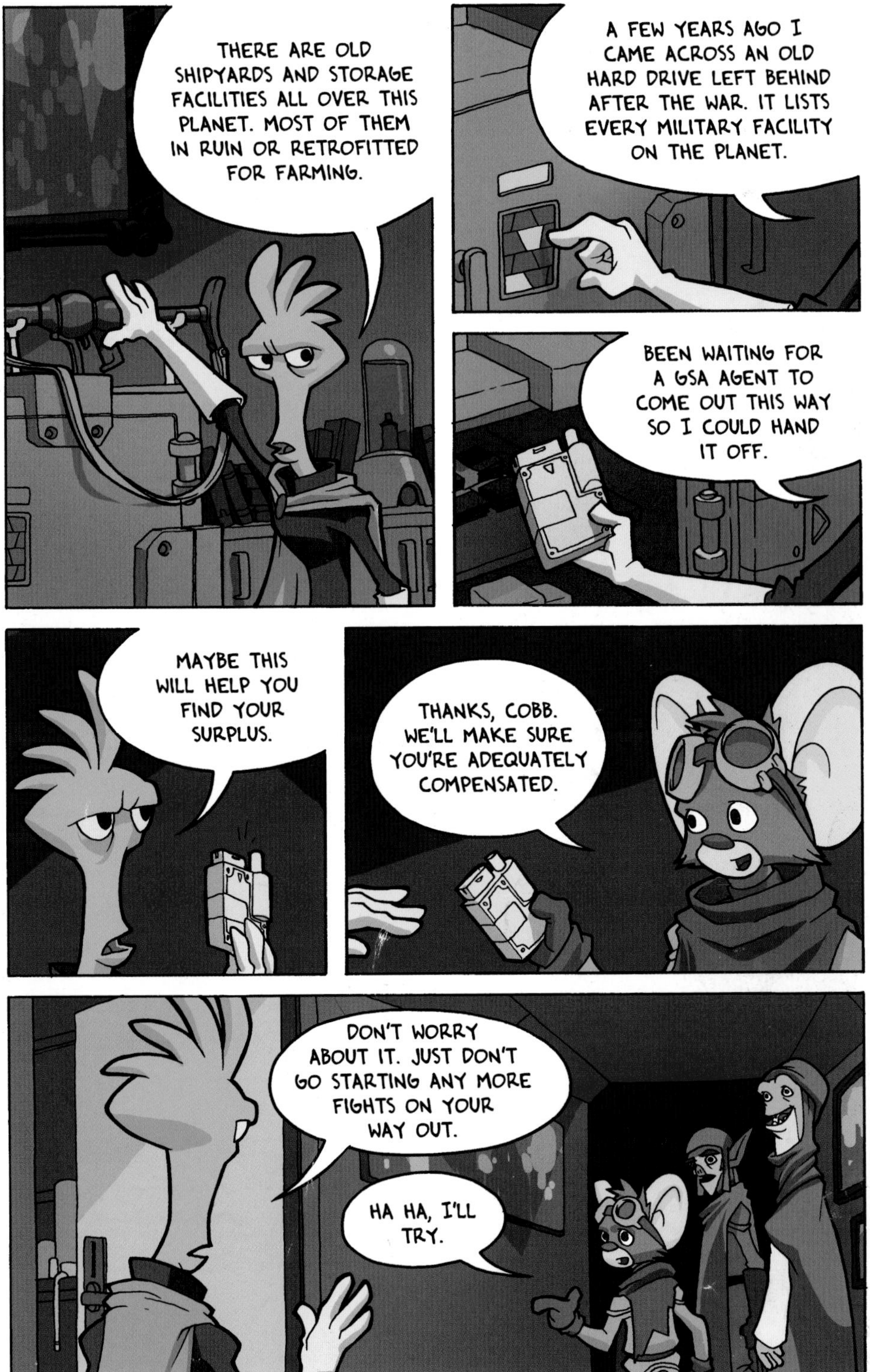
THERE ARE OLD SHIPYARDS AND STORAGE FACILITIES ALL OVER THIS PLANET. MOST OF THEM IN RUIN OR RETROFITTED FOR FARMING.
A FEW YEARS AGO I CAME ACROSS AN OLD HARD DRIVE LEFT BEHIND AFTER THE WAR. IT LISTS EVERY MILITARY FACILITY ON THE PLANET.
BEEN WAITING FOR A GSA AGENT TO COME OUT THIS WAY SO I COULD HAND IT OFF.
MAYBE THIS WILL HELP YOU FIND YOUR SURPLUS.
THANKS, COBB. WE'LL MAKE SURE YOU'RE ADEQUATELY COMPENSATED.
DON'T WORRY ABOUT IT. JUST DON'T GO STARTING ANY MORE FIGHTS ON YOUR WAY OUT.
HA HA, I'LL TRY.

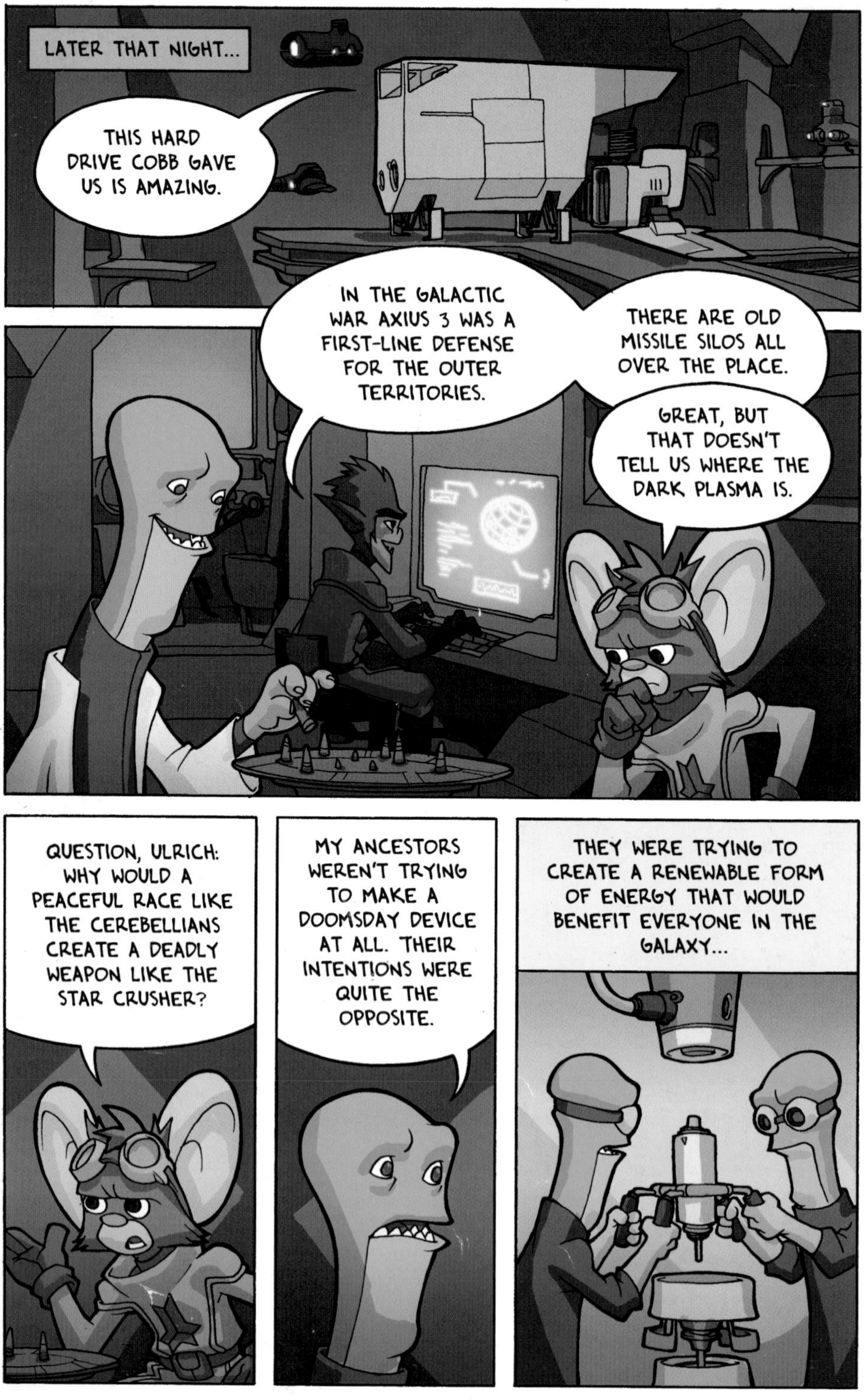
LATER THAT NIGHT...
THIS HARD DRIVE COBB GAVE US IS AMAZING.
IN THE GALACTIC WAR AXIUS 3 WAS A FIRST-LINE DEFENSE FOR THE OUTER TERRITORIES.
THERE ARE OLD MISSILE SILOS ALL OVER THE PLACE.
GREAT, BUT THAT DOESN'T TELL US WHERE THE DARK PLASMA IS.
QUESTION, ULRICH: WHY WOULD A PEACEFUL RACE LIKE THE CEREBELLIANS CREATE A DEADLY WEAPON LIKE THE STAR CRUSHER?
MY ANCESTORS WEREN'T TRYING TO MAKE A DOOMSDAY DEVICE AT ALL. THEIR INTENTIONS WERE QUITE THE OPPOSITE.
THEY WERE TRYING TO CREATE A RENEWABLE FORM OF ENERGY THAT WOULD BENEFIT EVERYONE IN THE GALAXY...

THEIR GOAL WAS TO TAKE THE FINITE BUT POWERFUL SUPPLY OF DARK PLASMA AND TURN IT INTO AN INFINITE SUPPLY OF ENERGY.

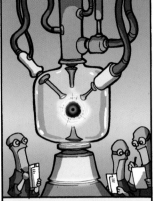

IN THEIR EXPERIMENTS THEY DISCOVERED THAT ORGANIC MATTER, WHEN FUSED WITH DARK PLASMA, TURNED ITSELF INTO PURE ENERGY.

IMAGINE A DARK PLASMA-INFUSED TREE THAT GREW HIGHLY ENERGIZED FRUIT POWERFUL ENOUGH TO FUEL A FLEET OF SPACE CRUISERS.

BUT EVERY EXPERIMENT ENDED IN FAILURE. THE PLASMA-CHARGED MATTER COULDN'T HANDLE THE PURE ENERGY. IT COLLAPSED ON ITSELF, CREATING A BLACK HOLE EVERY TIME.

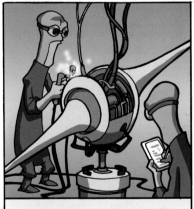

THE MILITARY HEARD OF THE CEREBELLIAN EXPERIMENTS AND DEMANDED THE TECHNOLOGY BE TURNED INTO A WEAPON, THE STAR CRUSHER.

SPIES THEN TOOK THE TECH TO THE OTHER SIDE AND **BOOM**...

HALF THE GALAXY DESTROYED.

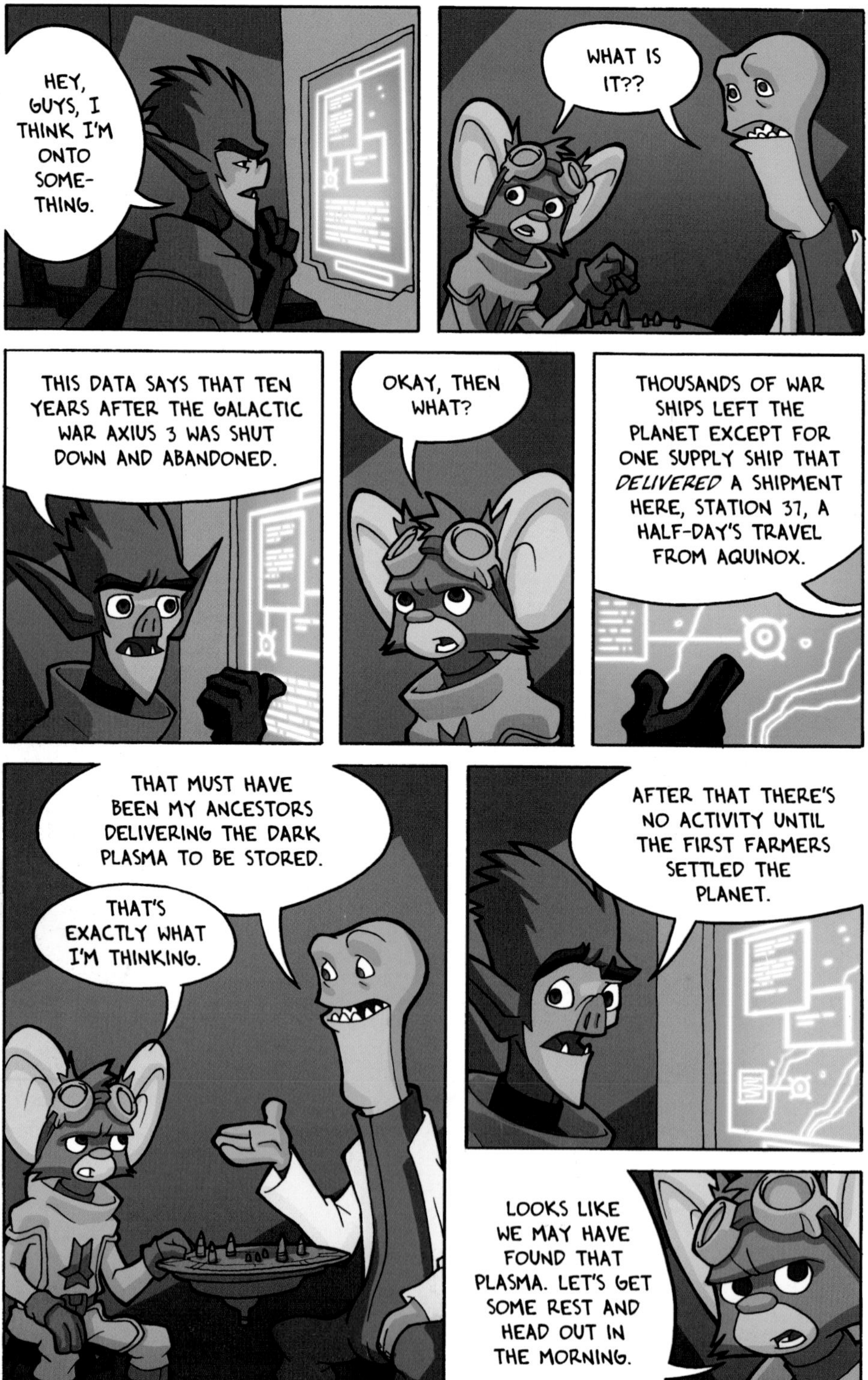
HEY, GUYS, I THINK I'M ONTO SOME-THING.
WHAT IS IT??
THIS DATA SAYS THAT TEN YEARS AFTER THE GALACTIC WAR AXIUS 3 WAS SHUT DOWN AND ABANDONED.
OKAY, THEN WHAT?
THOUSANDS OF WAR SHIPS LEFT THE PLANET EXCEPT FOR ONE SUPPLY SHIP THAT *DELIVERED* A SHIPMENT HERE, STATION 37, A HALF-DAY'S TRAVEL FROM AQUINOX.
THAT MUST HAVE BEEN MY ANCESTORS DELIVERING THE DARK PLASMA TO BE STORED.
THAT'S EXACTLY WHAT I'M THINKING.
AFTER THAT THERE'S NO ACTIVITY UNTIL THE FIRST FARMERS SETTLED THE PLANET.
LOOKS LIKE WE MAY HAVE FOUND THAT PLASMA. LET'S GET SOME REST AND HEAD OUT IN THE MORNING.

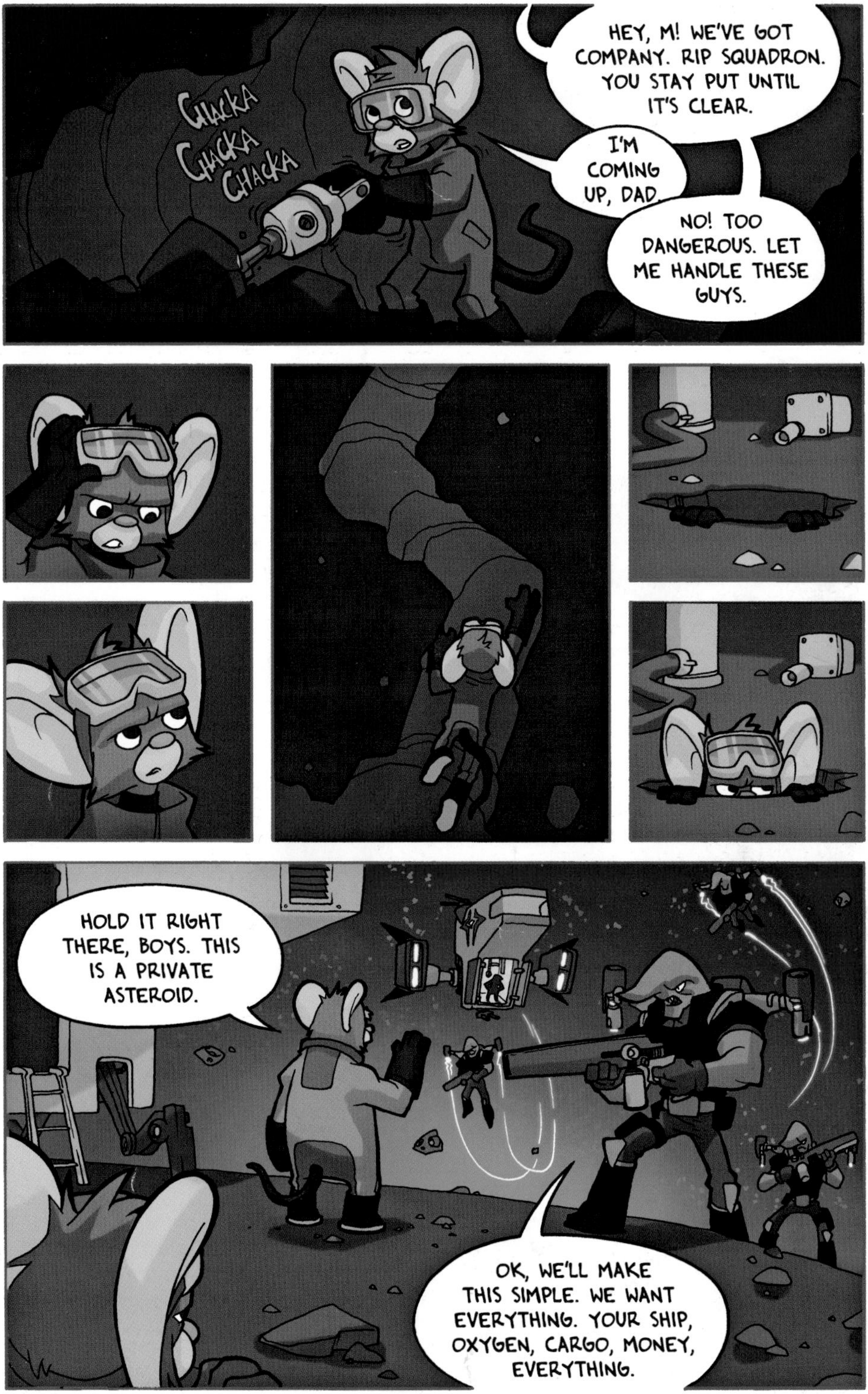
CHACKA CHACKA CHACKA
HEY, M! WE'VE GOT COMPANY. RIP SQUADRON. YOU STAY PUT UNTIL IT'S CLEAR.
I'M COMING UP, DAD.
NO! TOO DANGEROUS. LET ME HANDLE THESE GUYS.
HOLD IT RIGHT THERE, BOYS. THIS IS A PRIVATE ASTEROID.
OK, WE'LL MAKE THIS SIMPLE. WE WANT EVERYTHING. YOUR SHIP, OXYGEN, CARGO, MONEY, EVERYTHING.

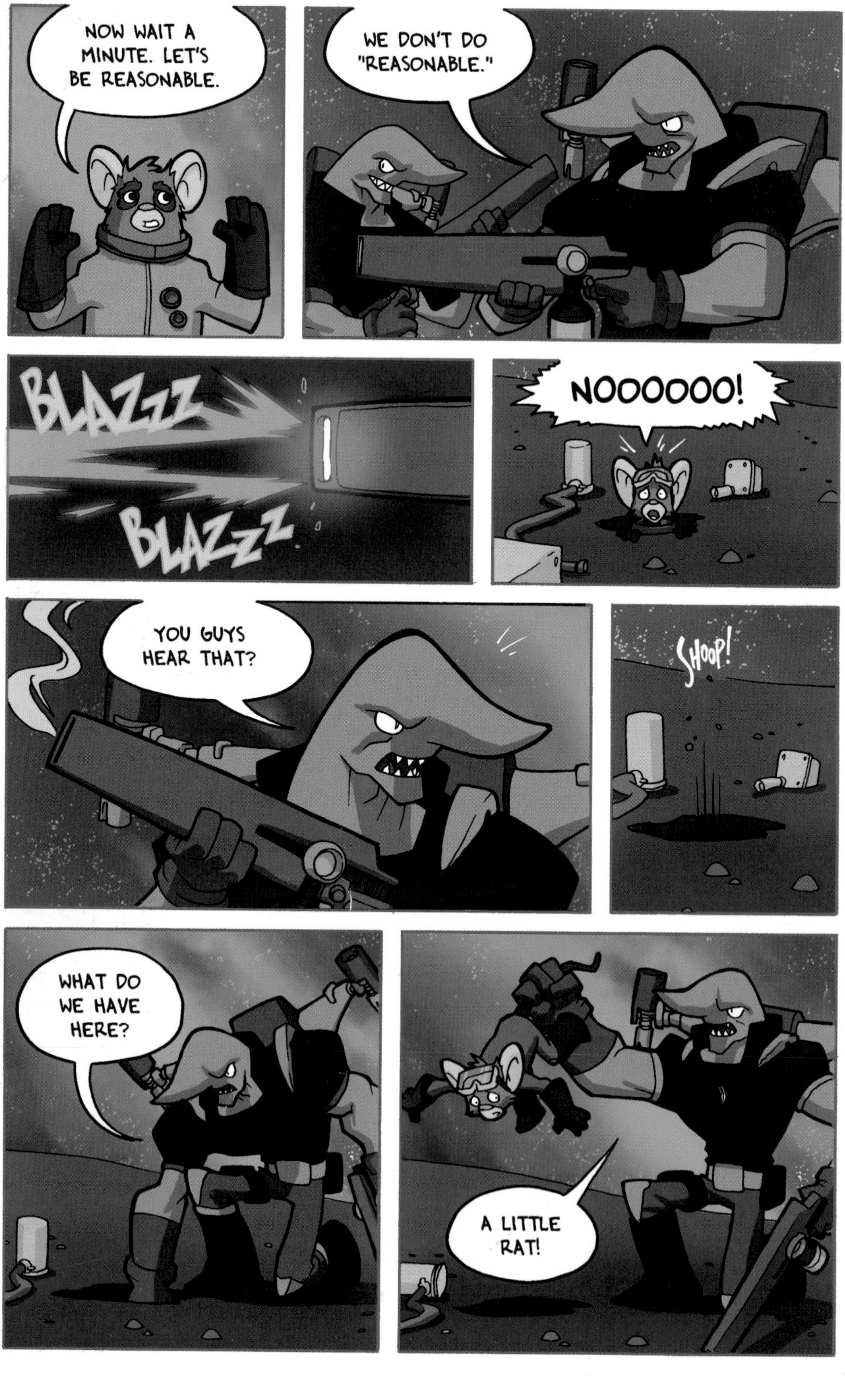
NOW WAIT A MINUTE. LET'S BE REASONABLE.
WE DON'T DO "REASONABLE."
BLAZZZ
BLAZZZ
NOOOOOO!
YOU GUYS HEAR THAT?
SHOOP!
WHAT DO WE HAVE HERE?
A LITTLE RAT!

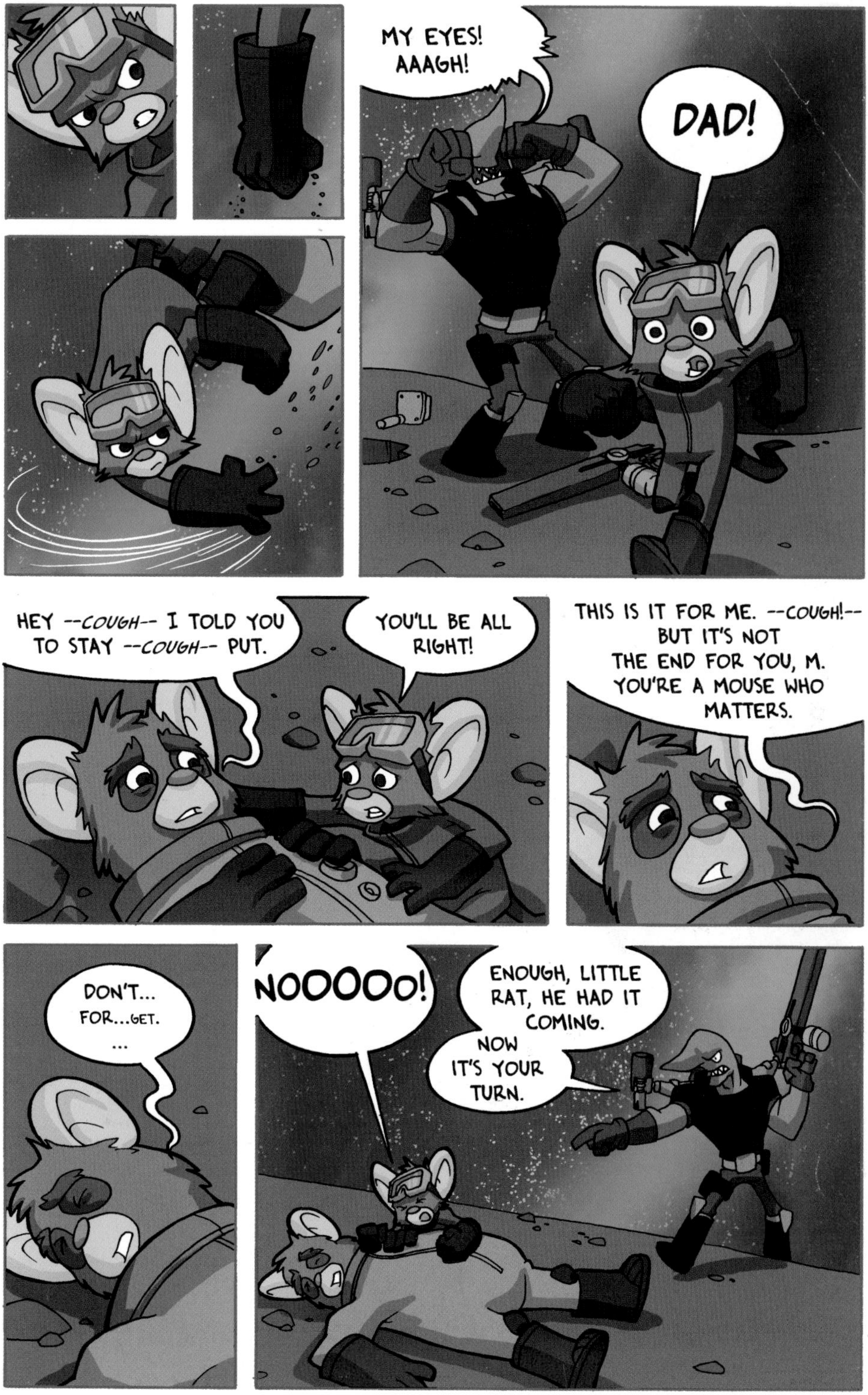
MY EYES! AAAGH!
DAD!
HEY --COUGH-- I TOLD YOU TO STAY --COUGH-- PUT.
YOU'LL BE ALL RIGHT!
THIS IS IT FOR ME. --COUGH!-- BUT IT'S NOT THE END FOR YOU, M. YOU'RE A MOUSE WHO MATTERS.
DON'T... FOR...GET. ...
NOOOOO!
ENOUGH, LITTLE RAT, HE HAD IT COMING.
NOW IT'S YOUR TURN.

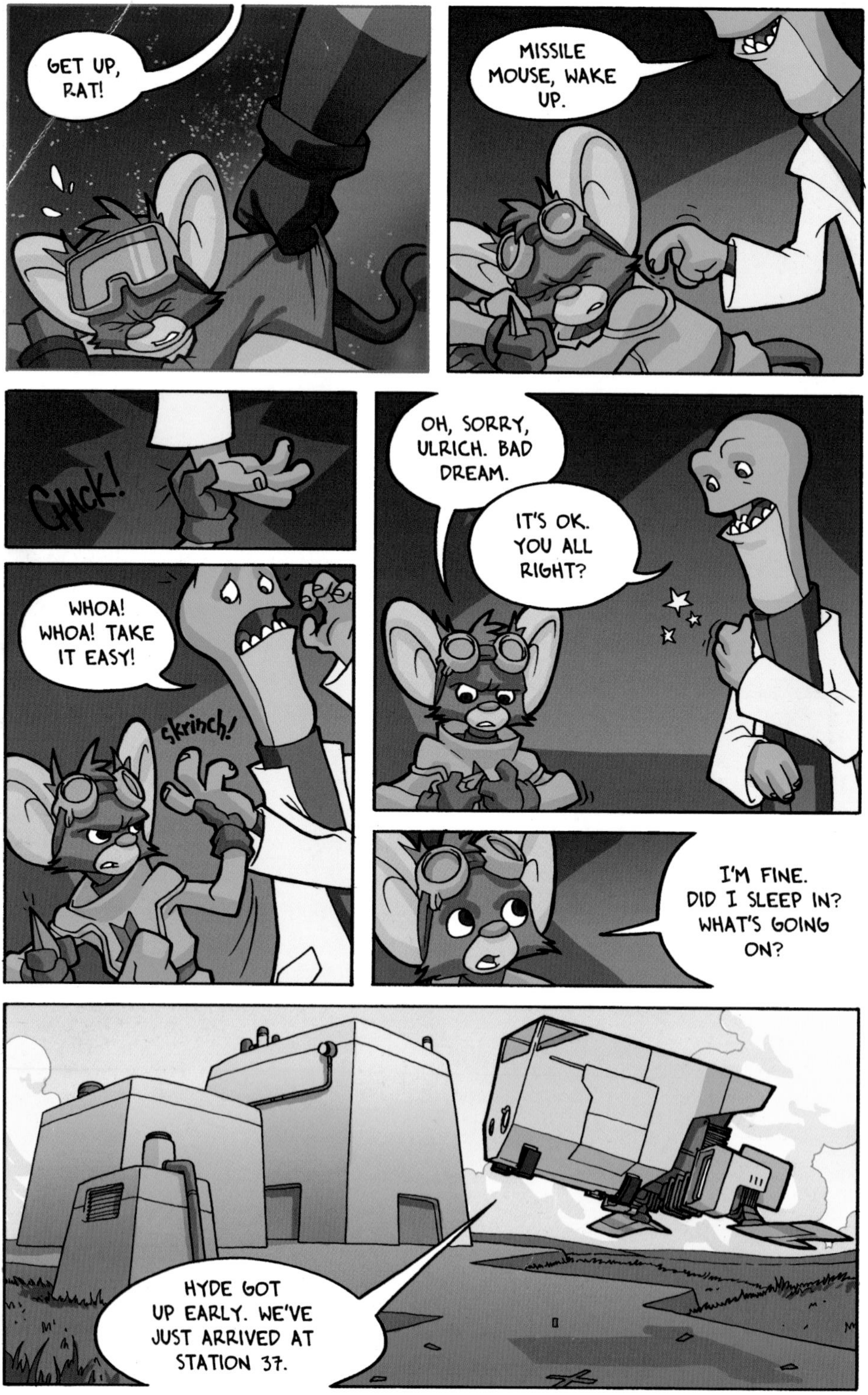
GET UP, RAT!
MISSILE MOUSE, WAKE UP.
CHACK!
OH, SORRY, ULRICH. BAD DREAM.
IT'S OK. YOU ALL RIGHT?
WHOA! WHOA! TAKE IT EASY!
skrinch!
I'M FINE. DID I SLEEP IN? WHAT'S GOING ON?
HYDE GOT UP EARLY. WE'VE JUST ARRIVED AT STATION 37.

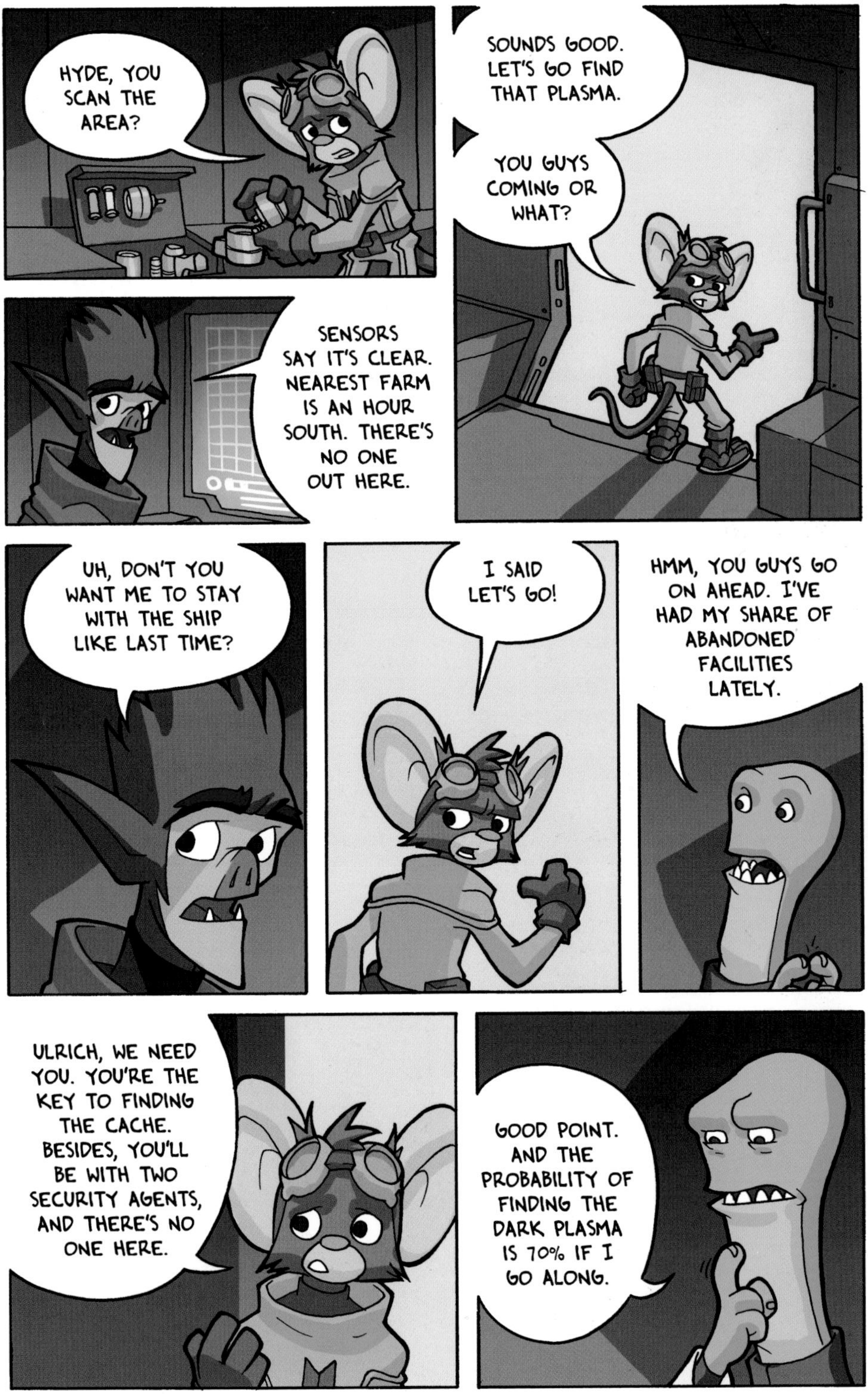
HYDE, YOU SCAN THE AREA?
SOUNDS GOOD. LET'S GO FIND THAT PLASMA.
YOU GUYS COMING OR WHAT?
SENSORS SAY IT'S CLEAR. NEAREST FARM IS AN HOUR SOUTH. THERE'S NO ONE OUT HERE.
UH, DON'T YOU WANT ME TO STAY WITH THE SHIP LIKE LAST TIME?
I SAID LET'S GO!
HMM, YOU GUYS GO ON AHEAD. I'VE HAD MY SHARE OF ABANDONED FACILITIES LATELY.
ULRICH, WE NEED YOU. YOU'RE THE KEY TO FINDING THE CACHE. BESIDES, YOU'LL BE WITH TWO SECURITY AGENTS, AND THERE'S NO ONE HERE.
GOOD POINT. AND THE PROBABILITY OF FINDING THE DARK PLASMA IS 70% IF I GO ALONG.

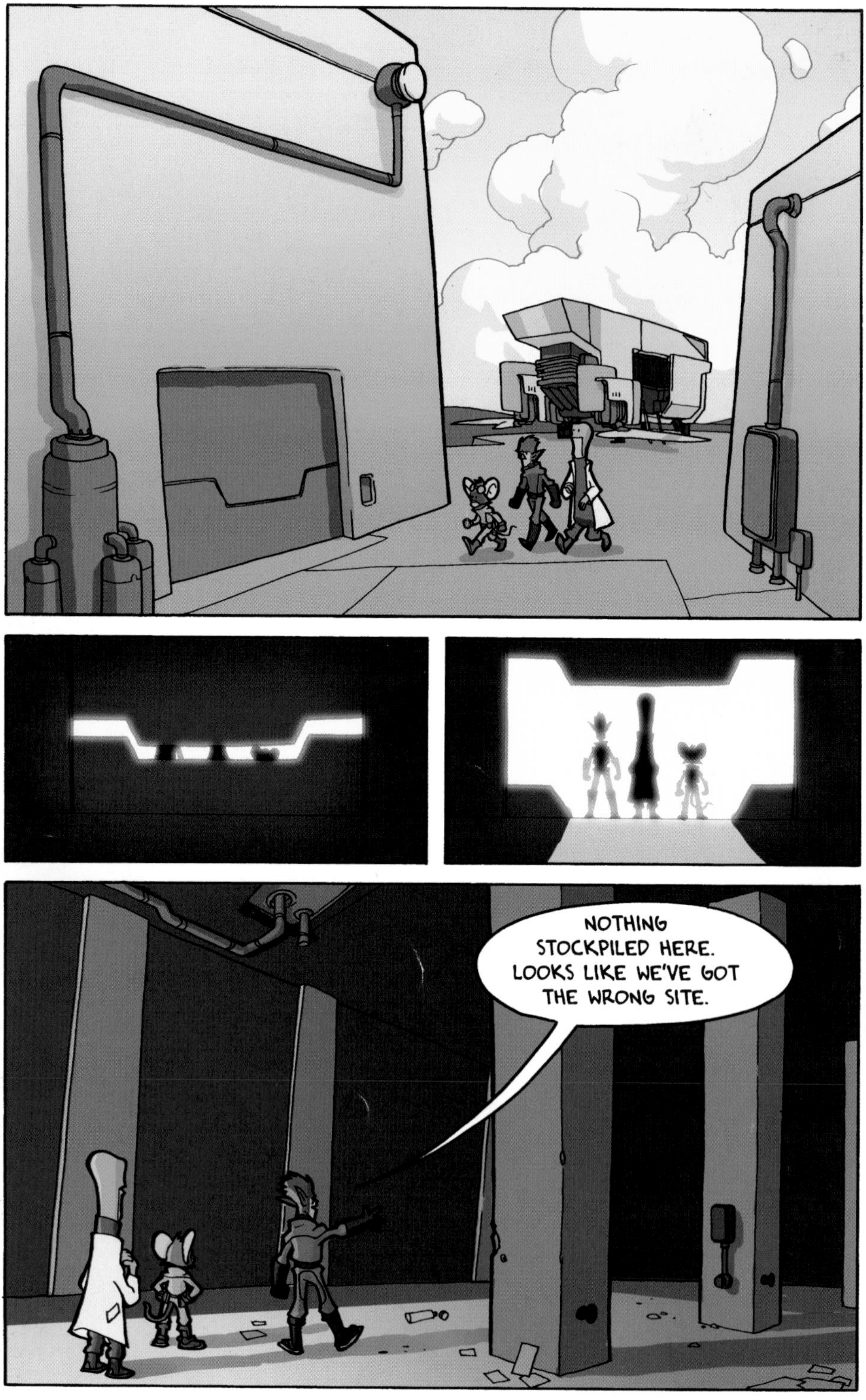
NOTHING STOCKPILED HERE. LOOKS LIKE WE'VE GOT THE WRONG SITE.

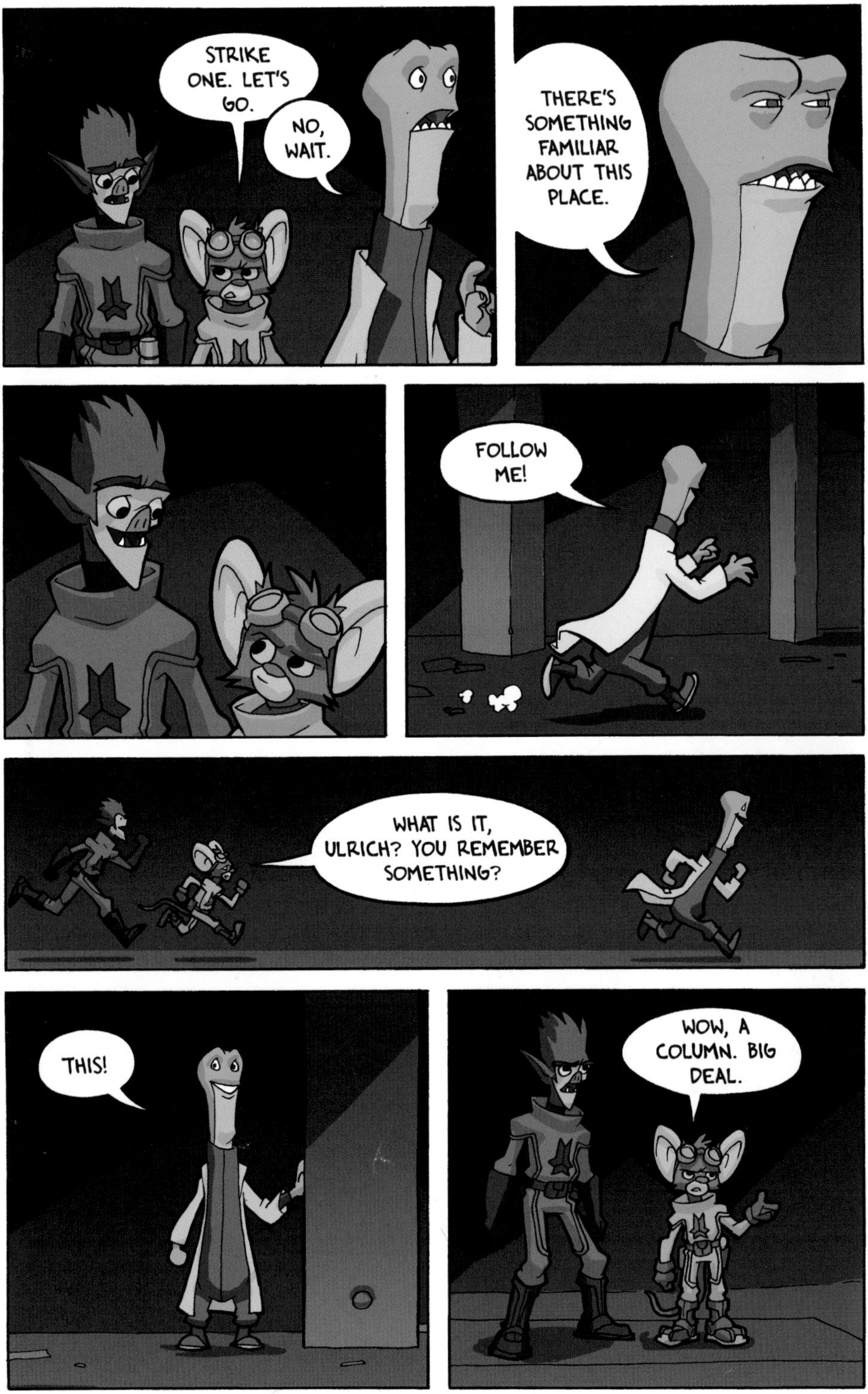
STRIKE ONE. LET'S GO.
NO, WAIT.
THERE'S SOMETHING FAMILIAR ABOUT THIS PLACE.
FOLLOW ME!
WHAT IS IT, ULRICH? YOU REMEMBER SOMETHING?
THIS!
WOW, A COLUMN. BIG DEAL.

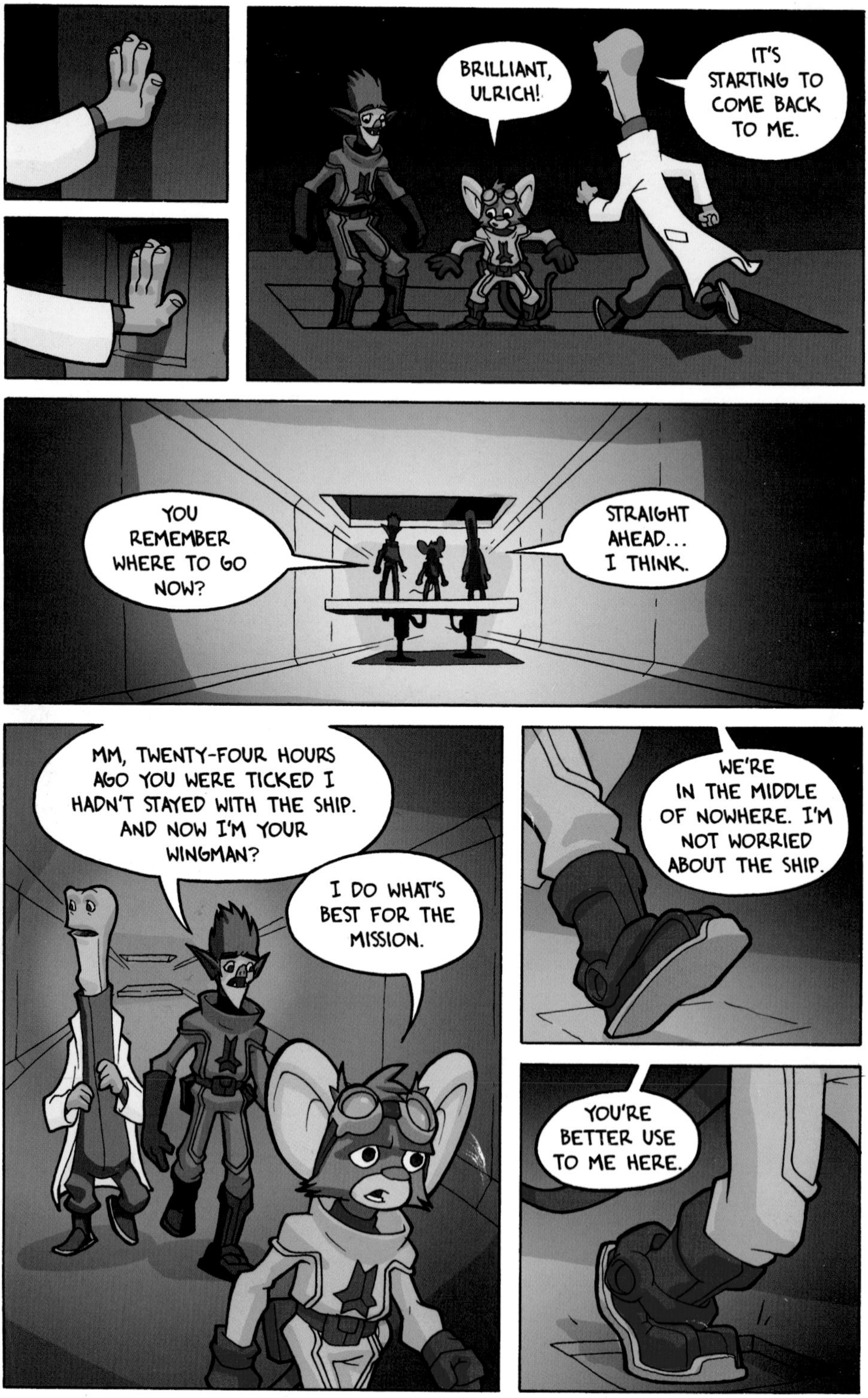
BRILLIANT, ULRICH!
IT'S STARTING TO COME BACK TO ME.
YOU REMEMBER WHERE TO GO NOW?
STRAIGHT AHEAD... I THINK.
MM, TWENTY-FOUR HOURS AGO YOU WERE TICKED I HADN'T STAYED WITH THE SHIP. AND NOW I'M YOUR WINGMAN?
I DO WHAT'S BEST FOR THE MISSION.
WE'RE IN THE MIDDLE OF NOWHERE. I'M NOT WORRIED ABOUT THE SHIP.
YOU'RE BETTER USE TO ME HERE.

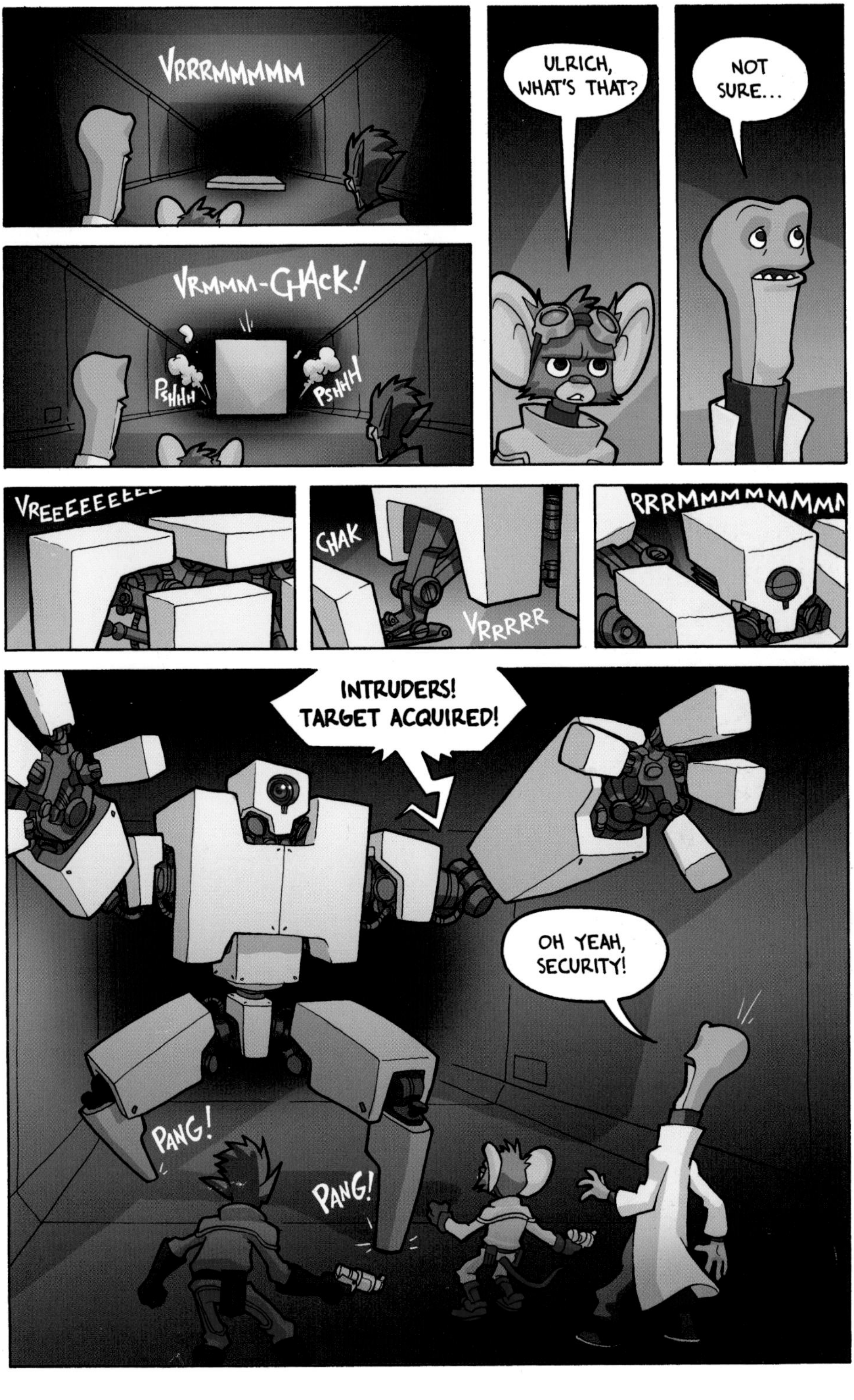
VRRRMMMMM
VRMMM-CHACK!
PSHHH
PSHHH
ULRICH, WHAT'S THAT?
NOT SURE...
VREEEEEEEEE
CHAK
VRRRRR
RRRMMMMMMMMM
INTRUDERS! TARGET ACQUIRED!
OH YEAH, SECURITY!
PANG!
PANG!

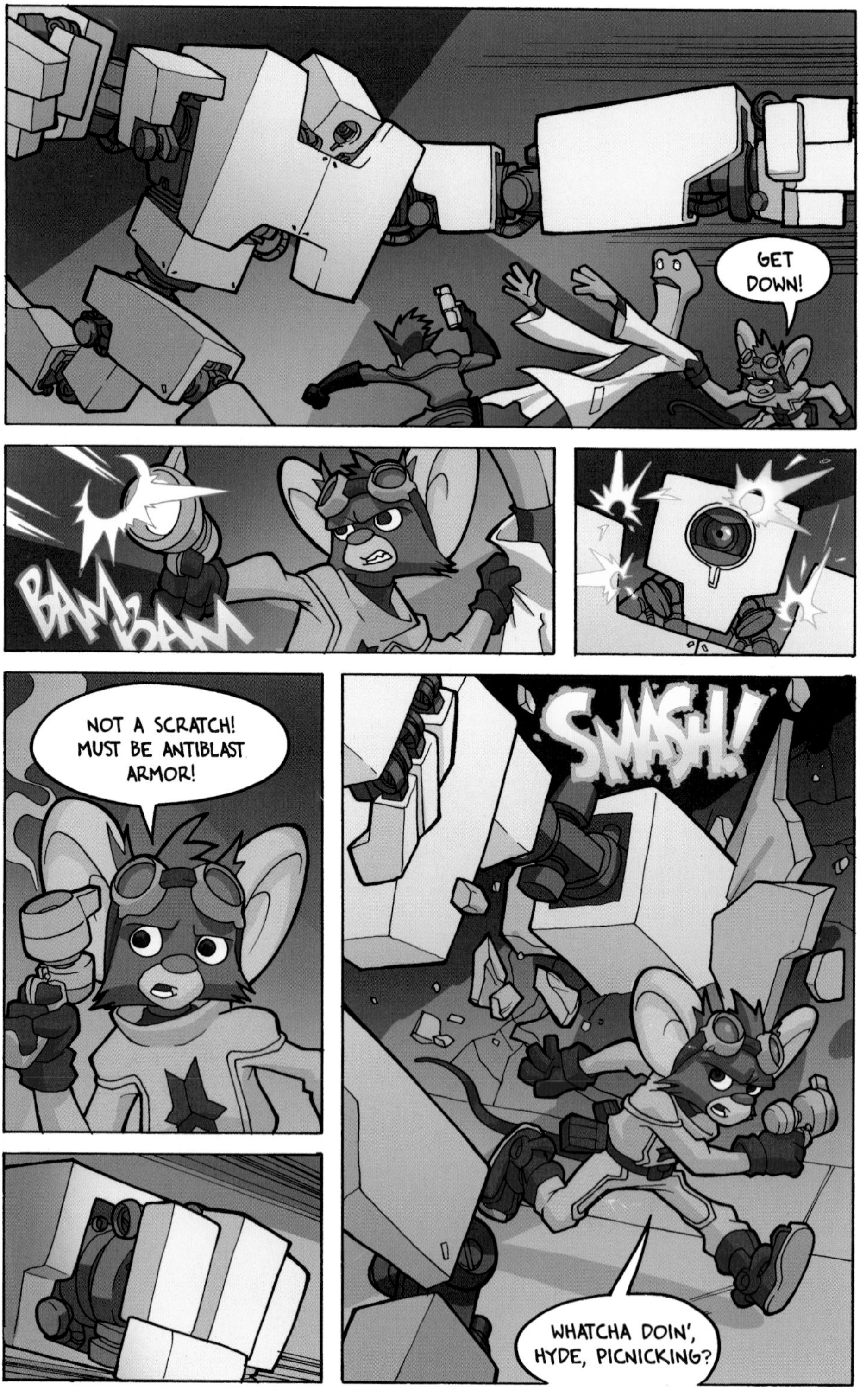
GET DOWN!
BAM BAM
NOT A SCRATCH! MUST BE ANTIBLAST ARMOR!
SMASH!
WHATCHA DOIN', HYDE, PICNICKING?

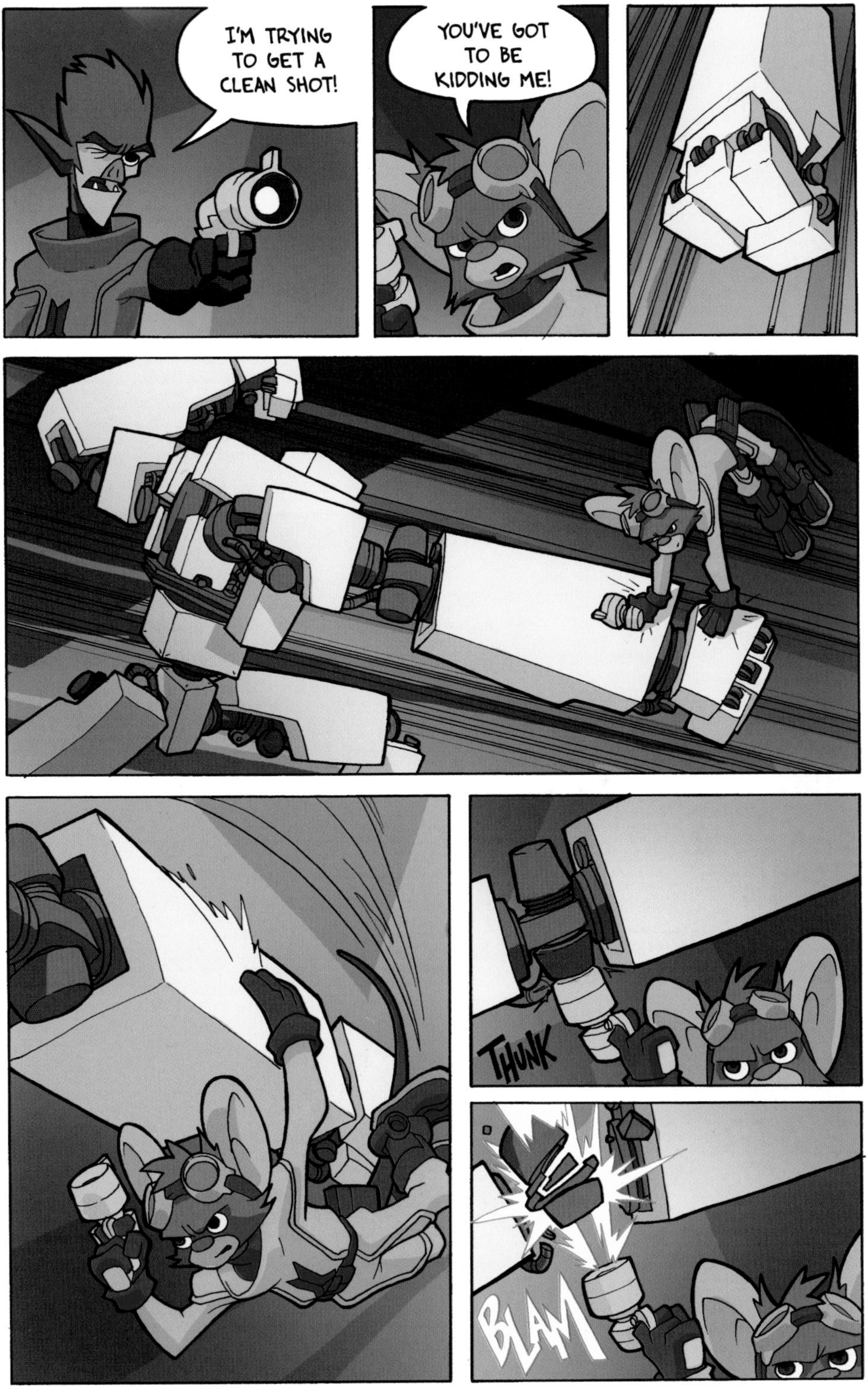
I'M TRYING TO GET A CLEAN SHOT!
YOU'VE GOT TO BE KIDDING ME!
THUNK
BLAM

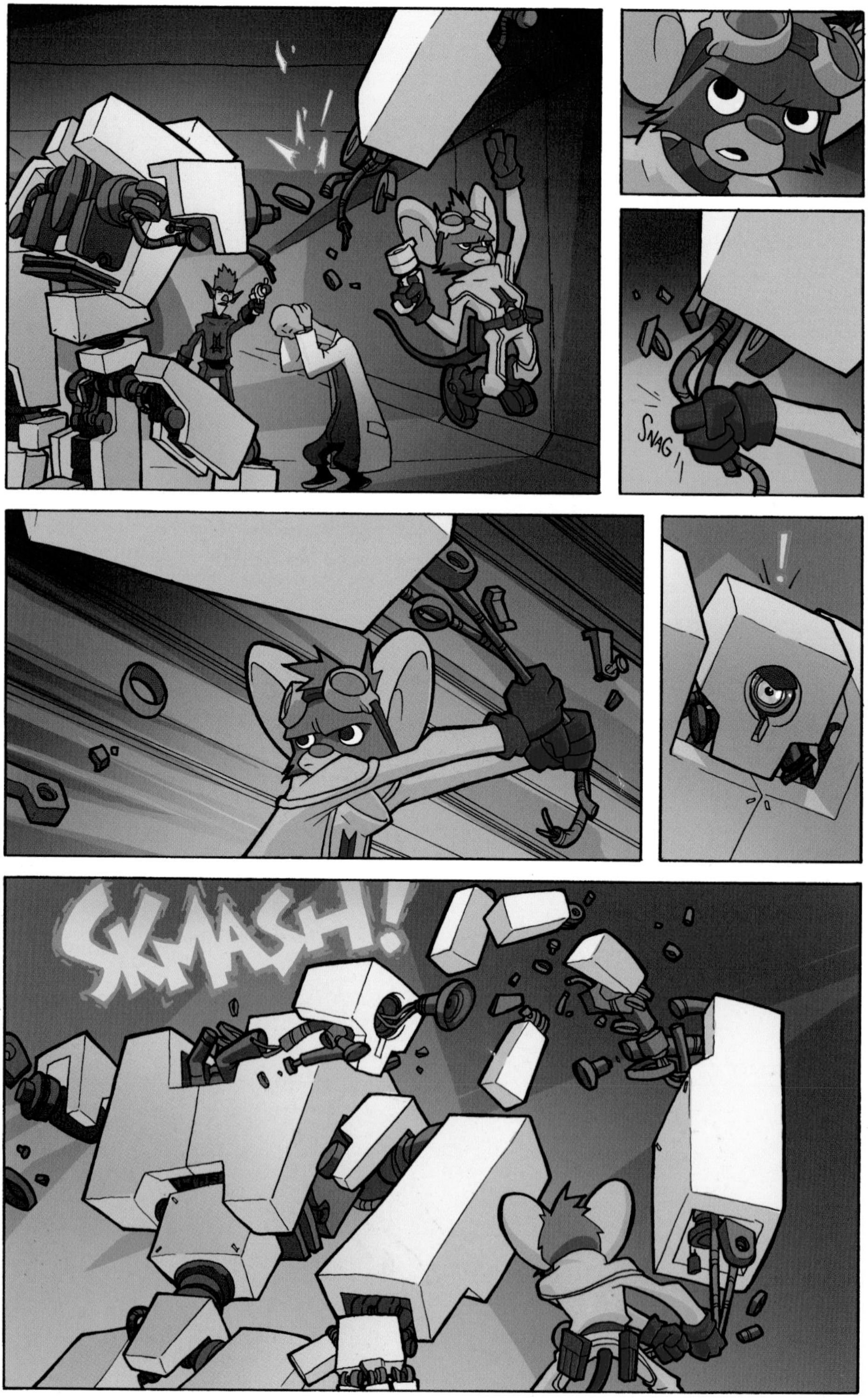
SNAG
!
SMASH!

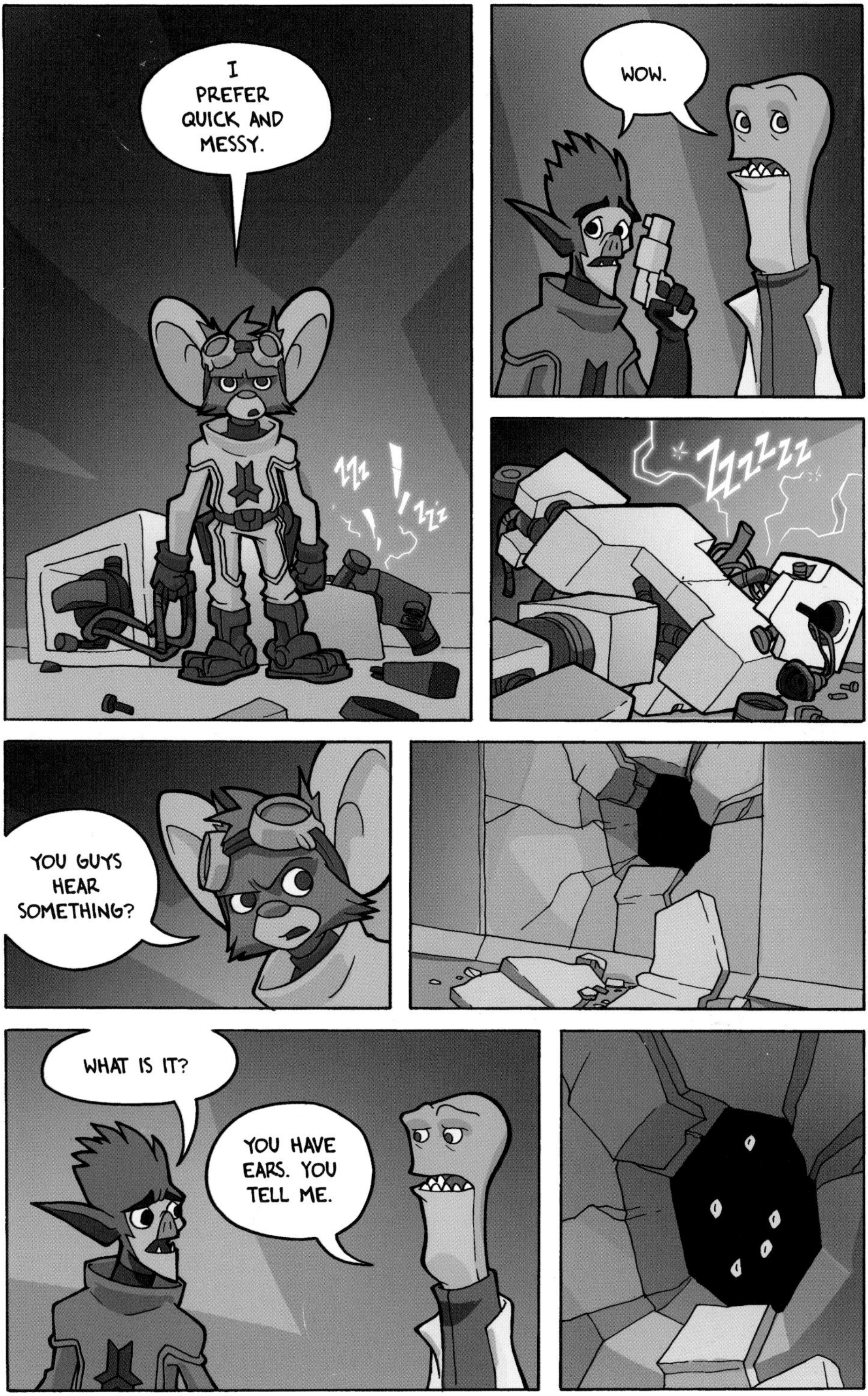
I PREFER QUICK AND MESSY.
WOW.
YOU GUYS HEAR SOMETHING?
WHAT IS IT?
YOU HAVE EARS. YOU TELL ME.

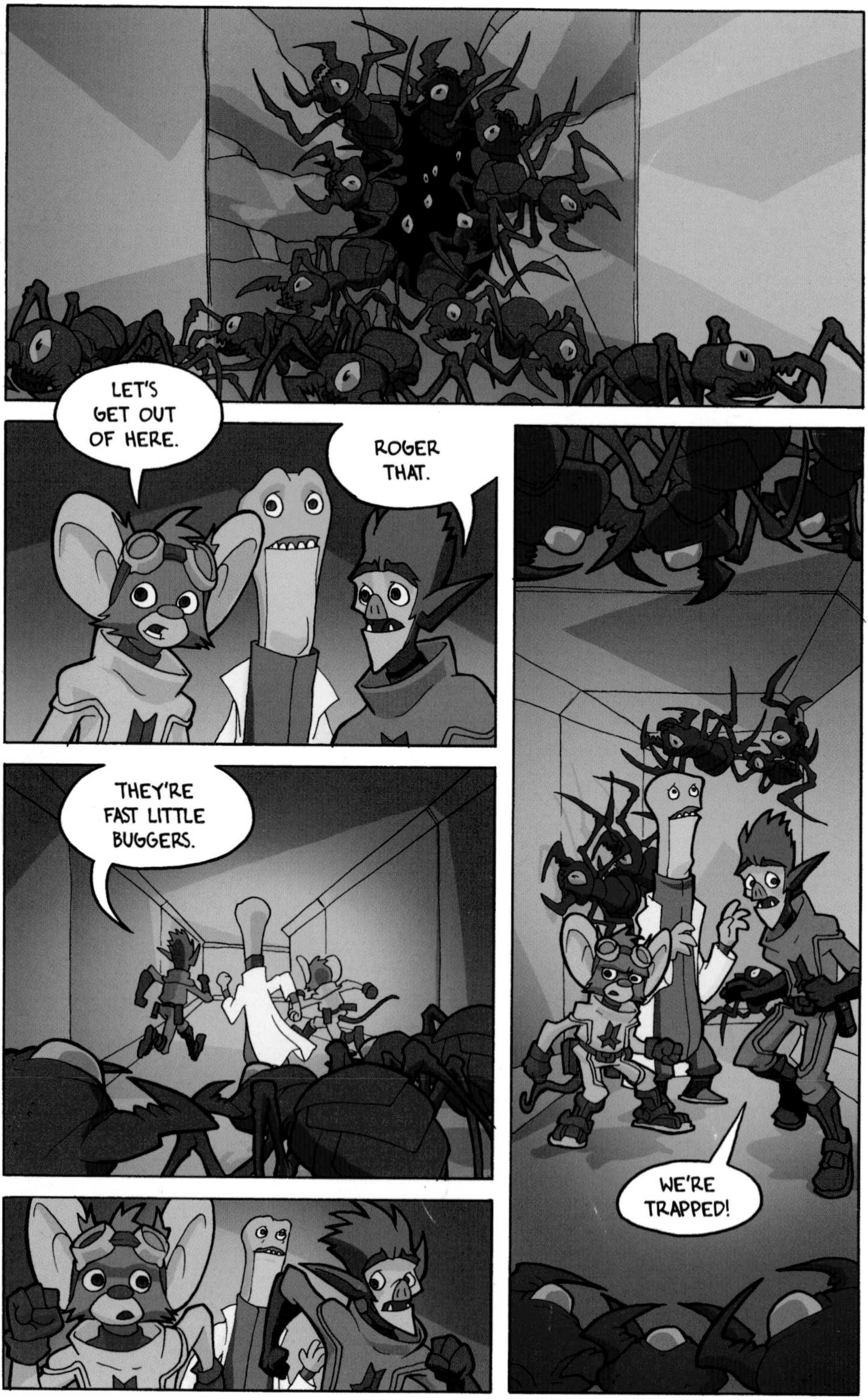
LET'S GET OUT OF HERE.
ROGER THAT.
THEY'RE FAST LITTLE BUGGERS.
WE'RE TRAPPED!

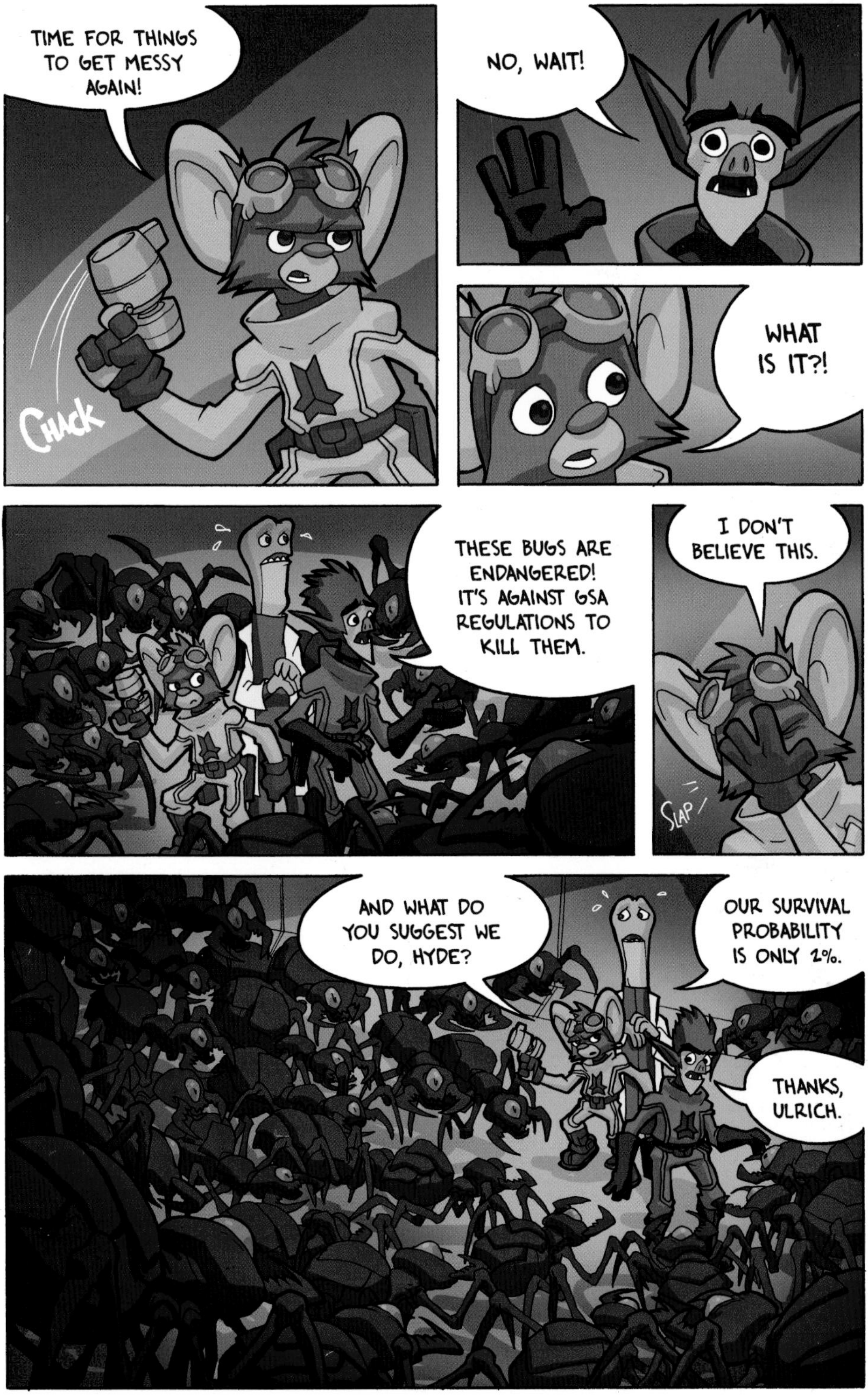
TIME FOR THINGS TO GET MESSY AGAIN!
CHACK
NO, WAIT!
WHAT IS IT?!
THESE BUGS ARE ENDANGERED! IT'S AGAINST GSA REGULATIONS TO KILL THEM.
I DON'T BELIEVE THIS.
SLAP!
AND WHAT DO YOU SUGGEST WE DO, HYDE?
OUR SURVIVAL PROBABILITY IS ONLY 2%.
THANKS, ULRICH.

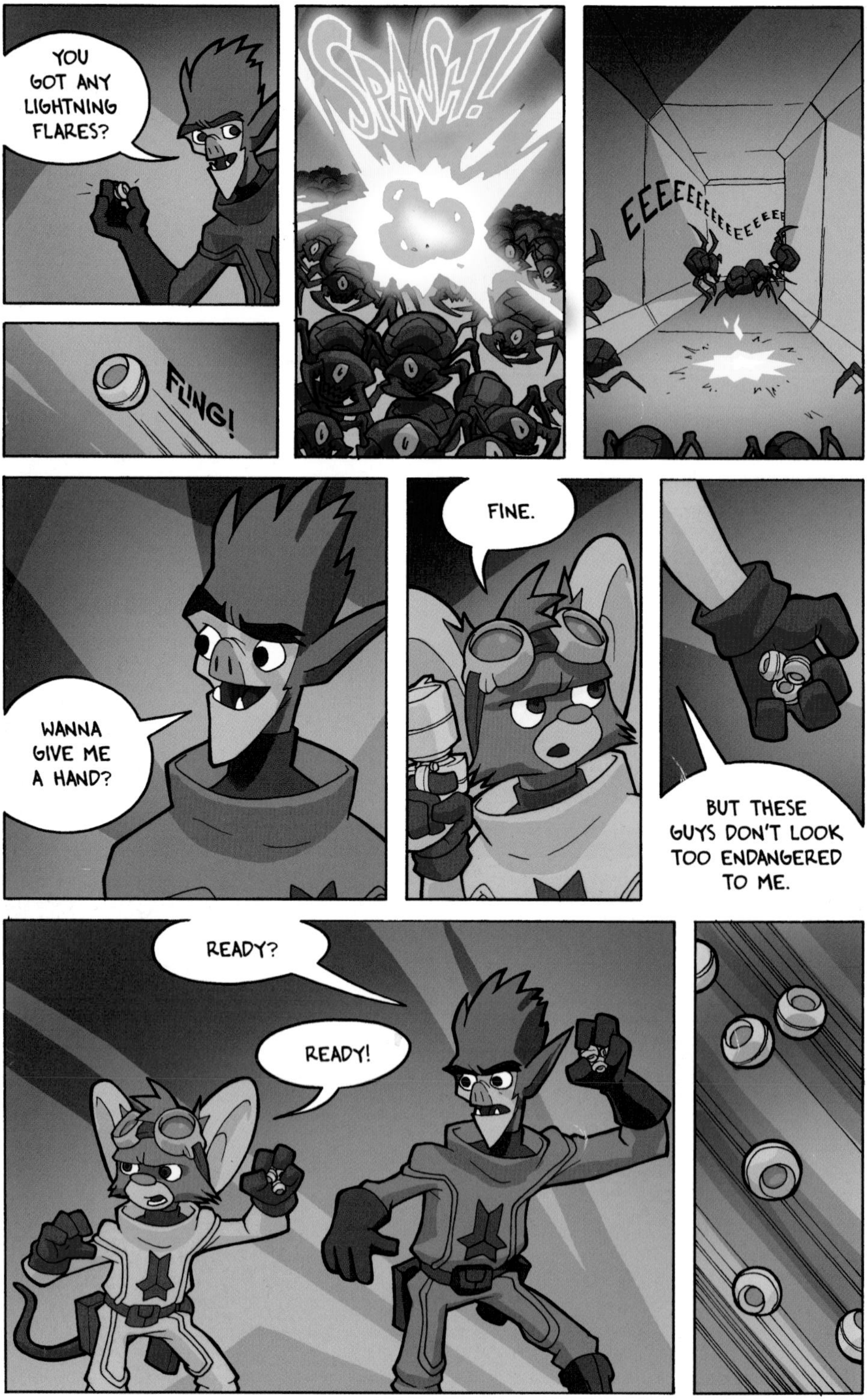
YOU GOT ANY LIGHTNING FLARES?
FLING!
SPASH!!
EEEEEEEEEEEEEEEE
WANNA GIVE ME A HAND?
FINE.
BUT THESE GUYS DON'T LOOK TOO ENDANGERED TO ME.
READY?
READY!

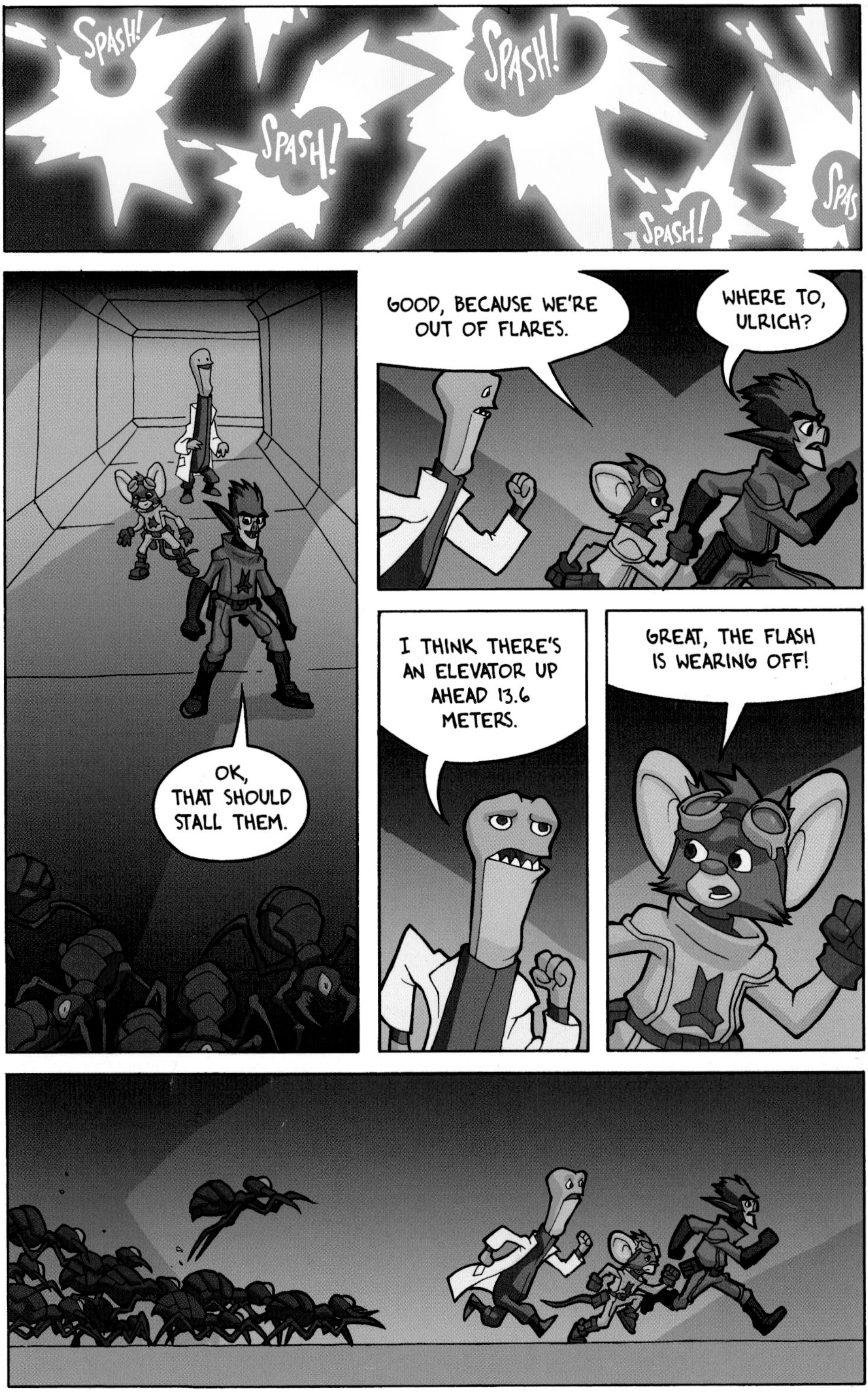
SPASH!
SPASH!
SPASH!
SPASH!
SPAS
OK, THAT SHOULD STALL THEM.
GOOD, BECAUSE WE'RE OUT OF FLARES.
WHERE TO, ULRICH?
I THINK THERE'S AN ELEVATOR UP AHEAD 13.6 METERS.
GREAT, THE FLASH IS WEARING OFF!

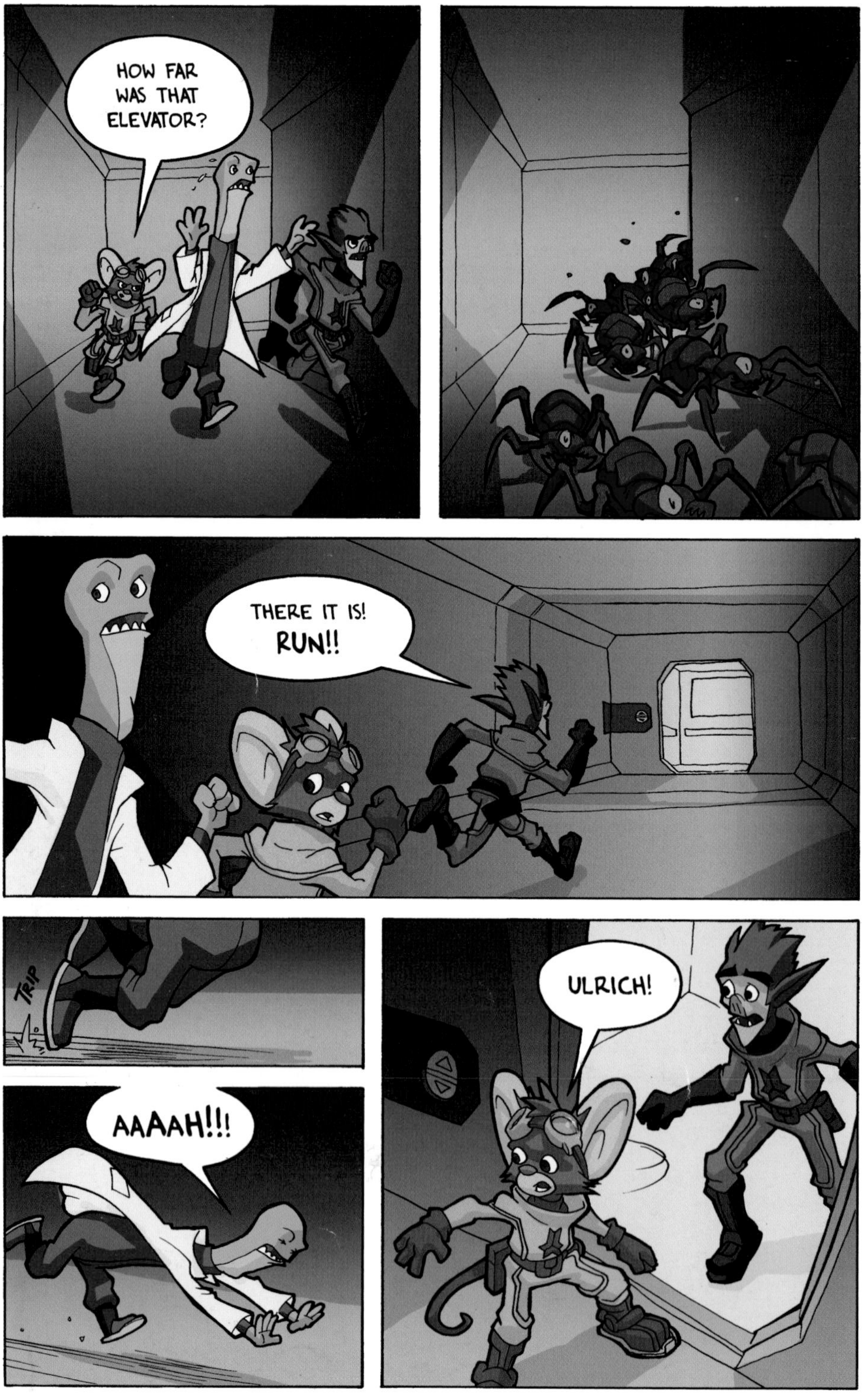
HOW FAR WAS THAT ELEVATOR?
THERE IT IS! RUN!!
TRIP
AAAAH!!!
ULRICH!

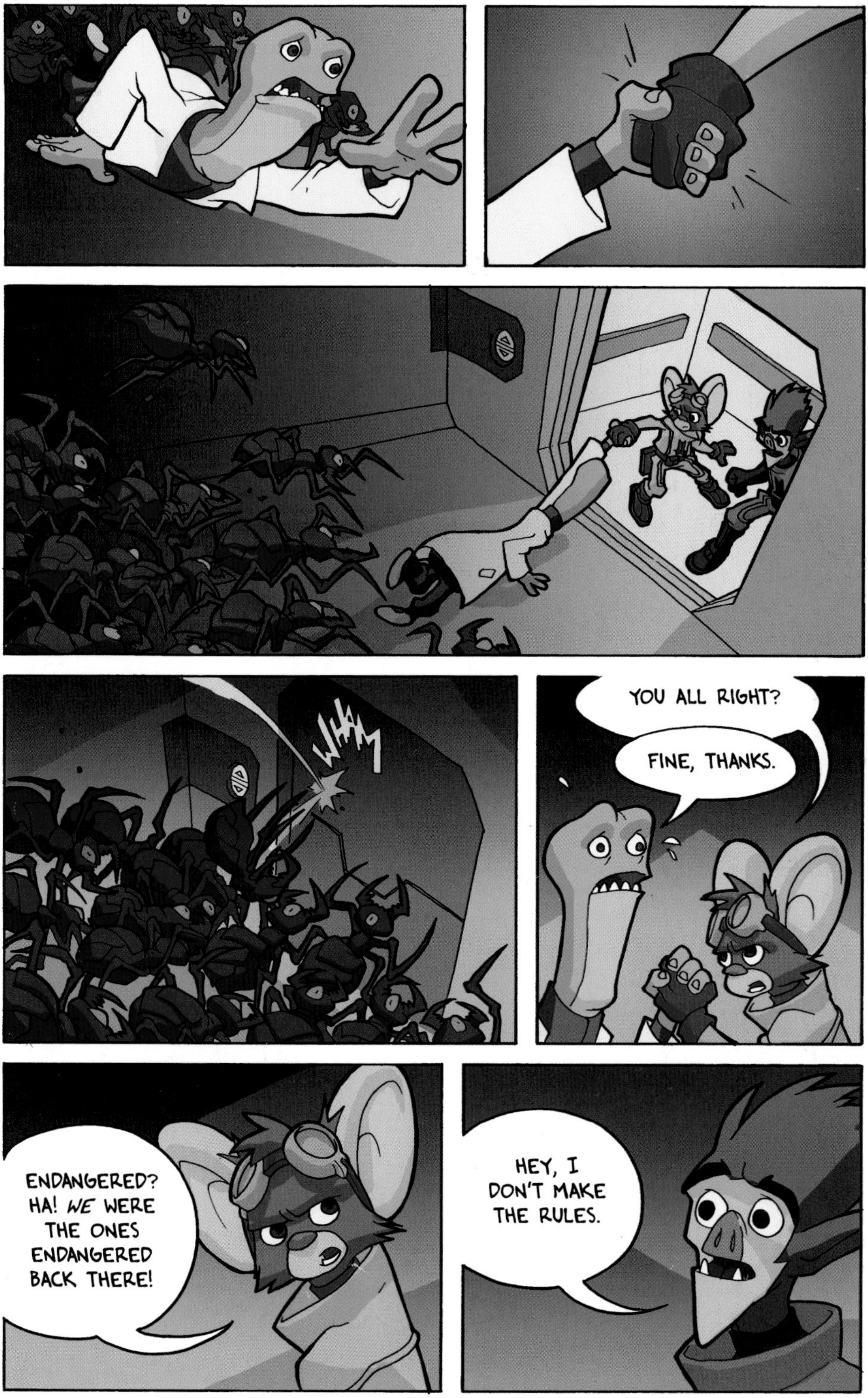
WHAM
YOU ALL RIGHT?
FINE, THANKS.
ENDANGERED? HA! *WE* WERE THE ONES ENDANGERED BACK THERE!
HEY, I DON'T MAKE THE RULES.

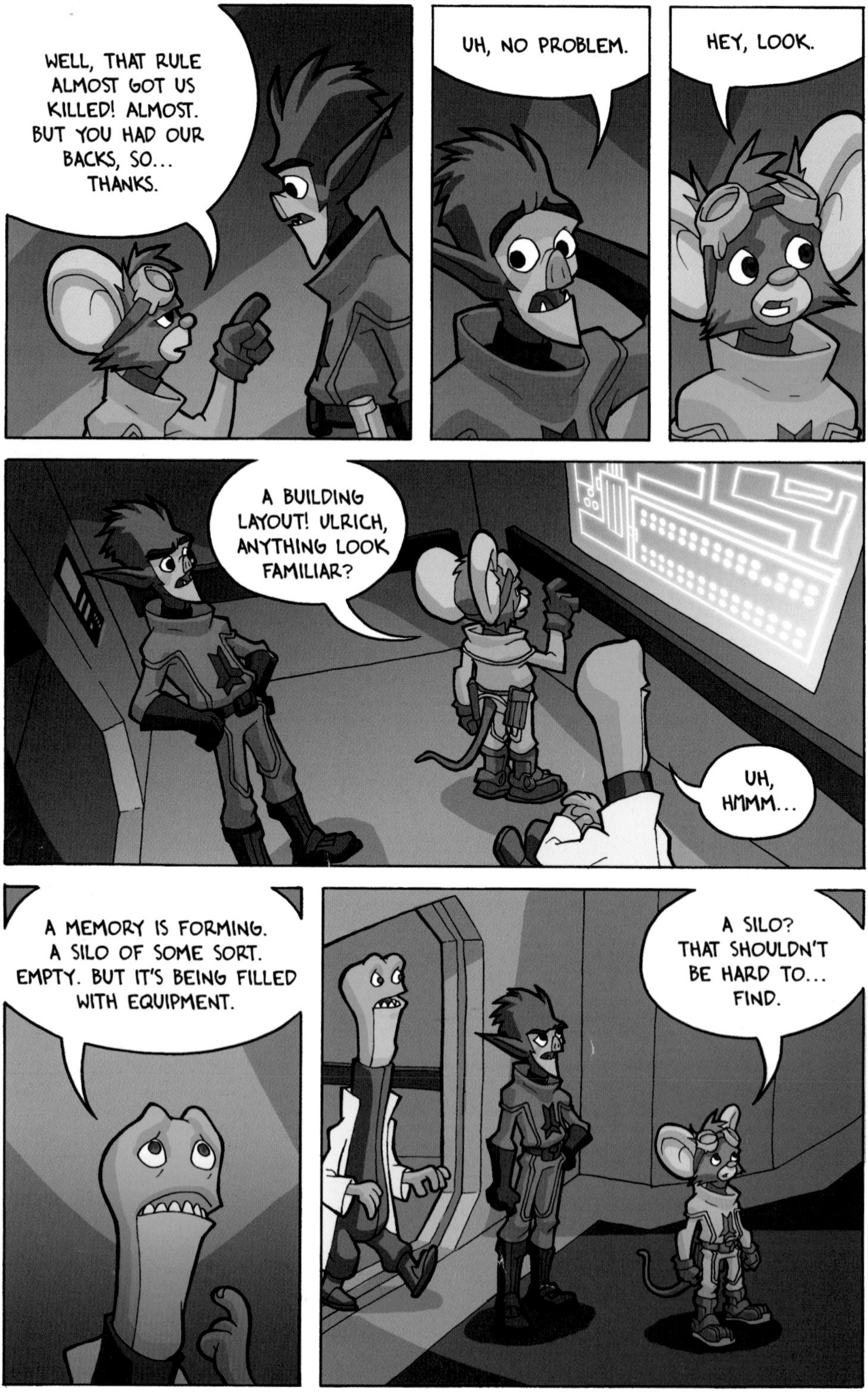
WELL, THAT RULE ALMOST GOT US KILLED! ALMOST. BUT YOU HAD OUR BACKS, SO... THANKS.
UH, NO PROBLEM.
HEY, LOOK.
A BUILDING LAYOUT! ULRICH, ANYTHING LOOK FAMILIAR?
UH, HMMM...
A MEMORY IS FORMING. A SILO OF SOME SORT. EMPTY. BUT IT'S BEING FILLED WITH EQUIPMENT.
A SILO? THAT SHOULDN'T BE HARD TO... FIND.

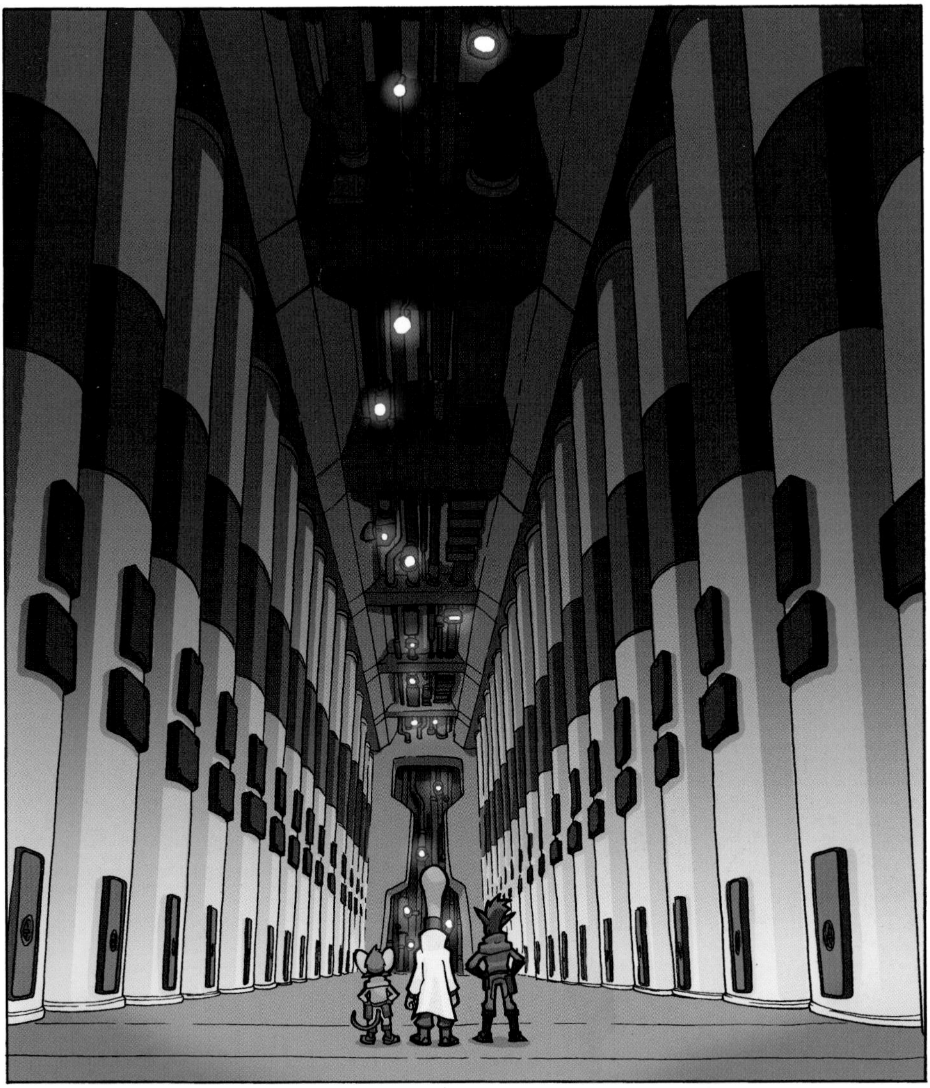

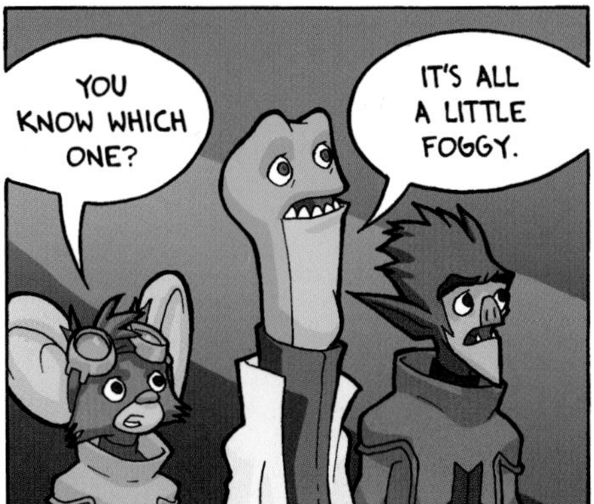
YOU KNOW WHICH ONE?
IT'S ALL A LITTLE FOGGY.

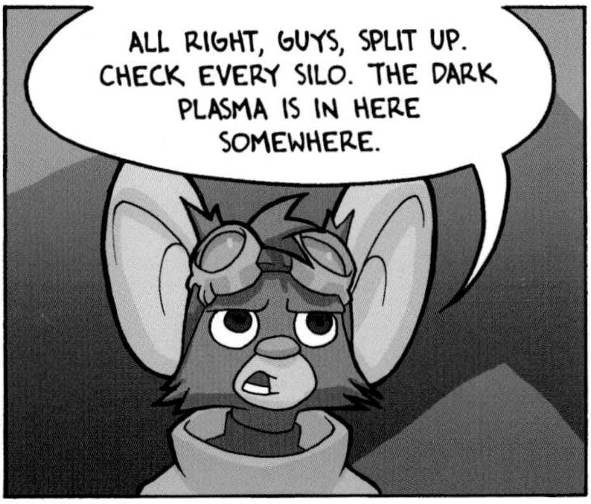
ALL RIGHT, GUYS, SPLIT UP. CHECK EVERY SILO. THE DARK PLASMA IS IN HERE SOMEWHERE.

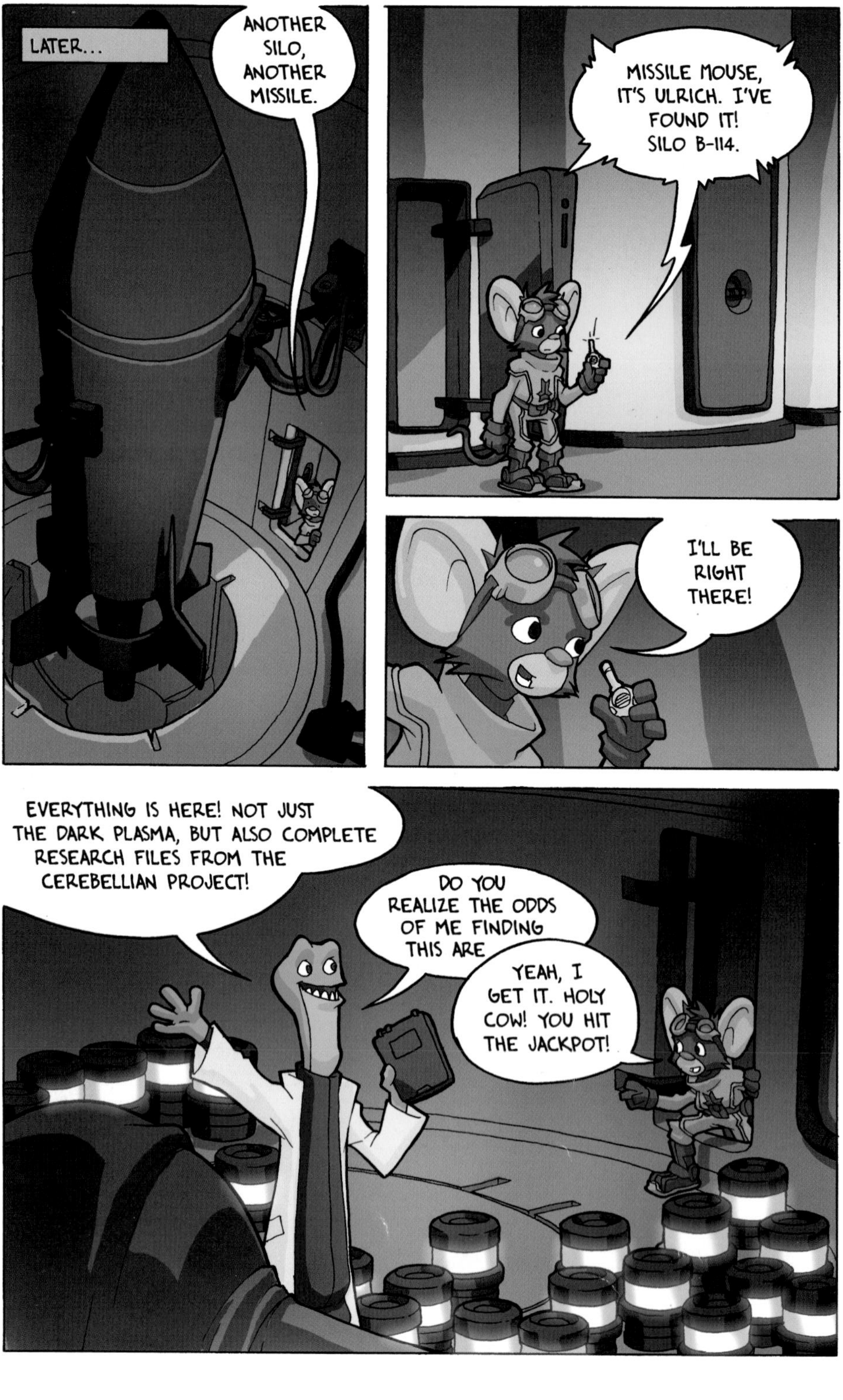
LATER...
ANOTHER SILO, ANOTHER MISSILE.
MISSILE MOUSE, IT'S ULRICH. I'VE FOUND IT! SILO B-114.
I'LL BE RIGHT THERE!
EVERYTHING IS HERE! NOT JUST THE DARK PLASMA, BUT ALSO COMPLETE RESEARCH FILES FROM THE CEREBELLIAN PROJECT!
DO YOU REALIZE THE ODDS OF ME FINDING THIS ARE
YEAH, I GET IT. HOLY COW! YOU HIT THE JACKPOT!

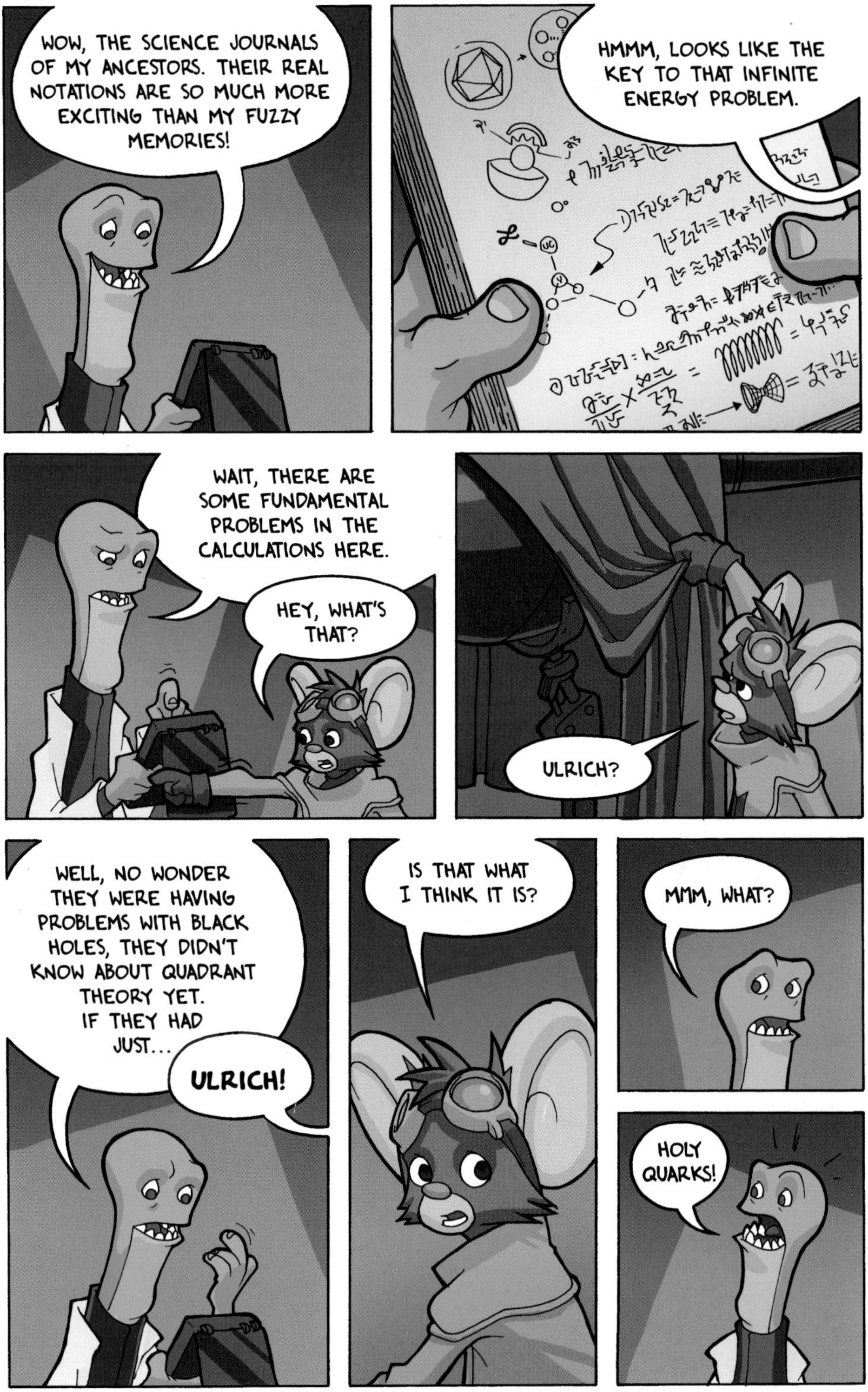
WOW, THE SCIENCE JOURNALS OF MY ANCESTORS. THEIR REAL NOTATIONS ARE SO MUCH MORE EXCITING THAN MY FUZZY MEMORIES!
HMMM, LOOKS LIKE THE KEY TO THAT INFINITE ENERGY PROBLEM.
WAIT, THERE ARE SOME FUNDAMENTAL PROBLEMS IN THE CALCULATIONS HERE.
HEY, WHAT'S THAT?
ULRICH?
WELL, NO WONDER THEY WERE HAVING PROBLEMS WITH BLACK HOLES, THEY DIDN'T KNOW ABOUT QUADRANT THEORY YET. IF THEY HAD JUST...
ULRICH!
IS THAT WHAT I THINK IT IS?
MMM, WHAT?
HOLY QUARKS!

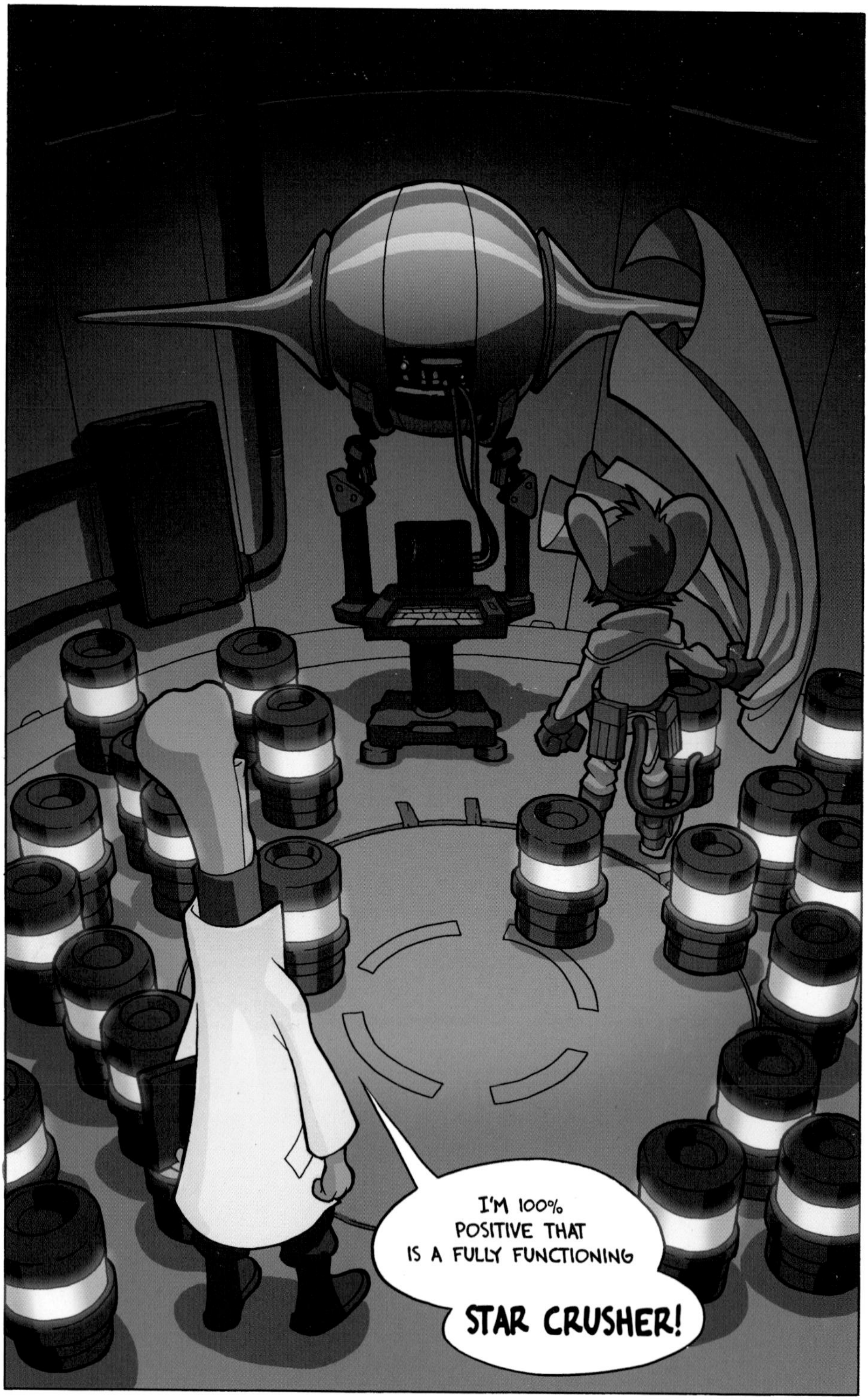
I'M 100% POSITIVE THAT IS A FULLY FUNCTIONING
STAR CRUSHER!

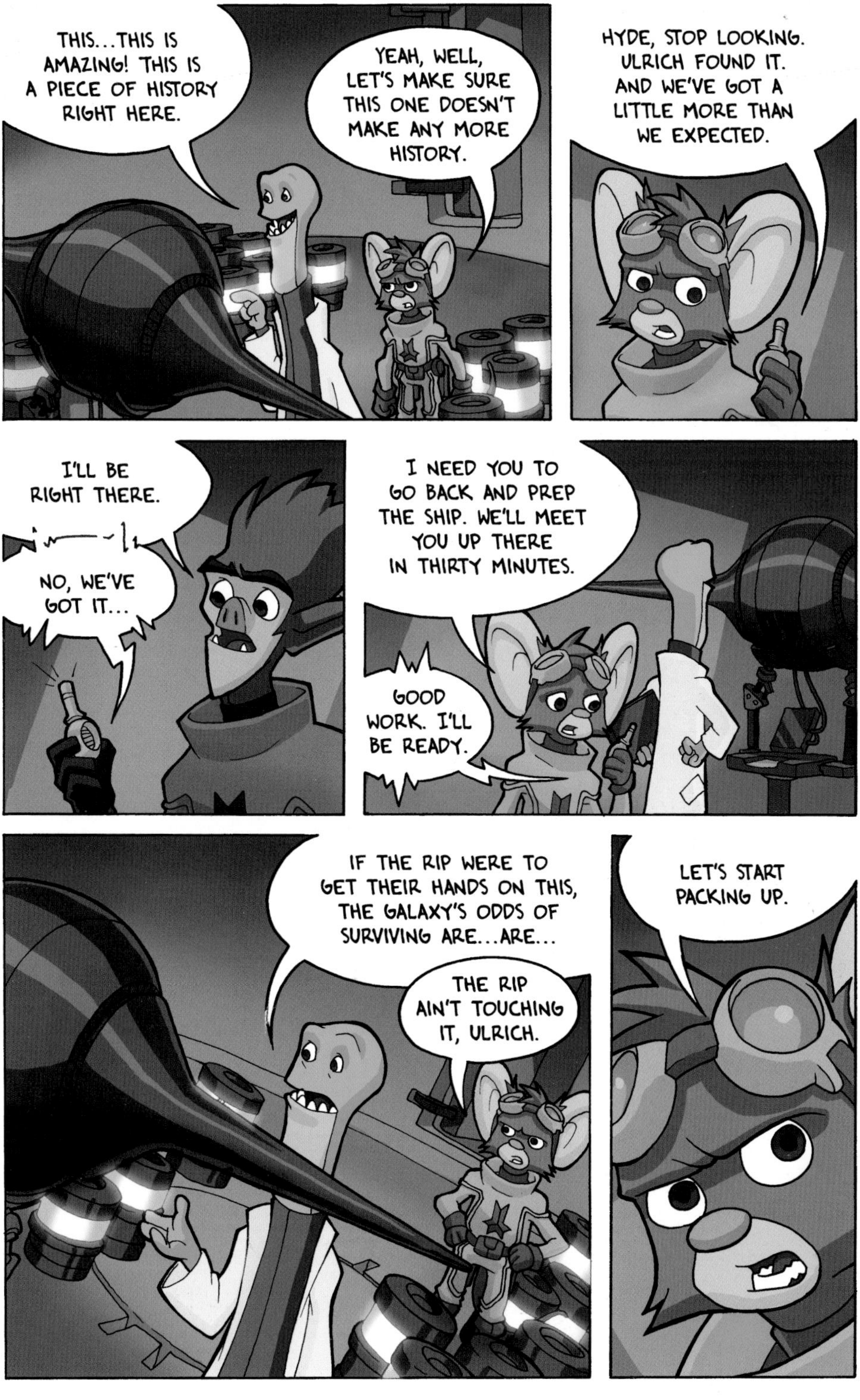
THIS...THIS IS AMAZING! THIS IS A PIECE OF HISTORY RIGHT HERE.
YEAH, WELL, LET'S MAKE SURE THIS ONE DOESN'T MAKE ANY MORE HISTORY.
HYDE, STOP LOOKING. ULRICH FOUND IT. AND WE'VE GOT A LITTLE MORE THAN WE EXPECTED.
I'LL BE RIGHT THERE.
NO, WE'VE GOT IT...
I NEED YOU TO GO BACK AND PREP THE SHIP. WE'LL MEET YOU UP THERE IN THIRTY MINUTES.
GOOD WORK. I'LL BE READY.
IF THE RIP WERE TO GET THEIR HANDS ON THIS, THE GALAXY'S ODDS OF SURVIVING ARE...ARE...
THE RIP AIN'T TOUCHING IT, ULRICH.
LET'S START PACKING UP.

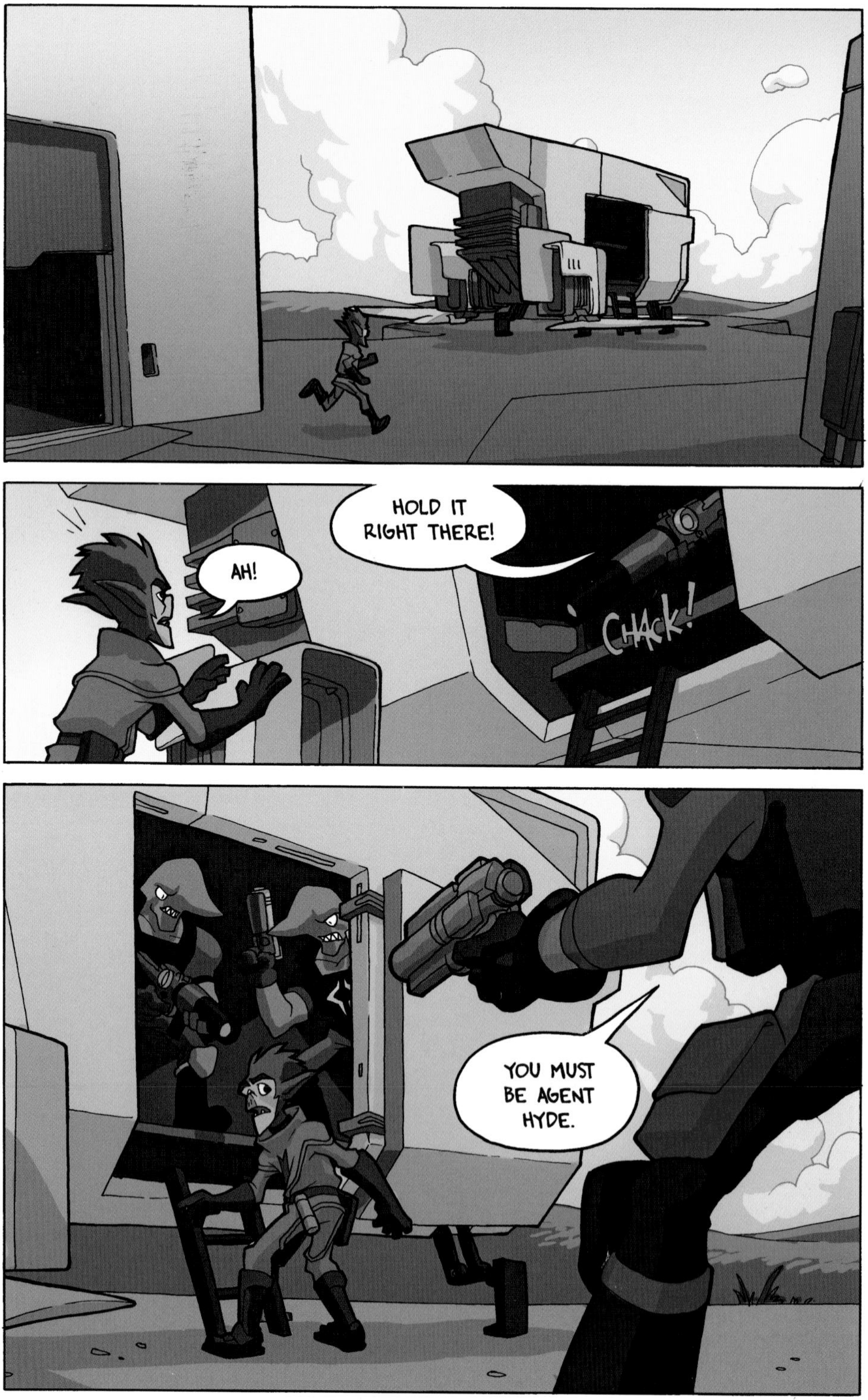
HOLD IT RIGHT THERE!
AH!
CHACK!
YOU MUST BE AGENT HYDE.

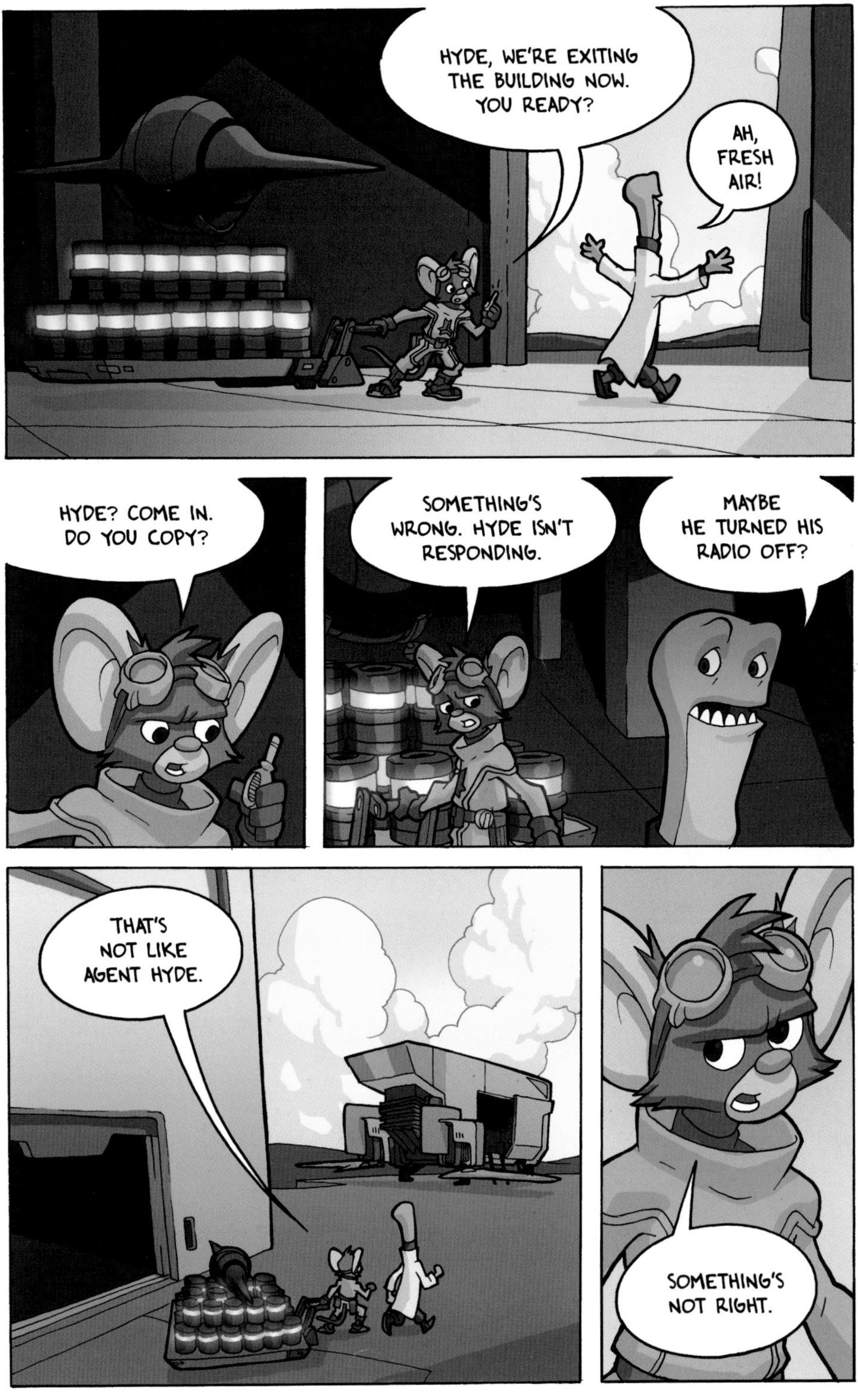
HYDE, WE'RE EXITING THE BUILDING NOW. YOU READY?
AH, FRESH AIR!
HYDE? COME IN. DO YOU COPY?
SOMETHING'S WRONG. HYDE ISN'T RESPONDING.
MAYBE HE TURNED HIS RADIO OFF?
THAT'S NOT LIKE AGENT HYDE.
SOMETHING'S NOT RIGHT.

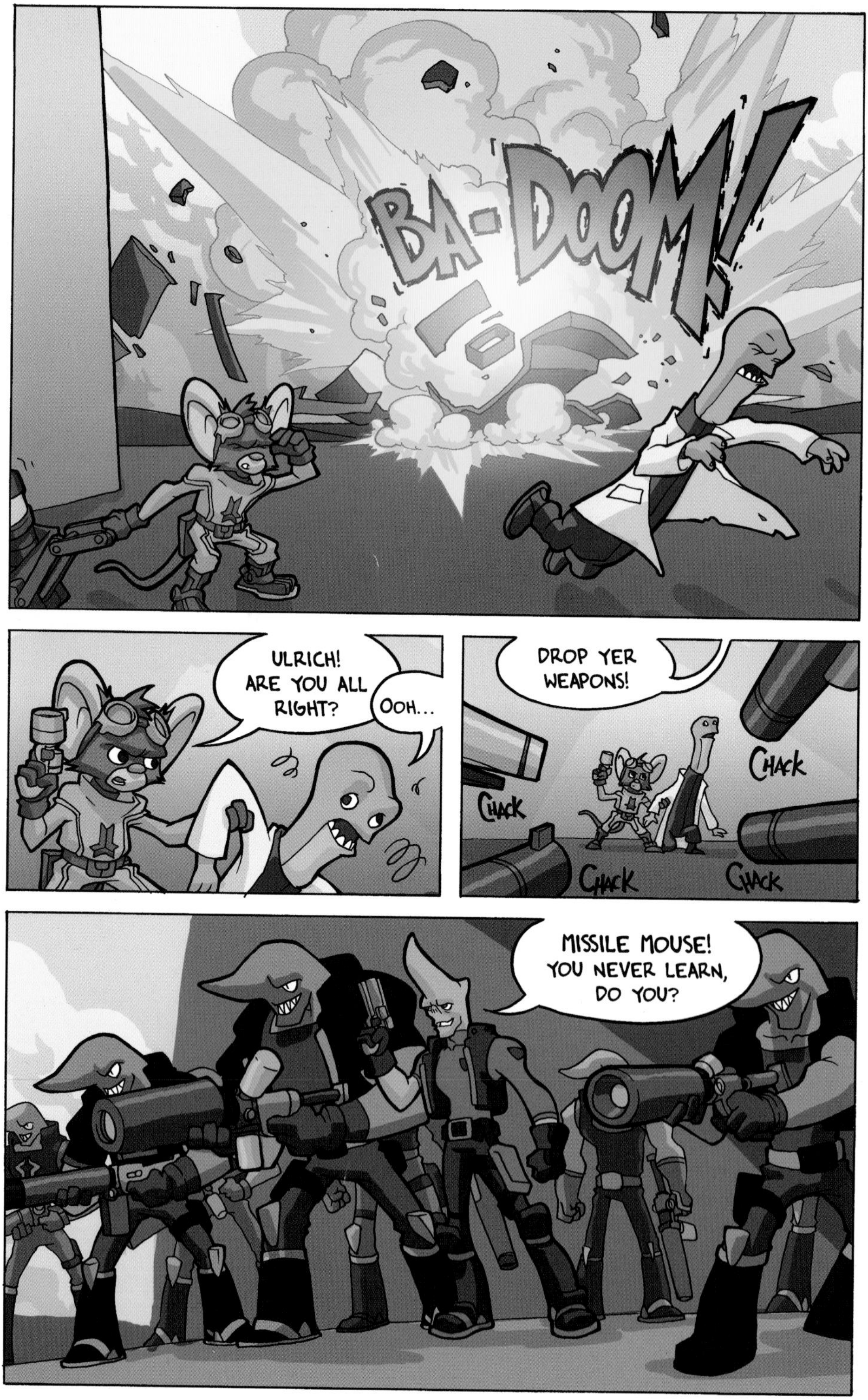
BA-DOOM!
ULRICH! ARE YOU ALL RIGHT?
OOH...
DROP YER WEAPONS!
CHACK
CHACK
CHACK
CHACK
MISSILE MOUSE! YOU NEVER LEARN, DO YOU?

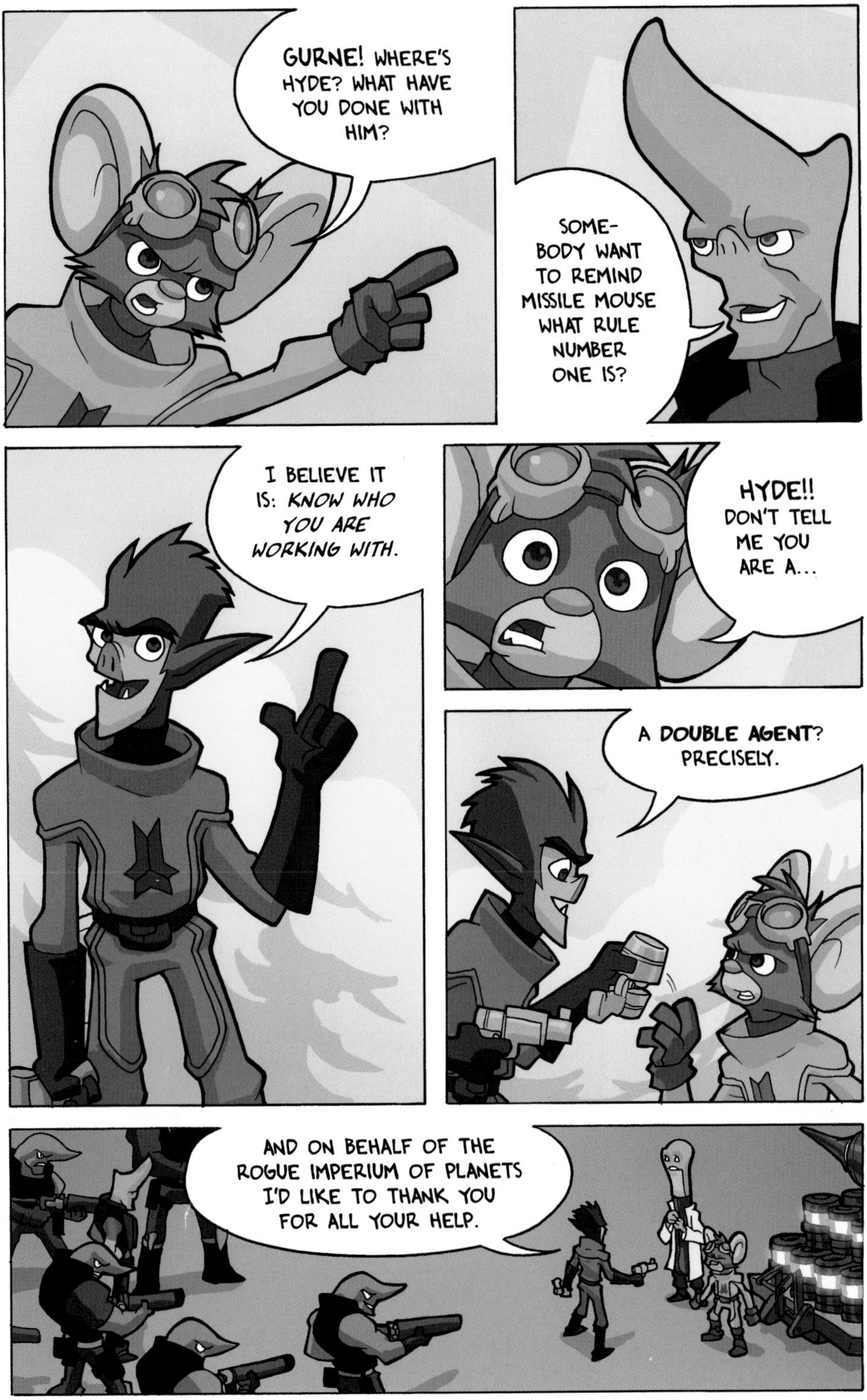
GURNE! WHERE'S HYDE? WHAT HAVE YOU DONE WITH HIM?
SOME-BODY WANT TO REMIND MISSILE MOUSE WHAT RULE NUMBER ONE IS?
I BELIEVE IT IS: KNOW WHO YOU ARE WORKING WITH.
HYDE!! DON'T TELL ME YOU ARE A...
A DOUBLE AGENT? PRECISELY.
AND ON BEHALF OF THE ROGUE IMPERIUM OF PLANETS I'D LIKE TO THANK YOU FOR ALL YOUR HELP.

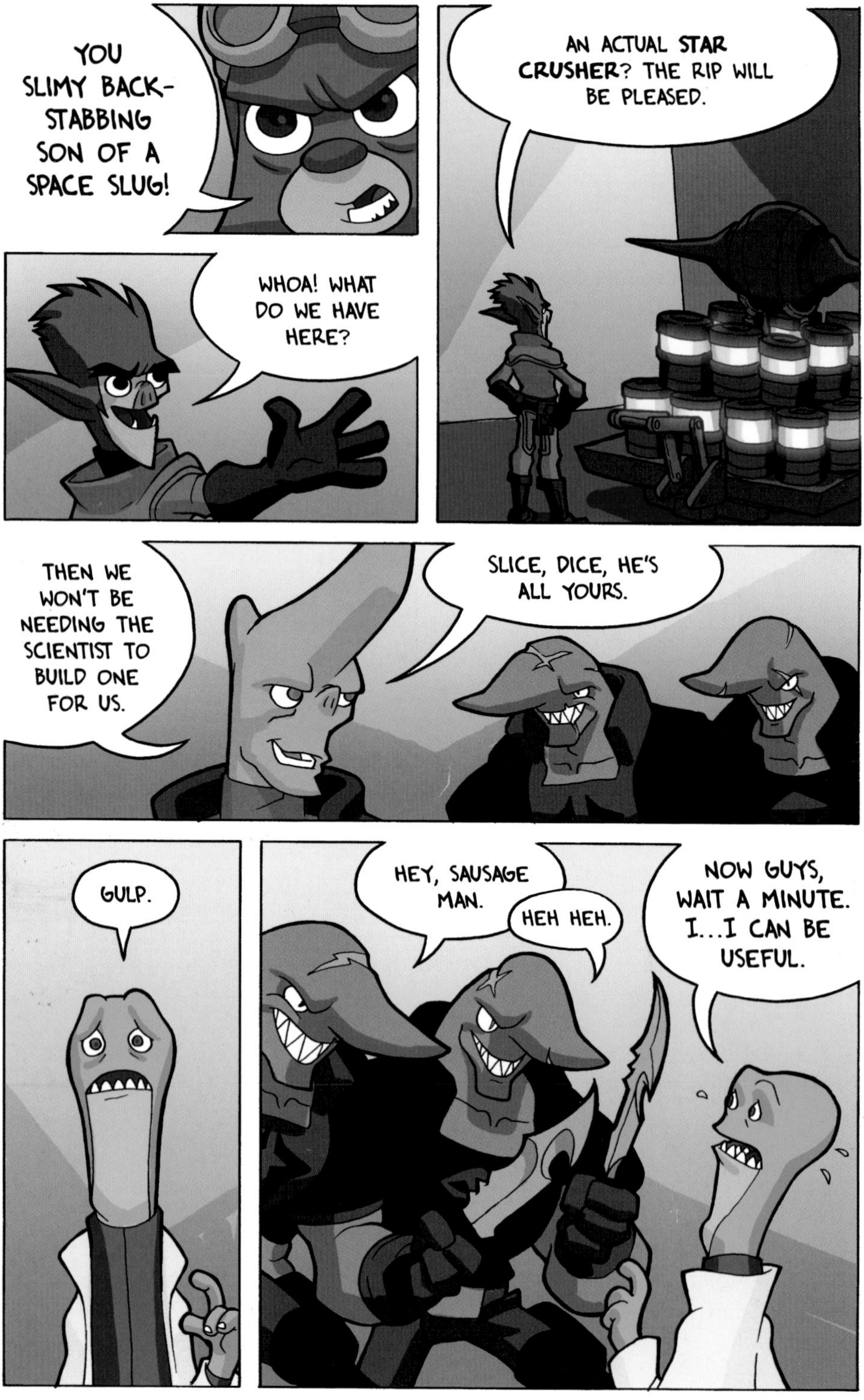
YOU SLIMY BACK-STABBING SON OF A SPACE SLUG!
AN ACTUAL STAR CRUSHER? THE RIP WILL BE PLEASED.
WHOA! WHAT DO WE HAVE HERE?
THEN WE WON'T BE NEEDING THE SCIENTIST TO BUILD ONE FOR US.
SLICE, DICE, HE'S ALL YOURS.
GULP.
HEY, SAUSAGE MAN.
HEH HEH.
NOW GUYS, WAIT A MINUTE. I...I CAN BE USEFUL.

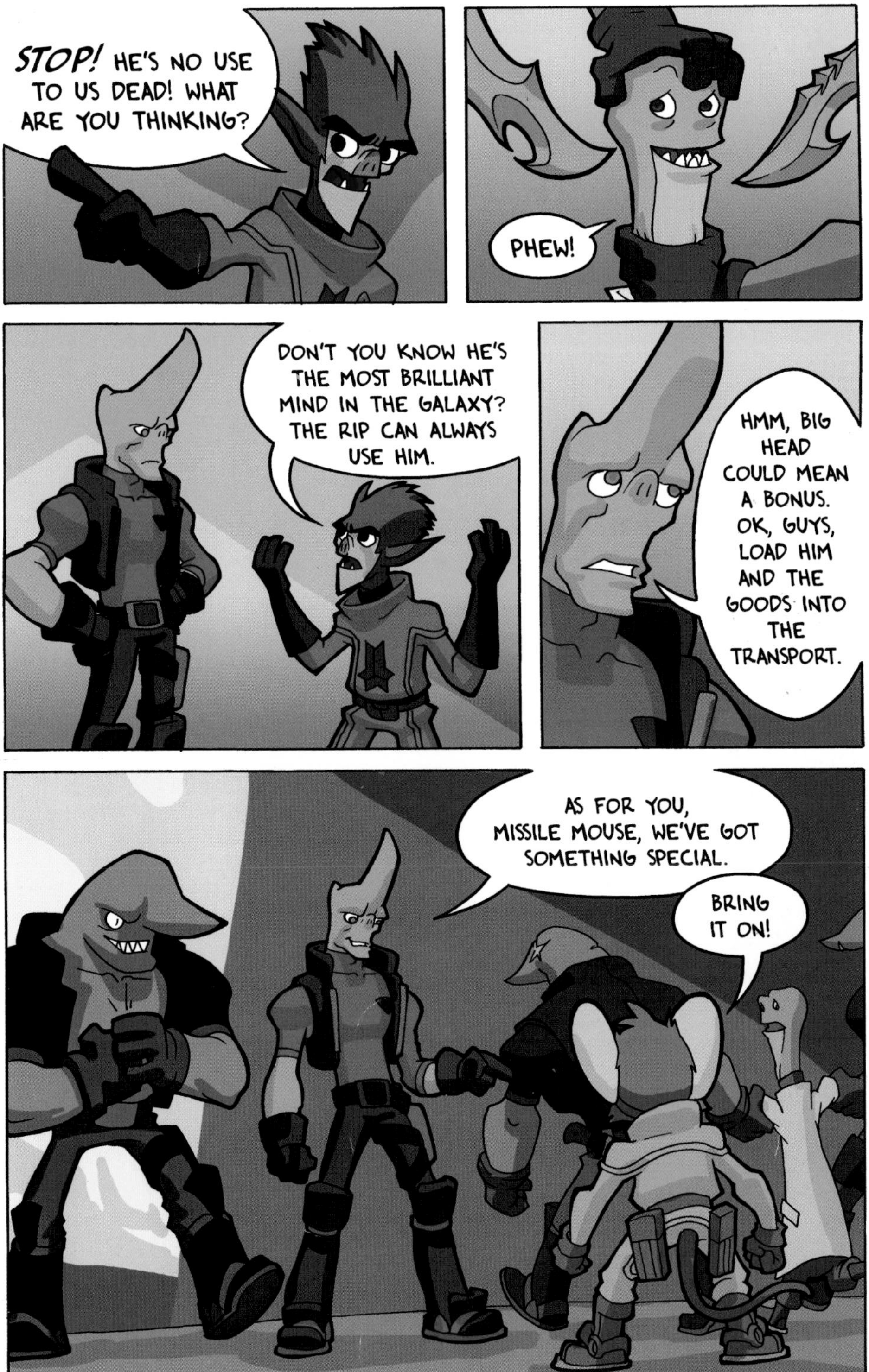
STOP! HE'S NO USE TO US DEAD! WHAT ARE YOU THINKING?
PHEW!
DON'T YOU KNOW HE'S THE MOST BRILLIANT MIND IN THE GALAXY? THE RIP CAN ALWAYS USE HIM.
HMM, BIG HEAD COULD MEAN A BONUS. OK, GUYS, LOAD HIM AND THE GOODS INTO THE TRANSPORT.
AS FOR YOU, MISSILE MOUSE, WE'VE GOT SOMETHING SPECIAL.
BRING IT ON!

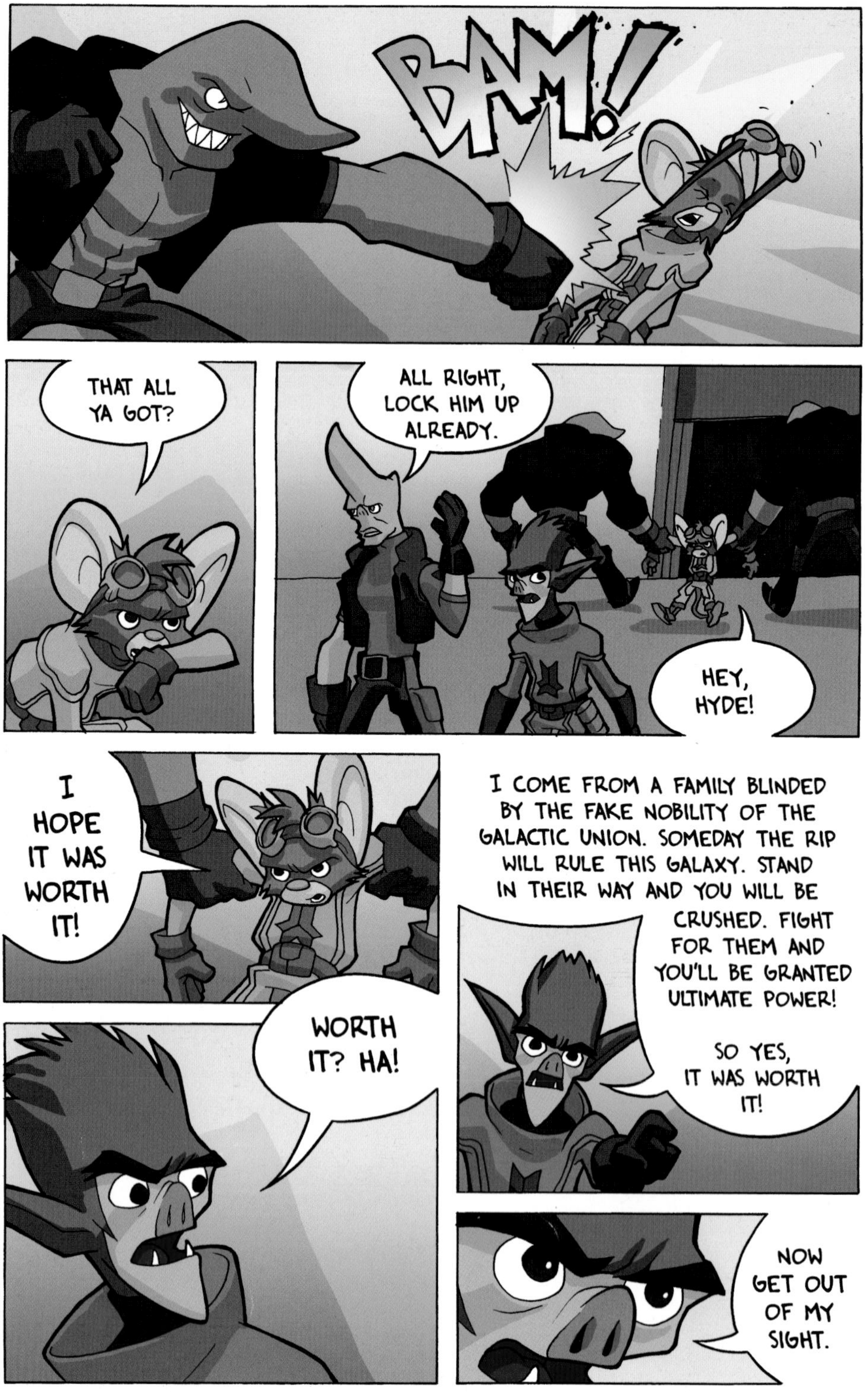

BAM!
THAT ALL YA GOT?
ALL RIGHT, LOCK HIM UP ALREADY.
HEY, HYDE!
I HOPE IT WAS WORTH IT!
WORTH IT? HA!
I COME FROM A FAMILY BLINDED BY THE FAKE NOBILITY OF THE GALACTIC UNION. SOMEDAY THE RIP WILL RULE THIS GALAXY. STAND IN THEIR WAY AND YOU WILL BE CRUSHED. FIGHT FOR THEM AND YOU'LL BE GRANTED ULTIMATE POWER!
SO YES, IT WAS WORTH IT!
NOW GET OUT OF MY SIGHT.

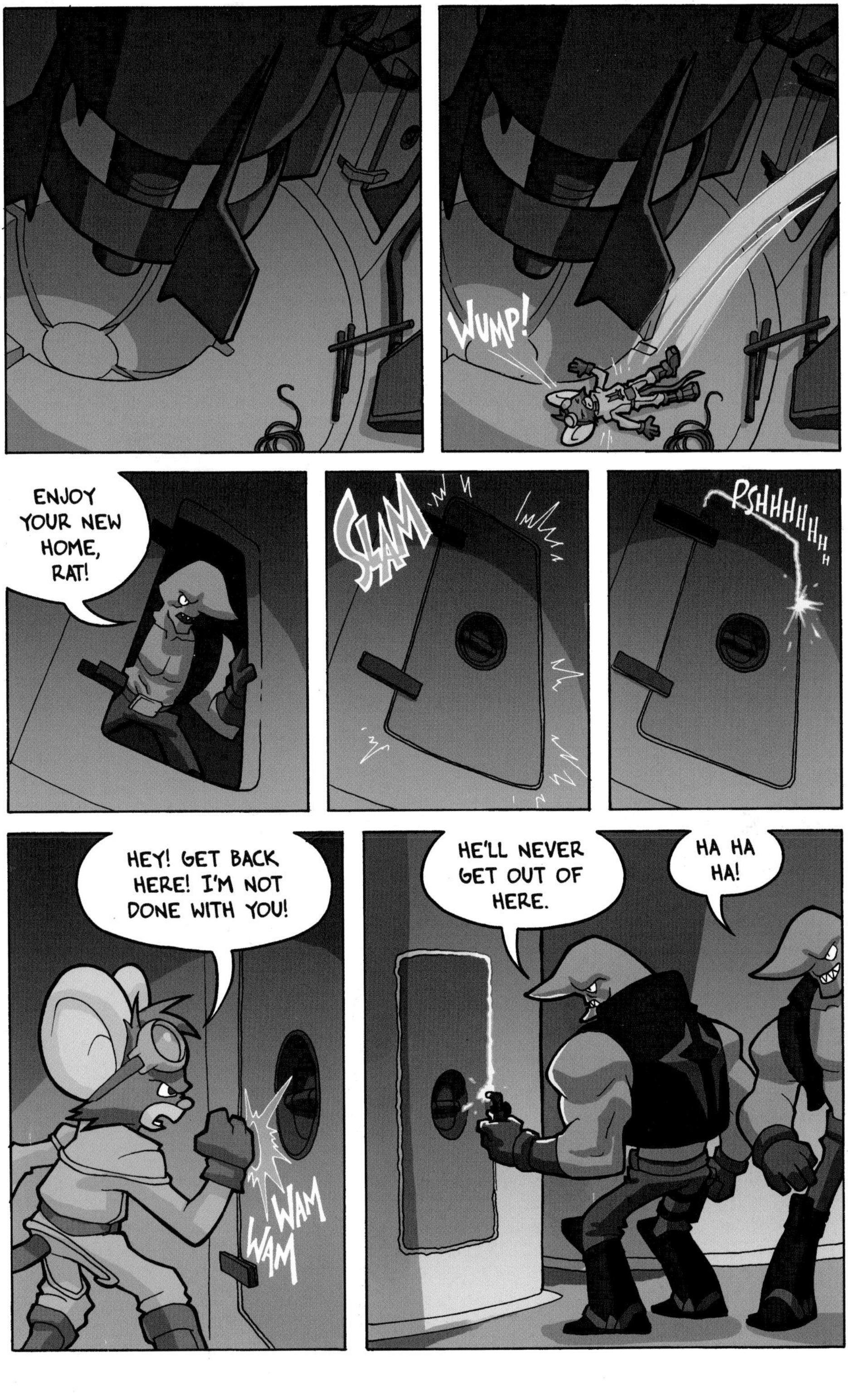
WUMP!
ENJOY YOUR NEW HOME, RAT!
SLAM
PSHHHHHHH
HEY! GET BACK HERE! I'M NOT DONE WITH YOU!
WAM WAM
HE'LL NEVER GET OUT OF HERE.
HA HA HA!

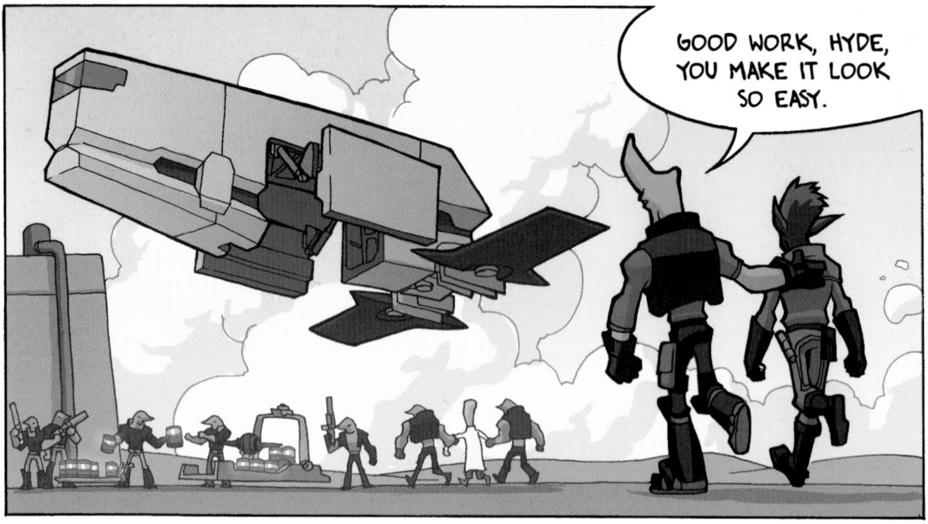
GOOD WORK, HYDE, YOU MAKE IT LOOK SO EASY.

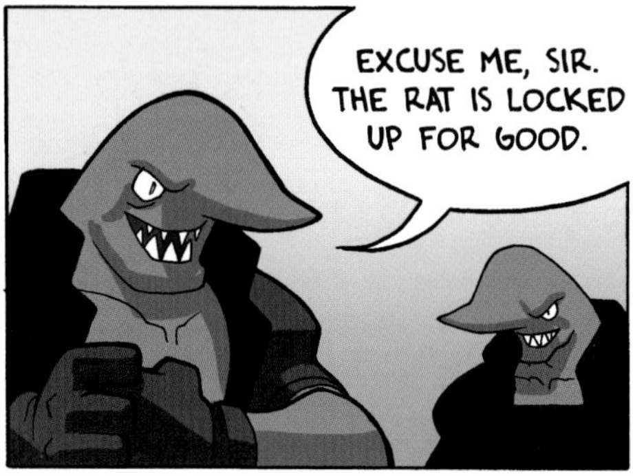
EXCUSE ME, SIR. THE RAT IS LOCKED UP FOR GOOD.

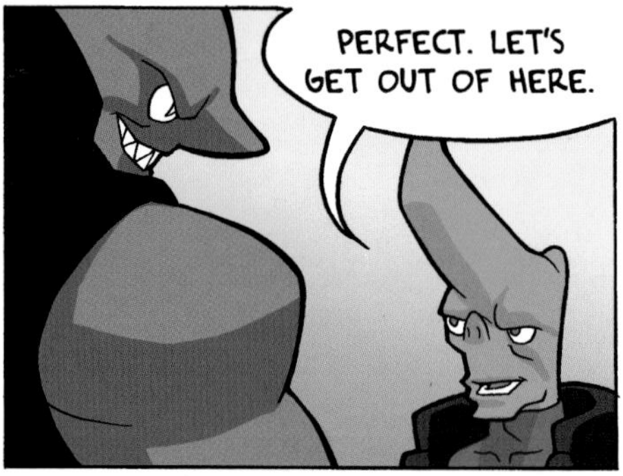
PERFECT. LET'S GET OUT OF HERE.

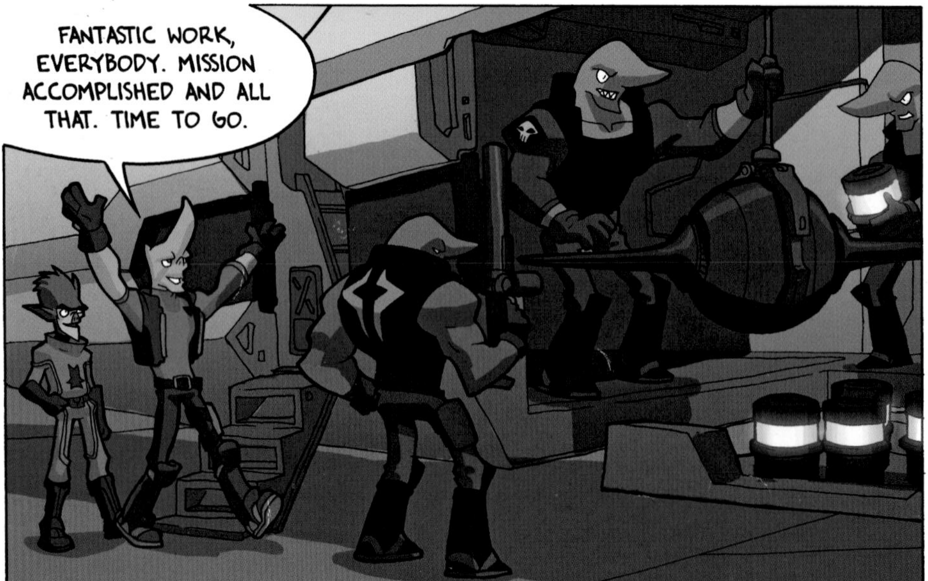
FANTASTIC WORK, EVERYBODY. MISSION ACCOMPLISHED AND ALL THAT. TIME TO GO.

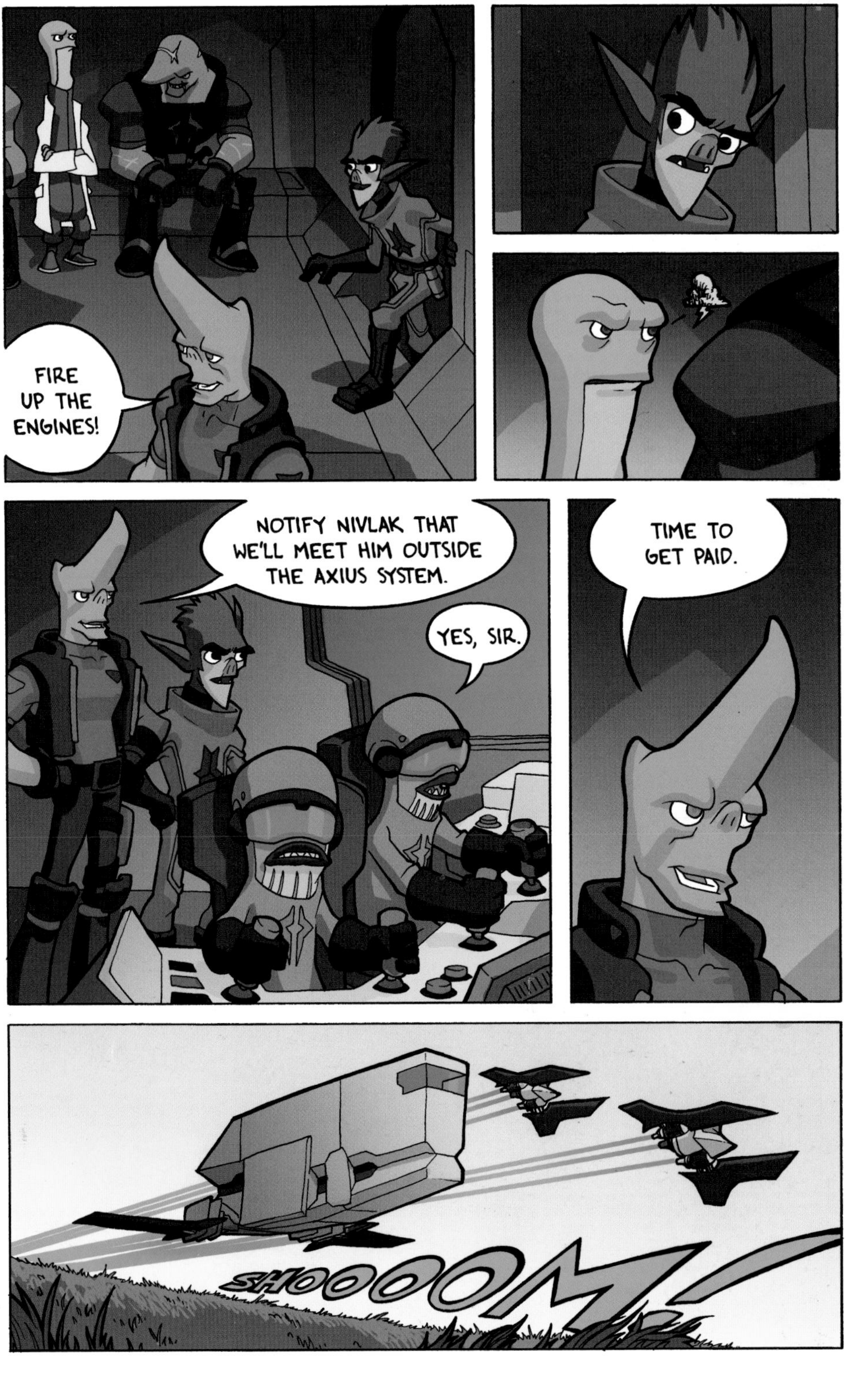
FIRE UP THE ENGINES!
NOTIFY NIVLAK THAT WE'LL MEET HIM OUTSIDE THE AXIUS SYSTEM.
YES, SIR.
TIME TO GET PAID.
SHOOOOOM!

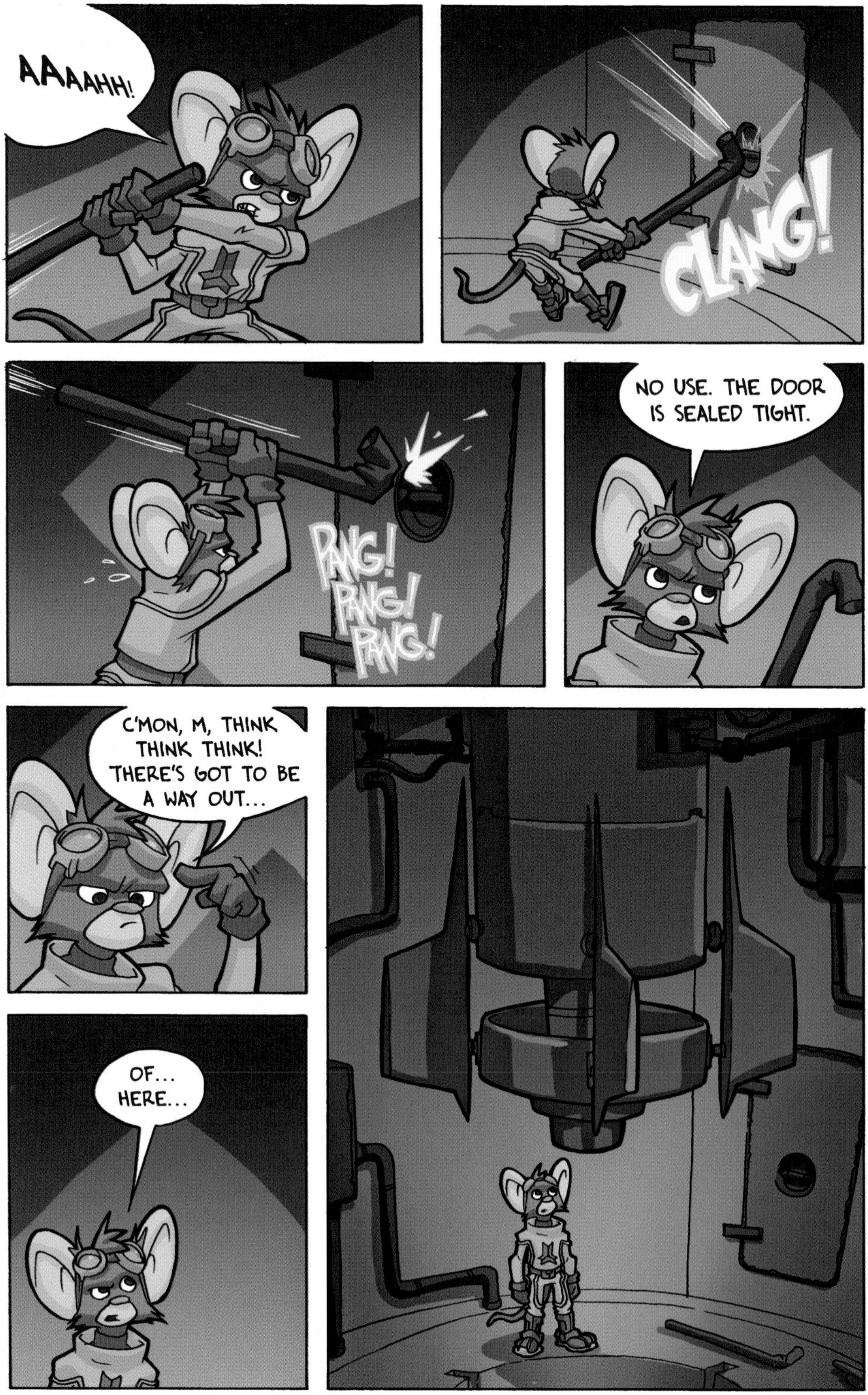
AAAAHH!
CLANG!
PANG! PANG! PANG!
NO USE. THE DOOR IS SEALED TIGHT.
C'MON, M, THINK THINK THINK! THERE'S GOT TO BE A WAY OUT...
OF... HERE...

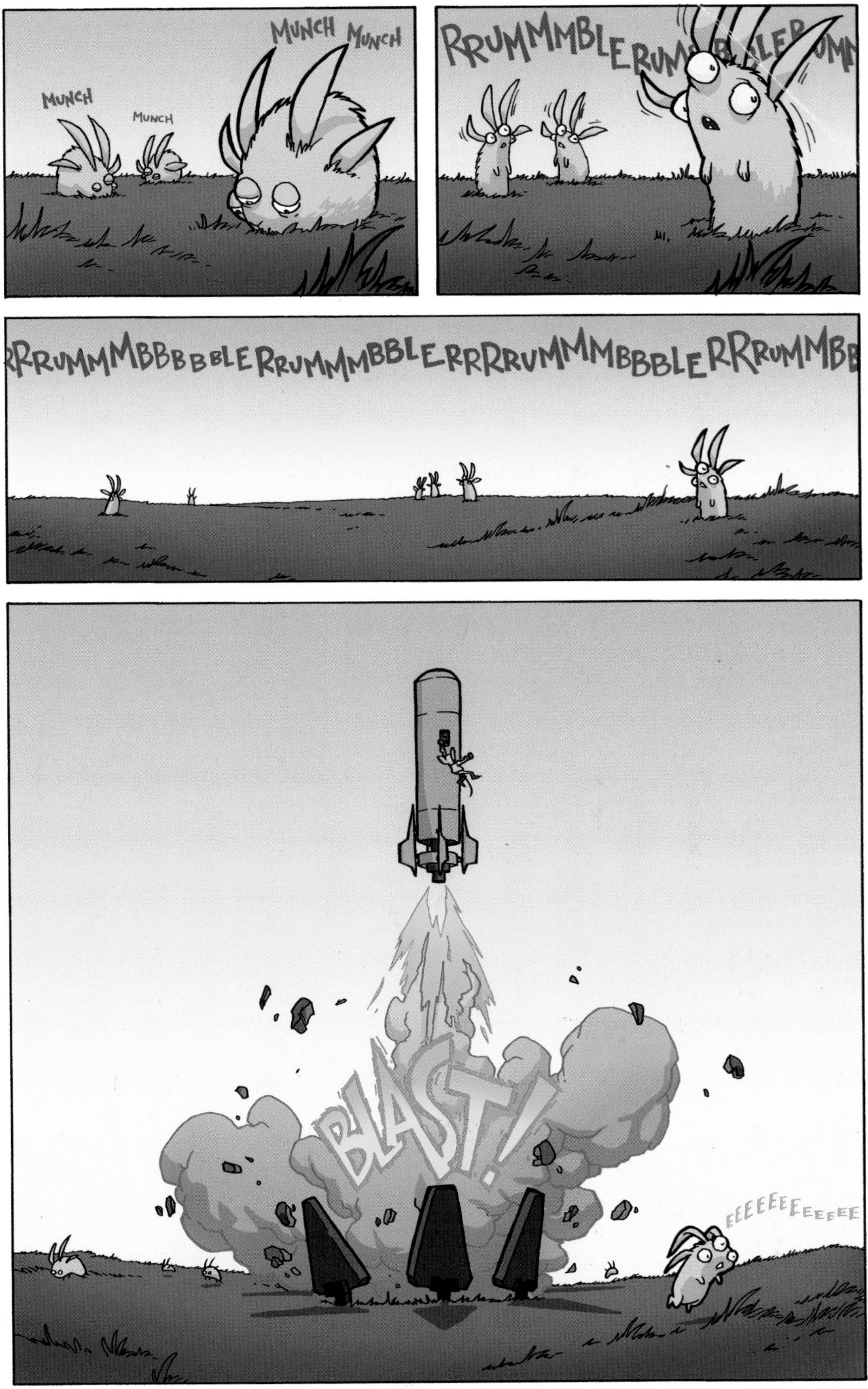
MUNCH MUNCH
MUNCH
MUNCH
RRUMMMBLERUM
RRUMMMBBBBBLERRUMMMMBBLERRRRUMMMMBBBLERRRUMMB
BLAST!
EEEEEEEEEEEE

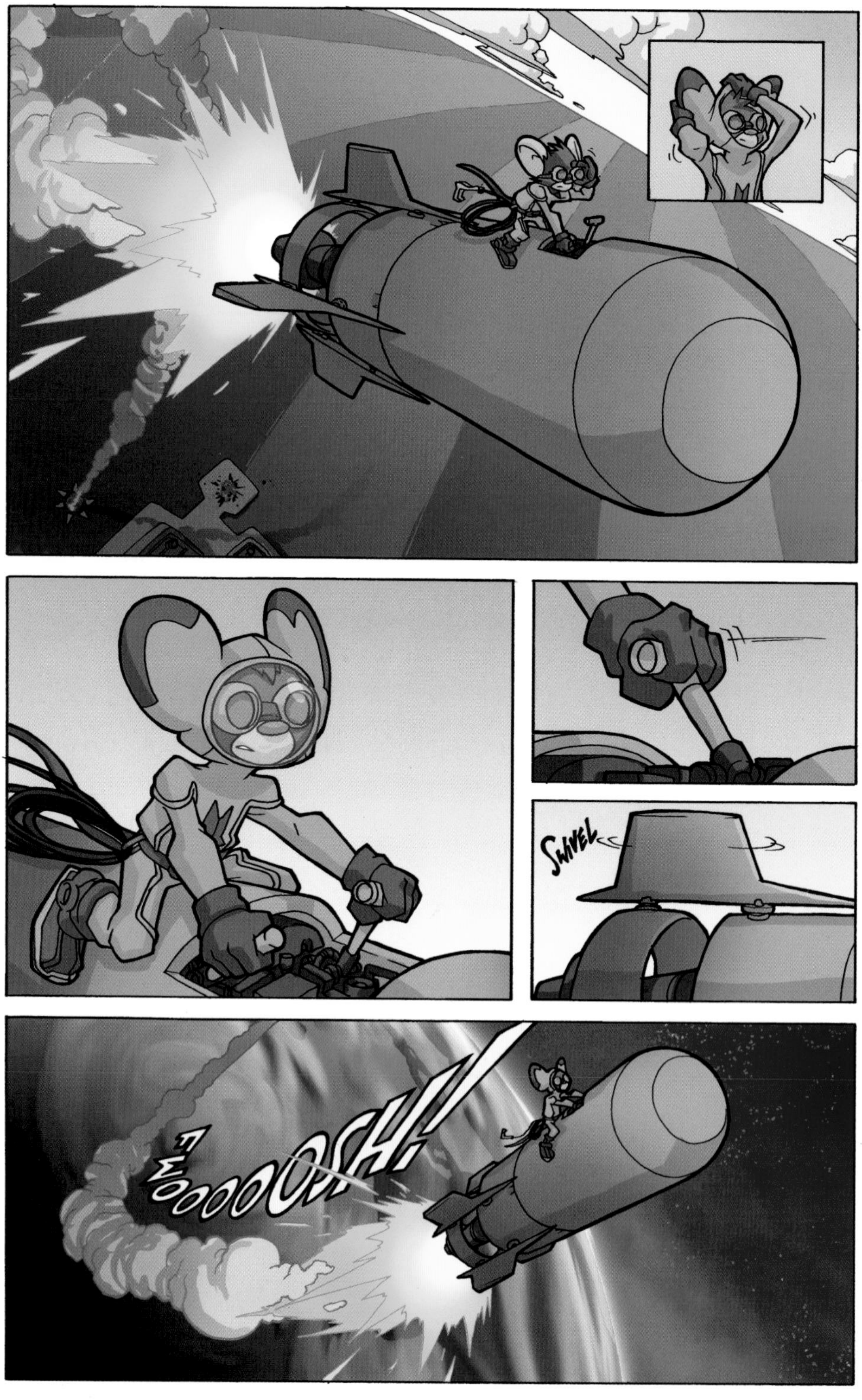
SWIVEL
FWOOOOOSH!

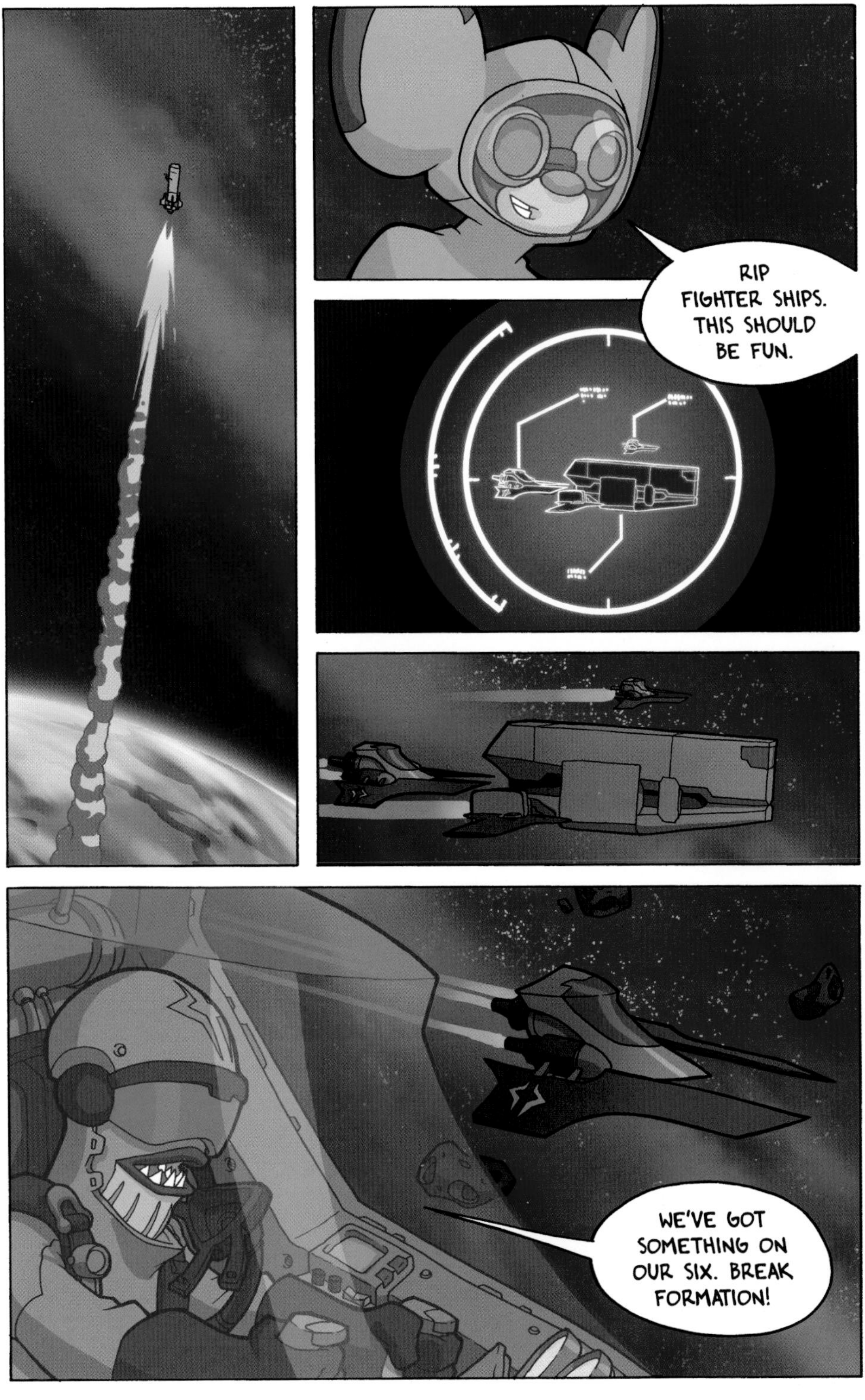
RIP FIGHTER SHIPS. THIS SHOULD BE FUN.
WE'VE GOT SOMETHING ON OUR SIX. BREAK FORMATION!

WHAT IN SPACE DO WE HAVE HERE?

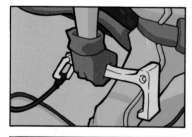

ZAF

ZAF

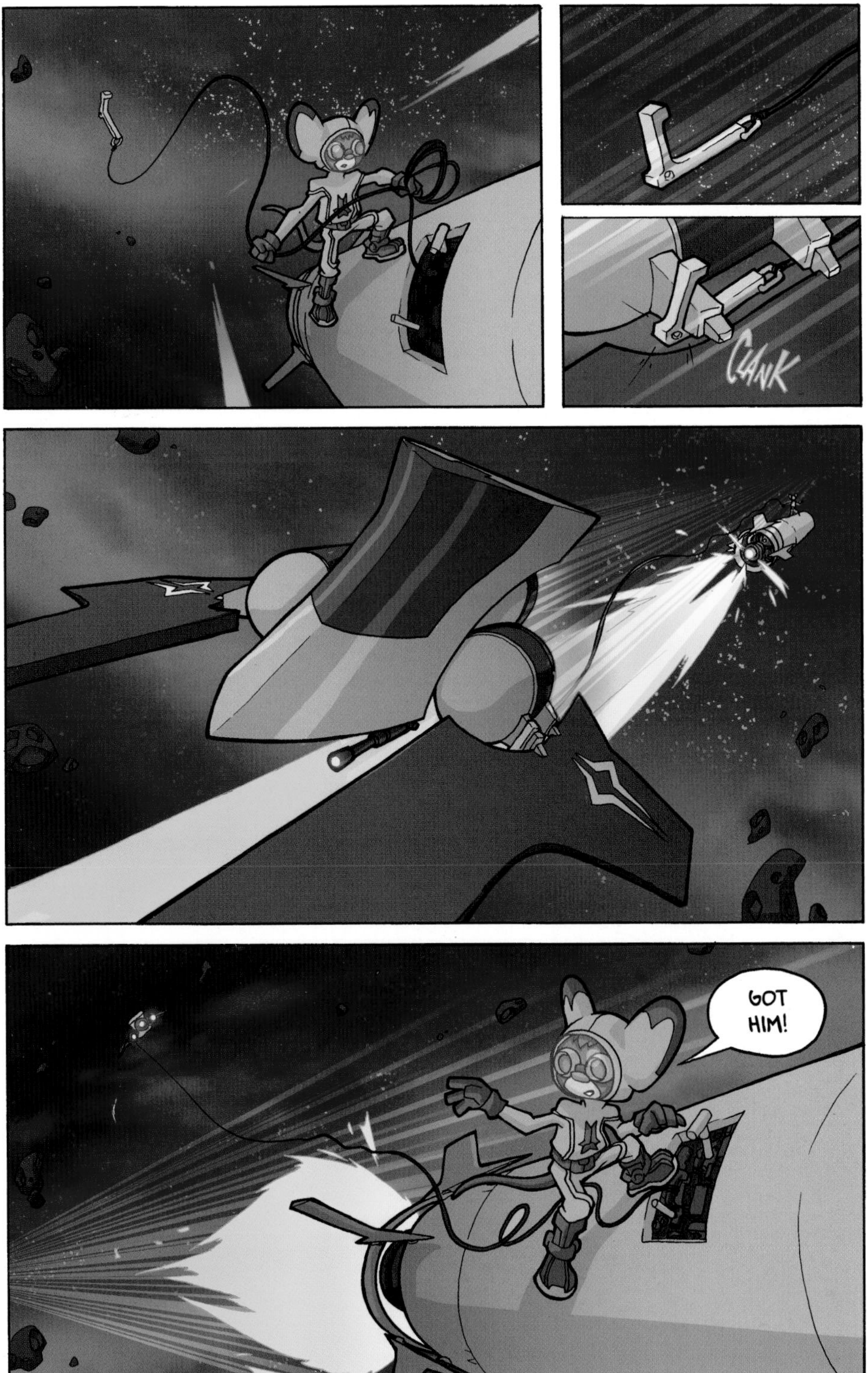
CLANK
GOT HIM!

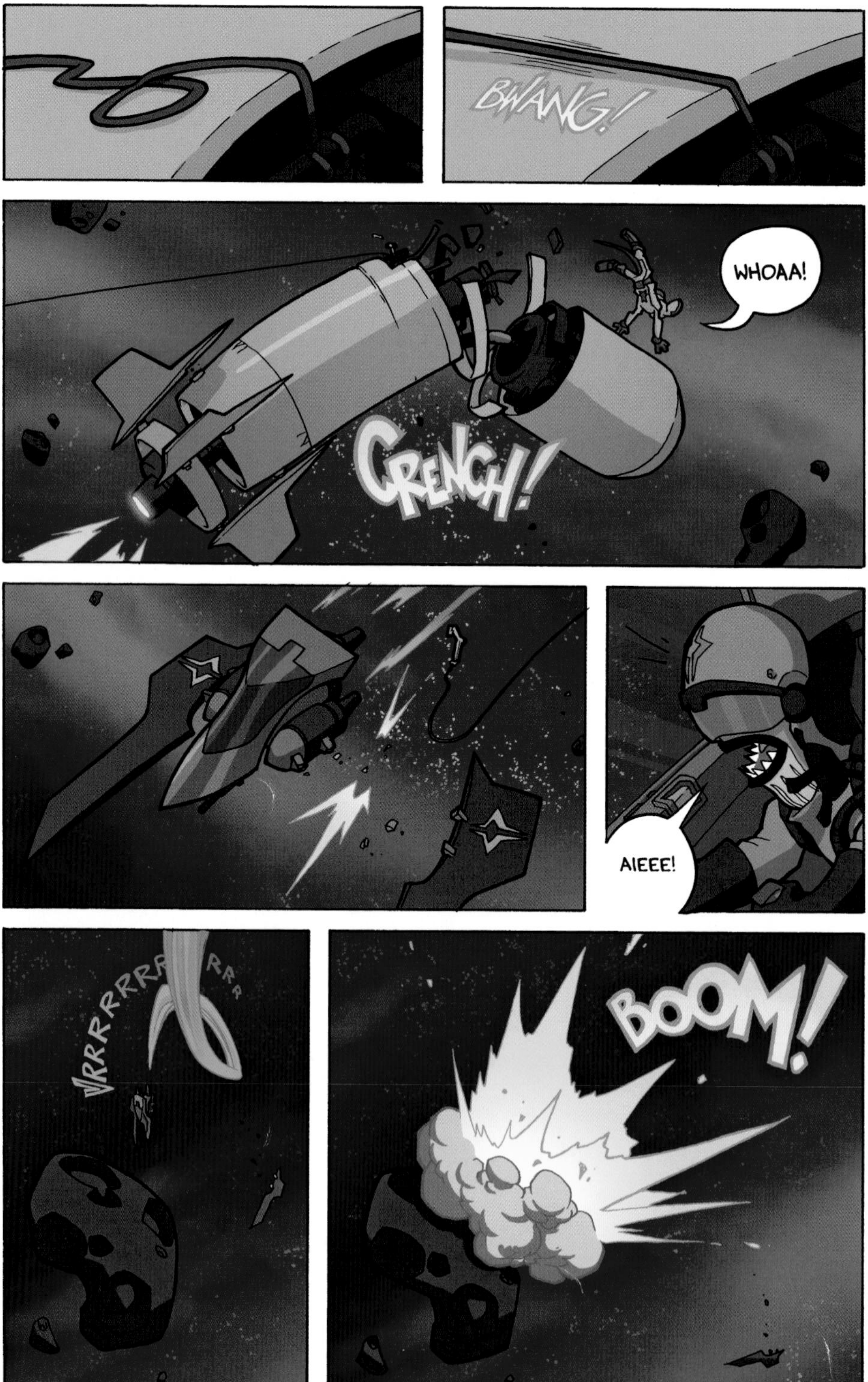
BWANG!
WHOAA!
CRENCH!
AIEEE!
VRRRRRRRRRRR
BOOM!

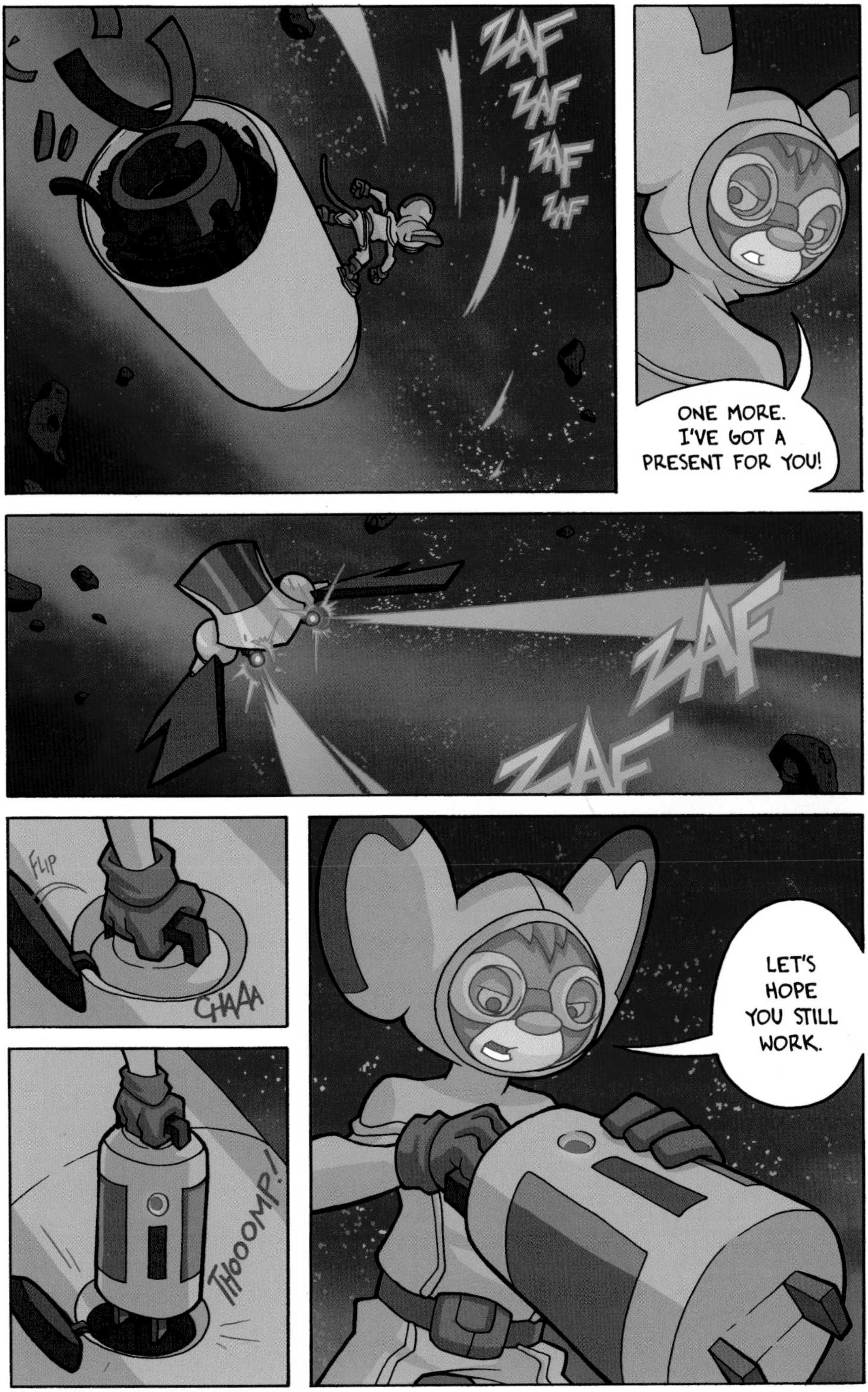
ZAF ZAF ZAF ZAF
ONE MORE. I'VE GOT A PRESENT FOR YOU!
ZAF ZAF
FLIP
CHAAA
THOOOMP!
LET'S HOPE YOU STILL WORK.

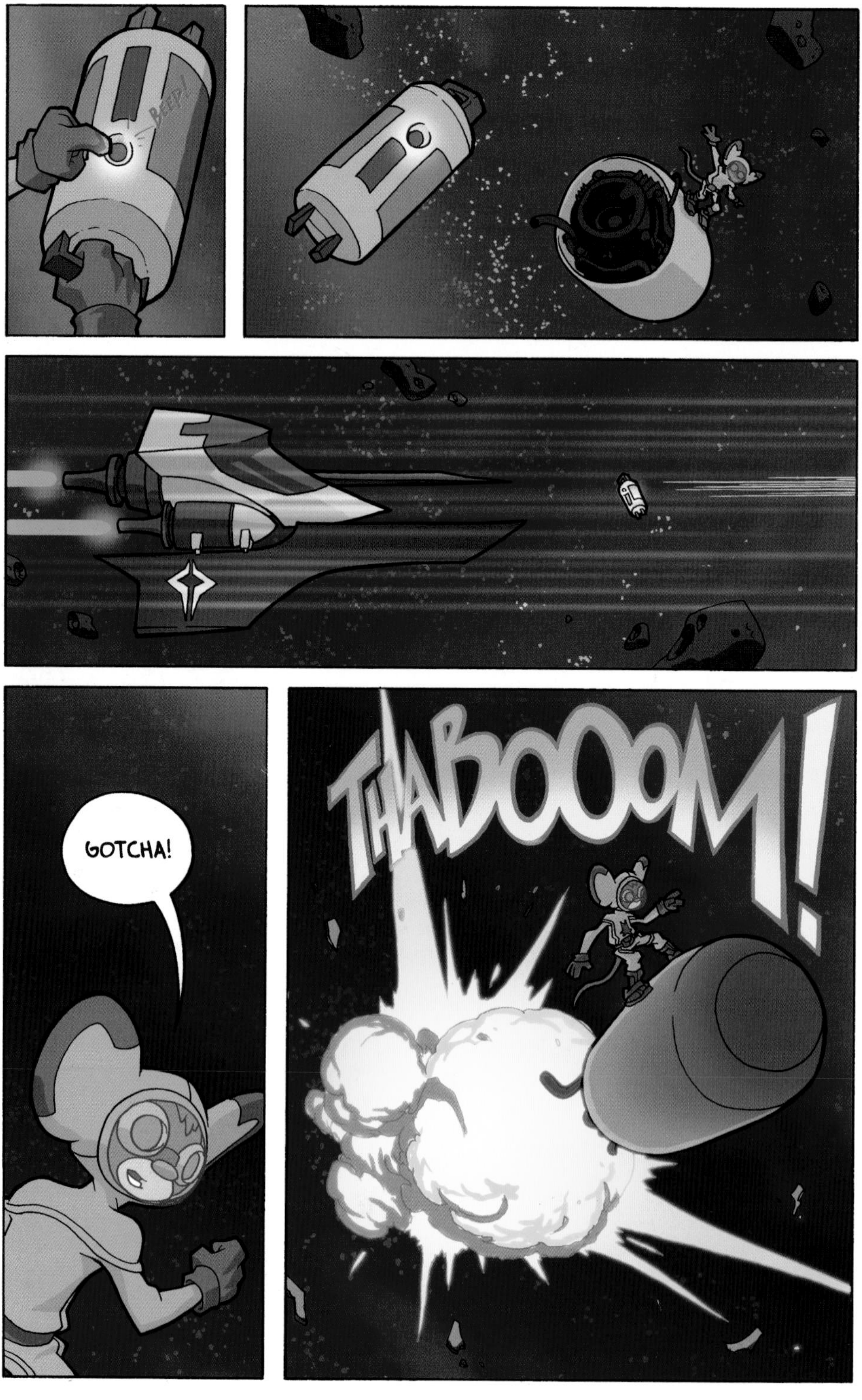
BEEP!
GOTCHA!
THABOOOM!

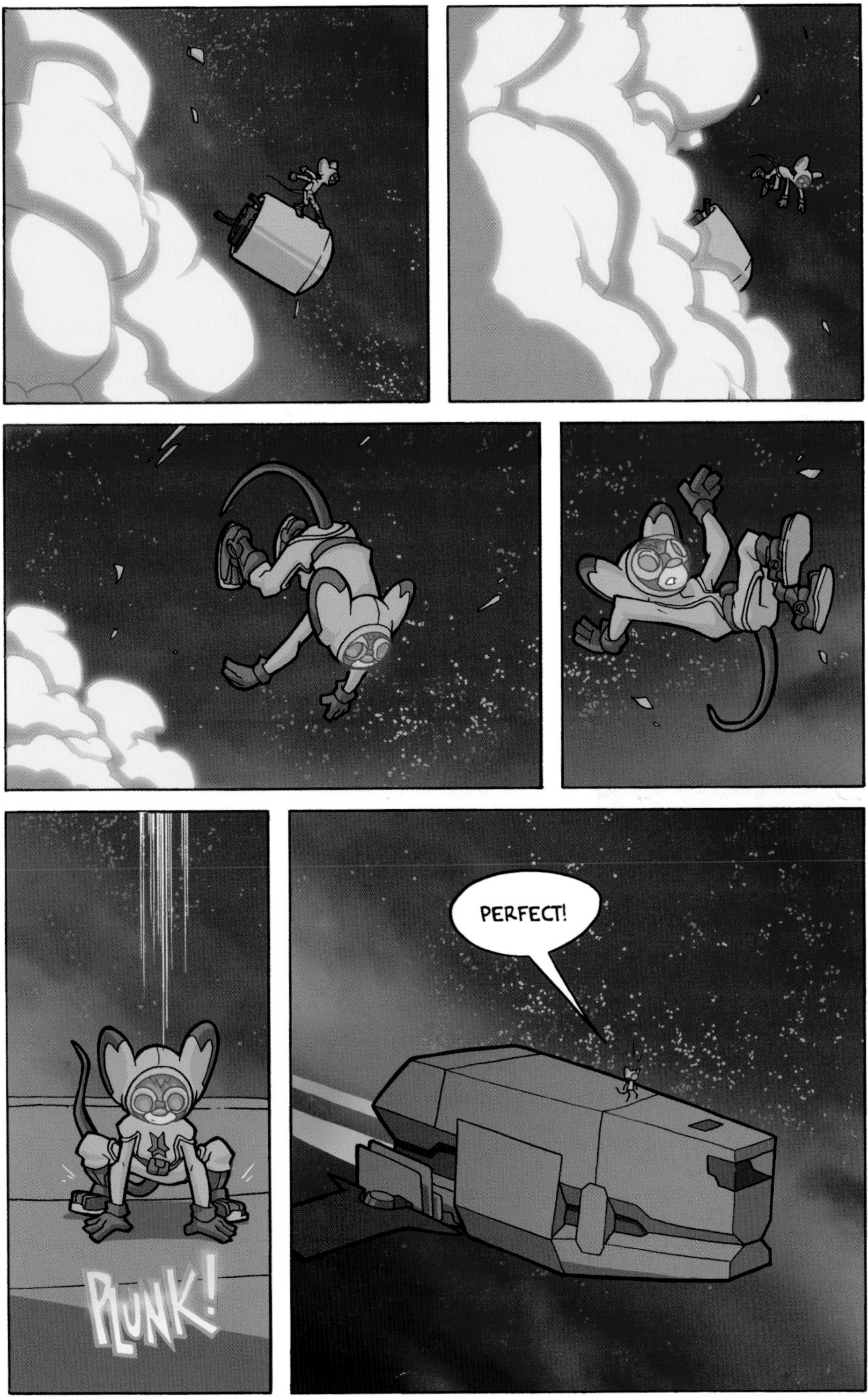
PLUNK!
PERFECT!

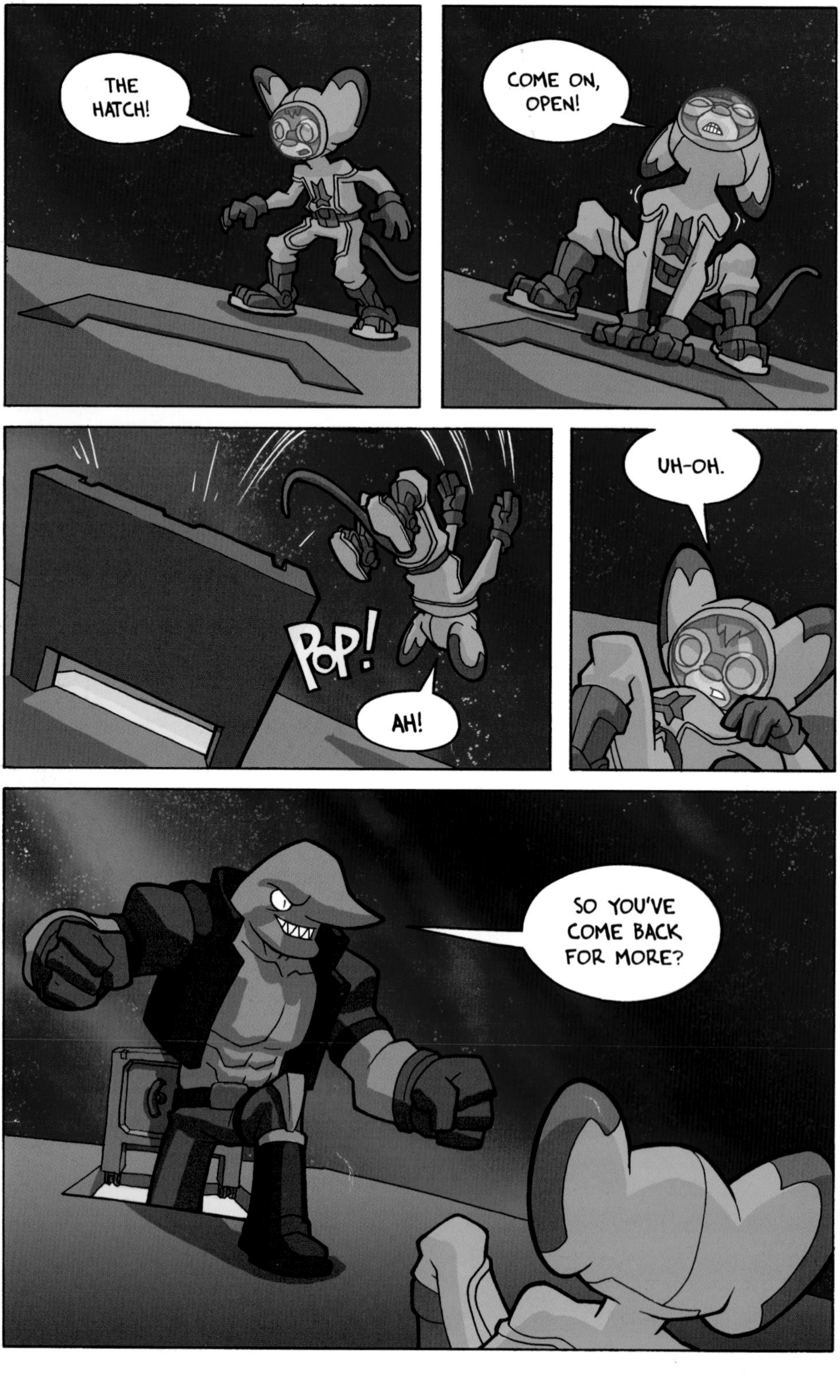
THE HATCH!
COME ON, OPEN!
POP!
AH!
UH-OH.
SO YOU'VE COME BACK FOR MORE?

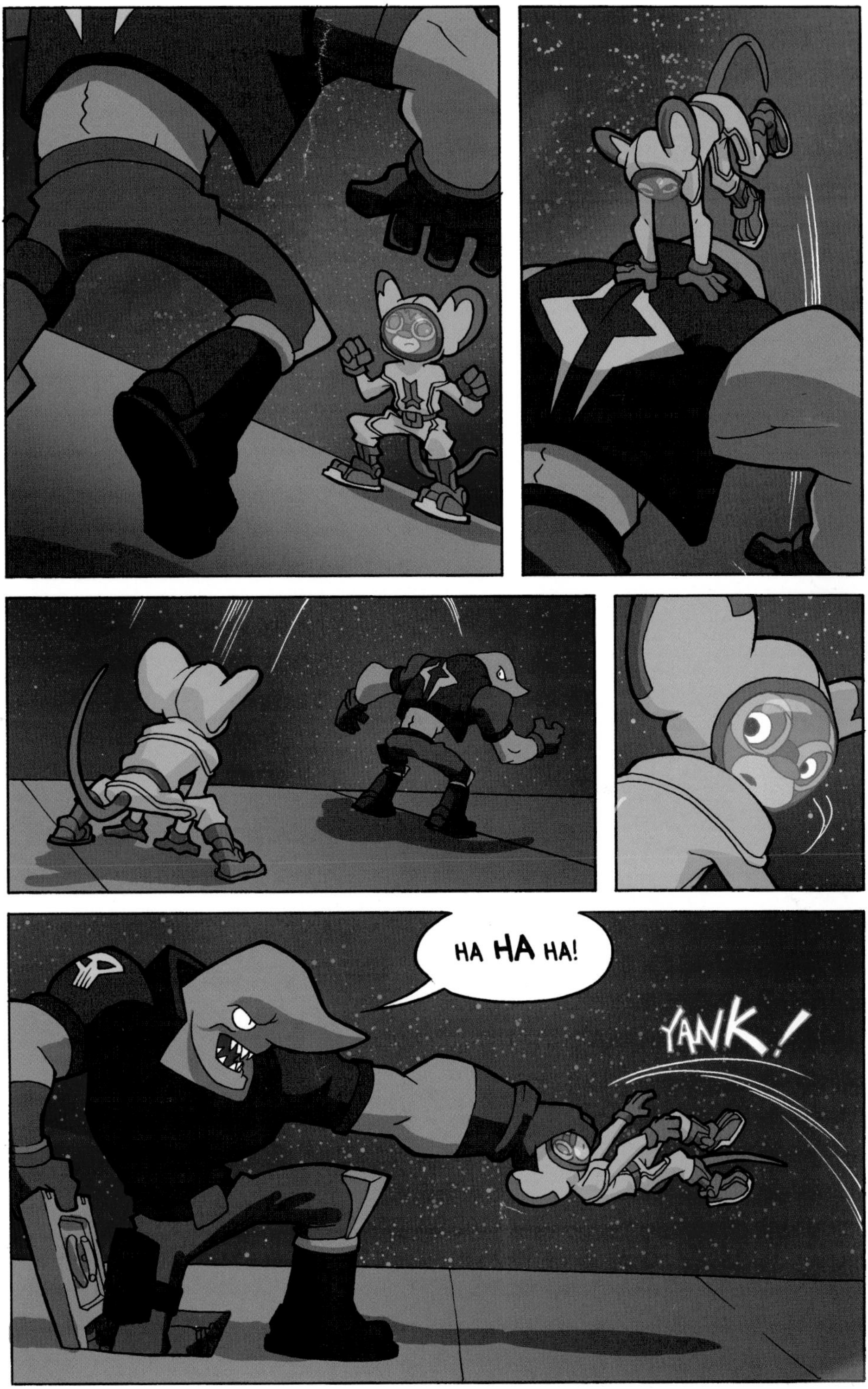

HA HA HA!
YANK!

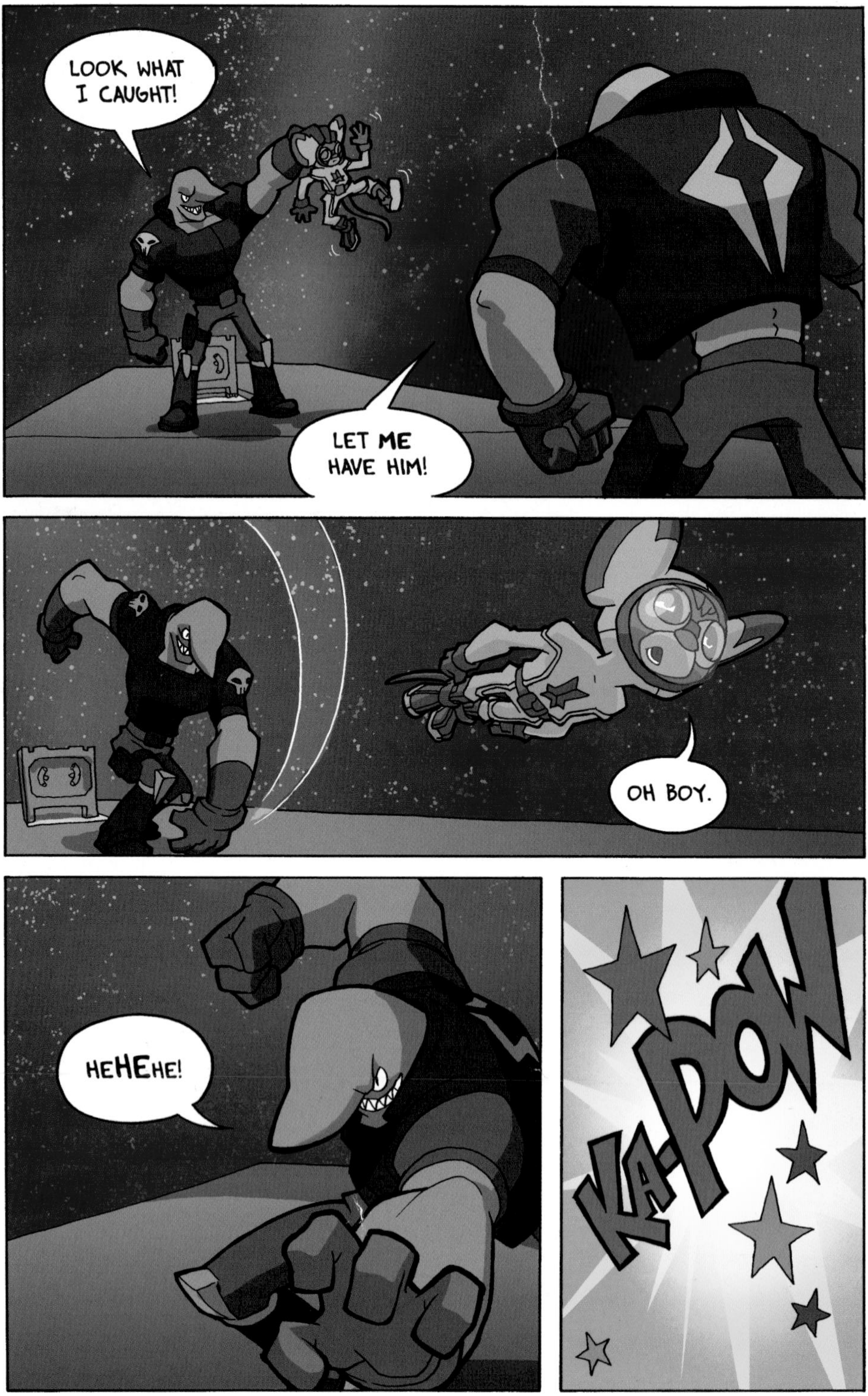
LOOK WHAT I CAUGHT!
LET ME HAVE HIM!
OH BOY.
HEHEHE!
KA-POW

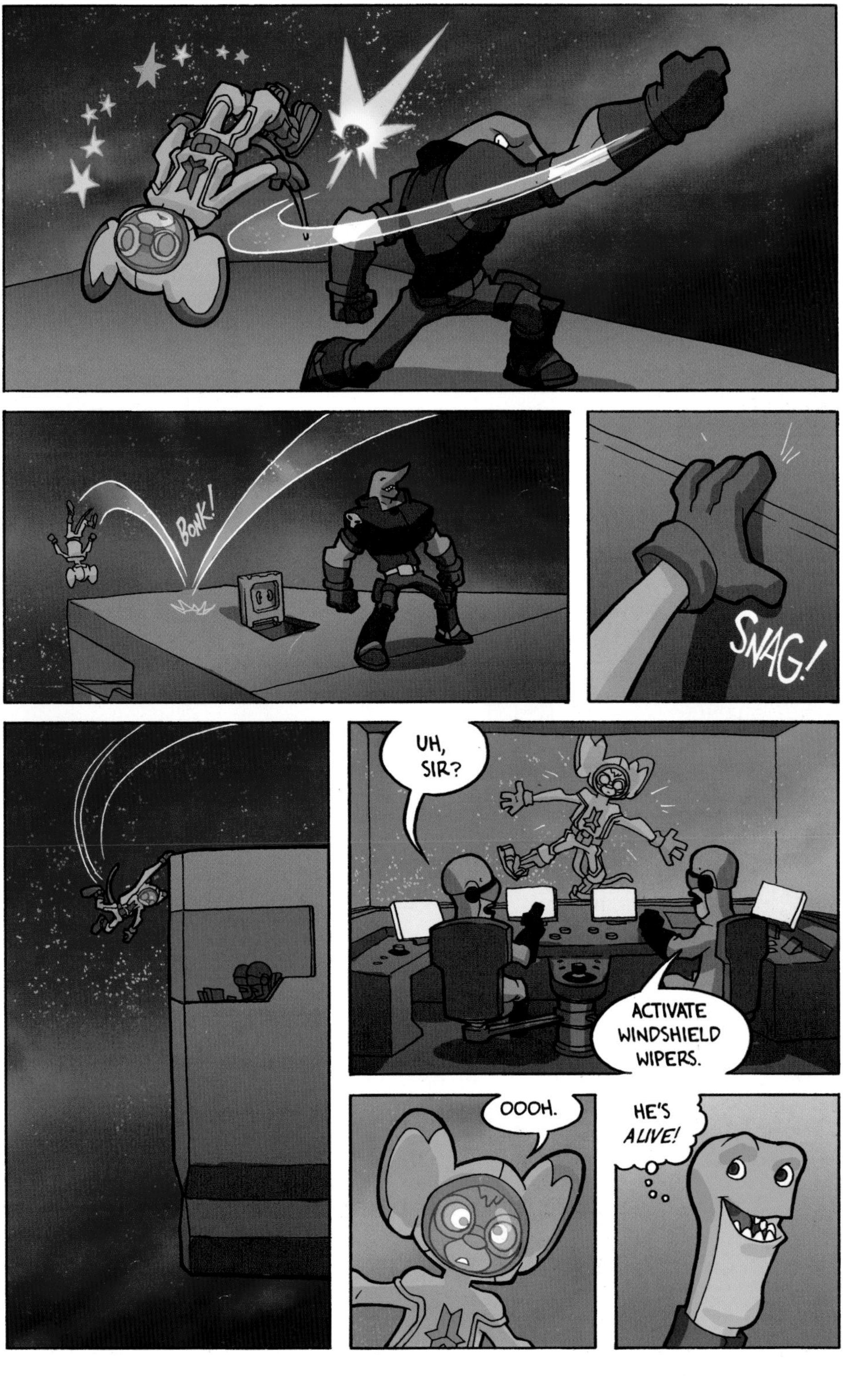
BONK!
SNAG!
UH, SIR?
ACTIVATE WINDSHIELD WIPERS.
OOOH.
HE'S ALIVE!

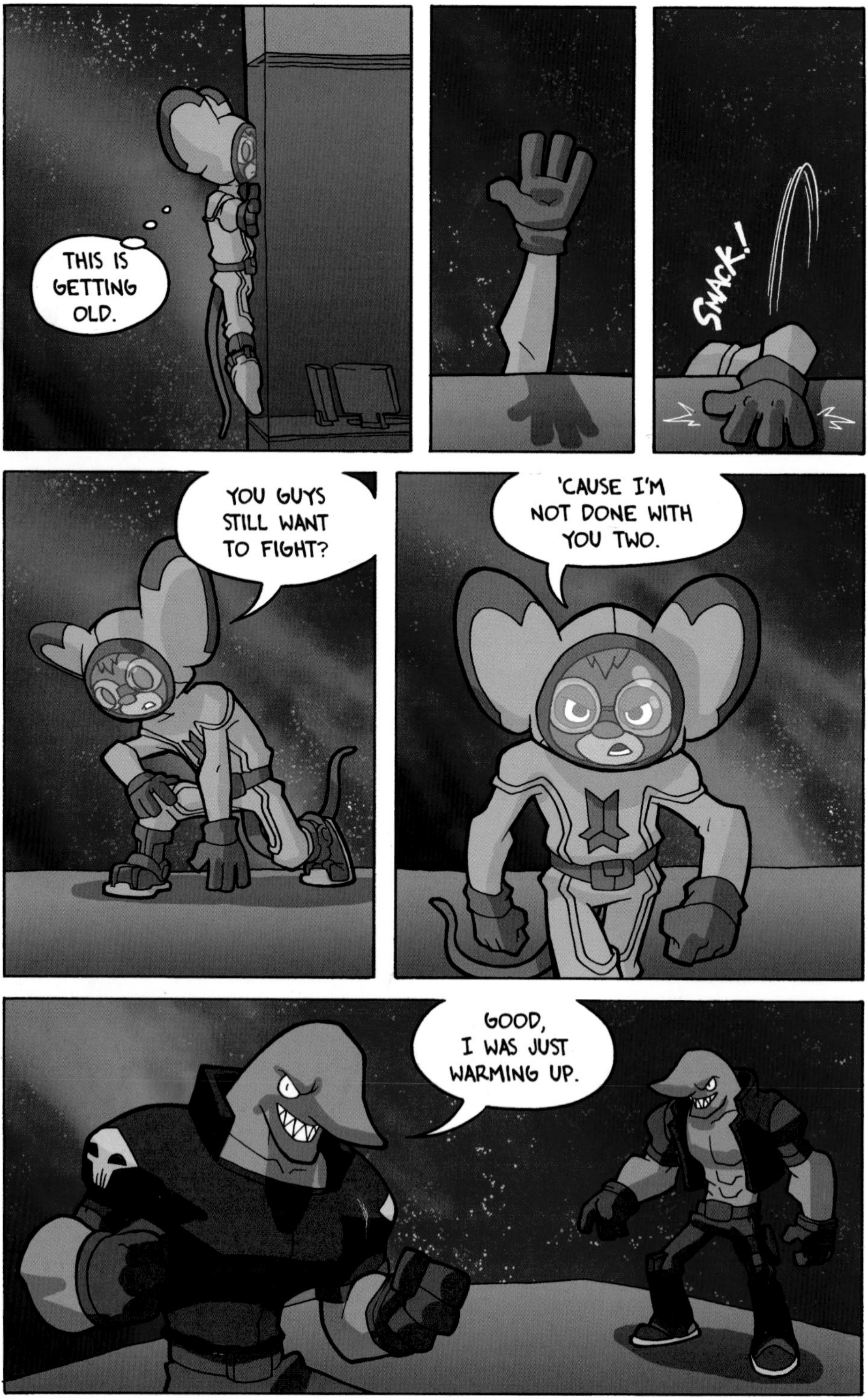
THIS IS GETTING OLD.
SMACK!
YOU GUYS STILL WANT TO FIGHT?
'CAUSE I'M NOT DONE WITH YOU TWO.
GOOD, I WAS JUST WARMING UP.

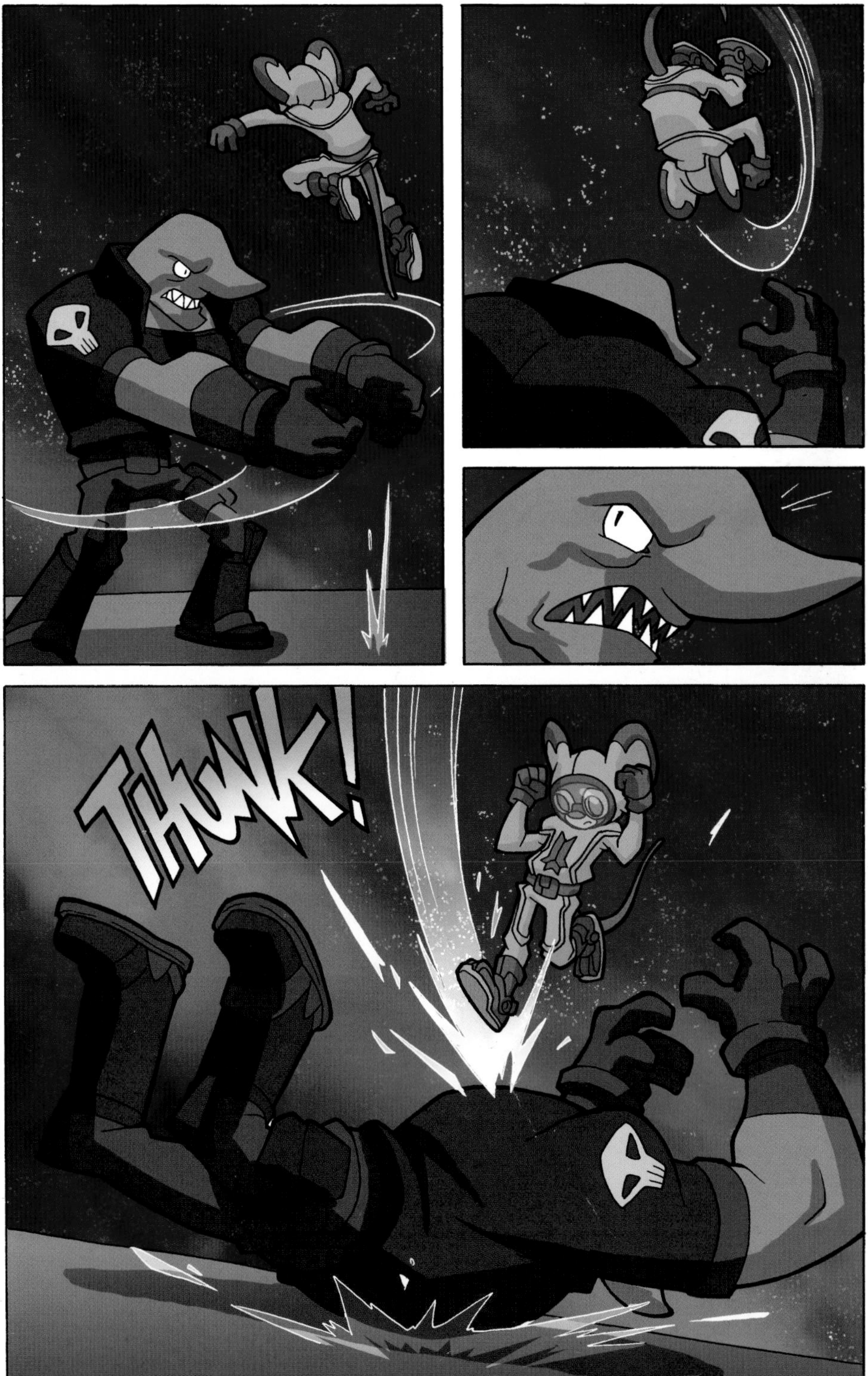
THUNK!

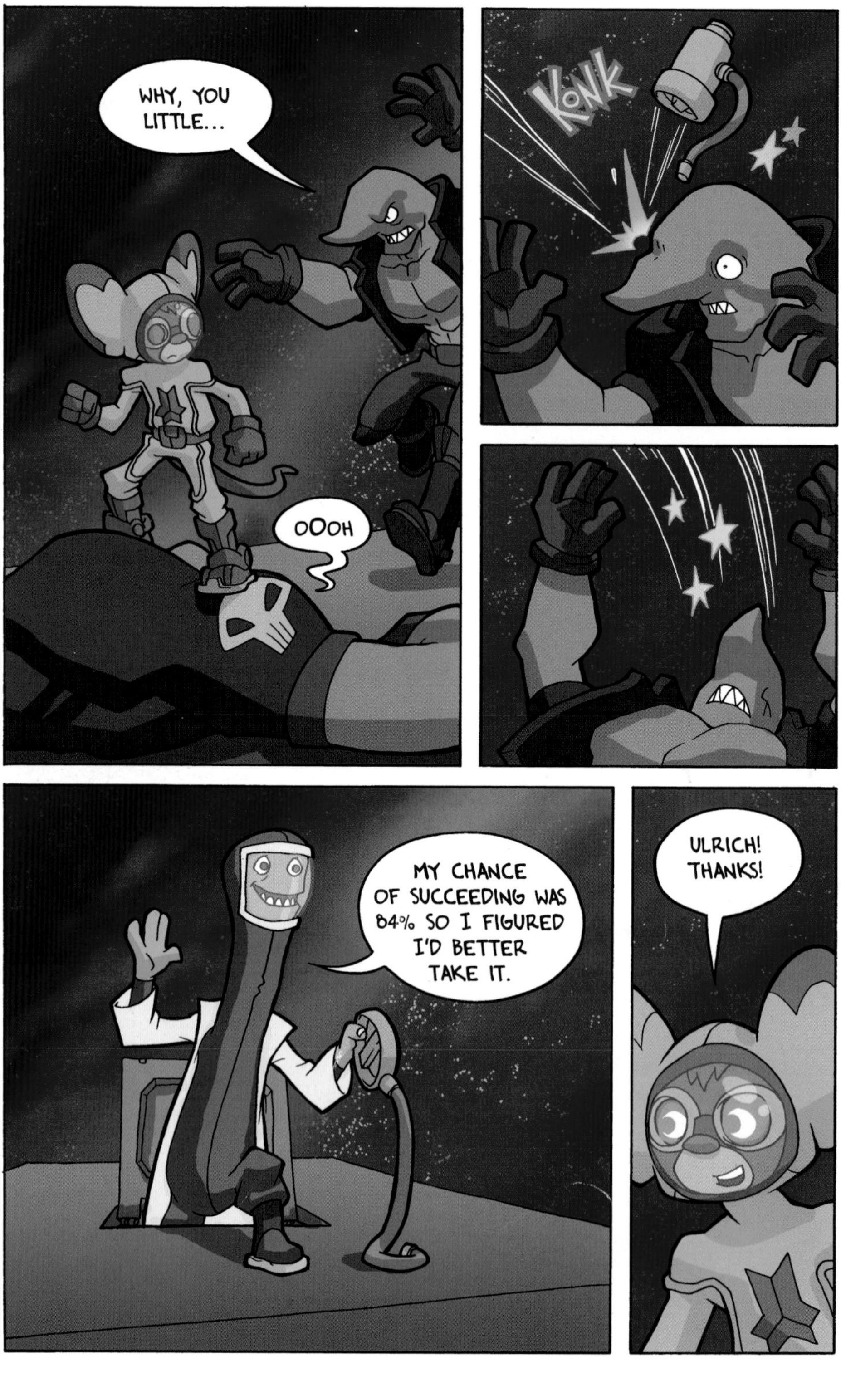
WHY, YOU LITTLE...
OOOH
KONK
MY CHANCE OF SUCCEEDING WAS 84% SO I FIGURED I'D BETTER TAKE IT.
ULRICH! THANKS!

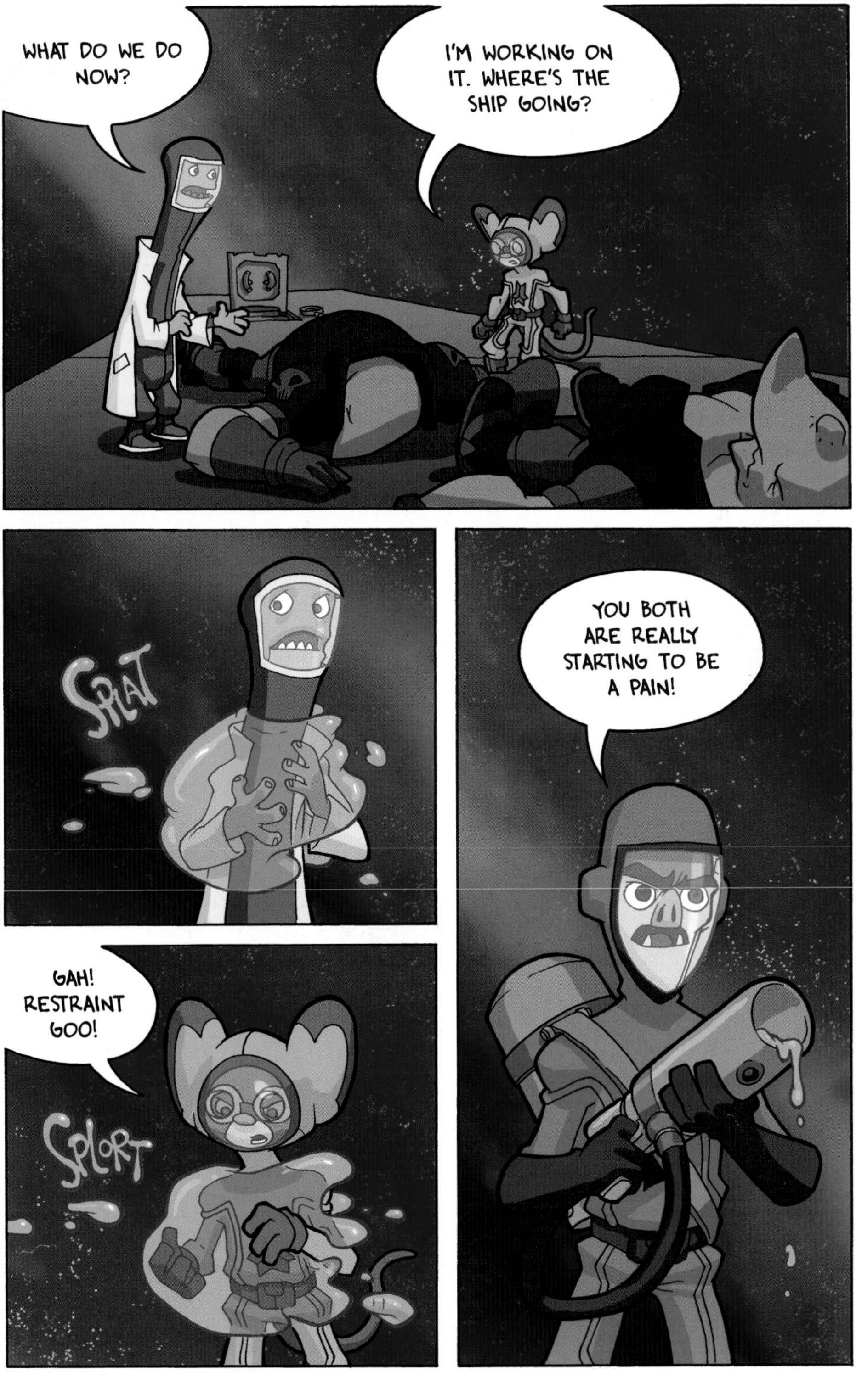
WHAT DO WE DO NOW?
I'M WORKING ON IT. WHERE'S THE SHIP GOING?
SPLAT
YOU BOTH ARE REALLY STARTING TO BE A PAIN!
GAH! RESTRAINT GOO!
SPLORT

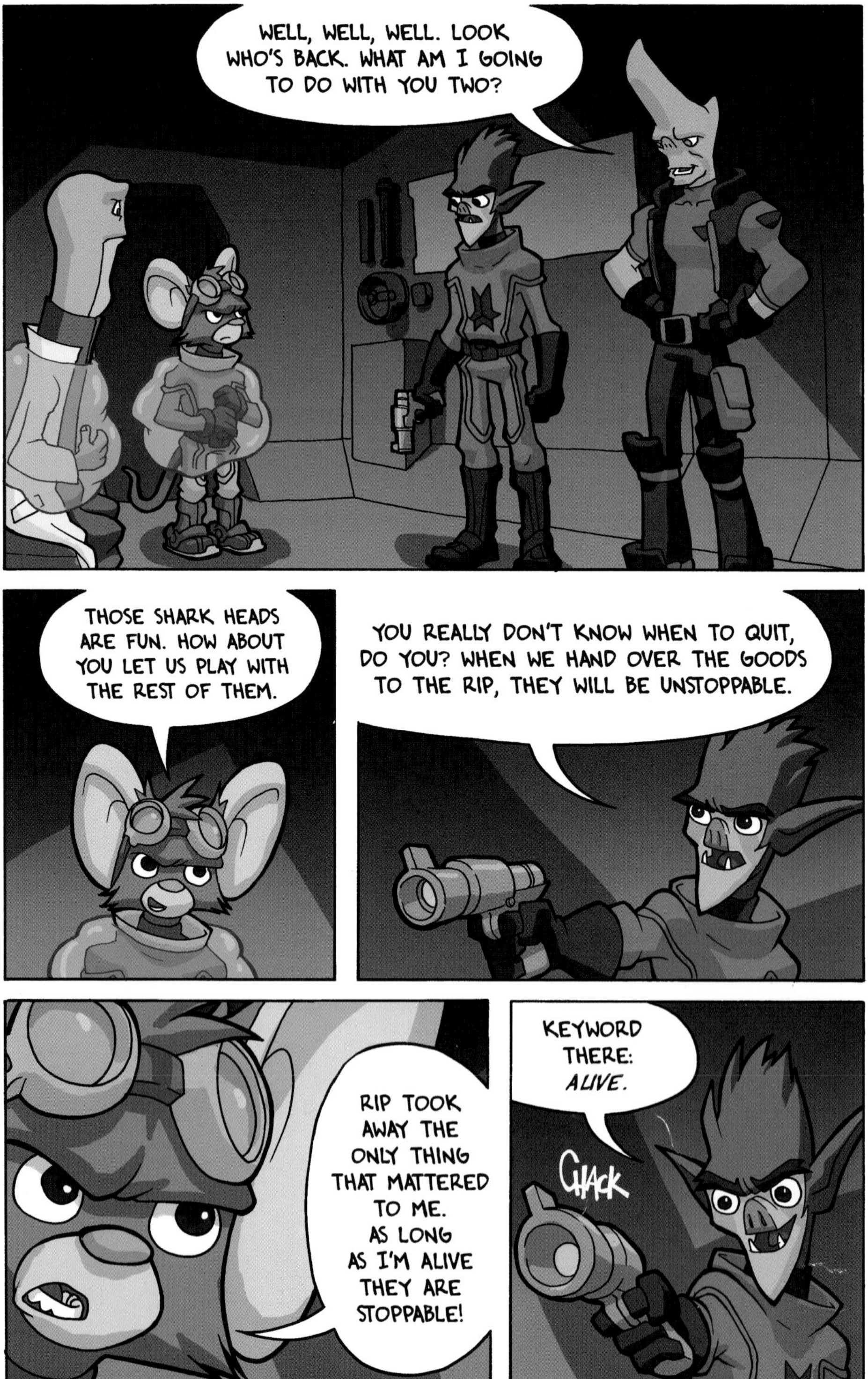
WELL, WELL, WELL. LOOK WHO'S BACK. WHAT AM I GOING TO DO WITH YOU TWO?
THOSE SHARK HEADS ARE FUN. HOW ABOUT YOU LET US PLAY WITH THE REST OF THEM.
YOU REALLY DON'T KNOW WHEN TO QUIT, DO YOU? WHEN WE HAND OVER THE GOODS TO THE RIP, THEY WILL BE UNSTOPPABLE.
RIP TOOK AWAY THE ONLY THING THAT MATTERED TO ME. AS LONG AS I'M ALIVE THEY ARE STOPPABLE!
KEYWORD THERE: *ALIVE*.
CHACK

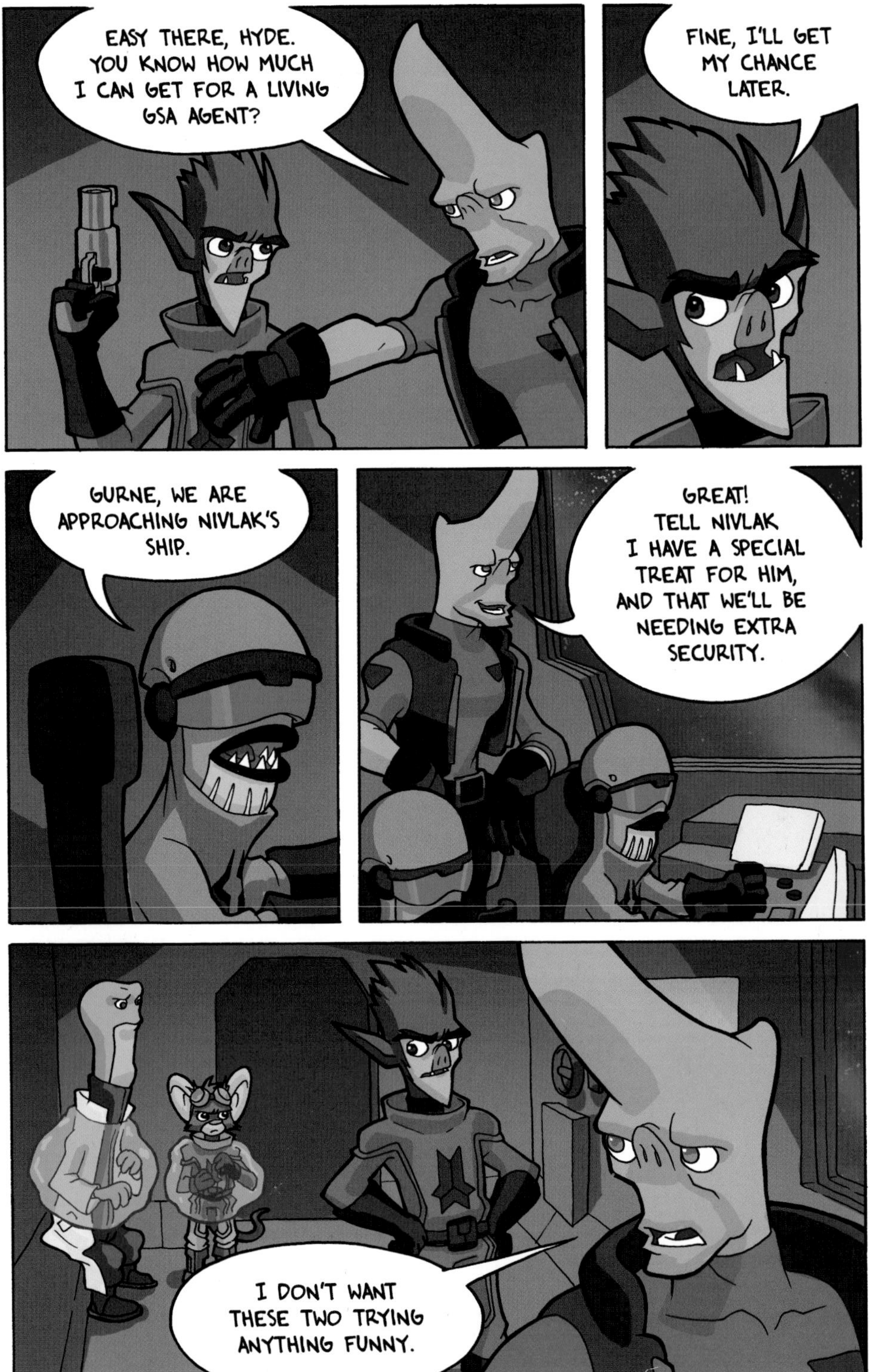
EASY THERE, HYDE. YOU KNOW HOW MUCH I CAN GET FOR A LIVING GSA AGENT?
FINE, I'LL GET MY CHANCE LATER.
GURNE, WE ARE APPROACHING NIVLAK'S SHIP.
GREAT! TELL NIVLAK I HAVE A SPECIAL TREAT FOR HIM, AND THAT WE'LL BE NEEDING EXTRA SECURITY.
I DON'T WANT THESE TWO TRYING ANYTHING FUNNY.

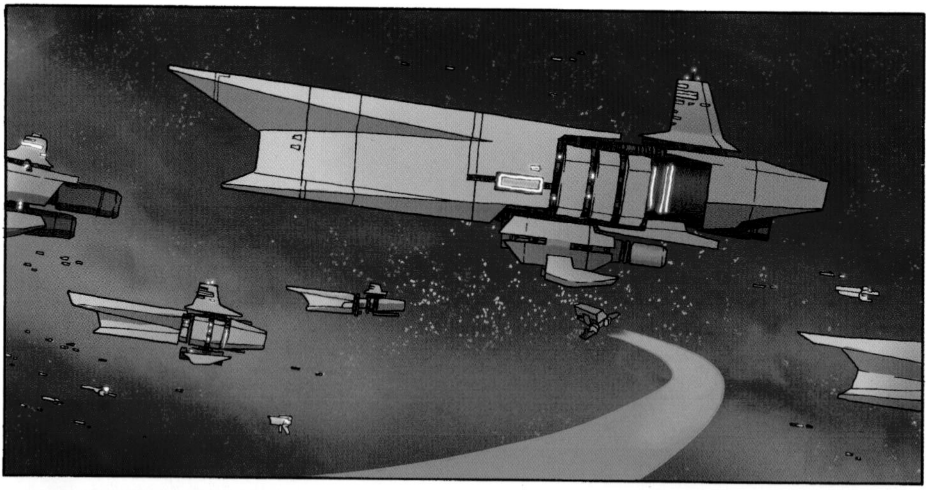

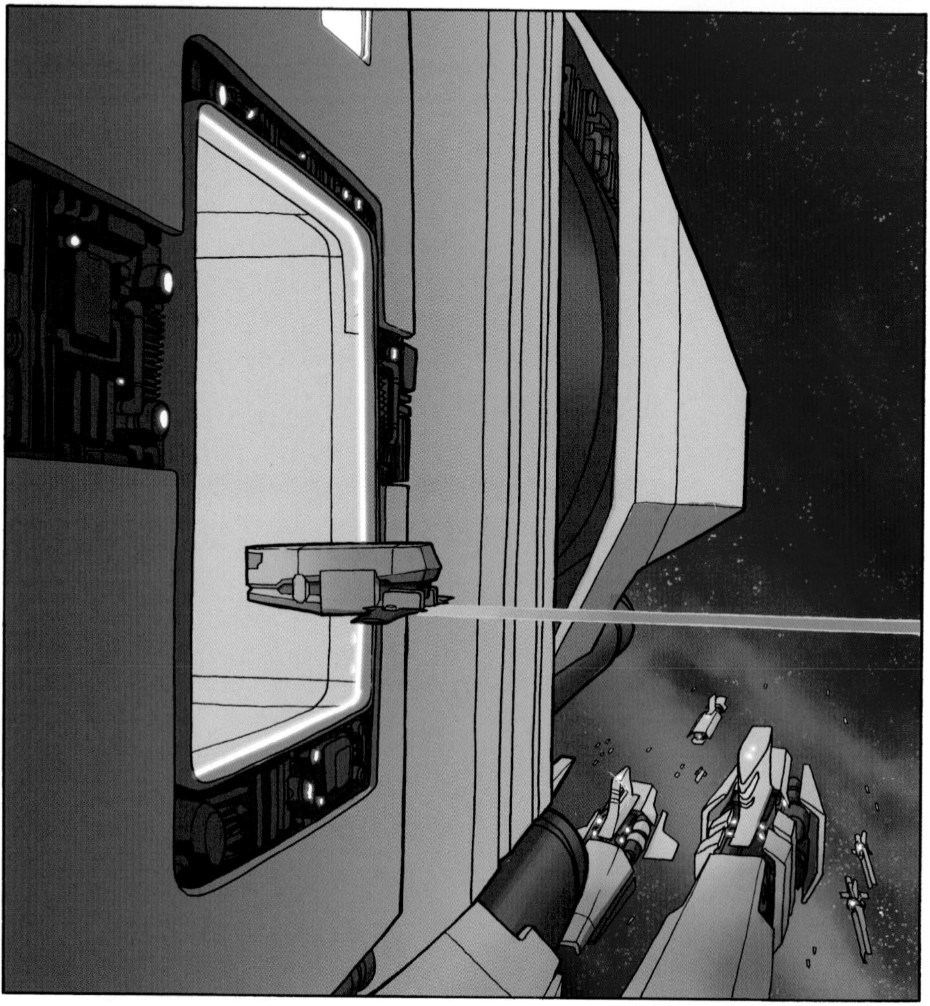

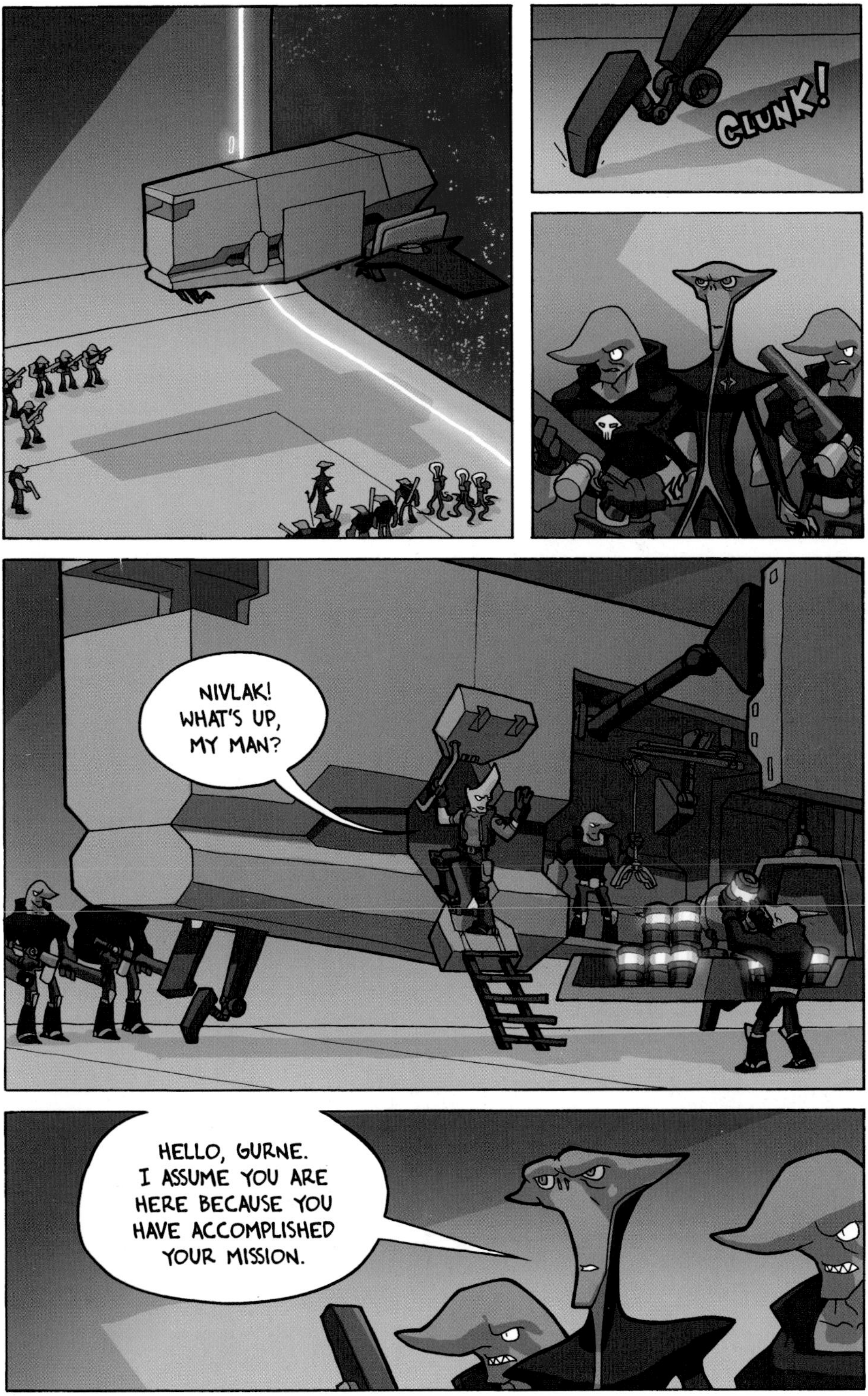
CLUNK!
NIVLAK! WHAT'S UP, MY MAN?
HELLO, GURNE. I ASSUME YOU ARE HERE BECAUSE YOU HAVE ACCOMPLISHED YOUR MISSION.

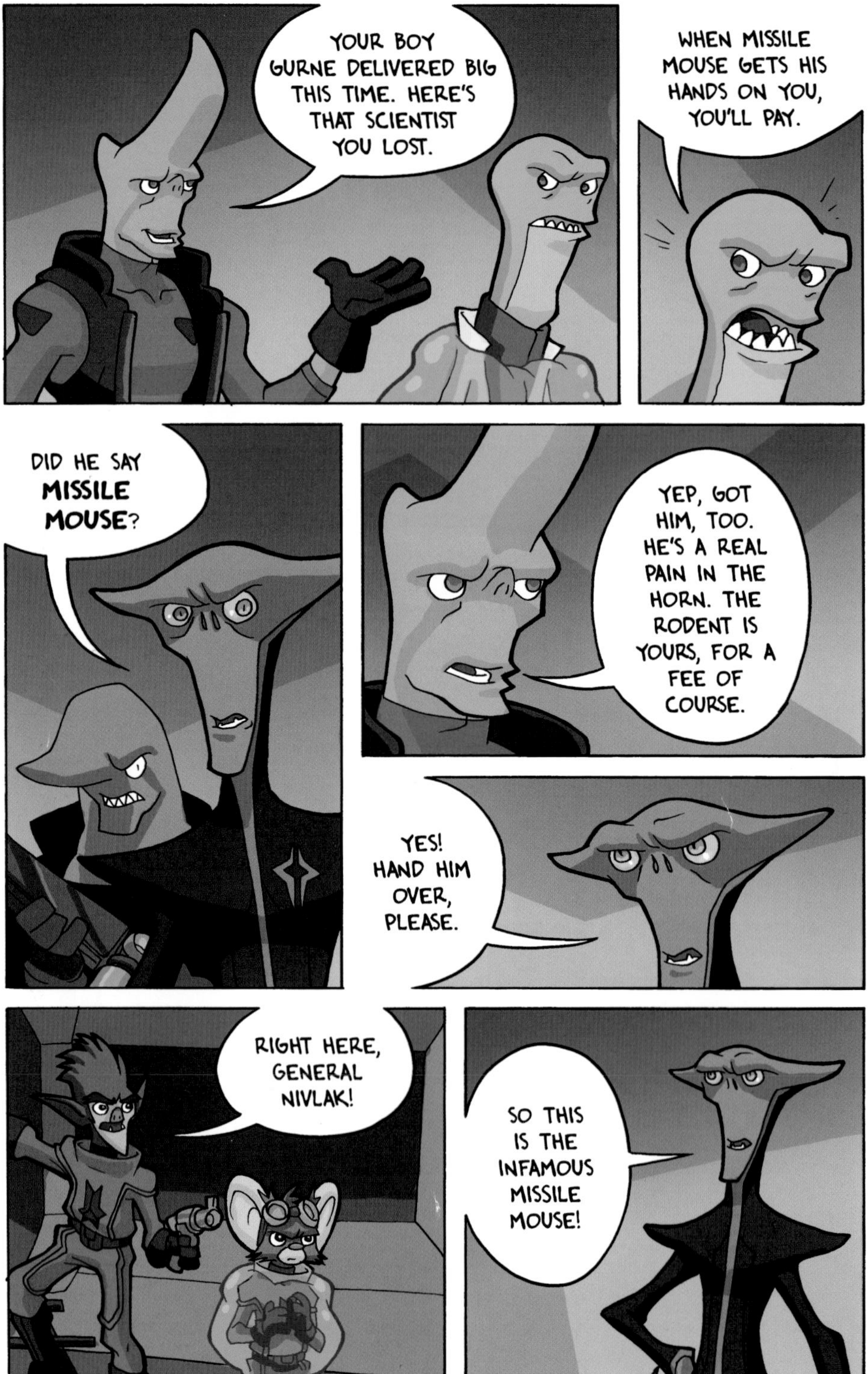
YOUR BOY GURNE DELIVERED BIG THIS TIME. HERE'S THAT SCIENTIST YOU LOST.
WHEN MISSILE MOUSE GETS HIS HANDS ON YOU, YOU'LL PAY.
DID HE SAY **MISSILE MOUSE**?
YEP, GOT HIM, TOO. HE'S A REAL PAIN IN THE HORN. THE RODENT IS YOURS, FOR A FEE OF COURSE.
YES! HAND HIM OVER, PLEASE.
RIGHT HERE, GENERAL NIVLAK!
SO THIS IS THE INFAMOUS MISSILE MOUSE!

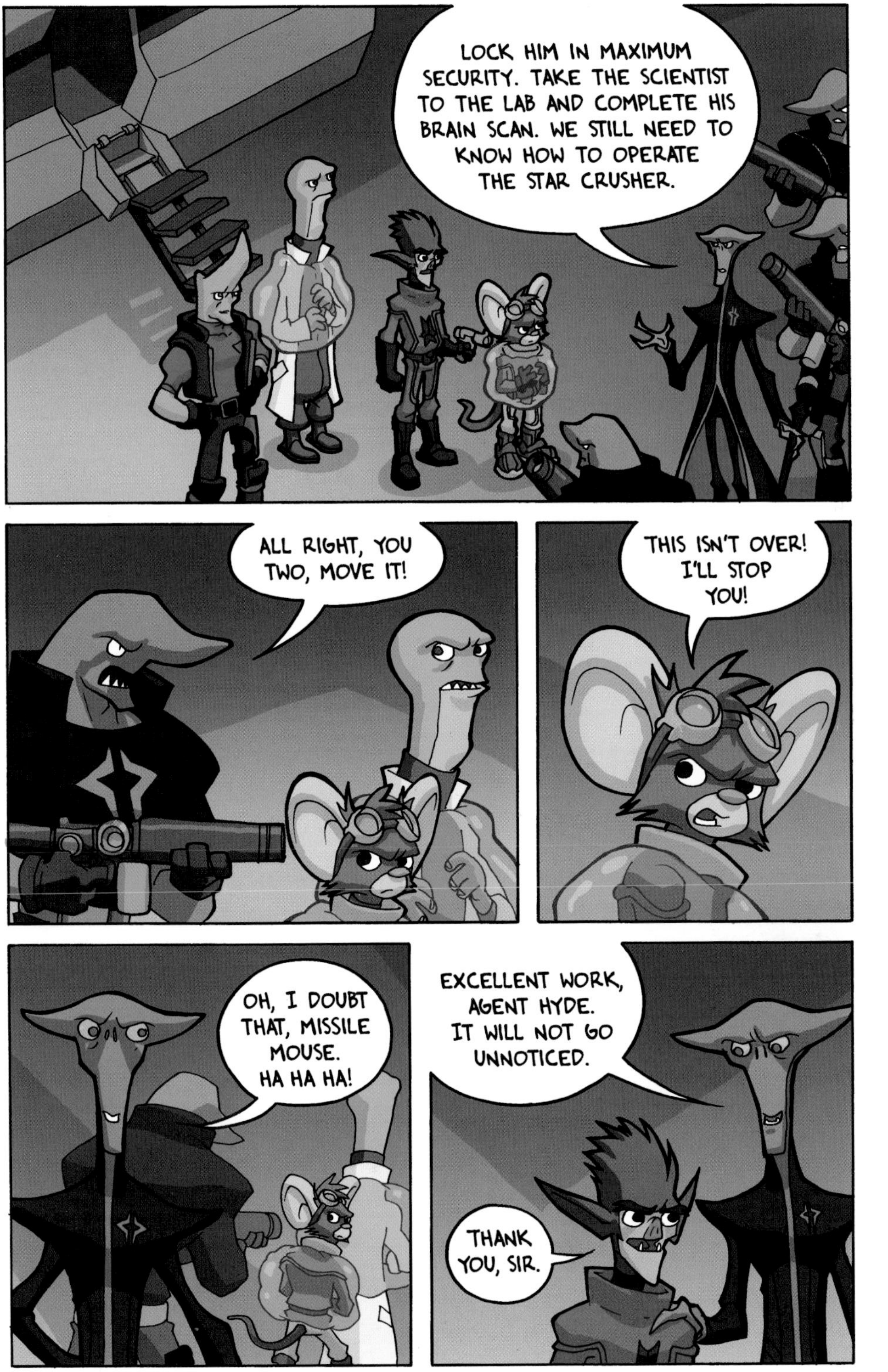
LOCK HIM IN MAXIMUM SECURITY. TAKE THE SCIENTIST TO THE LAB AND COMPLETE HIS BRAIN SCAN. WE STILL NEED TO KNOW HOW TO OPERATE THE STAR CRUSHER.
ALL RIGHT, YOU TWO, MOVE IT!
THIS ISN'T OVER! I'LL STOP YOU!
OH, I DOUBT THAT, MISSILE MOUSE. HA HA HA!
EXCELLENT WORK, AGENT HYDE. IT WILL NOT GO UNNOTICED.
THANK YOU, SIR.

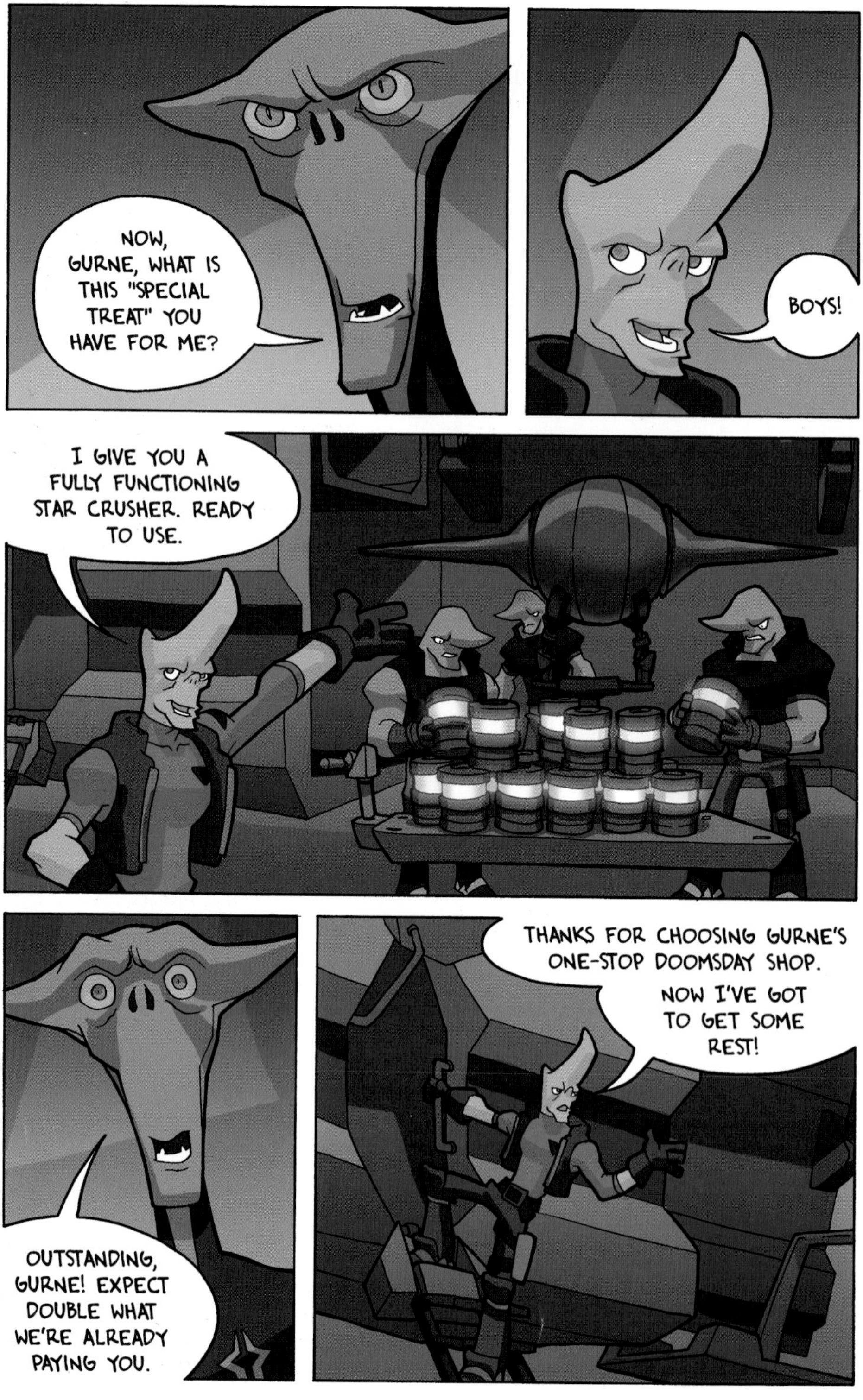
NOW, GURNE, WHAT IS THIS "SPECIAL TREAT" YOU HAVE FOR ME?
BOYS!
I GIVE YOU A FULLY FUNCTIONING STAR CRUSHER. READY TO USE.
OUTSTANDING, GURNE! EXPECT DOUBLE WHAT WE'RE ALREADY PAYING YOU.
THANKS FOR CHOOSING GURNE'S ONE-STOP DOOMSDAY SHOP.
NOW I'VE GOT TO GET SOME REST!

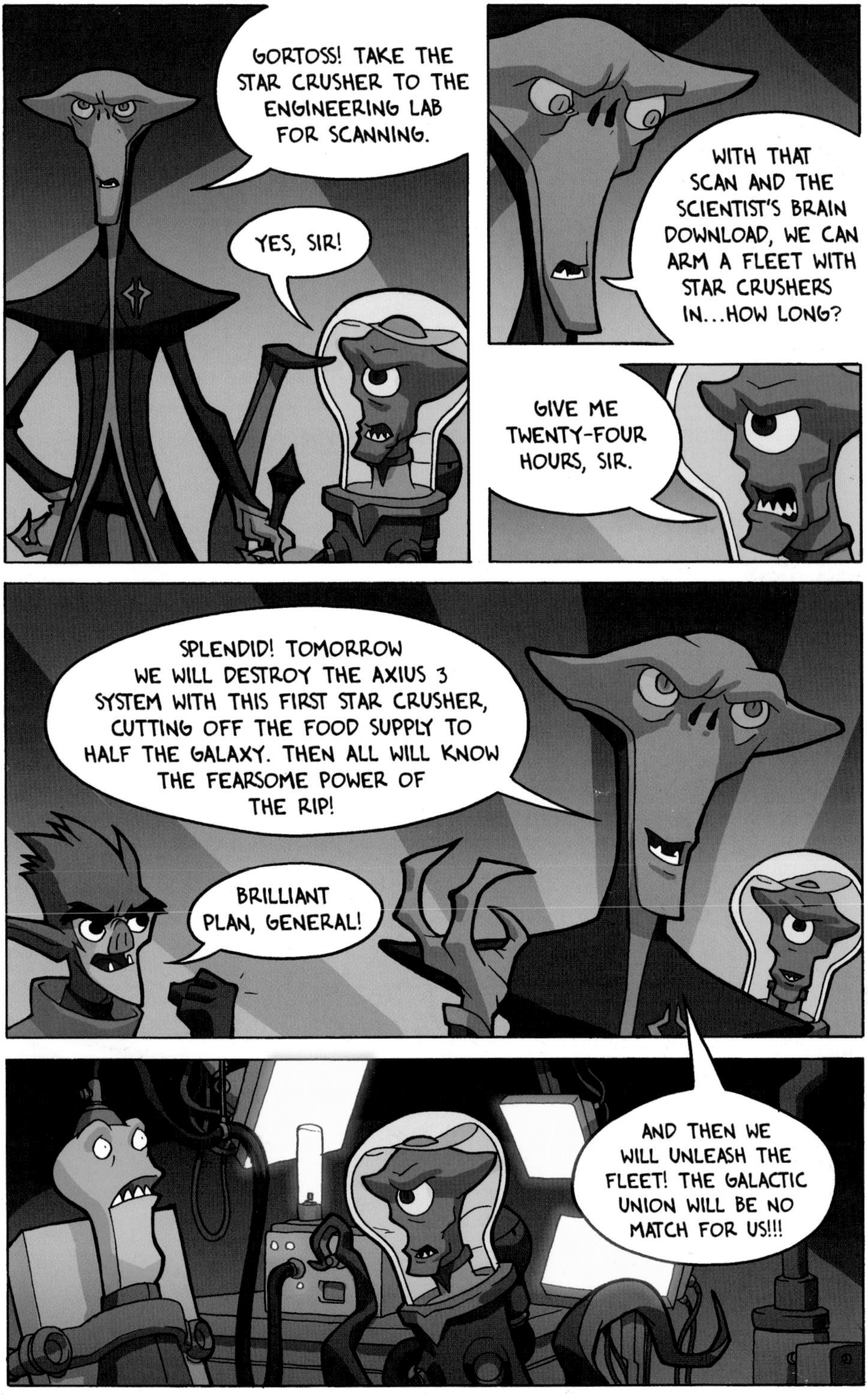
GORTOSS! TAKE THE STAR CRUSHER TO THE ENGINEERING LAB FOR SCANNING.
YES, SIR!
WITH THAT SCAN AND THE SCIENTIST'S BRAIN DOWNLOAD, WE CAN ARM A FLEET WITH STAR CRUSHERS IN...HOW LONG?
GIVE ME TWENTY-FOUR HOURS, SIR.
SPLENDID! TOMORROW WE WILL DESTROY THE AXIUS 3 SYSTEM WITH THIS FIRST STAR CRUSHER, CUTTING OFF THE FOOD SUPPLY TO HALF THE GALAXY. THEN ALL WILL KNOW THE FEARSOME POWER OF THE RIP!
BRILLIANT PLAN, GENERAL!
AND THEN WE WILL UNLEASH THE FLEET! THE GALACTIC UNION WILL BE NO MATCH FOR US!!!

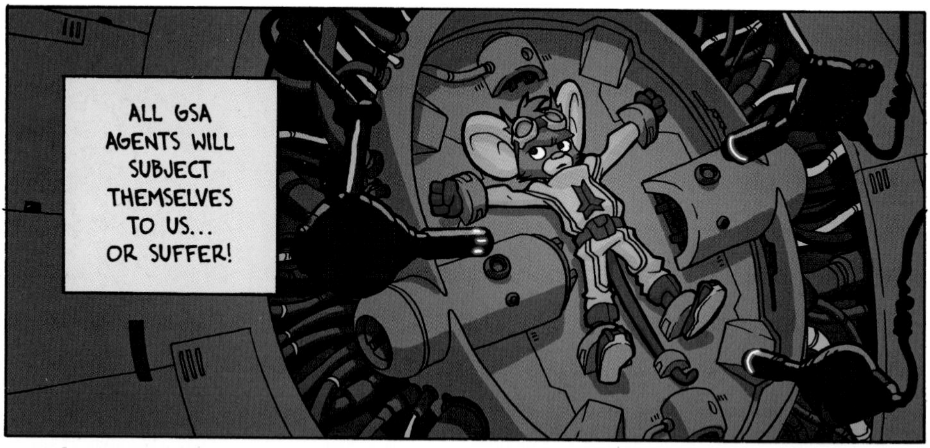
ALL GSA AGENTS WILL SUBJECT THEMSELVES TO US... OR SUFFER!

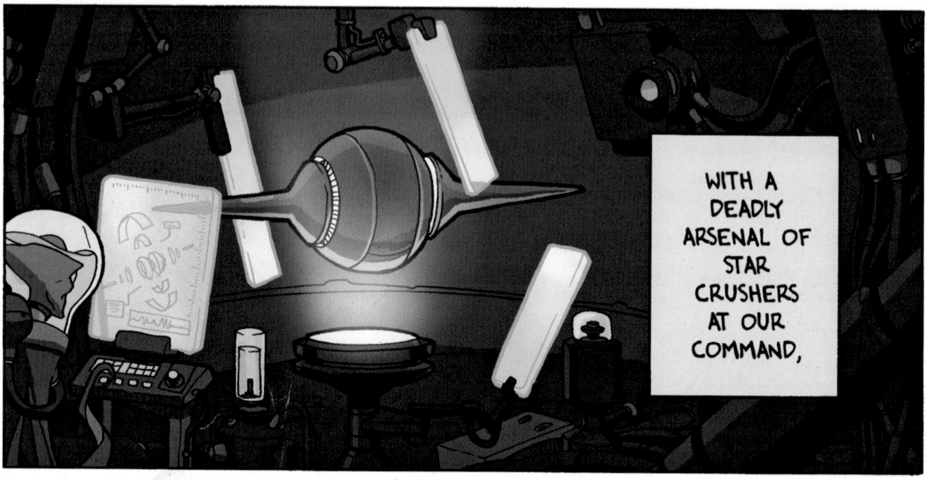
WITH A DEADLY ARSENAL OF STAR CRUSHERS AT OUR COMMAND,

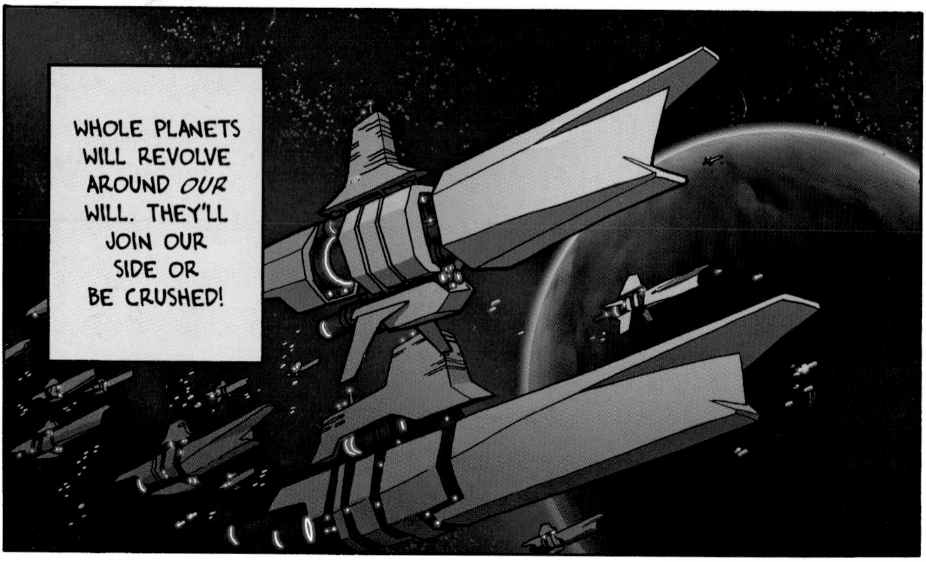
WHOLE PLANETS WILL REVOLVE AROUND *OUR* WILL. THEY'LL JOIN OUR SIDE OR BE CRUSHED!

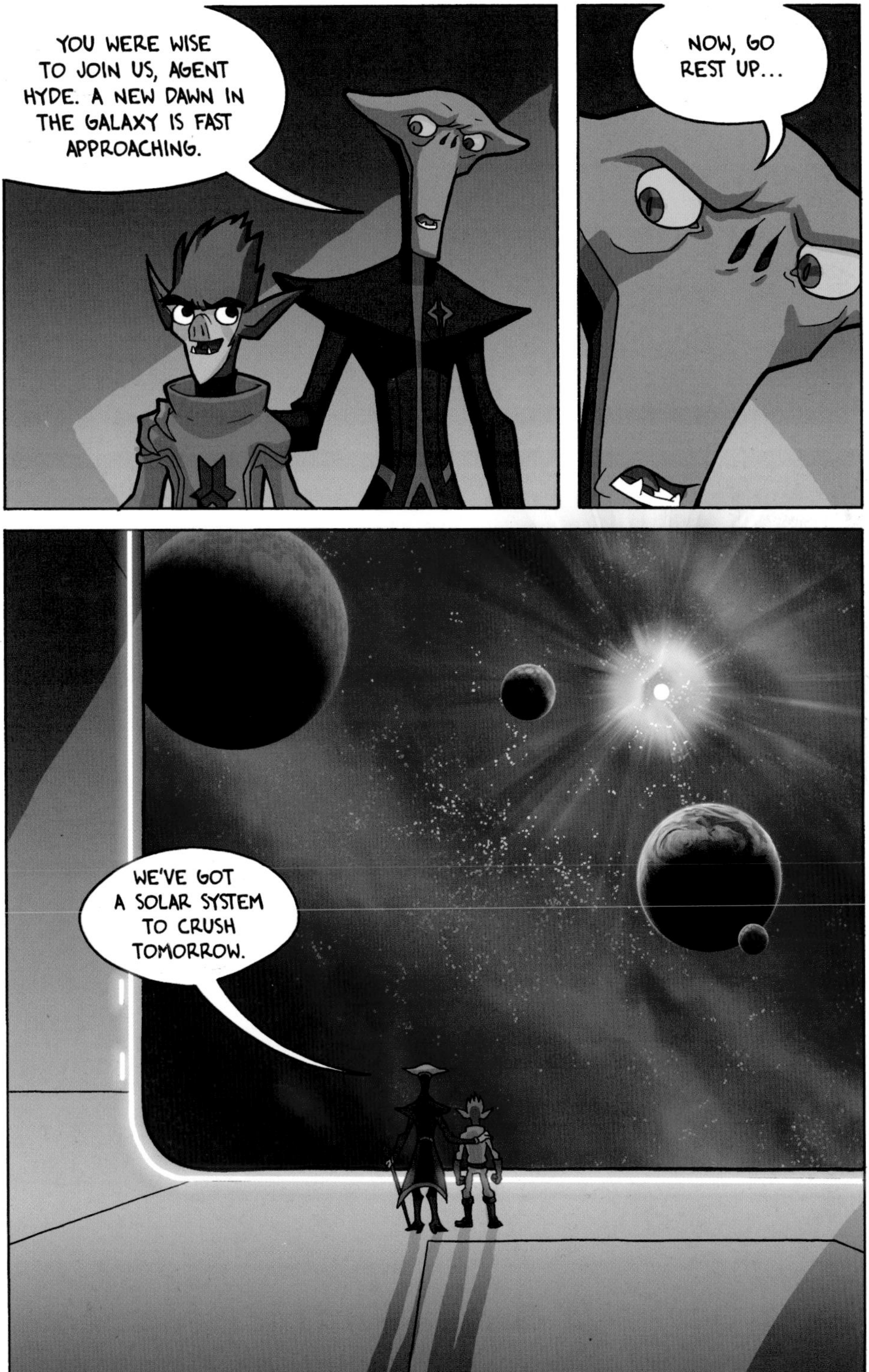
YOU WERE WISE TO JOIN US, AGENT HYDE. A NEW DAWN IN THE GALAXY IS FAST APPROACHING.
NOW, GO REST UP...
WE'VE GOT A SOLAR SYSTEM TO CRUSH TOMORROW.

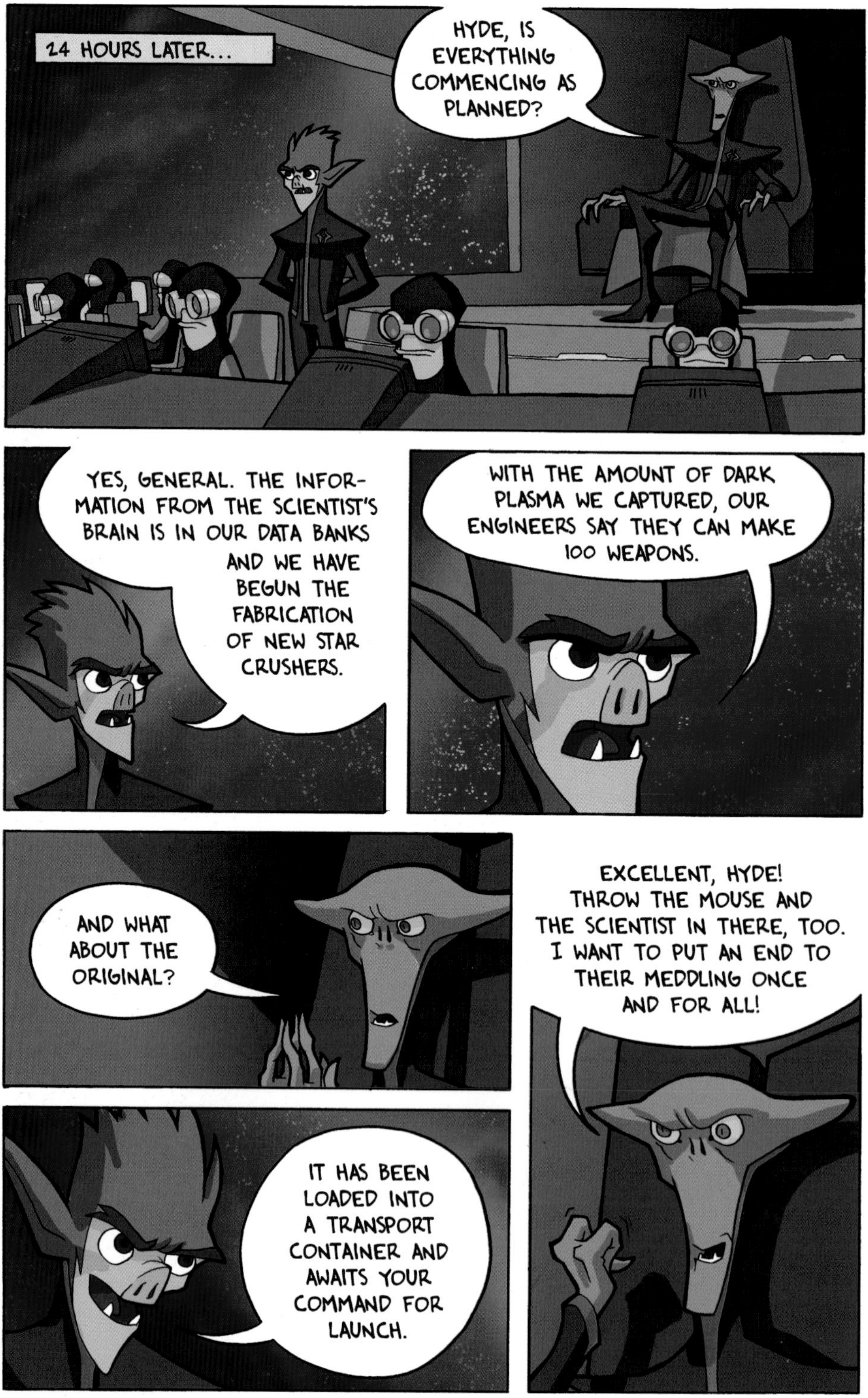
24 HOURS LATER...
HYDE, IS EVERYTHING COMMENCING AS PLANNED?
YES, GENERAL. THE INFOR-MATION FROM THE SCIENTIST'S BRAIN IS IN OUR DATA BANKS AND WE HAVE BEGUN THE FABRICATION OF NEW STAR CRUSHERS.
WITH THE AMOUNT OF DARK PLASMA WE CAPTURED, OUR ENGINEERS SAY THEY CAN MAKE 100 WEAPONS.
AND WHAT ABOUT THE ORIGINAL?
IT HAS BEEN LOADED INTO A TRANSPORT CONTAINER AND AWAITS YOUR COMMAND FOR LAUNCH.
EXCELLENT, HYDE! THROW THE MOUSE AND THE SCIENTIST IN THERE, TOO. I WANT TO PUT AN END TO THEIR MEDDLING ONCE AND FOR ALL!

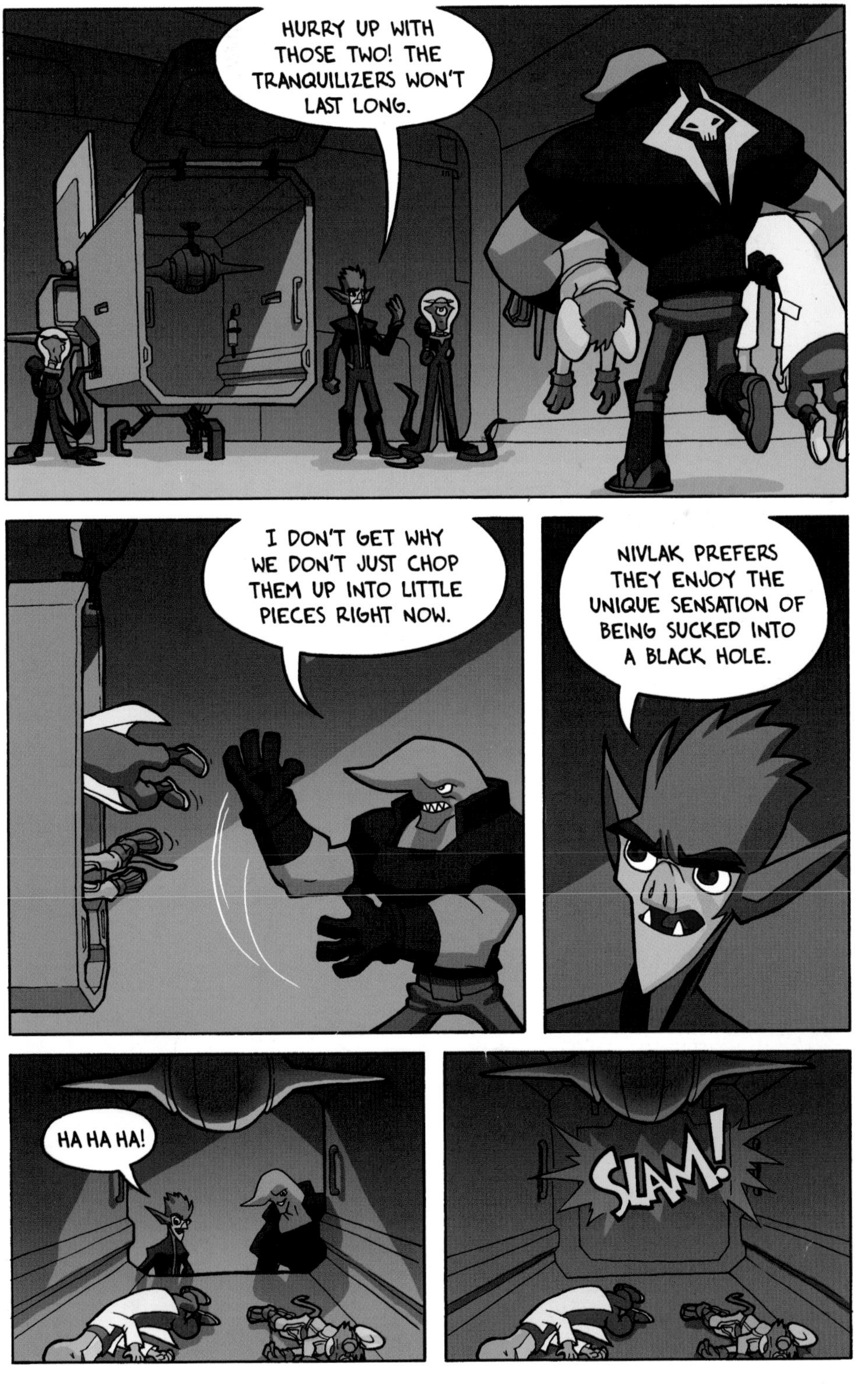
HURRY UP WITH THOSE TWO! THE TRANQUILIZERS WON'T LAST LONG.
I DON'T GET WHY WE DON'T JUST CHOP THEM UP INTO LITTLE PIECES RIGHT NOW.
NIVLAK PREFERS THEY ENJOY THE UNIQUE SENSATION OF BEING SUCKED INTO A BLACK HOLE.
HA HA HA!
SLAM!

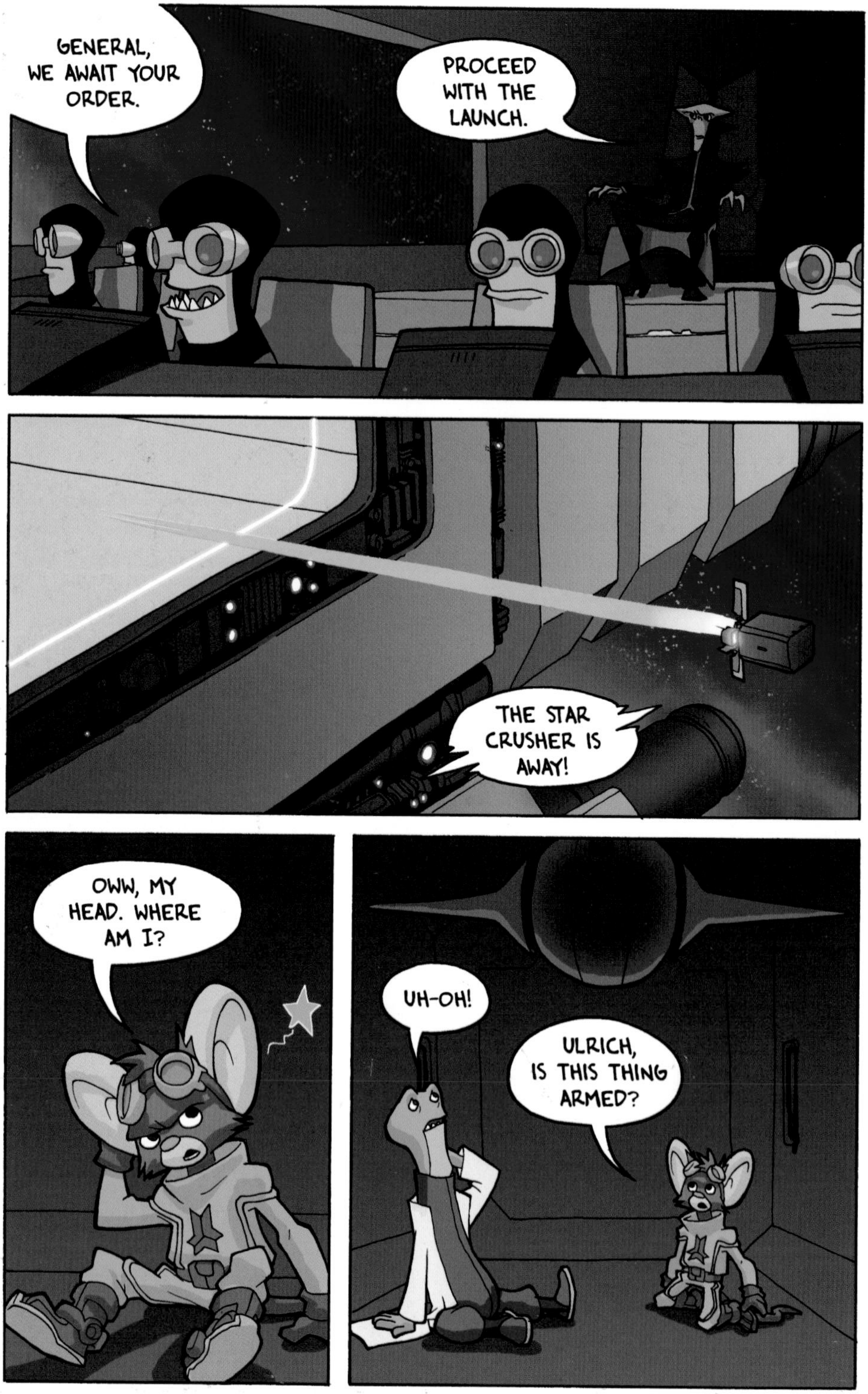
GENERAL, WE AWAIT YOUR ORDER.
PROCEED WITH THE LAUNCH.
THE STAR CRUSHER IS AWAY!
OWW, MY HEAD. WHERE AM I?
UH-OH!
ULRICH, IS THIS THING ARMED?

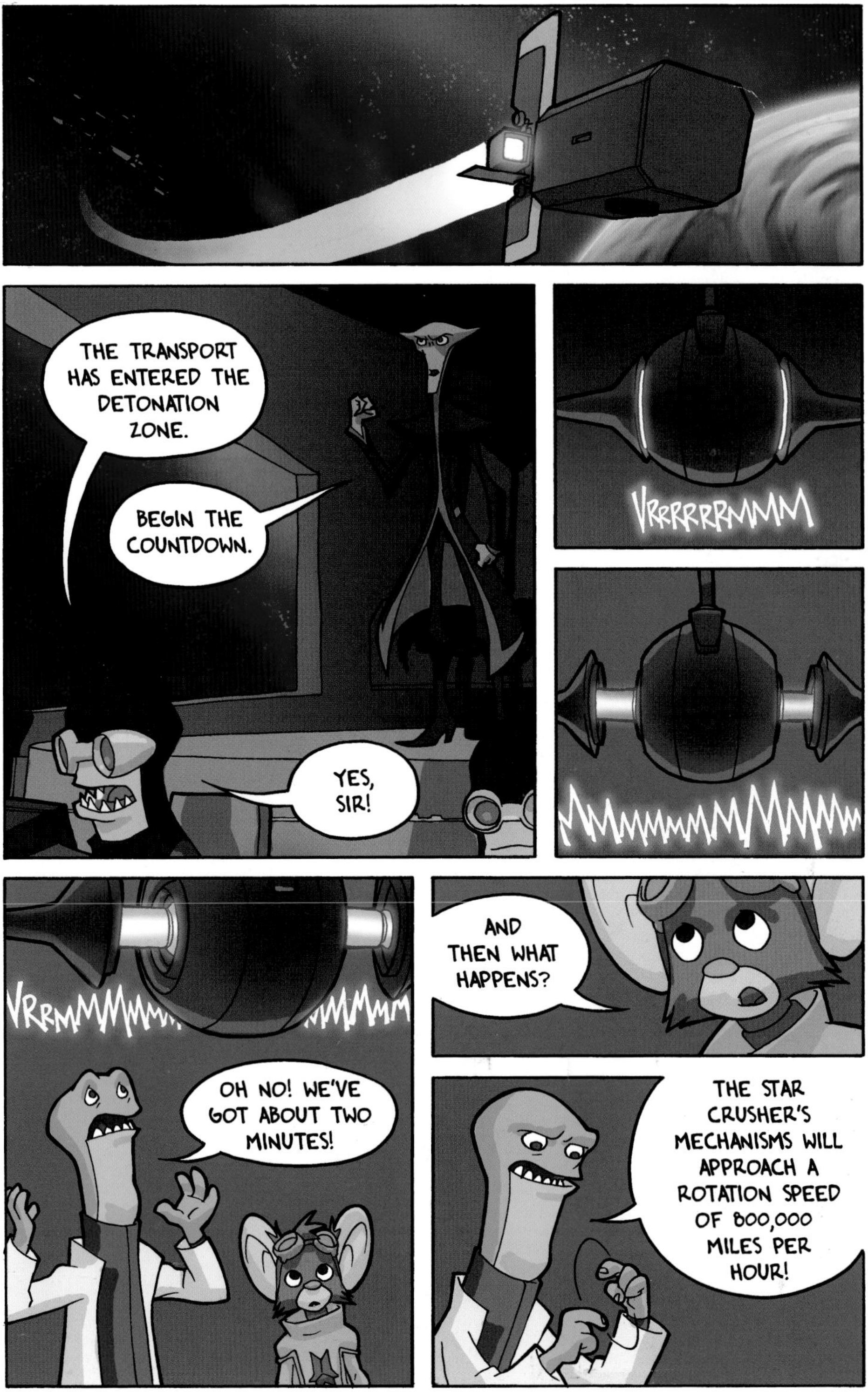
THE TRANSPORT HAS ENTERED THE DETONATION ZONE.
BEGIN THE COUNTDOWN.
YES, SIR!
VRRRRRRMMM
MMMMMMMMMMMMMMMMM
VRRMMMMMM
MMMMM
AND THEN WHAT HAPPENS?
OH NO! WE'VE GOT ABOUT TWO MINUTES!
THE STAR CRUSHER'S MECHANISMS WILL APPROACH A ROTATION SPEED OF 800,000 MILES PER HOUR!

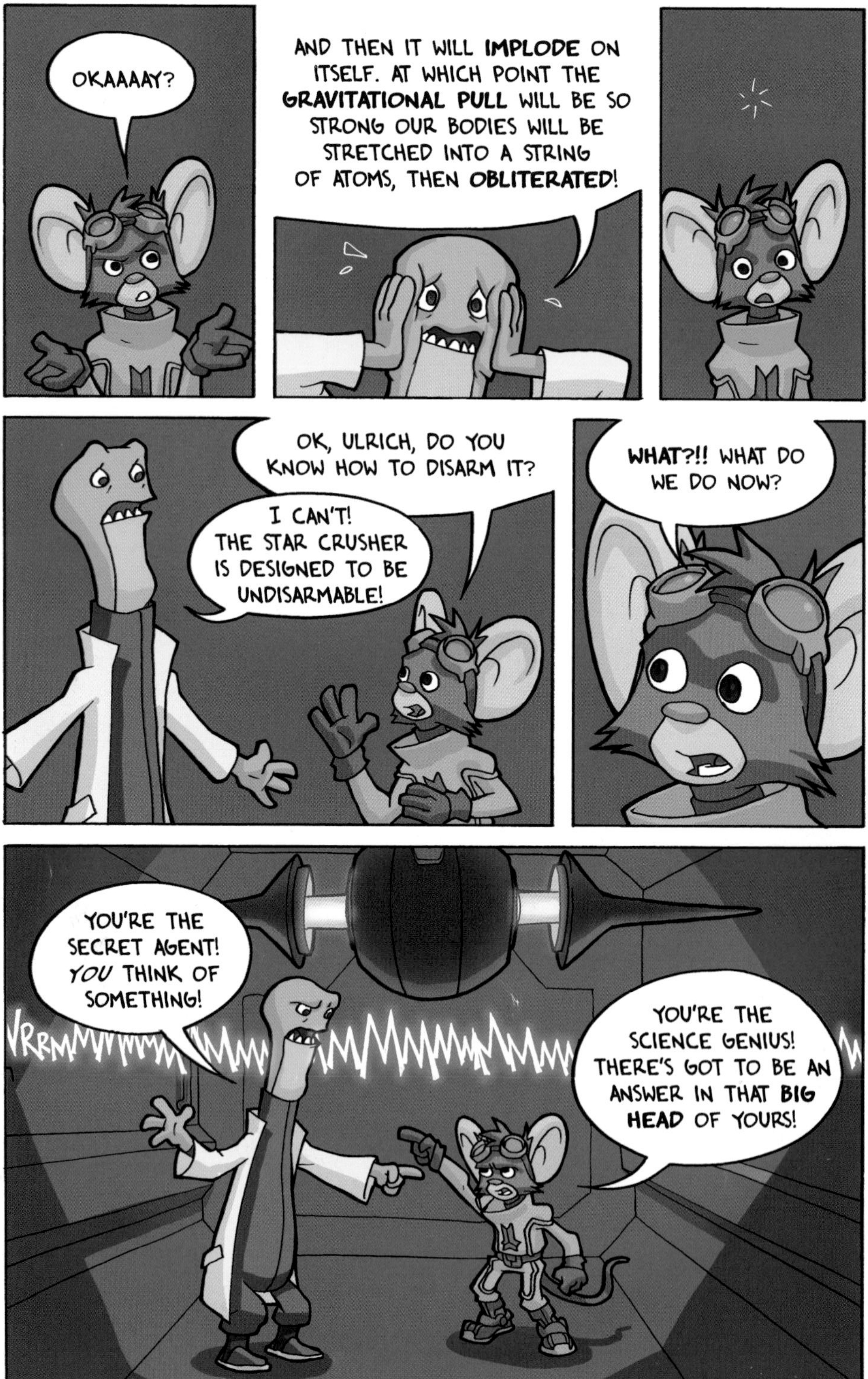
OKAAAAY?
AND THEN IT WILL IMPLODE ON ITSELF. AT WHICH POINT THE GRAVITATIONAL PULL WILL BE SO STRONG OUR BODIES WILL BE STRETCHED INTO A STRING OF ATOMS, THEN OBLITERATED!
OK, ULRICH, DO YOU KNOW HOW TO DISARM IT?
I CAN'T! THE STAR CRUSHER IS DESIGNED TO BE UNDISARMABLE!
WHAT?!! WHAT DO WE DO NOW?
YOU'RE THE SECRET AGENT! YOU THINK OF SOMETHING!
VRRMMMMMMM
YOU'RE THE SCIENCE GENIUS! THERE'S GOT TO BE AN ANSWER IN THAT BIG HEAD OF YOURS!

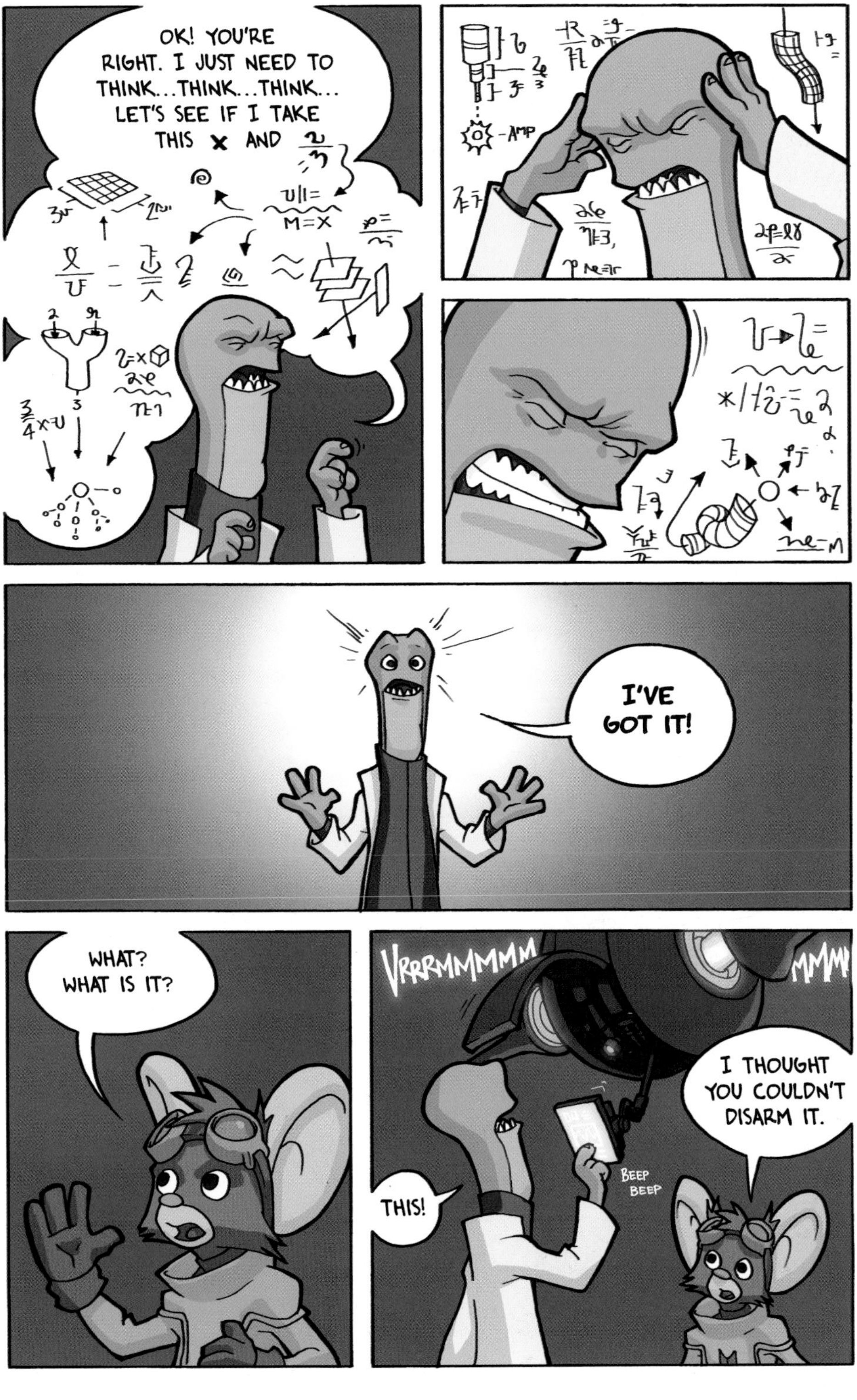
OK! YOU'RE RIGHT. I JUST NEED TO THINK...THINK...THINK... LET'S SEE IF I TAKE THIS x AND
I'VE GOT IT!
WHAT? WHAT IS IT?
VRRRMMMMM
MMM
I THOUGHT YOU COULDN'T DISARM IT.
THIS!
BEEP BEEP

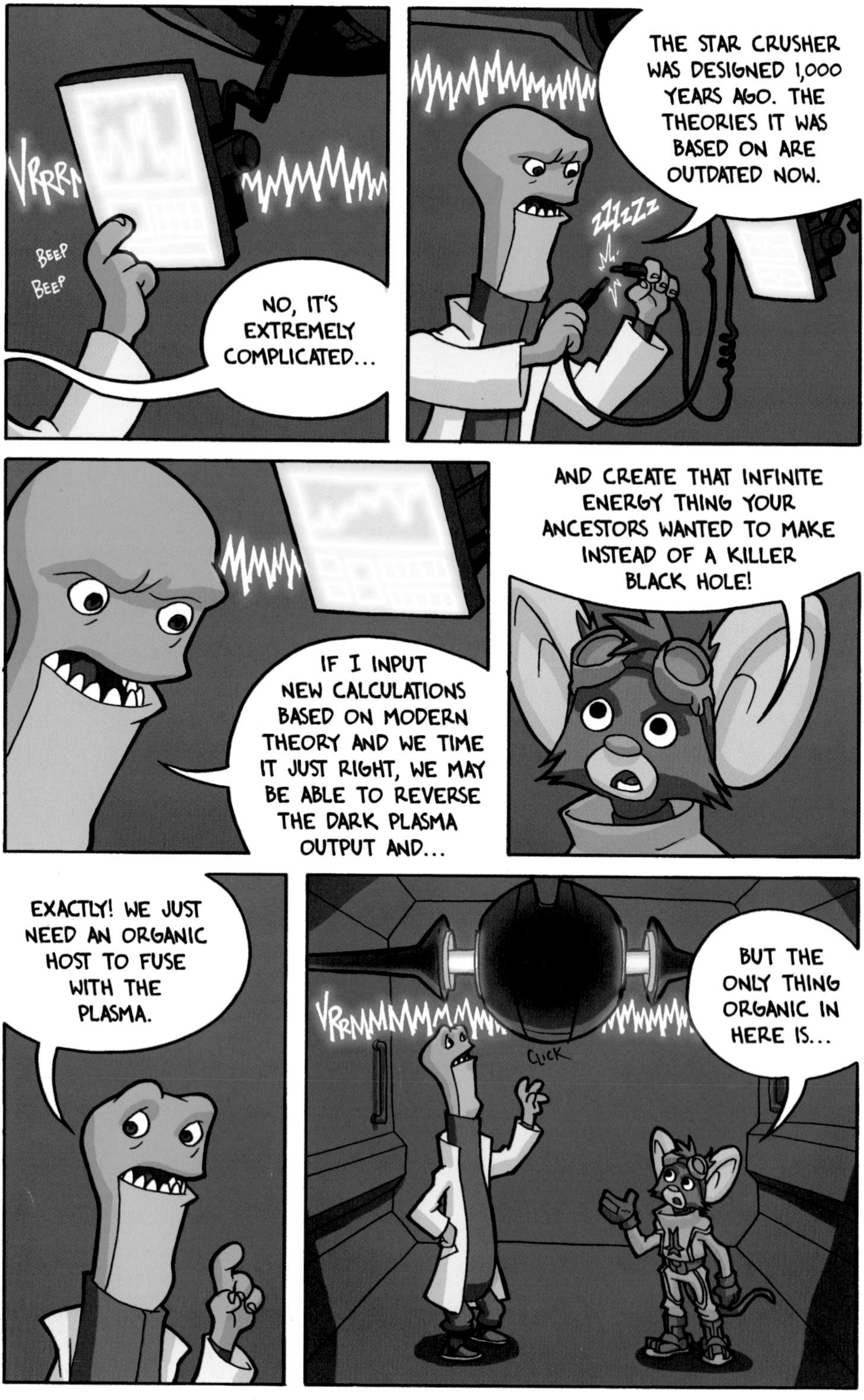
VRRR
BEEP
BEEP
NO, IT'S EXTREMELY COMPLICATED...
THE STAR CRUSHER WAS DESIGNED 1,000 YEARS AGO. THE THEORIES IT WAS BASED ON ARE OUTDATED NOW.
IF I INPUT NEW CALCULATIONS BASED ON MODERN THEORY AND WE TIME IT JUST RIGHT, WE MAY BE ABLE TO REVERSE THE DARK PLASMA OUTPUT AND...
AND CREATE THAT INFINITE ENERGY THING YOUR ANCESTORS WANTED TO MAKE INSTEAD OF A KILLER BLACK HOLE!
EXACTLY! WE JUST NEED AN ORGANIC HOST TO FUSE WITH THE PLASMA.
CLICK
BUT THE ONLY THING ORGANIC IN HERE IS...

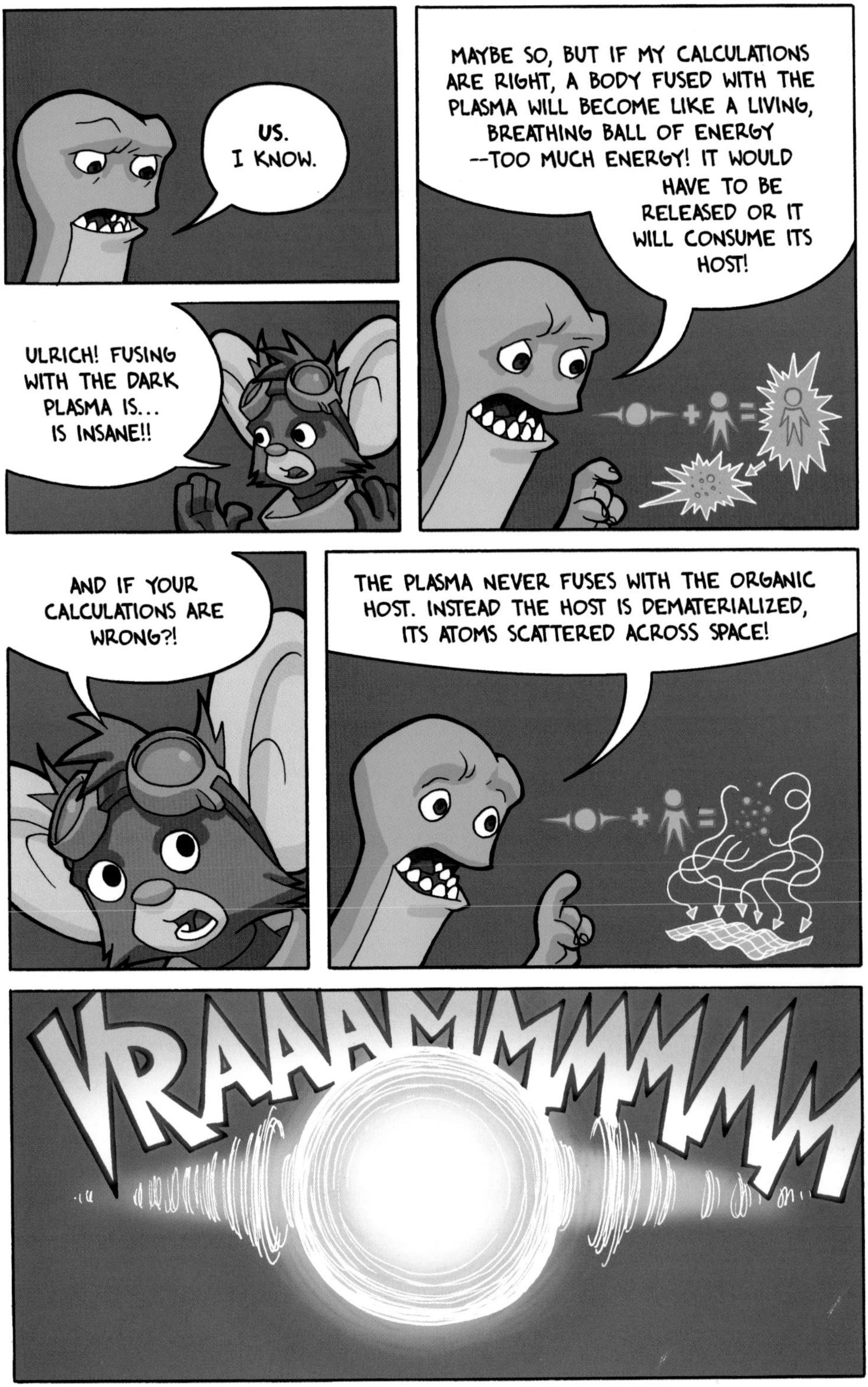
US. I KNOW.
ULRICH! FUSING WITH THE DARK PLASMA IS... IS INSANE!!
MAYBE SO, BUT IF MY CALCULATIONS ARE RIGHT, A BODY FUSED WITH THE PLASMA WILL BECOME LIKE A LIVING, BREATHING BALL OF ENERGY --TOO MUCH ENERGY! IT WOULD HAVE TO BE RELEASED OR IT WILL CONSUME ITS HOST!
AND IF YOUR CALCULATIONS ARE WRONG?!
THE PLASMA NEVER FUSES WITH THE ORGANIC HOST. INSTEAD THE HOST IS DEMATERIALIZED, ITS ATOMS SCATTERED ACROSS SPACE!
VRAAAMMMMMM

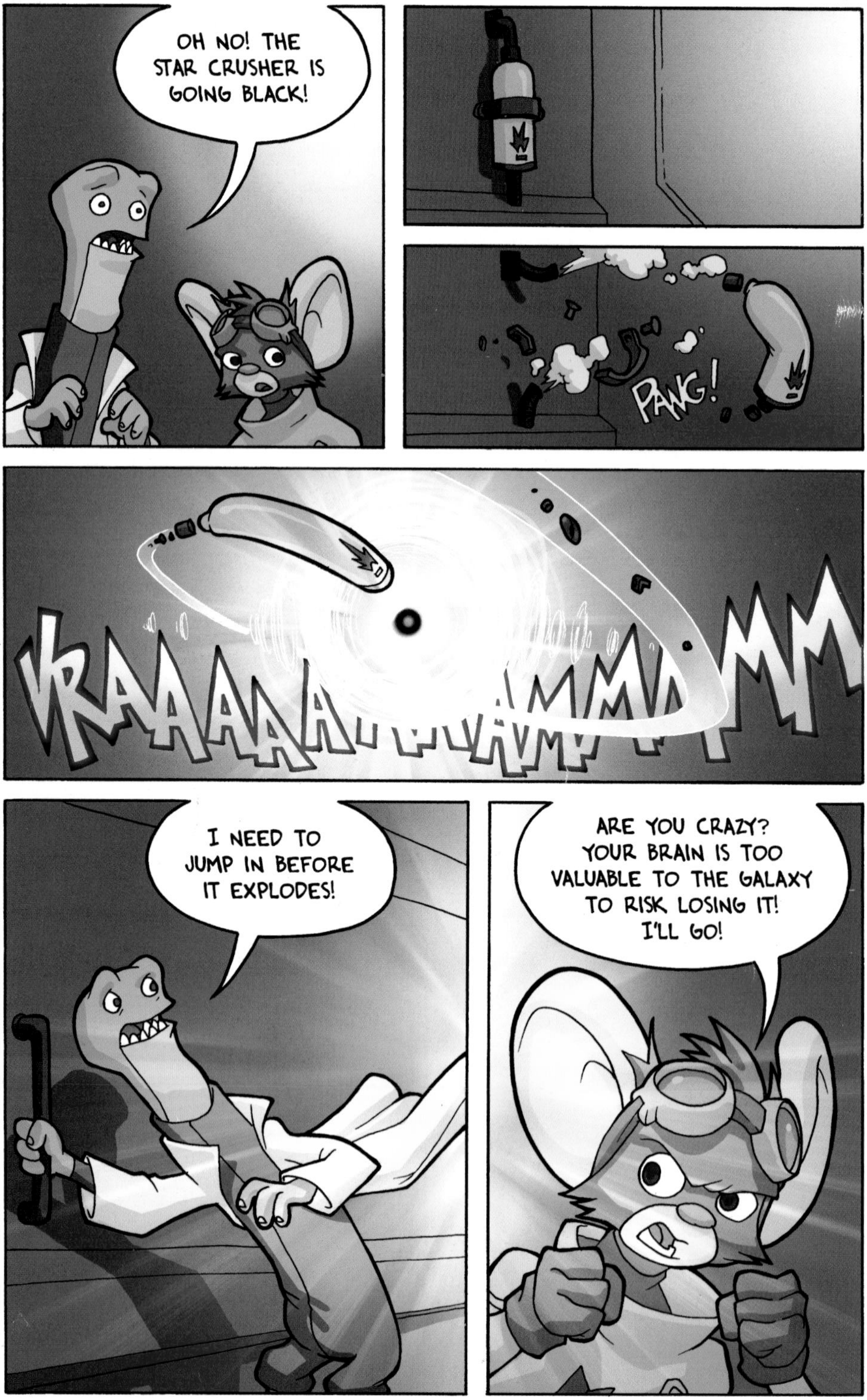
OH NO! THE STAR CRUSHER IS GOING BLACK!
PANG!
VRAAAAMMMMM
I NEED TO JUMP IN BEFORE IT EXPLODES!
ARE YOU CRAZY? YOUR BRAIN IS TOO VALUABLE TO THE GALAXY TO RISK LOSING IT! I'LL GO!

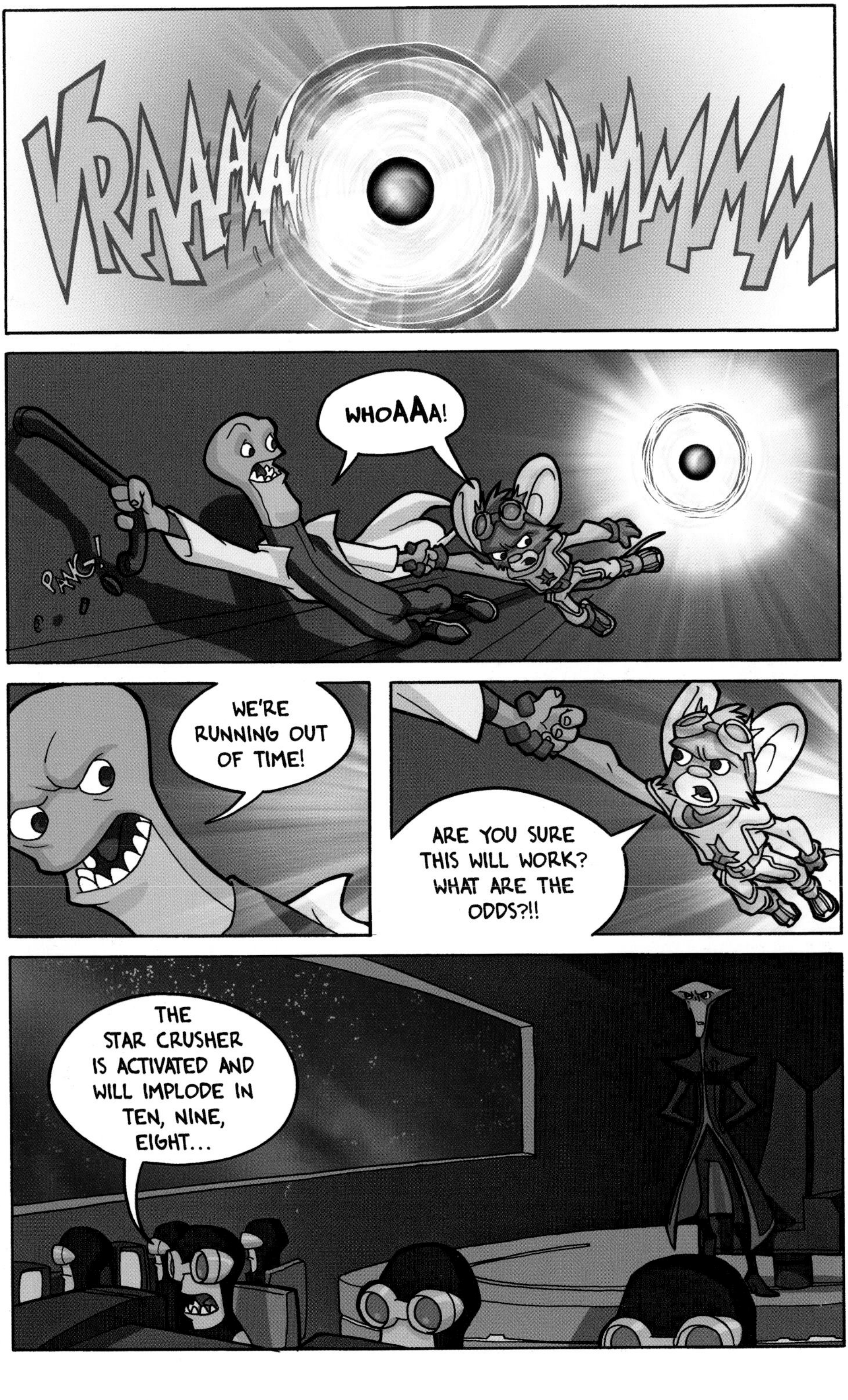
VRAAAAOMMMMM
WHOAAA!
PANG!
WE'RE RUNNING OUT OF TIME!
ARE YOU SURE THIS WILL WORK? WHAT ARE THE ODDS?!!
THE STAR CRUSHER IS ACTIVATED AND WILL IMPLODE IN TEN, NINE, EIGHT...

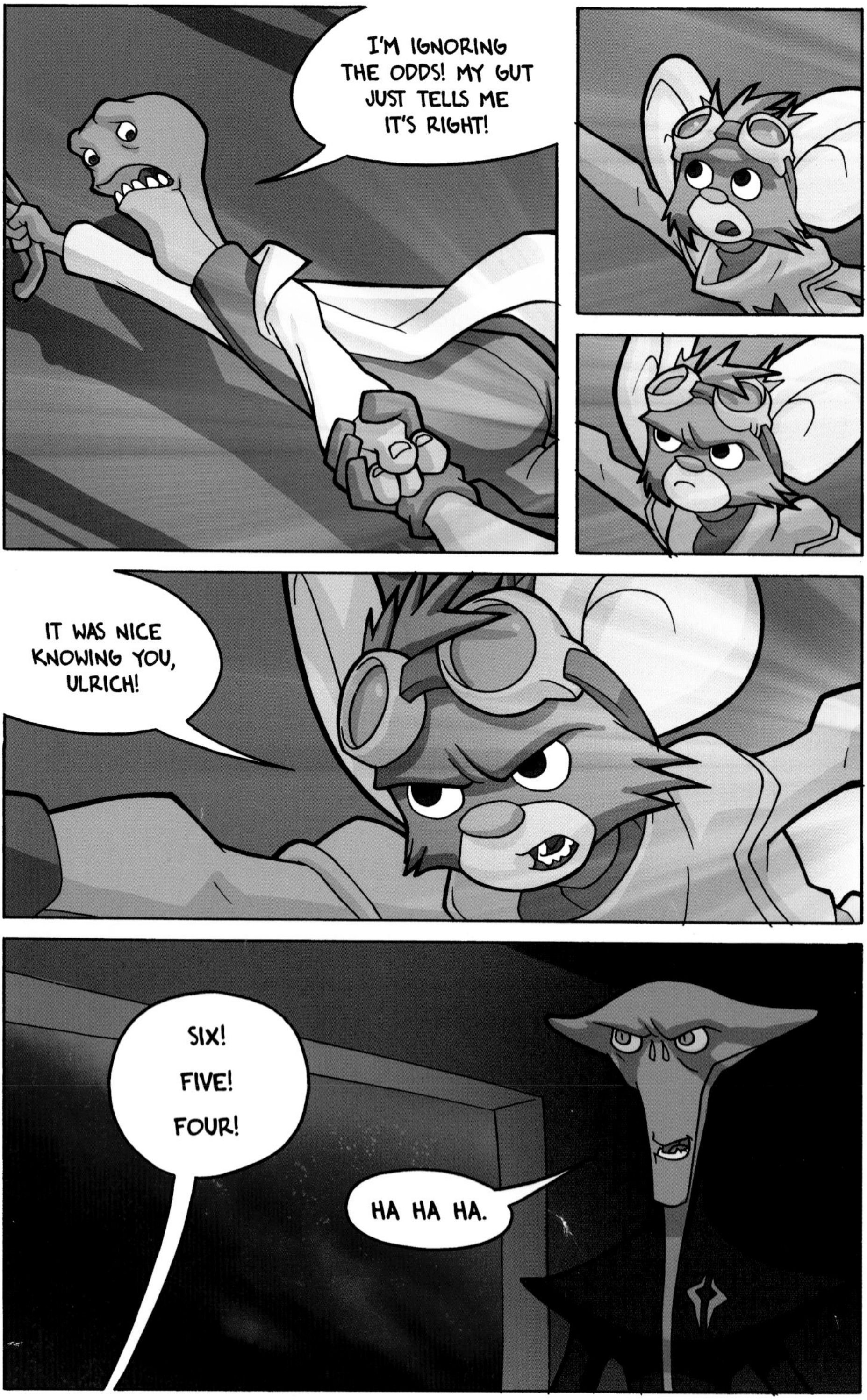
I'M IGNORING THE ODDS! MY GUT JUST TELLS ME IT'S RIGHT!
IT WAS NICE KNOWING YOU, ULRICH!
SIX! FIVE! FOUR!
HA HA HA.

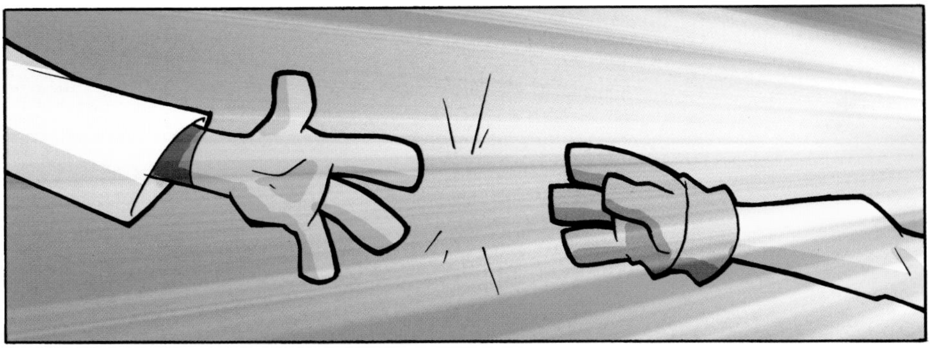

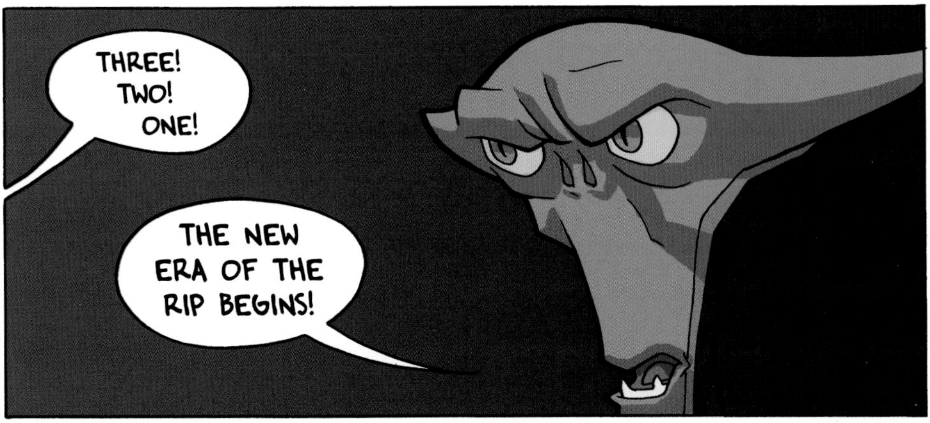
THREE!
TWO!
ONE!
THE NEW ERA OF THE RIP BEGINS!

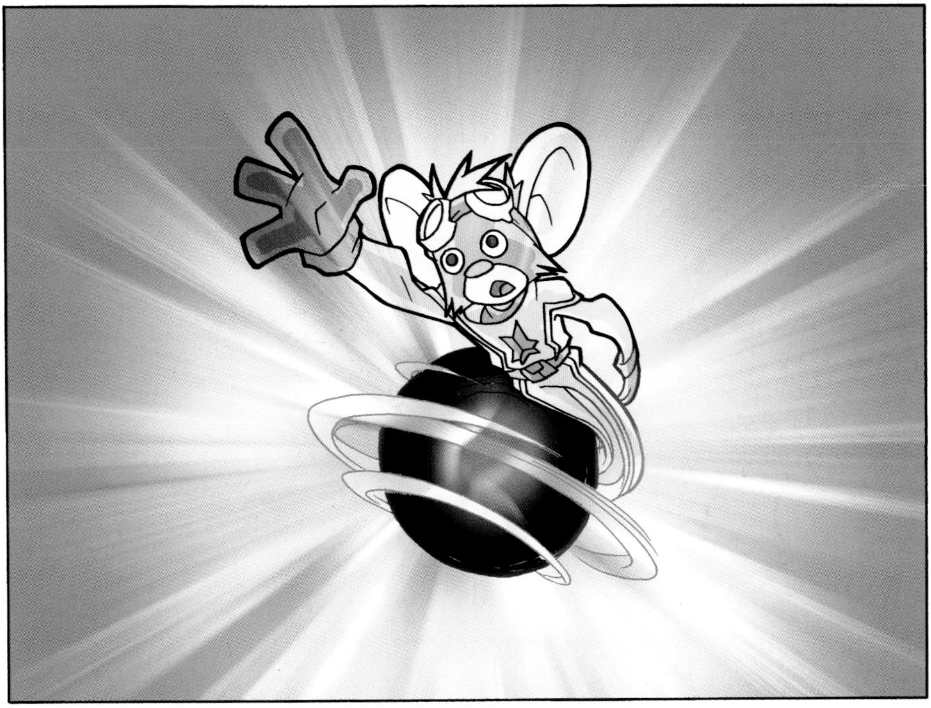

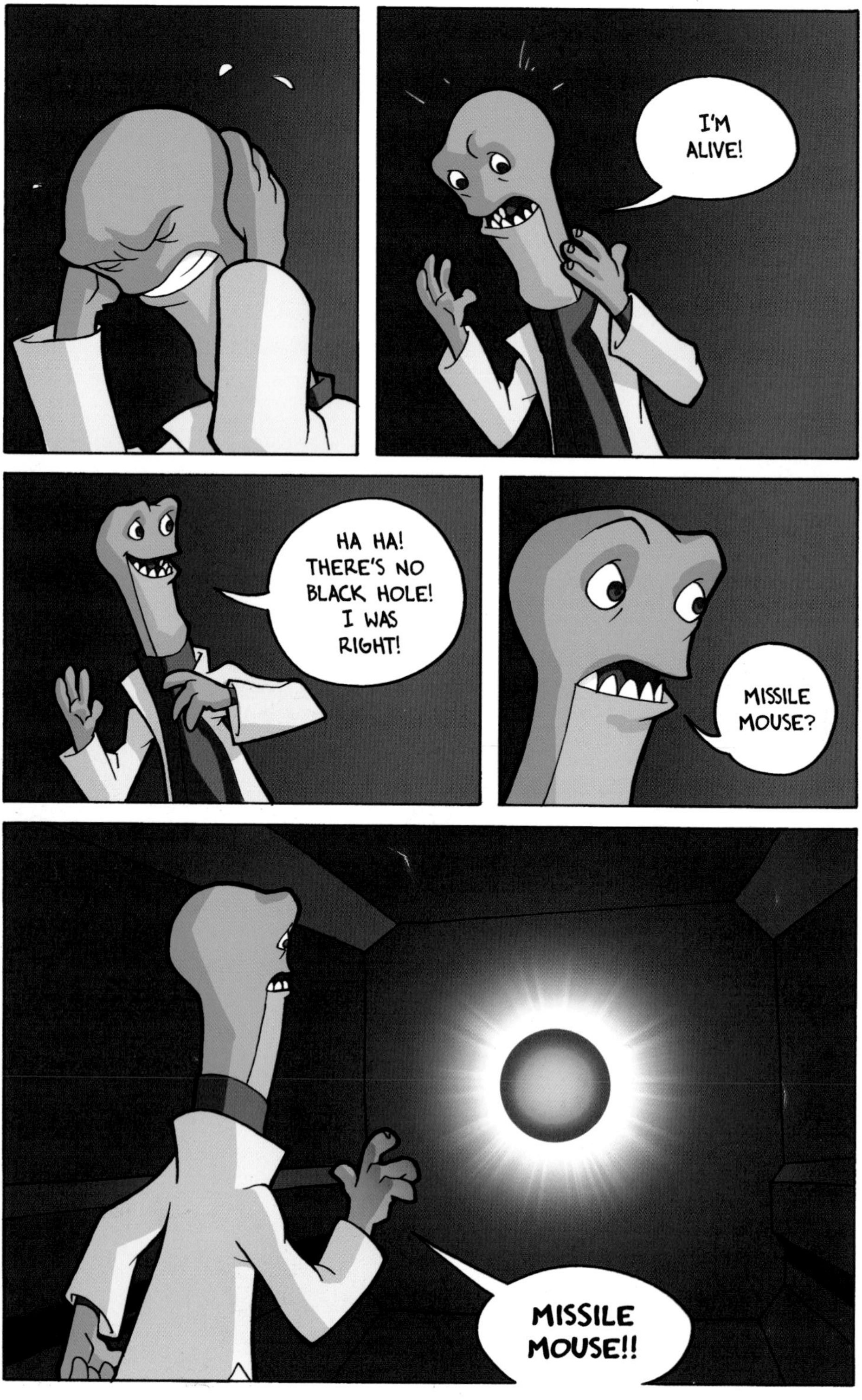
I'M ALIVE!
HA HA! THERE'S NO BLACK HOLE! I WAS RIGHT!
MISSILE MOUSE?
MISSILE MOUSE!!

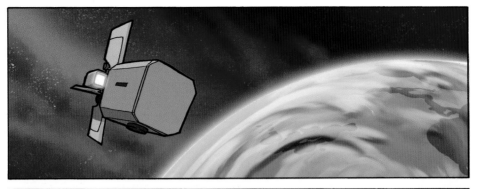

HYDE...

GENERAL?

CAN YOU EXPLAIN WHY MY STAR CRUSHER HAS NOT DETONATED?

WE ARE SENDING OUT A PROBE TO INVESTIGATE.

NO, I WANT YOU TO CHECK ON THIS PERSONALLY.

YES, SIR.

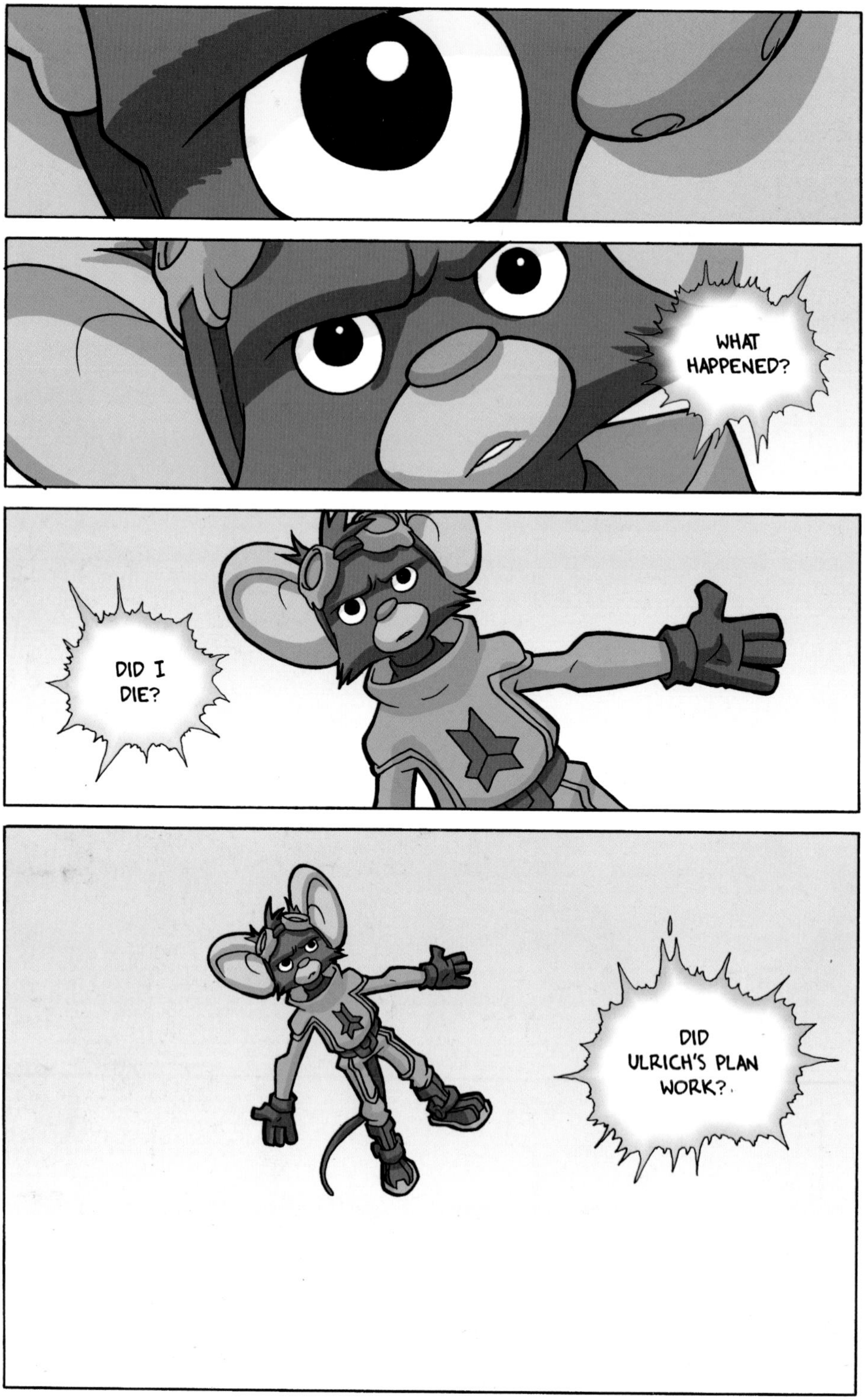
WHAT HAPPENED?
DID I DIE?
DID ULRICH'S PLAN WORK?

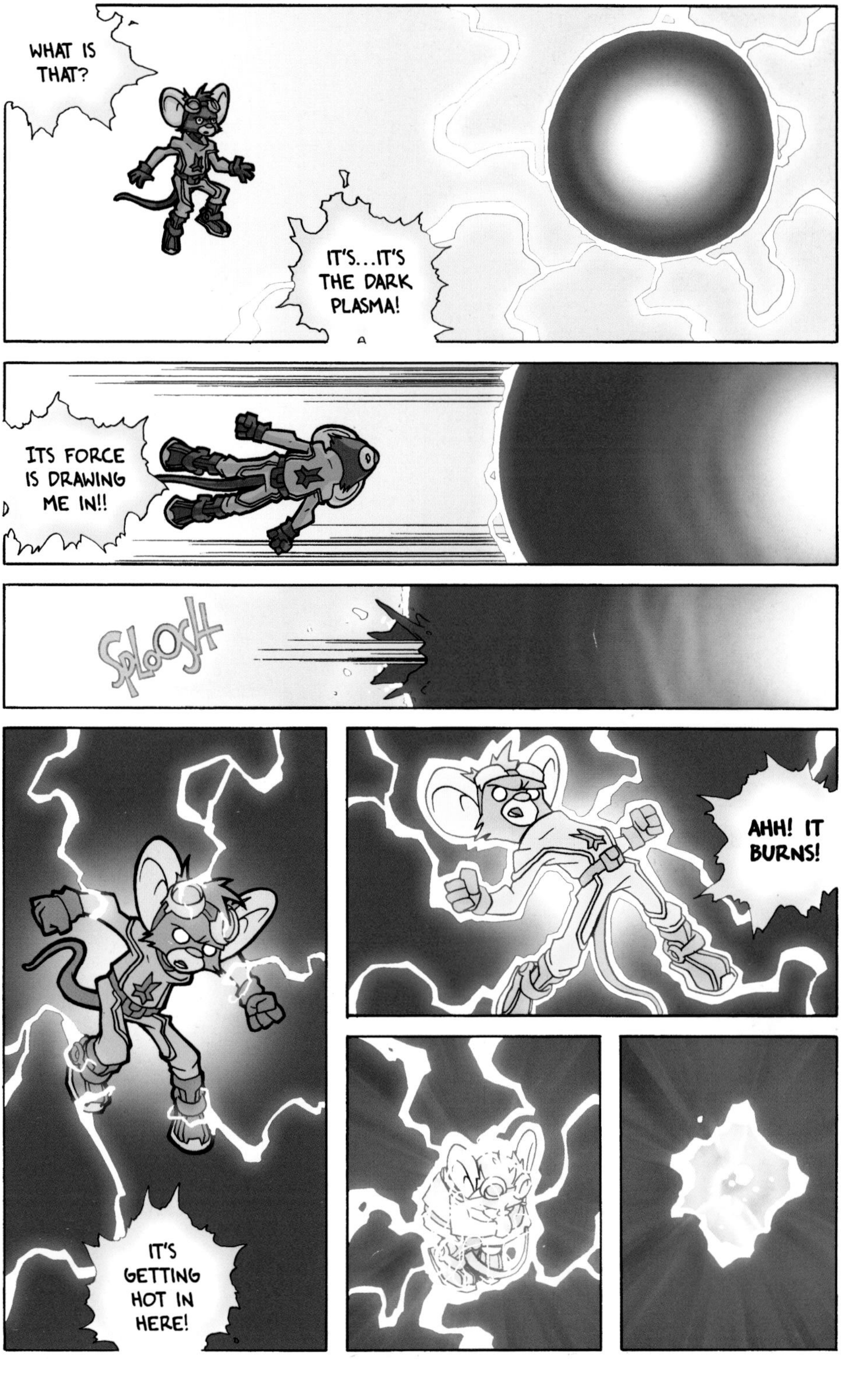
WHAT IS THAT?
IT'S...IT'S THE DARK PLASMA!
ITS FORCE IS DRAWING ME IN!!
SPLOOSH
AHH! IT BURNS!
IT'S GETTING HOT IN HERE!

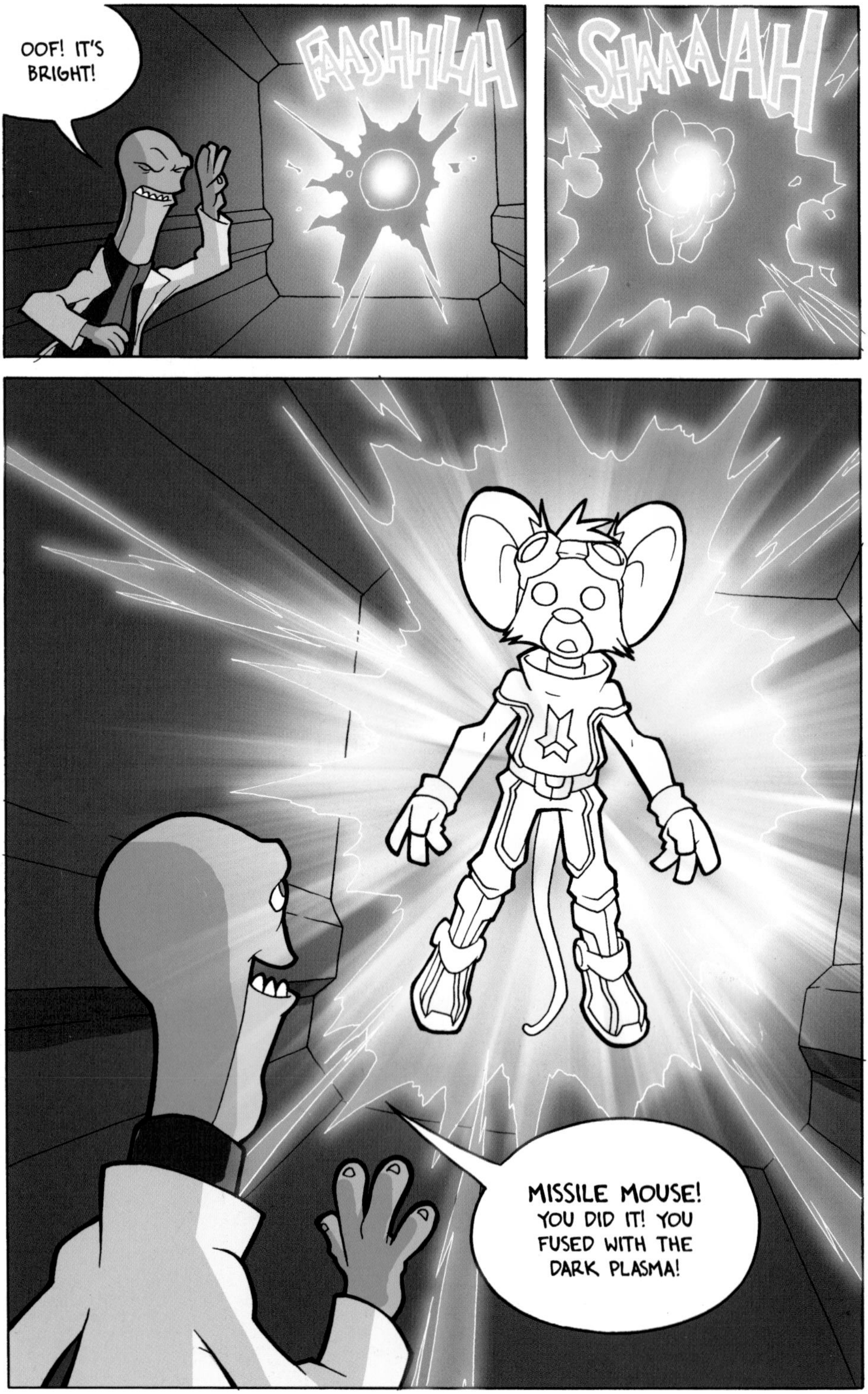
OOF! IT'S BRIGHT!
FAASHHHHH
SHAAAAAH
MISSILE MOUSE! YOU DID IT! YOU FUSED WITH THE DARK PLASMA!

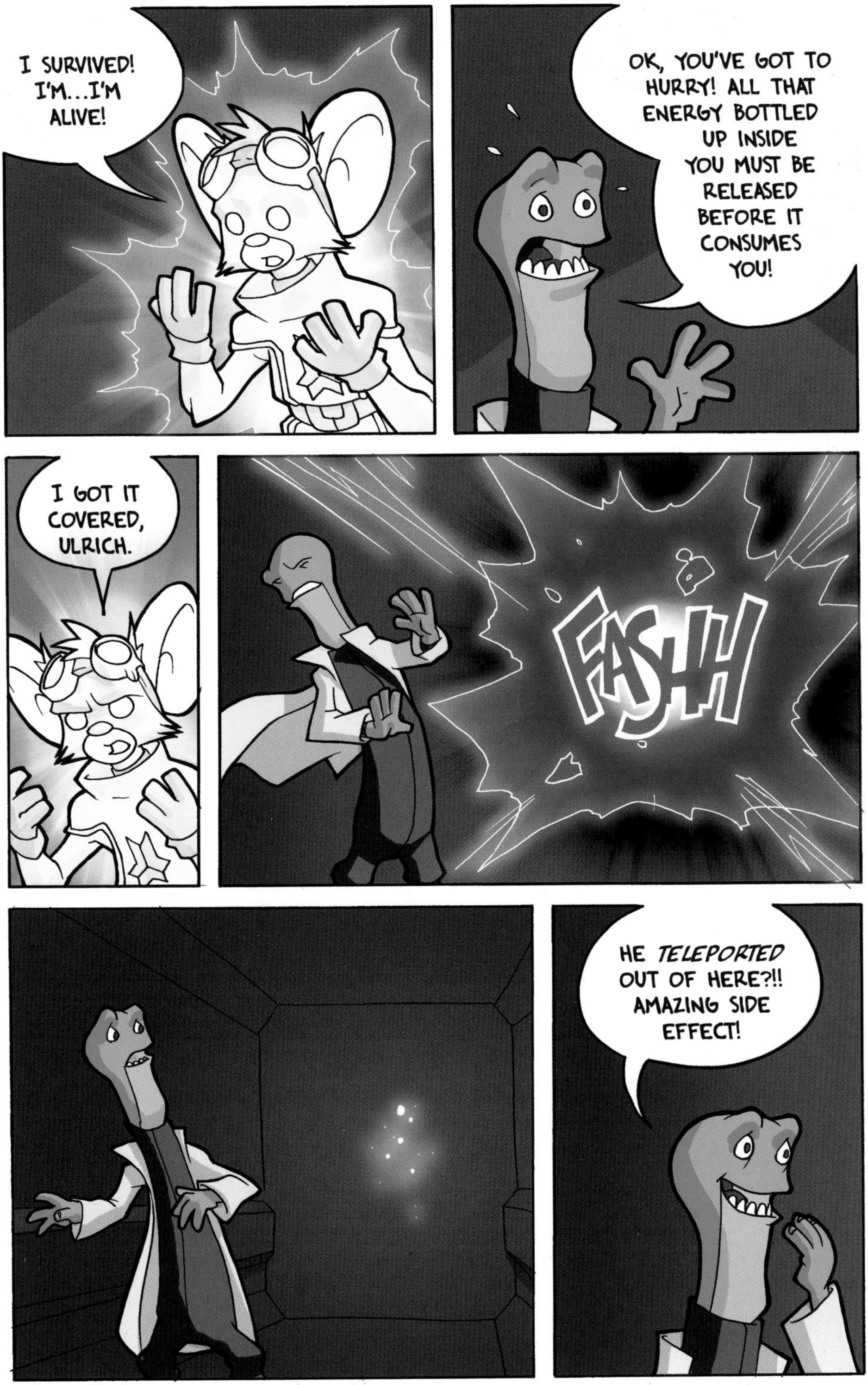
I SURVIVED! I'M...I'M ALIVE!
OK, YOU'VE GOT TO HURRY! ALL THAT ENERGY BOTTLED UP INSIDE YOU MUST BE RELEASED BEFORE IT CONSUMES YOU!
I GOT IT COVERED, ULRICH.
FASHH
HE *TELEPORTED* OUT OF HERE?!! AMAZING SIDE EFFECT!

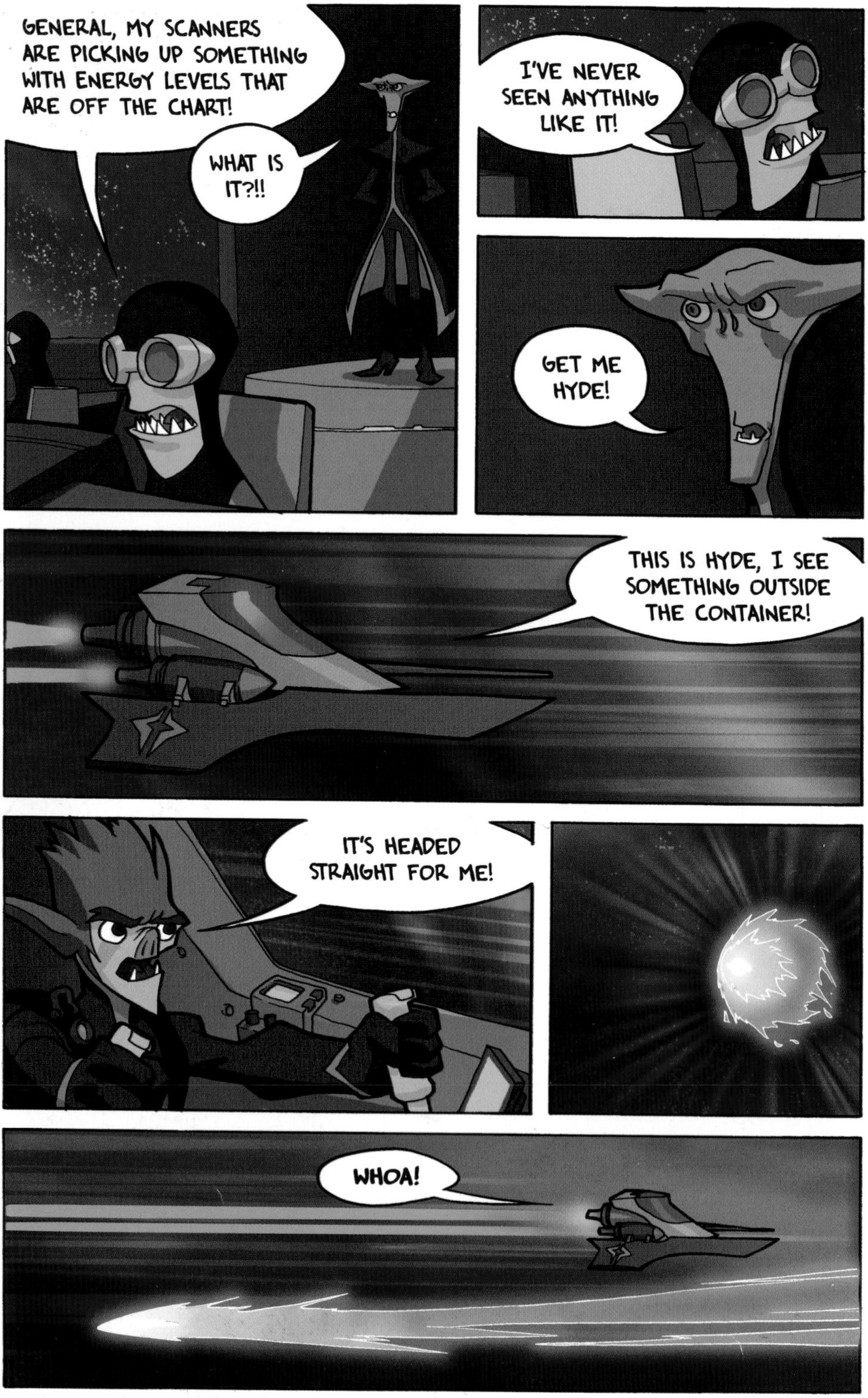
GENERAL, MY SCANNERS ARE PICKING UP SOMETHING WITH ENERGY LEVELS THAT ARE OFF THE CHART!
WHAT IS IT?!!
I'VE NEVER SEEN ANYTHING LIKE IT!
GET ME HYDE!
THIS IS HYDE, I SEE SOMETHING OUTSIDE THE CONTAINER!
IT'S HEADED STRAIGHT FOR ME!
WHOA!

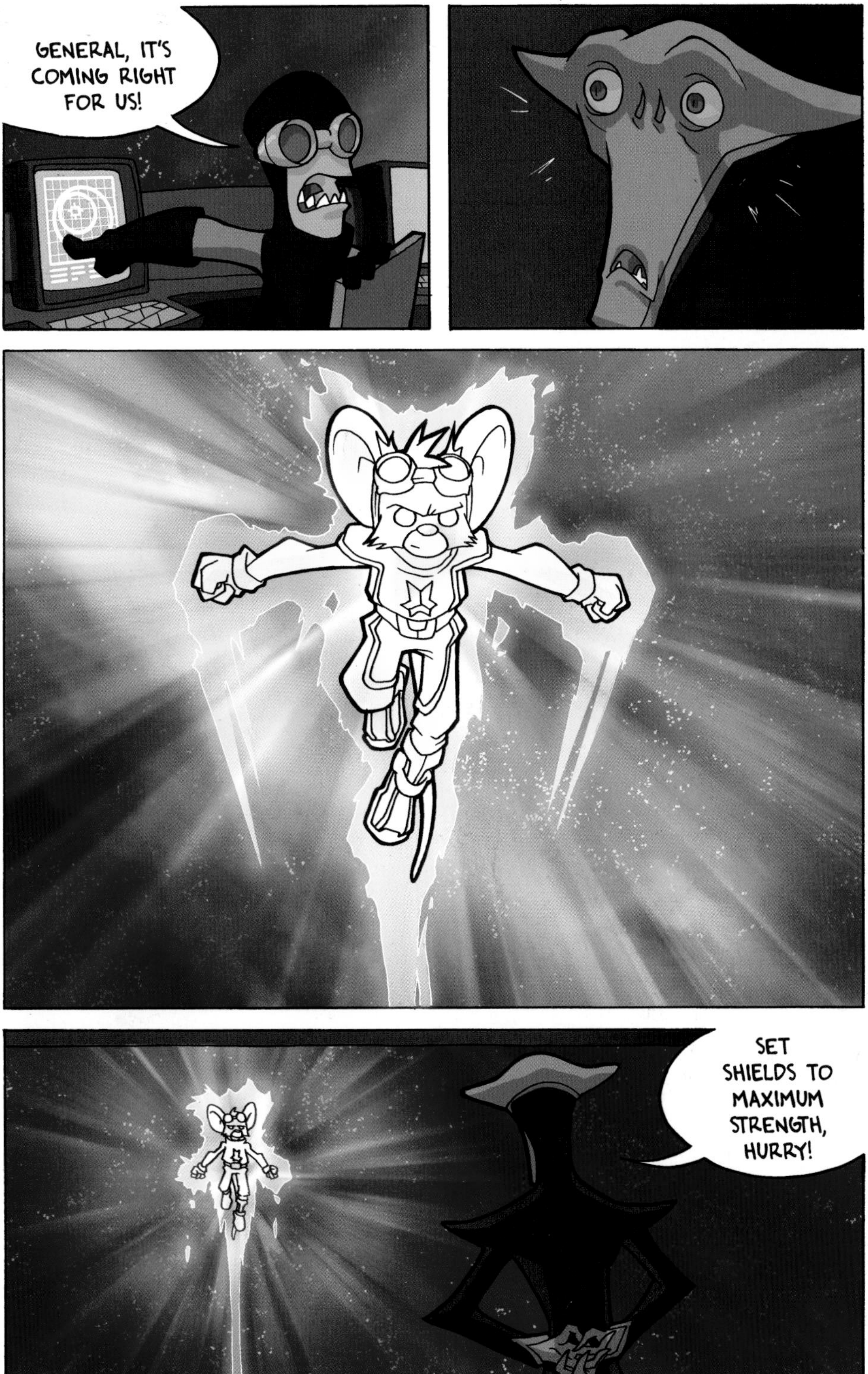
GENERAL, IT'S COMING RIGHT FOR US!
SET SHIELDS TO MAXIMUM STRENGTH, HURRY!

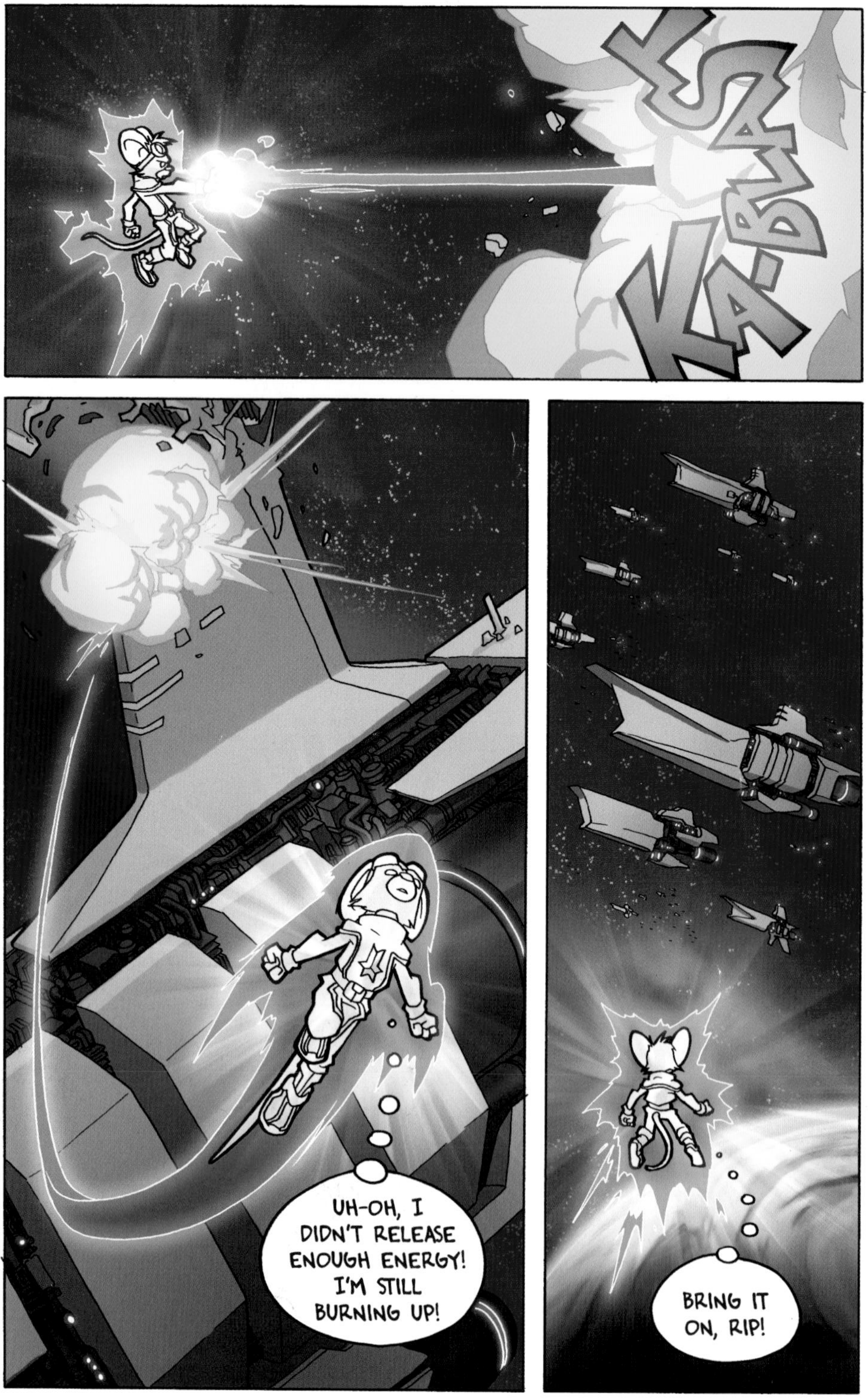
KA-BLAST
UH-OH, I DIDN'T RELEASE ENOUGH ENERGY! I'M STILL BURNING UP!
BRING IT ON, RIP!

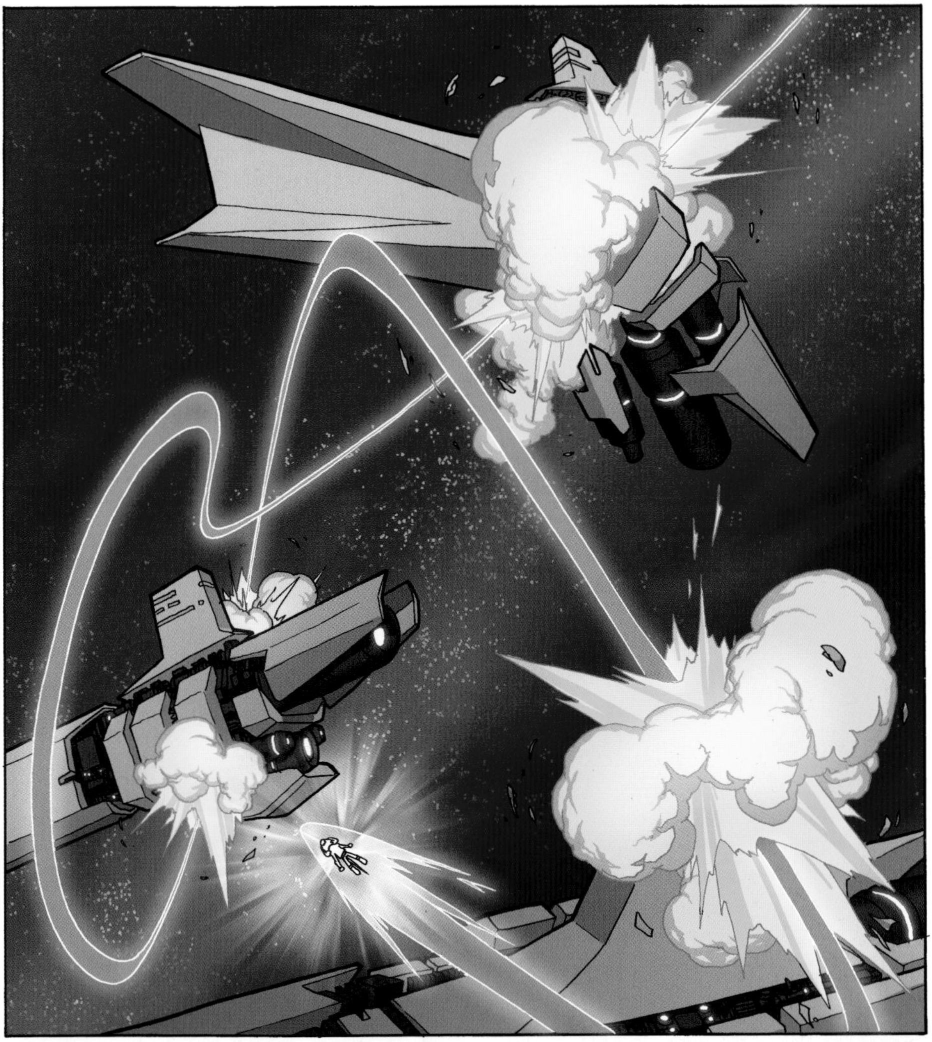

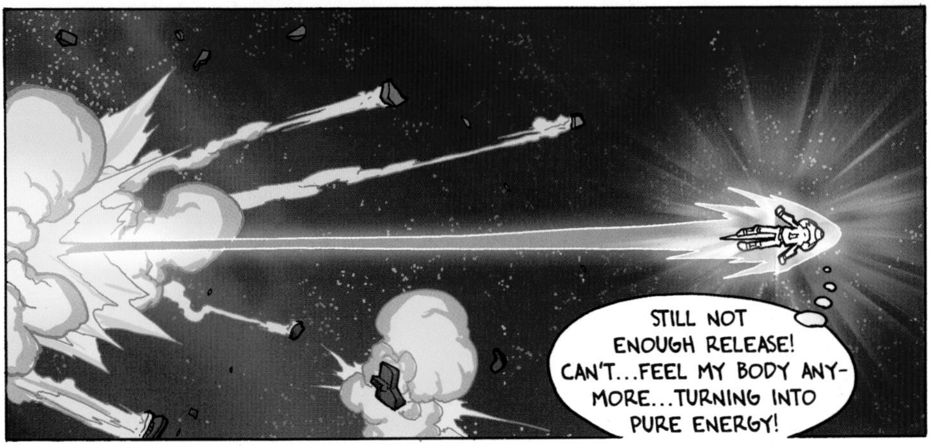
STILL NOT ENOUGH RELEASE! CAN'T...FEEL MY BODY ANY-MORE...TURNING INTO PURE ENERGY!

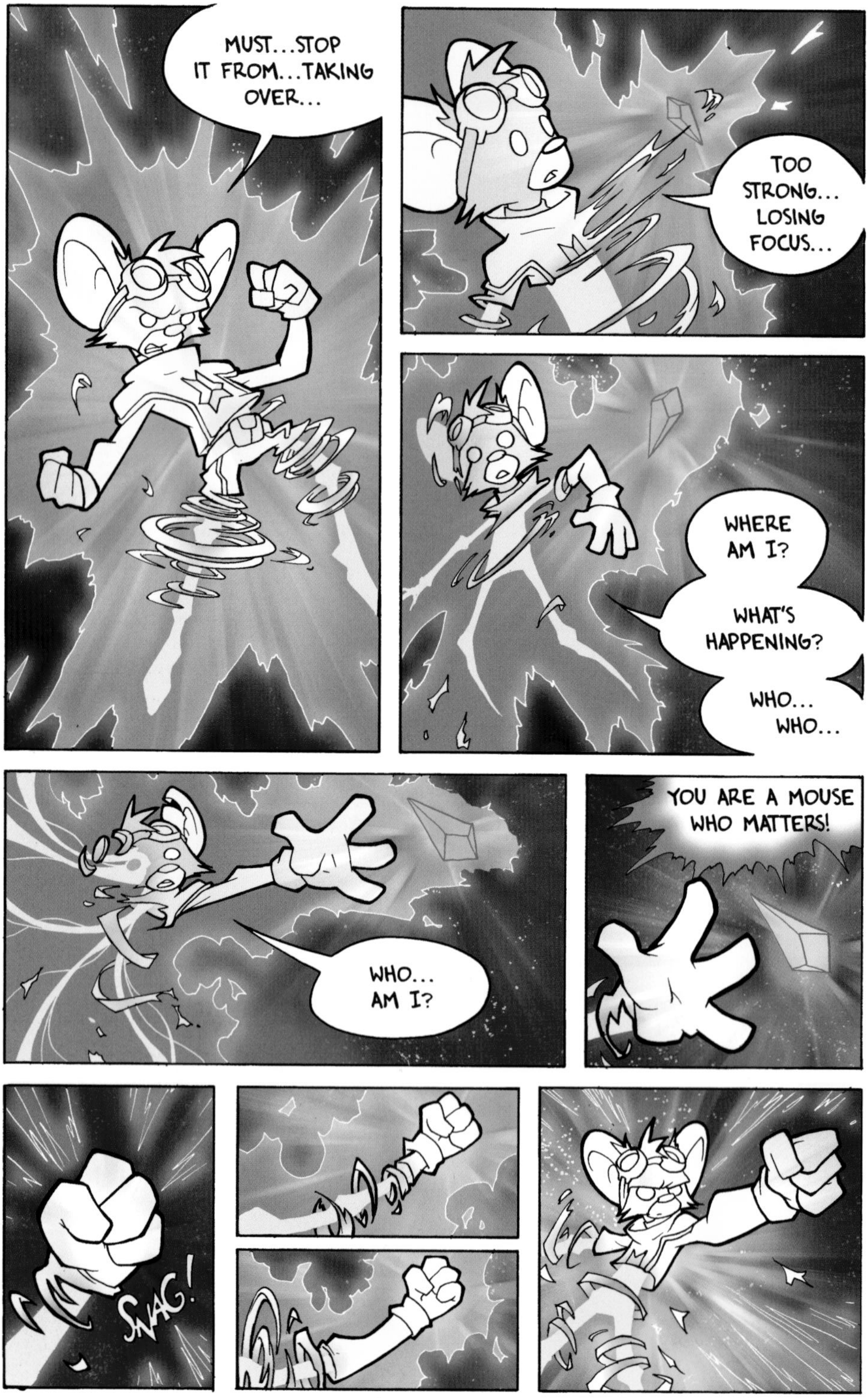
MUST...STOP IT FROM...TAKING OVER...
TOO STRONG... LOSING FOCUS...
WHERE AM I?
WHAT'S HAPPENING?
WHO... WHO...
WHO... AM I?
YOU ARE A MOUSE WHO MATTERS!
SNAG!

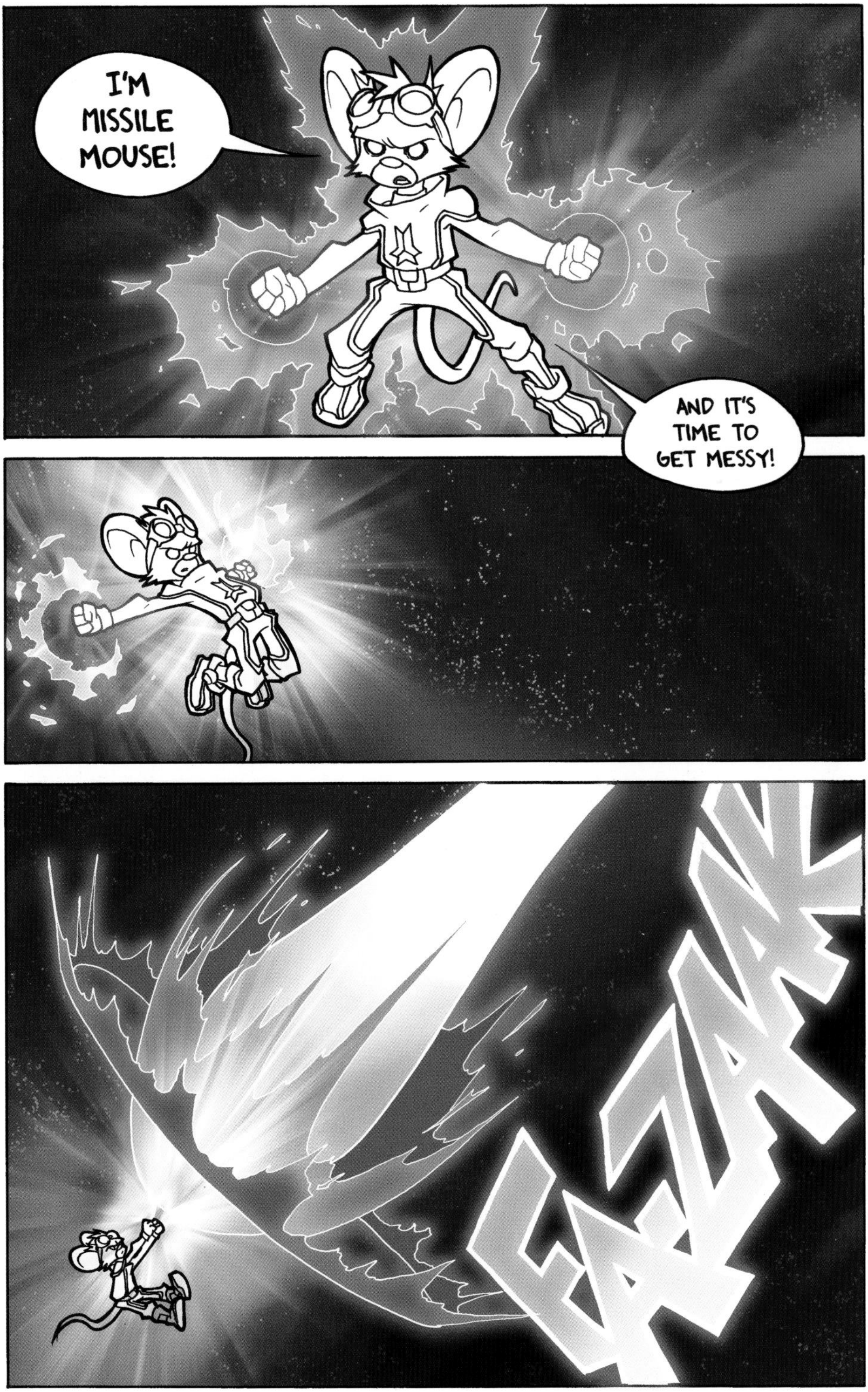
I'M MISSILE MOUSE!
AND IT'S TIME TO GET MESSY!

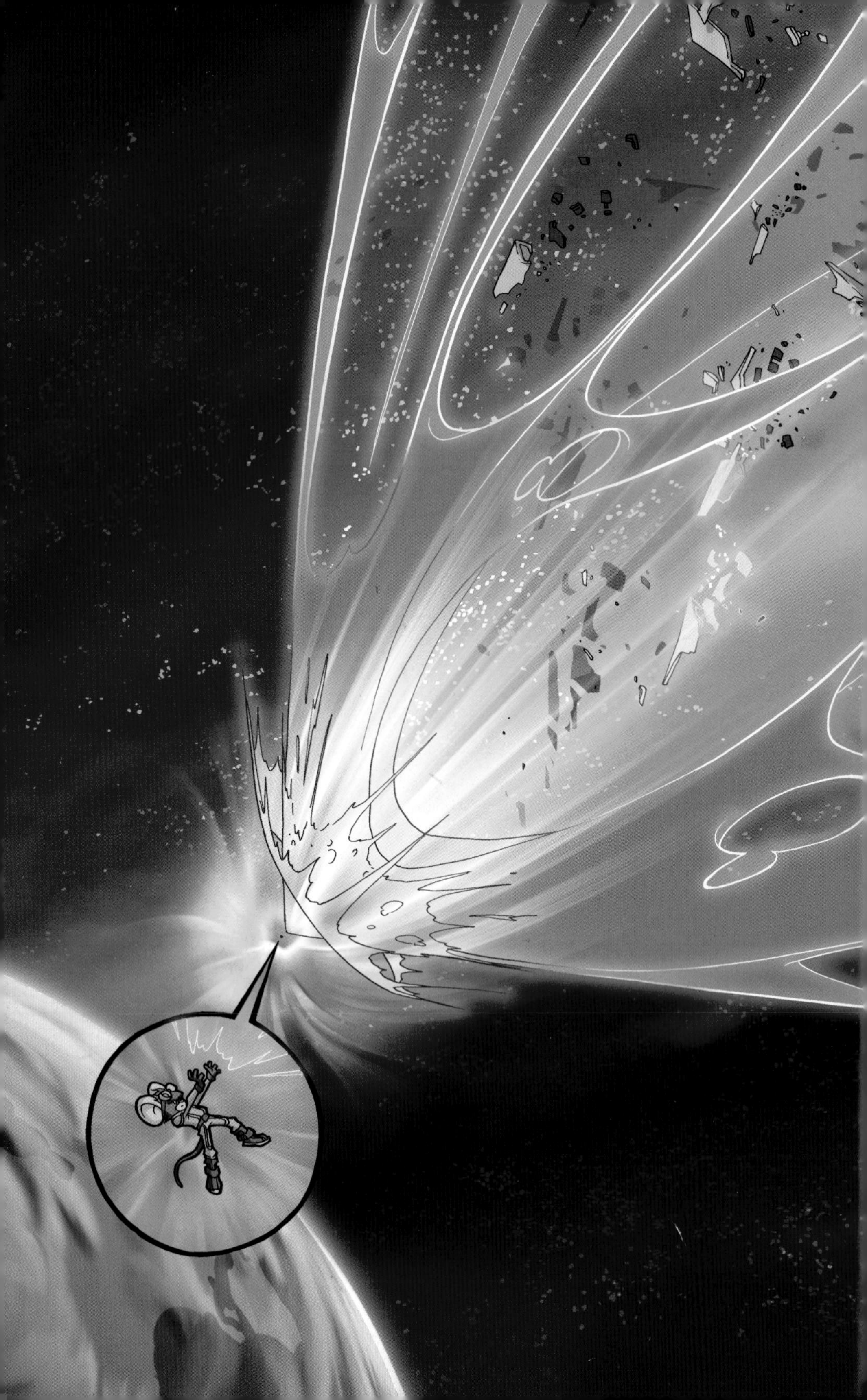

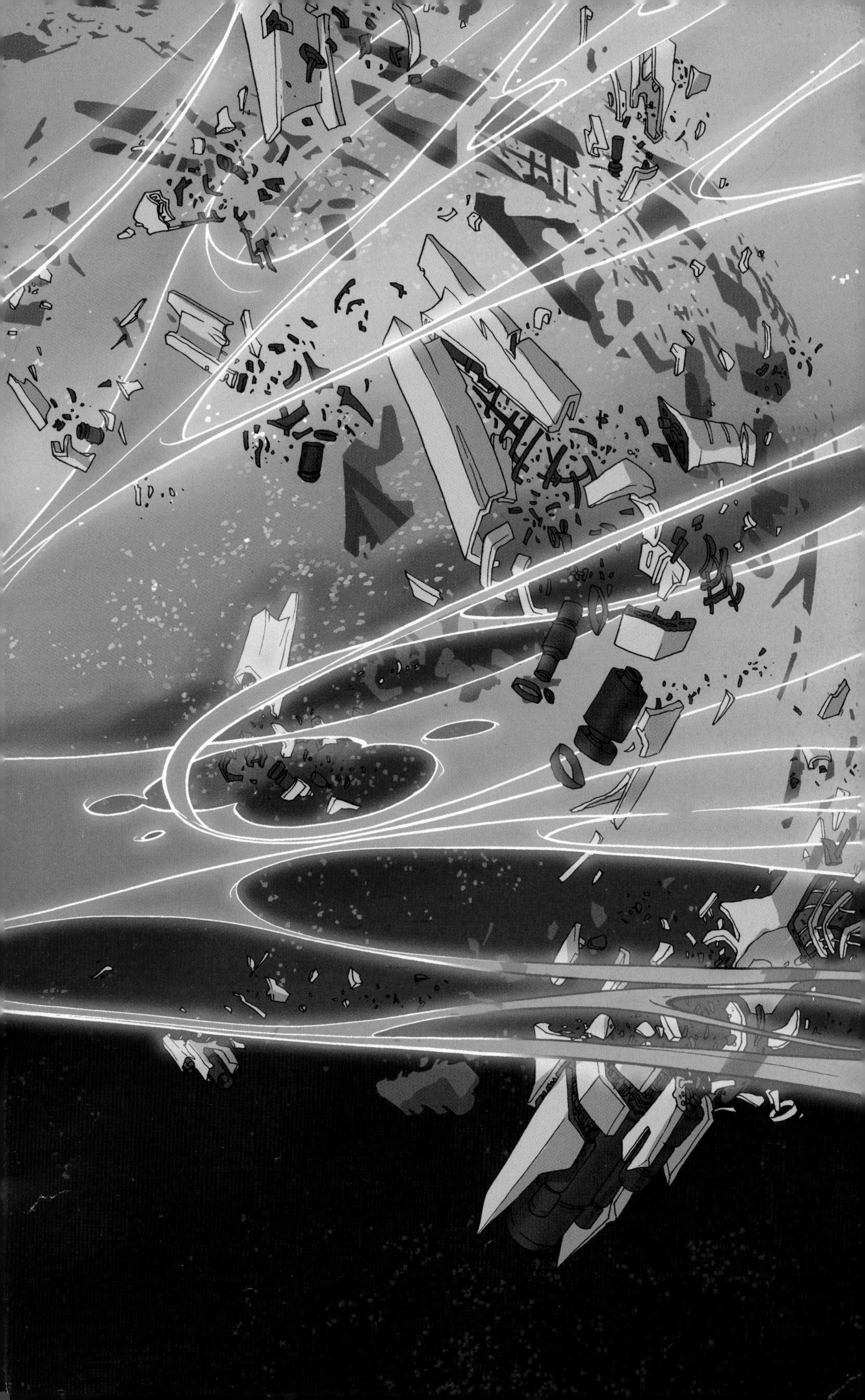

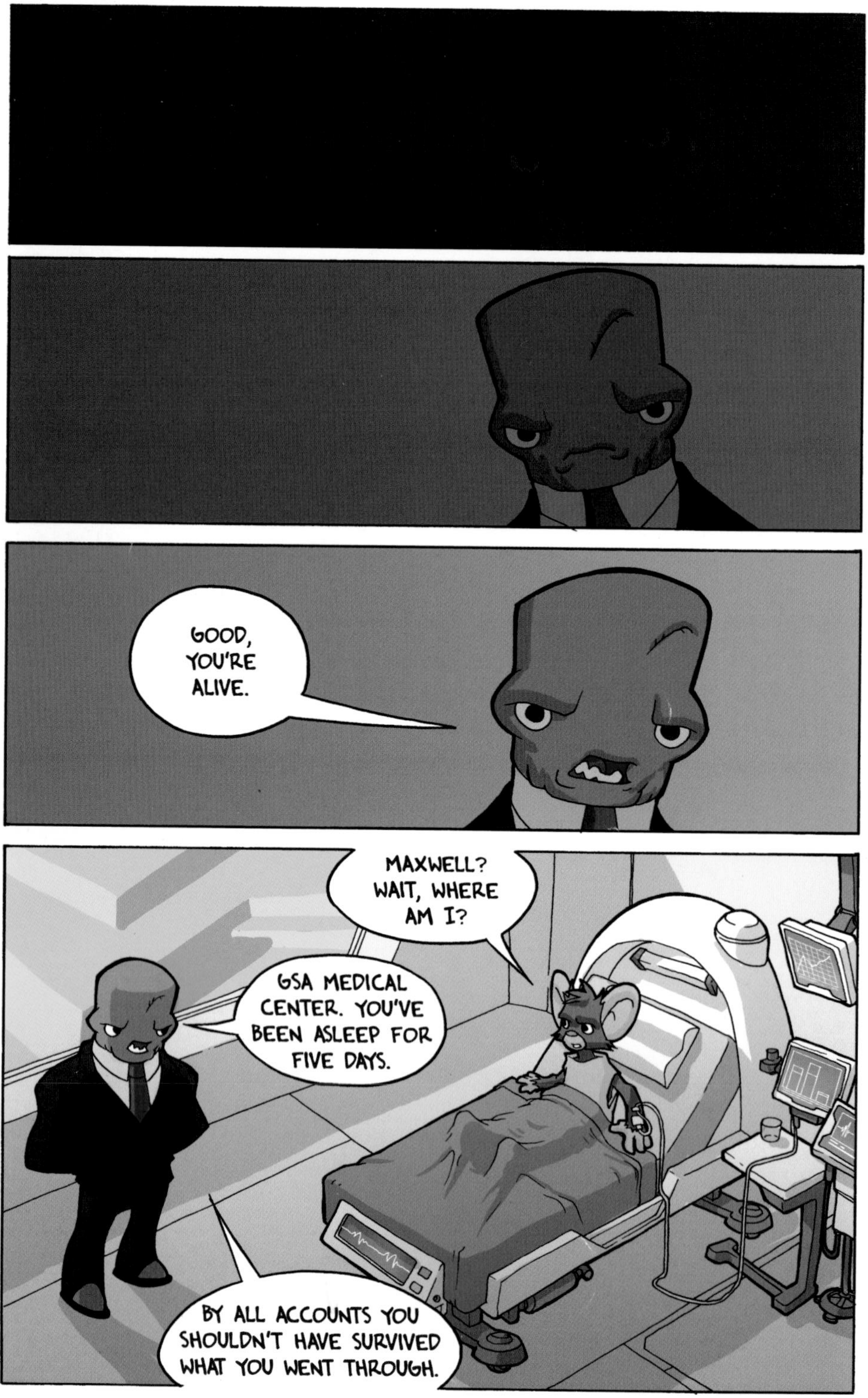
GOOD, YOU'RE ALIVE.
MAXWELL? WAIT, WHERE AM I?
GSA MEDICAL CENTER. YOU'VE BEEN ASLEEP FOR FIVE DAYS.
BY ALL ACCOUNTS YOU SHOULDN'T HAVE SURVIVED WHAT YOU WENT THROUGH.

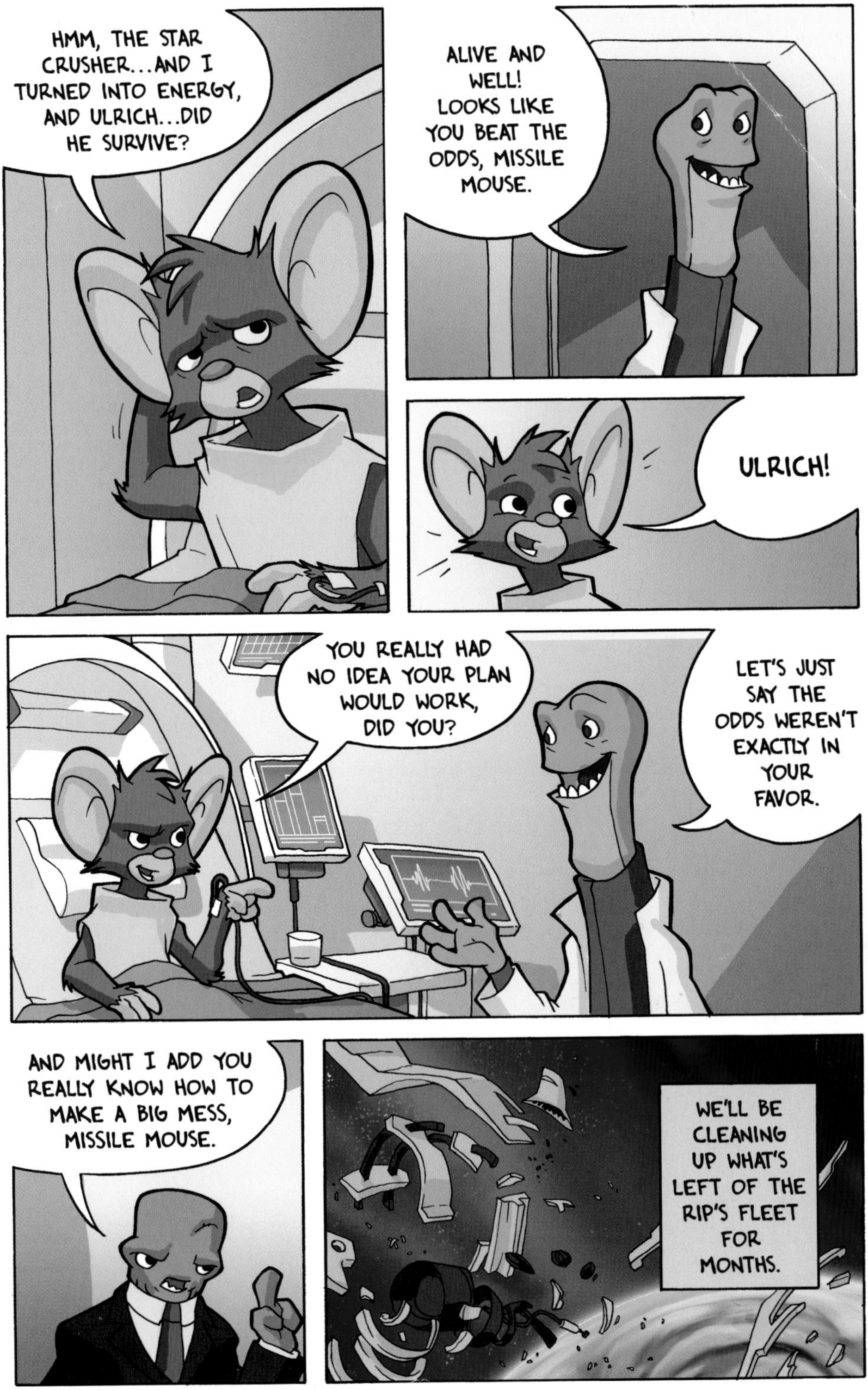
HMM, THE STAR CRUSHER...AND I TURNED INTO ENERGY, AND ULRICH...DID HE SURVIVE?
ALIVE AND WELL! LOOKS LIKE YOU BEAT THE ODDS, MISSILE MOUSE.
ULRICH!
YOU REALLY HAD NO IDEA YOUR PLAN WOULD WORK, DID YOU?
LET'S JUST SAY THE ODDS WEREN'T EXACTLY IN YOUR FAVOR.
AND MIGHT I ADD YOU REALLY KNOW HOW TO MAKE A BIG MESS, MISSILE MOUSE.
WE'LL BE CLEANING UP WHAT'S LEFT OF THE RIP'S FLEET FOR MONTHS.

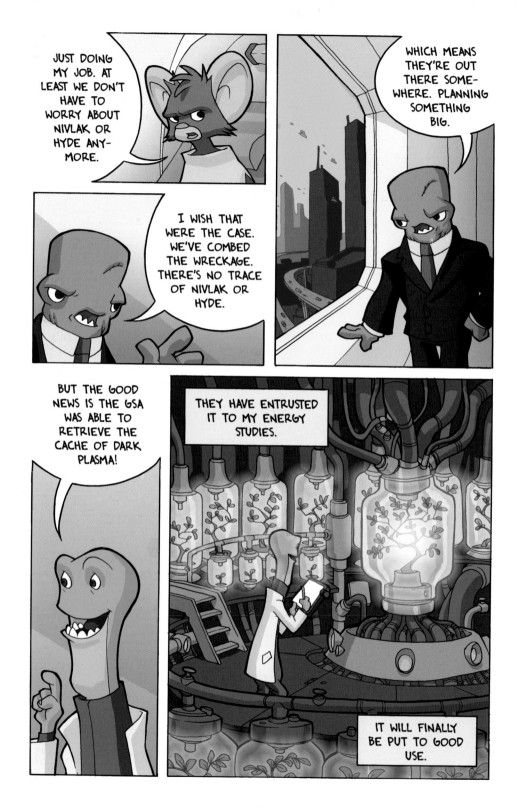

JUST DOING MY JOB. AT LEAST WE DON'T HAVE TO WORRY ABOUT NIVLAK OR HYDE ANYMORE.

WHICH MEANS THEY'RE OUT THERE SOMEWHERE. PLANNING SOMETHING BIG.

I WISH THAT WERE THE CASE. WE'VE COMBED THE WRECKAGE. THERE'S NO TRACE OF NIVLAK OR HYDE.

BUT THE GOOD NEWS IS THE GSA WAS ABLE TO RETRIEVE THE CACHE OF DARK PLASMA!

THEY HAVE ENTRUSTED IT TO MY ENERGY STUDIES.

IT WILL FINALLY BE PUT TO GOOD USE.

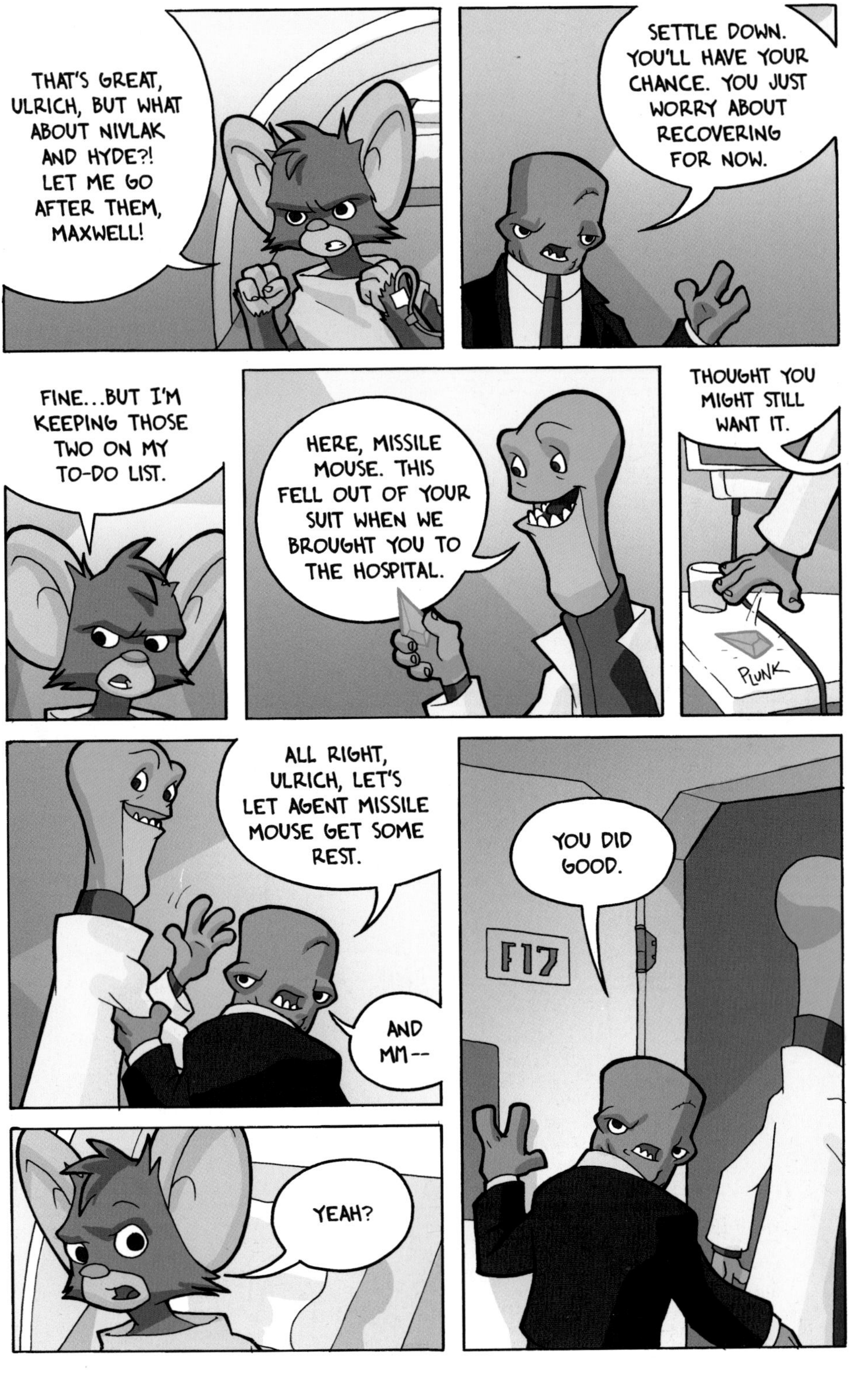
THAT'S GREAT, ULRICH, BUT WHAT ABOUT NIVLAK AND HYDE?! LET ME GO AFTER THEM, MAXWELL!
SETTLE DOWN. YOU'LL HAVE YOUR CHANCE. YOU JUST WORRY ABOUT RECOVERING FOR NOW.
FINE...BUT I'M KEEPING THOSE TWO ON MY TO-DO LIST.
HERE, MISSILE MOUSE. THIS FELL OUT OF YOUR SUIT WHEN WE BROUGHT YOU TO THE HOSPITAL.
THOUGHT YOU MIGHT STILL WANT IT.
PLUNK
ALL RIGHT, ULRICH, LET'S LET AGENT MISSILE MOUSE GET SOME REST.
AND MM--
YEAH?
YOU DID GOOD.
F17

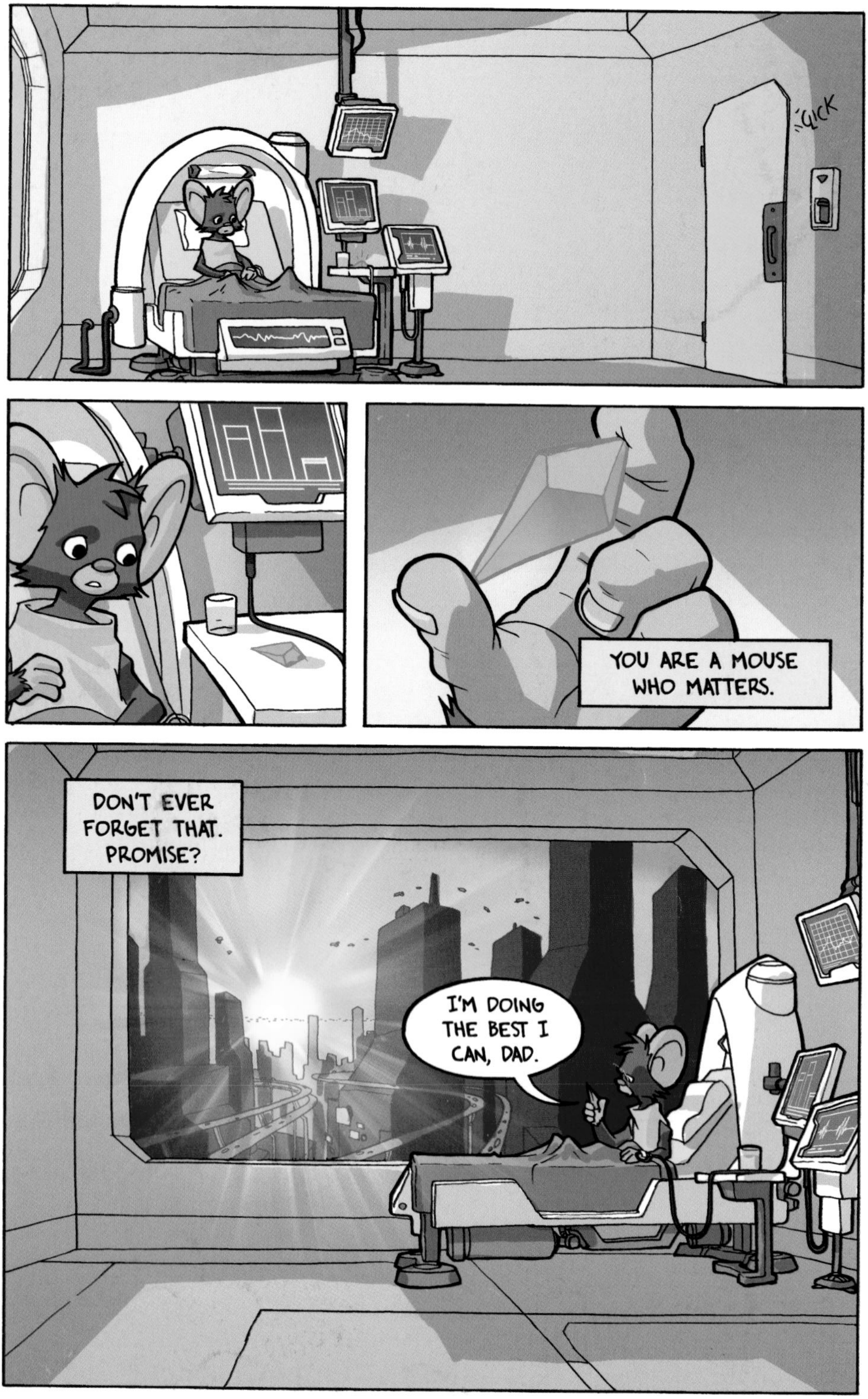
CLICK
YOU ARE A MOUSE WHO MATTERS.
DON'T EVER FORGET THAT. PROMISE?
I'M DOING THE BEST I CAN, DAD.

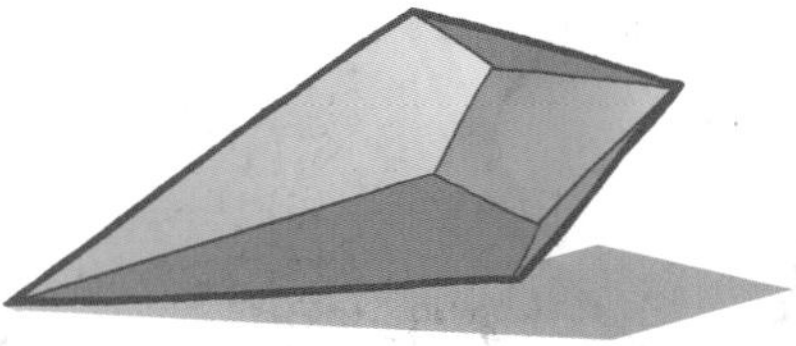

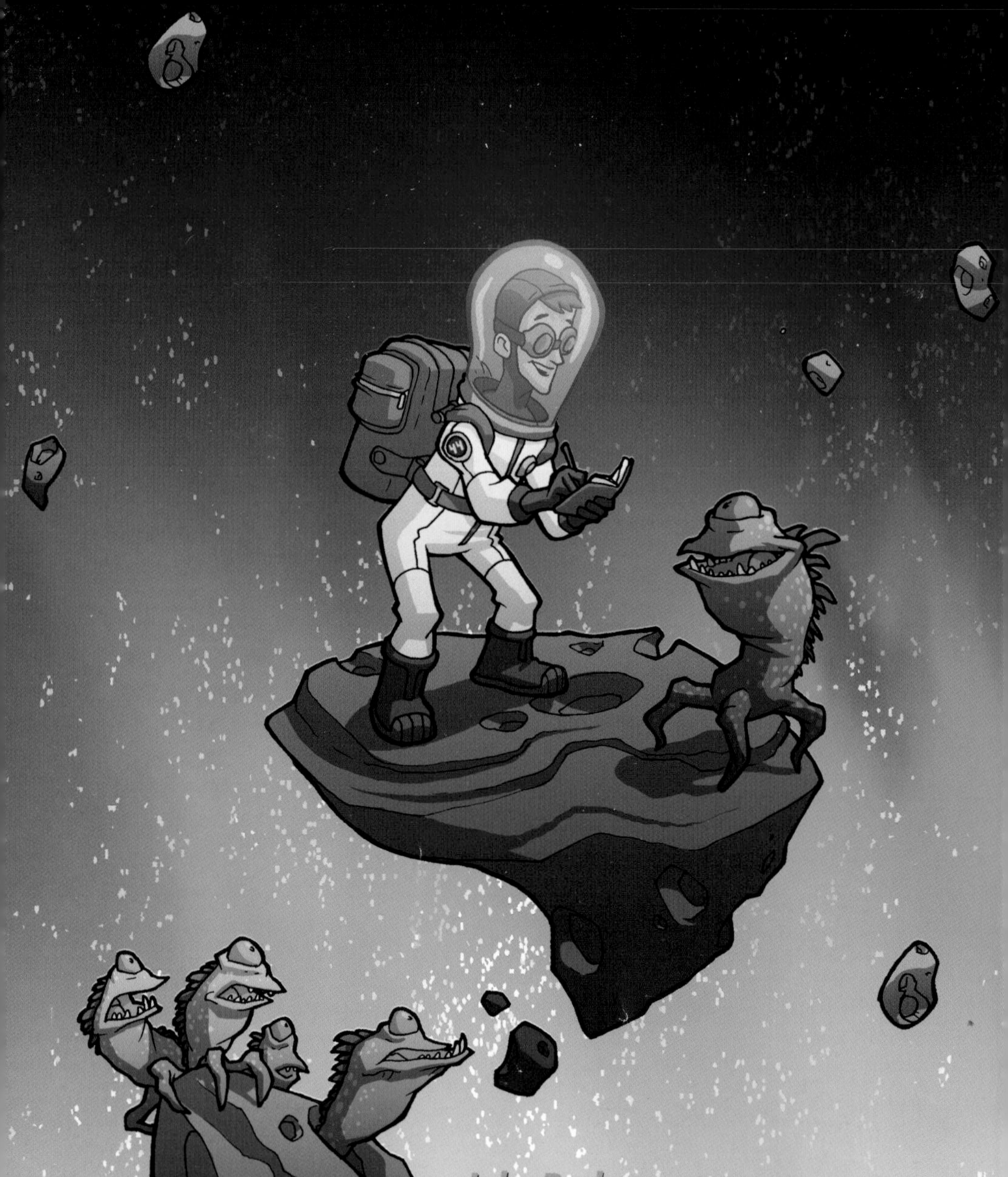

Jake Parker was born in Mesa, Arizona, and raised on a healthy diet of cereal, comic books, and Saturday morning cartoons. Now he draws comic books, works on animated films, and still eats lots of cereal. He's also done artwork for commercials, video games, kids' TV shows, and even a dinosaur exhibit for a museum. He currently lives in Cos Cob, Connecticut, with his wife and four kids, where he drew this book in his leaky basement.